THE
CROW

ShattErEd LiVES &
BrOken drEAMS

EDITED BY J. O'BARR AND ED KRAMER

DEL
REY

THE BALLANTINE PUBLISHING GROUP • NEW YORK

A Del Rey® Book
Published by The Ballantine Publishing Group

For Brandon

The editors would like to thank
Nancy and Robert Laughlin and Paul W. Cashman
for their invaluable assistance in preparing this tome.

C O N T E N T S

PREFACE

It has been nearly two decades since James O'Barr first painted the harlequin mask onto Eric Draven, and thereby conceived one of the most widely recognized gothic archetypes of today. What began as a comic book has evolved into a franchise of films, novels, merchandise, and even a new television series. But why?

Born of personal tragedy, the Crow warps together two of man's strongest emotions and desires—love and revenge. The antihero we have come to know, consciously or not, rejects conventional values and ideals to do ultimately what is right. Not because he wants to, but because he's fated to do so. And much like Elric, Michael Moorcock's Eternal Champion, the Crow is consumed by his own actions, only to be reborn again. A cycle that will continue for eternity.

In the collection before you, we have asked the genre's finest writers, artists, and poets to lend their voice to James O'Barr's vision. Many have integrated their own stories and characters with that of *The Crow*, to provide you with a most unique window into the psyche of a *new* chronic outlaw. You will be angered and fulfilled, satiated and left empty. But you won't be disappointed.

Ed Kramer
February 1988

FOREWORD

Remember that black bird Noah first sent out over the floodwaters? Remember how it never returned? How it just kept flying above the drowned horizons? Where did it go? The white bird that flew next brought back the olive leaf. Ever since then the dove has signified salvation. But what do you think is the significance of the black bird?

From the carbon diamond at the center of all living things open eyes watch. Black eyes. Not blinking.

Inspiration is the faithful happiness of that part of ourselves that is best fulfilled in hell and that precedes us there—our soul. Much inspiration has come to many souls in the last five years from James O'Barr's *The Crow*: this collection represents a glimpse of where the black bird has traveled.

The Crow's deathwatch begins when life itself becomes an illness: the incurable condition of being human. Words are too small. Everything we have created is too small. Cities, civilizations, planets themselves are too small before this vanishing. The real world that the white bird reveals is not enough. Its future offers nothing. And worse yet—its past can never be changed. To be wholly human we need a deeper memory of ourselves. And so we look to the transphenomenal world and its emblem since Paleolithic time—the Crow.

He is bigger than death. His dark eyes have outstared the void. His shadow nailed to the heart of the atom falls across veils of stars. Full of emptiness he returns over the vast waters from the forgotten country. Killing is a celebration to him. And through O'Barr's evocation he avenges the innocent dead. He stalks the crimson road of the slain. He mourns lost love so ardently that desire and death become one in a gallery of memories floored with blood.

The Crow is looking for you. He was looking for James O'Barr and found him on the dead white page, hungering for the impossible. Blood became ink. And that strange ink continues its transformations in other hands. They shape healing out of what cannot be changed.

The Crow is looking for you. If he finds you he will seize you with claws that are your own wounds. He may jam you into the worm dirt—into the phylogenetic depths of the psyche. Or he may carry you through a tunnel of fire to his nest inside the sun.

The flight may take a wrong turn. Phantoms. Gargoyles screaming. And the furious animosity and cold rage peculiar to the human animal. Hold on. The journey is ouroboric. You return to where you began. And if you are lucky you will be left with one or more black feathers. With these quills of night you may barter for all the meaning in your life.

This volume gathers other souls the Crow has found. These are the feathers they brought back. In their hands the touched and untouchable pain turns blood to ink again. And again the Crow flies, uplifting us with his vision of the forgotten country. These stories and images are fantasies. They are not real. They are more than real. For the true wordless reality of all that is possible in our lives we must seek the white bird. But to do the impossible—to free souls imprisoned in hell—to make music from notes of the dead bell—to meet again the dead we have lost—to meet the dead—we need the Crow.

Uplifting. Up above the floodwaters. In the void. In the mysterious domain of pure potential. In the realm of the unreal. Flying through the sacred nothing. We cross the shaman's sky. The Crow is our guide. His darkness knows the way through darkness.

Bitterness, depression, shattering despair are the transfiguring powers that eventually accompany each of us during our brief provisional lives. The Crow vision first won by people in the brutal ice ages enfolds us in a strength wider than our personal damage. The dark bird drifts through the antilife. The life of the imagination where the dead are brought back to us piece by piece.

Each of these images and tales is a match flare in the mist-swarming night of the soul. By their illuminations, we may see what we may never see.

A black bird flying through darkness.

Across the world of the white bird Noah's children are slain every hour and the secret spirit watches without blinking. Something very different is going on over the wide celestial waters of the Crow. In the far country. Where the dead are tongued with fire. The Crow is an ethical finality. He is the dream-carrier of holy retribution. He knows every devil was born in heaven. He understands that love is stronger than death. And in the name of love he delivers justice to the wicked.

A. A. Attanasio
Kalama Valley, 1997

INTRODUCTION: THE CROW THEORY

A. A. Attanasio

For a hundred thousand years, the greatest of the gods was the Crow. The dream carrier who brought civilization to the people in Paleolithic times. Mammoth-ivory carvings found over a vast area from Europe to the Near East depict a goddess with the raptor traits of a carrion bird: three-fingered talons and a beaked face—a predator Crow with breasts.

About ten thousand years ago, when the goddess became a god, the same winged omnivore continued as chief deity almost everywhere: the Archaic Greeks called him Cronos. Literally, the Crow. The tireless traveler and hunger machine. The Romans renamed him Saturn, God of Time. The sun god Apollo, whose name means the destroyer, was another Greek avatar of the Crow. As was the Norse king of the gods, Odin. To the Celts, as well as to aboriginal American nations, this scavenger bird carried the cosmic significance of the great benefactor, the creator of the visible world. The Germanic and Siberian tribes similarly worshiped the Crow as an oracular healer. And in China, the black-feathered predator was the first of the imperial emblems, representing yang, the sun, and the vitality of the emperor.

At our human limits, when we've gone as far as our bodies and imagination can take us, we meet the eternal ones—the powers that built our flesh out of the mineral accidents of creation and that are now building our individual fates out of time and the accidents of our hearts. They are as spaceless and timeless as numbers and yet, as with numbers, all order in space and time comes from them. In a glare of earthlight, the Crow emerges out of the super-real. He is the appetite of the eternal ones for the mortal powers of the world.

J. O'Barr's *The Crow* is an excarnation of this celestial devourer. This Crow is the same melancholy avenger who castrated his father (Uranus), king of the mountains, ten thousand years ago in the first kingdoms, the brutal Aryan war camps of Indo-Europe. He is immemorially old—and inconsolable. Because he is his own hades. Ghosts dwell in him. His clown-white and feminine features harken back to the ivory Crow-goddess of a hundred thousand years ago. The maker as the taker, the blood-drained face of mama death, her ghost crows descending to pluck the souls from our corpses.

The blood remembers this. What O'Barr adds is the acid-burn of city apocalypse. The physical dread of our animal grief in the asphalt canyons where death pretends to be life. By this immediacy, O'Barr creates rough, spare, sinewy, and rapid arcs of vision and makes a simple supernatural tale of revenge a poison-cure to the complete absence of imagination in mindless violence.

Tears. Salty blood. Bone shards and the sludge of brains attend this vision of the transcendental mystery of the Crow. It is how the dead are tongued with fire. It is an unnaturally natural way to express what the dead have no speech for. Shadows of ink play with motionless motions on the emptiness of the page and a Crow wakes in the heart. It is an illusion and a voluptuous truth about why we are unfinished and cannot fly.

And, because the hand really is no different from what it creates, it is also O'Barr's personal truth—a ritual. Done for us.

As with every true ritual, it is a killing floor. The more sacred the ritual, the more messy and gruesome the bloodletting. Saturn disemboweled. Odin pierced and hanging from the storm tree. The Crow creating a zombie to destroy dozens of violent, evil lives. This purging of evil is a primordial fantasy prominent even at the deepest range of consciousness—because it is rooted in the suzerain truth that we are all equal before death. No mortal has the right to take another's body or life. Yet people are raped and killed every hour. The whole world is infected, and the innermost secret spirit inside the recesses of inert matter watches without blinking.

The Crow is this chthonic spirit's long fantasy. Four billion years of raw food eaten alive has made the animal mind we have inherited a wild, hungry happiness. Life feeds voraciously on the silences of the dead. Behold our species's ravening of planetary resources. We are already, all of us, survivors of the aftermath. In our ignorance and tameless greed we have raped and killed the only woman the Crow ever loved. Now his scar-split mask fills the world, and each of us is one of his casualties.

Fleas

Iggy Pop

There is a pain in life
which visits us all.
Of course, we want to know why.

Why?

If this pain be unjust,
then actions are futile,
living is joking,
and the world is bad.

If our pain reflects justice,
then it follows to spend our lives
rooting out our faults
one by one without end,
like street dogs forever
with fleas.

Spooky, Codeine and the Dead Man

James O'Barr

JO'B '98

S pooky Stone cooked up the heroin in his lucky bottle cap, the bottom of which was thick with black carbon. After a time he slipped a long cold shiny needle into his last fat vein, the tourniquet shading his arm a flush lavender. He fell back on his ratty bed as the opiate spread through his body; Monkey Island screaming, God French-kissing his skull sockets. The euphoria of oblivion settled over him like warm blankets.

For a moment, before Morpheus poured sick dreams into his head, he thought about the dead man.

S pooky Stone and Apache Rick were doing the Hispanic girl in the storeroom of Ahmad's Stop and Go. She wasn't really cooperating, that was until Rick had given her a full roundhouse, and then she was crying through blood and spit and pieces of tooth and cooperating. Spooky had lured her into the back room by offering to smoke some rocks with her, and then Rick tackled her with a bear hug. Ahmad put the CLOSED sign in the window and bolted the door. He didn't care to participate but wanted to videotape the action. Spooky and Rick, sick bravado pumping like adrenaline, readily agreed as long as their faces didn't appear on the recording.

The girl had gone hysterical on them, kicking and convulsing, finally vomiting and wetting herself. Spooky, who was forcing himself into her from behind, fell back in disgust, shouting profanities and curses at her. His revulsion roiled into anger and he began kicking her furiously in the back, in the rib cage. She seemed to lose consciousness momentarily.

Ahmad continued to videotape the assault, maneuvering around for better angles on the violence.

Apache Rick was doubled over, clutching his groin where the girl had bitten him out of spasmodic fear. The whites of her eyes clouded over with blood and she gasp-whispered for mercy.

A sudden quiet hushed over the storeroom. The kerosene space heater stalled and a rush of icy October chill wafted through the room.

Everyone turned toward the rear door as the ghost slipped out of the shadows, out of nothing and into everything. Spooky's eyes went wide, comical, and Apache Rick stood erect, a thin rope of saliva swaying from his lower lip. Ahmad dropped his Sony camcorder and backed toward the entrance.

The ghost looked seven feet tall. He walked slowly toward the center of the room and the bare overhead bulb glanced off his forehead and began spinning crazily, casting shadows like dancing jesters, ceiling to floor, up and down. The specter's face was ash-white and his eyes and lips were lined in kohl like a circus clown's, a forced smile painted on his mouth. His long, shaggy black hair looked like ravens crawling up his shoulders.

He laughed and it sounded like a tomb closing, low, almost subsonic. Spooky could feel it in his bones; it felt like pure fear.

"The sins you make by two and two must be paid for one by one," the dead man said.

"What the fuck does that mean?" asked Spooky, his voice quivering.

This is when things started to speed up.

Apache Rick went for the nine millimeter he usually had tucked down the back of his jeans, but he'd laid it on a nearby shelf as his pants were down. Ahmad tripped backward over a case of malt liquor and cursed Allah in some Middle Eastern dialect.

The ghost raised his hands toward heaven and the sleeves of his black leather trench coat fell back to his elbows. His forearms were covered with a hundred razor cuts, all sloppily sewn up with carpet thread. They looked like railroad tracks holding the bone and muscle together, a ghastly sight—some of the lacerations were still wide open, the red tissue underneath hot with infection.

"Forgive them, Lord, for they know not what they do," he whispered. "They need your forgiveness."

"I don't need nothin' from your white ass," Rick sputtered, angry with fear.

"I'm not *offering* anything," he said, glaring, "I'm *delivering* slow death."

Spooky and Rick both thought they saw a black bird lofting about his shoulders but it just wouldn't seem to come into focus.

"Do you remember me, Apache Rick?" the dead man asked, his voice a thousand-year-old wind.

"Nope," Rick said, inching his way toward his handgun, "I sure don't, but I can tell you you're gonna be in a world of hurt for stickin' your nose in my business."

"One year ago . . . ," he continued, oblivious or uncaring of Rick's threat, "you . . . and five of your accomplices . . . you raped and killed an angel . . ."

"Man, I had nothin' to do with that . . . that was them other niggers . . ." Spooky jumped in, a desperate attempt to distance himself from something that he knew, down in his soul, there were going to be horrific consequences for. Rick and the other Apaches had fucked over this guy's domain, and now it was time to pay. *This kind of shit always comes back to bite you in the ass,* he thought, *and I wasn't in on it.*

"Me neither, man! I wasn't even *in* this country!" Ahmad interjected.

"Who the fuck are you?" Rick shouted, outrage tinged in his voice. "That bitch got what was coming to her and her pansy-ass boyfriend, too. Called Five Oh on us for something that was none of her bidness. Fuck her and fuck you. She your sister? Guy your brother? You fuck with the Apaches and shit rains down on your head hard. That's the facts."

He was six inches away from the gun now. If he kicked the spic bitch again that should give him the moment. His eyes shifted from the ghost to the gun, back again.

"I am the boyfriend," the dead man said, "and you put a bullet in the back of my head."

"Shit, shit, shit," Spooky said, "this ain't happenin'."

This is when the ghost went insane. "I begged you not to hurt her," he said. He was crying. "Please, please don't hurt her—" Now his voice was a scream. "Monsters!" he wailed. He began spinning and shaking, waving his arms like an epileptic seizure. Cans and jars crashed to the floor, whole shelves came down, he was a hurricane of rage. "MONSTERS!"

The dead man suddenly had a Colt Python .357 pistol in his hand, or perhaps it was always there. In any event, it was Apache Rick's last moment to draw breath. The ghost casually took aim and the gun discharged like rolling thunder, bright as lightning.

Rick's head exploded in a scarlet blossom, brain matter and skull fragments stinging Spooky's cheeks in a hot wet spray. Spooky fell to his knees saying, "fuck, fuck, fuck," like some Detroit good-luck mantra. He padded around the storeroom floor on his knees trying vainly to locate Rick's handgun. His chant metamorphosed into "Jesus, Jesus, Jesus."

Rick took a staggering step forward, his body still unaware that its head was no longer issuing commands. Blood jetted outward in a warm fan, drenching the storeroom shelves and their wares. He slowly came to his knees and then flopped over on the Hispanic girl, who began a new round of hysterics, trying unsuccessfully to dislodge the corpse. The ghost walked over and, with a booted foot, kicked Rick's body off the girl.

Ahmad and Spooky were frozen. Smoke settled through the room and everyone's ears rang like church bells.

The ghost knelt down and put a gentle hand on the girl's shoulder. She shuddered instinctively, but calm washed over her when she looked into his sad eyes. They were two different colors of blue—the left iris ruptured into a crystal slush.

"What is your name, princess?" he asked, all the calmness of an ocean in his words.

She looked up at him through tears and mouthed, "Anna."

"Everything's going to be all right now, Anna." He half smiled. "No one's going to hurt you anymore, I promise."

Ahmad found Rick's gun before Spooky did. With a trembling hand he leveled it at the ghost. "You come into my place, you fuck, and blow away this nigger over somethin' that don't even concern me."

The dead man turned and looked up slowly, fury boiling in his veins.

"This . . . *This* concerns you," he said, gesturing toward Anna. He started to rise, big as the sun, heavy as an orbit.

Ahmad fired the gun and the ghost tumbled over, his raincoat billowing up like smoke.

It was quiet as a grave for a moment afterward. Ahmad's thoughts raced like greyhounds. What the hell was he going to do with the bodies? Shit, the girl was going to have to be capped, too. *Damn, what a fuckin' nightmare.* Goddamn crazy white-faced fool. "You in this up to your ass, too, Spooky, this shit on your hands, too."

Anna began sobbing softly.

"Fuck," Ahmad said, and stepped over Rick, aiming the pistol at her head.

The dead man rose. Crimson etched his face like a claw, a gaping hole in his forehead. Blood oozed down his nose to hang in a thick drop. His tongue snaked up and licked it free. "You're going to die," he laughed.

Ahmad tried to fire the gun again but he was weak with fear and his sweat-slick finger kept sliding off the trigger. Finally, he got a firm grip and began firing wildly. Bottles and canned foods began exploding, spraying everything in glass, alcohol, and thick brown fluids.

The ghost walked directly into the gunfire, raised the Colt and shot Ahmad square in the face. He tumbled over backward, his feet going overhead, a trail of thick gore mimicking the movement, the force of the shot propelling his body into the next room.

Spooky dropped to his knees. "Don't kill me, don't kill me, please," he begged. "I'll do anything you say."

"I'm not going to kill you . . . now," the dead man said, ejecting the clip out of Rick's gun. He thumbed the live shell out of the chamber and it thumped off Spooky's head. "You have until midnight to make amends between God and yourself."

He's gonna let me go. Spooky was elated.

The dead man picked up Anna and left into the cold night. It was four hours till midnight.

Spooky's cigarette tumbled out of his mouth and the hot ashes sprayed the bedsheets. *They were filthy anyway,* he thought.

He considered leaving the city but he had no car, nowhere to go. No, if the dead man found him, he'd deal with it. Heroin didn't necessarily make him brave, only ambivalent.

He fished the smoke out of the covers and settled back against the wall. He finally nodded into a warm opiate dream.

In the dream he was driving. He wasn't sure, but he thought it was Blackie's car: an Oldsmobile Cutlass Supreme. It was dusk and he was speeding through the ghetto, blowing red lights and stop signs like they didn't exist. The roads appeared to be deserted. He saw no pedestrians or homeless people. He fumbled with a near empty pack of Kools, breaking two cigarettes before finally luring one out and getting it lit. It started to rain and he successfully found the wipers on the turn signal switch after turning on the radio and rear defroster, raising the antenna, and pitching the lumbar support into an incredibly uncomfortable position.

After a time it was dark, in his dream, and he turned on the lights at the same moment he remembered the codeine.

There was a brown prescription bottle lying on the passenger seat. He snatched it up and read the label: Tylenol #4 with codeine. He smiled; it was a full bottle, thirty tablets. He thumbed the top off and dumped four or five pills into his mouth. Codeine was a good high, a sister drug to morphine, but, Jesus, it tasted like shit, he thought. He was crunching on the white tabs when the police lights caught his attention. Shit, he was doing nearly 75 mph through a residential section. The lights cycled blue-red-blue-red and he thought he could hear a siren wailing around him. The Tylenols were stuck in his throat. He accelerated—75 to 80 to 85. He tried to think of a car named after an animal and couldn't come up with one.

They were out of the city now, on the expressway at speeds nearing 100 mph. The police car was right on his bumper. He got an idea to discourage the cop: he jammed on the brakes and the police car slammed into his rear and pieces of taillight and bumper guards fell away as he accelerated again.

Spooky decided to eat a few more Tylenols: if he was going to spend the night in jail, he was going to feel good doing it. Reaching over he found that the lid had come off the bottle and the tablets were falling down into the seat. He dug his fingers around the seat belt and tried to palm some of the pills. At the same instant he glanced at the speedometer: 105 mph. The rain was hitting the windshield like bullets. The Cutlass started to vibrate at the wheels or frame, he wasn't sure which.

The police car rammed him again and the rear window shattered. The siren was deafening now.

Why couldn't he think of a car named after an animal?

The speedometer read 110 mph now. A molding blew off the front end and whipped over the roof like a javelin.

He managed to get a few more Tylenols into his mouth.

The speedometer read 120 mph now and there was no pedal left. He stomped on it, pounding it into the floor pan.

"Come on! Come on!" He hammered on the steering wheel. The car shook like a blender and was nearly airborne.

Suddenly there was a figure in the road. He instinctively went for the brake but the car's velocity wouldn't slow.

The figure in the road was the dead man from earlier that night. Spooky screamed and the Cutlass hit the ghost like it was a brick wall.

In slow motion: the front end of the Cutlass wrapped around the lone figure. The fenders, hood, and grille all collapsed as if the ghost were a tree. The car's sheet metal folded around him in an iron caress.

The dead man slowly raised his arms in a Christ-like pose. A smile washed down his face.

The impact lifted Spooky off the seat, propelled bottles and trash that were in the back forward. In his peripheral vision, Spooky saw the little white Tylenol pills fly past him and burst into tiny dust clouds.

Just before he smashed through the windshield he thought, *Buick . . . Buick Wildcat . . .*

Spooky shot awake in bed, covered in cold sweat. *Just a dream,* he thought. A dream. He glanced over at the small alarm clock laying next to his works on the nightstand. Twelve o'clock midnight. His breath came in bursts.

The dead man stood at the front of his bed. "Guess what?" the ghost said.

Goings Forth

James S. Dorr

"Since the trickster's antics have a way of leading to acts of
creation, he is susceptible of being treated as a god, even if he has
the personality of a devil."

"Raven's preoccupation is hunger."
—John Bierhorst, *The Mythology of North America*

Raven, Rook, Crow, Jackdaw,
Carrion Crow in the dim mists of Europe,
his names were many;
called Geb in the flatness of Nile-watered Egypt
he married the Sky,
his back carried verdure;
separated by Ra-Atum from his bride, still he was able to
      father children,
Osiris who he, after, made Pharaoh in his stead—
Khenti Amenti, the "Lord of the Westerners," those who had
      passed forth—
Set—"Evil Brother"—and Isis and Nephthys,
Horus the Elder;
by Plutarch identified as the Greek Cronus,
he governed Time, he the father-castrator,
the eater of children so new life might blossom.

But Raven's father, so states a tale of the Northwest Coast
      tribesmen,
was shamed by the great appetite of his son, engendered by
      licking the scabs of the wounded,
and so handed him a Crow-suit of black feathers,
and named him Wigyet—"Giant"—
and handed him a seed-filled bladder
and sent him forth,
telling him thus to sow berries to cover the mainland,
and fish eggs to fill its streams,
so that there might nevermore be hunger . . .

And farther East, Crow taught the Iroquois Nation the
planting of corn . . .

And yet was not himself filled:

In Europe, as Odin, he, one-eyed, sent forth the Hunt,
Wild, of his Valkyrs collecting the souls of men;
Southward, in Egypt, now woman-formed—see the wings!—
set forth as Isis to visit the chieftain, Ra, of her wronged
        father—
Ra-Atum, he of the Sun, aged now and trembling—
and, through her sorcery, beguiled with a serpent's bite,
stinging him cruelly,
in such way he knew not the method to cure himself
until she, wheedling, took from him his secret name,
and, thus, the Sun's power;
so too the son of a brother of Cronus, Prometheus,
stole Heaven's fire;
as, later, Isis with her husband-brother ruled over the souls
of those "gone forth by daylight"—

As, so the tales tell us, Wigyet decided that food would be
*   better sought*
if there were daylight,
and so, flying through the clouds, found the daughter of
*   Heaven's Chief about to drink from a bucket.*
He thus changed himself to the leaf of a cedar and, floating
*   within and so swallowed by her, he made her pregnant.*
In this way Crow was born into the Sky's house and,
finding light hung in a box from its ceiling,
he stole it to Earth with him where, when he came upon frog
*   people night fishing,*
he demanded as his share a candlefish.

This they refused him and so, in spite, he broke the box of
    Day open,
thus flooding the world with light.

As, on Crete, Icarus, Geb-like sought to approach his bride,
    the Sky,
and, decked out in feather-wings made by his father, flew up
    to Ra's throne room
and, singed by the Sun's heat—
his feather-coat blackened—
fell down to the sea;
and black feathers whirlwinded over the ocean to cover three
    continents;
more, as the Sun's boat sailed west to its setting—

And Wigyet, the tales say, as Bearer of Light wandered
    forth till he met Stone and Elderberry,
arguing as to which one might give birth first.
Soon tiring of this, Raven touched Elderberry and so she
    delivered;
and so people die soon instead of enduring, as Stone's
    children might have.

Yet Crow was not sated.

As Isis discovered her husband's corpse, slain by Set,
yet through her magic could animate it, enough to lie by it,
and so delivered the Osirian Horus—
Hor-sa-iset, the Infant Avenger—
and hid him from Set, her husband's brother, until he
    reached manhood.

And War was invented!

God battled god with lance and pruning scythe,
gutting the vanquished,
until at last Horus, having lost one eye—
just as the Moon's eye winks monthly to darkness—
castrated his uncle.

And, cawing, Crow glided the field of flesh, seeking souls,
Valkyrlike lifting them,
fetching them in his beak into the tunnels of Going-Forth-
      Under-Earth
where hearts are measured by a single feather—
to balance or not balance—
be saved or eaten . . .

And thirty-six tales in all are told of Raven,
of ribaldry, gluttony, spitefulness, killing,
and one more tale, finally,
in which the Bearer of Light sends a summons to all the
      world's monsters
to join him in feasting on a distant island,
and, trapping them there, the Trickster turns all to stone.
Turns himself with them.
Yet others say, still, somewhere beyond the mountains,
to the East—to the rising Sun—he lies yet,
ready to share food with wanderers . . .

As Crow, no night-bird he, yet decked in Night's plumage,
turned chthonic now in his ways,
guiding souls' Goings-Forth to death's completion—
assisting those sundered, like Geb and his Sky Bride
unjustly, by others—
and, always, avenging;
coursing his way over continents, islands,
he trails Atum's sun-barque through basalt-faced alleyways
      gleaming beneath the moon;
slab-sided pyramids peopled, as in Egypt, often with those
      dying;
deafened with music, bright, blinded in neon;
and always seeking
to balance,
to not balance—

As elderberries grow rife on men's graves—

   still Crow remains, hungered.

THE BLOOD-RED SEA

WILLIAMSON

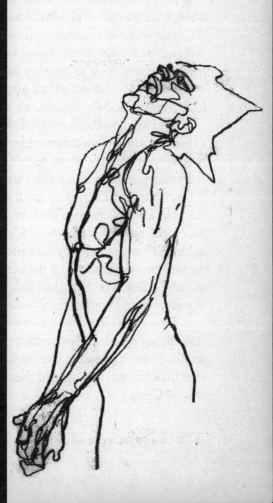

*B*lood-red. Yes, that was what he should have called it. But he had not seen blood before. He had tasted it, of course, just as he had tasted wine, but the taste of blood had no beauty in it, while the taste of wine did. Thus, the sea, what should be the most beautiful sight of all, as he thought then and knew now, had become wine-red as the sun rose and set upon it.

Red. That was all his pupils had told the singer.

—It's red, master. The setting sun makes the clouds red, and then the sea turns red as well.

Even Timaeus could say little more:

—It is the red of apples, master, and sometimes the pink of the inside of shells, and sometimes the red of the stone of certain cliffs.

Well, that was certainly edifying. Though blind, the singer knew that stone could be of many different colors.

And yet Timaeus had been the most promising pupil he had ever had. Though the youth had no gifts of song himself, he could nigh perfectly commit the singer's words to memory. Timaeus knew the two great songs, the first of war and the second of wandering, as surely as the singer did. And he had committed the new song to memory as well, the song of aspiration, the song on which the singer had worked for many years, his song of songs, his masterpiece. Only Timaeus and the singer knew that song. And it had died with them both.

That was how the singer finally knew the color of blood, by awakening next to Timaeus's body, with the great black bird sitting in the branches of the tree near him. In one moment, he was senseless, dwelling in the land of death, bereft not only of sight, as he had been all his life, but of touch and breath and life itself. And in the next moment, sensation had flooded back into his gashed and hacked body.

His eye sockets, their dead fruit plucked by the sword points of the renegades who had killed him, were filled anew, burning with the fire of the great golden orb whose light he had felt on his flesh but never before seen. He pressed his eyelids shut, but the burning ball remained glowing on the inside of them, a bright circle in the blackness, sending straight rays outward, blinding him with light rather than darkness.

Pressing his hand over his eyes, he turned his head away from the sun, and felt his bearded cheek rubbing against blades of grass. High grass surrounded him, embracing him on all sides, and he shielded his new, sighted eyes from the sun and opened them again.

—*Green.*

This was green, had to be green, for what grew all about him felt like grass, smelled like grass, and he knew that grass was what men called green, and though he expected the green of grass to be cool, it seemed hot to his unlearned eyes, as hot as the sun's touch upon him.

But there were other colors in the grass. The long, wide blades seemed touched by something else, by droplets that had clung and dried to the green. They were darker, a color the singer could not name, ignorant of what liquid, wine or water or milk or some exudation from tree or sky, had dropped thereon.

There were trees about him, too, but he had only a vague idea as to how close they were to him. He knew how big around trees were, and thought that perhaps that big oak might be thrice again the length of a man away. Then he heard the caw of a crow, and gazed upon his first living creature.

This was assuredly a crow, for he had touched both living and dead birds. He had been told that a crow was black, and black was the only color that he knew well, for it was what was seen when the eyes were closed or blinded. But he did not expect blackness to have this sheen to it. As the crow spread wide its wings, it seemed that blackness was many colors thrown over darkness.

Then the singer looked at his arm lying on the ground next to his body. The hand was still attached, and wasn't that wrong? Hadn't the renegades cut off his hands? Of course they had, because after the great pain in his left arm, he had felt upon it with his right hand, and discovered that there was nothing after the wrist, only hot blood that jetted against his right palm as he strove to hold it within his body.

And then they had laughed again, and cut off his right hand. They had done this, he recalled, but dimly, as of some other time and place, amidst the towers of the long-ago cities of which he had sung. They had killed him because he had tried to save Timaeus. He had heard the youth's screams, and cried out:

—No! I am only a singer, and he is my pupil! Don't harm him, I beg you!

But Timaeus shrieked all the louder, and from the renegades' bawdy oaths he knew that they were having the boy. The singer swung his staff toward where he guessed them to be, and connected with a hearty thud that made one of the attackers grunt with pain. It was then that he felt the sword sever his hand that held the staff. After they had cut off both hands, he had fallen to his knees, the weight of his body resting for a moment upon his stumps until the agony of the contact knocked him on his side. It was then that they had spitted his blind eyes, and stabbed at him with their swords, over and over, until the life left his body and all his senses were as dead as his sight.

As he was drifting into the land of the dead, he could only think of two things—the pity of Timaeus's dying, and the loss of the song of aspiration, the great song that could never now be sung, and he hated these men, these rene-gades, these cowards who attacked a youth and a blind man rather than their lord's enemies. He hated these creatures who took away, not only his life, but the greatest of his songs from the world.

Hate flooded through him as he died, and all he could think was:

—*This is not right. This is* not right!

Even as he was thinking it, he felt that it seemed a simple and childlike thought to be having, and wondered if the brave and swift Achilles would have had such a thought when he went down to death. Then, in the middle of that thought, the singer died.

And awoke.

It seemed to take only a moment, but now all was quiet, and it was day. The sun was shining brightly, too brightly for his new eyes, and the grass, green grass, was dappled with the strange, dark-colored drops. The singer turned, shielding his gaze from the sun with his hands, which Zeus had restored as well as his sight, and when he looked at what lay next to him, he knew at last what liquid had bathed the green grass.

It was the blood of the youth who lay only a few handbreadths away. The singer had never before seen flesh or blood, and it took a moment for him to realize that this thing next to him had been human. In his mind, he connect-ed the spatial features that he saw with what he had known of the human form from feeling of it with his hands, and knew it for what it was. It was not, how-ever, until he had crawled across to the body and placed his hand upon its face and hair that he whispered:

—Timaeus . . .

Timaeus had not come back from the land of the dead. His throat had been cut, and the swords had played about in his bowels. This then was blood, thought the singer. This then was red. It looked darker than he thought red would look. It was not the red of his rose-fingered dawn:

—*It is red, master, red like roses.*

He could smell roses, but the smell of their redness was not like the smell of the redness of blood. This was a briny, sour smell, a smell of death and loss and sorrow and stupidity, the smell of a song stopped in a throat opened by iron.

The singer heard the cry of the crow again, and he turned to look at it, but it came streaking over his head—his first sight of quick motion, unex-pected and unique in his memory. He gasped and pressed his face down into the grass, felt the stickiness of Timaeus's blood against his cheek and fore-head.

The crow screamed again, and he looked up to see it perching on

Timaeus's face, its claws clinging to his lips and jaws. It looked at him with sharp eyes, and the singer felt as though it were somehow challenging him, telling him about something he must do.

The crow's head bobbed as its eyes looked at the singer's hands, first one, and then the other, and then the singer knew that his rebirth, the regaining of his hands, and, most miraculously, his eyes, were due to this crow, and he knew beyond doubt who it was. He spoke the name:

—Zeus . . .

Of course. It was Zeus, king of all gods, come down to the world in the form of a crow, as he had come down so many other times in the shapes of beast and bird, to interpose himself and his justice in the realm of men. He had given the poet hands and eyes. He had brought him back from the everlasting blackness of Hades and given him life so that he could . . .

What? Sing his song, the great epic of aspiration and striving and triumph that had died when he and Timaeus had drunk of the renegades' iron? Or something else, something darker?

The crow's beak descended to the side of Timaeus's mouth, and it seemed to drink from the dark red blood that had dried on the boy's lip. Then the bird, Zeus, king of gods, lifted its head again and looked at the singer, and now its gaze was implacable. The singer knew its purpose and his own. The knowledge surged into his mind of what he should do, what he *must* do, for Zeus had brought him back from the dead, him, a simple singer, to take what was wrong, as boldly as Heracles had grasped the horns of the Cretan bull, and make it right once again.

The three men who had killed him and Timaeus, those who had silenced his song, must die. Only then could the singer rest in peace among the quiet dead.

He knew that it was true. He felt the torment of his and the youth's deaths in the taut sinews of his body, in the cold fire of the blood rushing through him, and the only thing that would assuage his torment, Zeus told him with the bird's beady eyes, was the sword, used against those who had slain him.

The god-crow startled him then by rising from Timaeus's body and flying into the air, flapping his dark wings across the sea of grass and descending some distance away. The singer followed.

The claws of the king of gods grasped a large bush, and beneath, the singer found a short sword, its leather hilt rotted until its green was lighter than that of the grass, its edge rusted to the color of Timaeus's blood. The singer reached for it, and was surprised when his hand grasped it so quickly. He had always been used to fumbling for things, and it was an unexpected delight to see his hand move to something and close upon it so easily, particularly this hand that had been severed. When the singer looked closely at his wrist, he could see a light, thin line where Zeus had reattached it.

The sword felt foreign in his hand, however, and he swung it through the air at the unspoken behest of Zeus. Immediately the god-crow arose and skimmed through the air, upward out of the bowl of land in which the singer stood, and in which he and Timaeus had met their deaths. The singer followed, holding the sword loosely at his side.

If this was what he had to do, then so be it. He truly hated the renegades, and wished their deaths. Perhaps if he accomplished this, if he fulfilled the will of Zeus, the god would allow him to remain on the earth long enough to teach his final song to another, or, better yet, to have the words written down by a scribe, as had been done with his other two songs, though unfaithfully, if the fragments of them that had been read to him were indicative. He had orally corrected the written texts whenever he could, but he could not know how many error-laden copies, twisted as rope and rotten as aged meat, existed.

—Oh Zeus, grant that, if I do your will and shed the blood of these men, I may sing my song one final time and leave it behind for men to hear, before I go down to Hades. Grant me this, mighty Zeus.

He followed the bird, his heart heavy with the thought of killing, but buoyed by hope as the sailor adrift on a roaring sea.

The heart of the singer lightened as he walked toward the rim of the hill. All about him were trees and weeds and flowers blooming in such colors whose names he could only guess. Some he had touched, and so recognized by their names, and remembered the colors that he had been told they possessed. So there was purple, there yellow, and that was pink. He paused to kneel down next to them as at shrines, and admire the hues that changed subtly, delicately on a single petal.

The god-crow called again. He looked up and saw it circling impatiently above his head. It seemed to want the singer to follow it, to go on and not stop to look at flowers. But when the singer looked at it, he could not help but stand amazed, marveling at the grace of the bird drifting through the sky, outlined against what he now knew to be blue, a pure color that seemed radiant, lit by itself as much as by the bright yellow ball of the sun. Clouds, *white* clouds, hung in the sky, round and puffy like great piles of cloths, and the singer laughed at the sight, at the sheer beauty of sky.

Zeus cried angrily, and swept about toward the rim of the hill. The singer followed, moving his legs faster and faster until he realized that he was running for the first time in his life, not feeling his way, but tirelessly barreling up the hill, which ended in a sharp line across the sky.

Had he been wrong? Was Zeus taking him to Olympus itself? Would he run off the very edge of the earth and soar into the sky with the god?

But as he arrived at the edge of sky and earth, he saw that his road went downward. Spread out below him was a vista that stopped him dead in his tracks, so that he tottered and almost fell, unused to such strength in his limbs.

It was the sea. The sea lay before him, its waves sparkling and glinting with new light. The entire surface of it, as far as he could see, was moving, shifting constantly, and though he had sailed on the sea, to see it at last was awesome and terrifying. It seemed a living thing, ready to swallow up any creature bold or foolish enough to set out upon it. He heard the familiar sound of the waves crashing upon the rocks, but now he *saw* them, white-tongued claws of water ripping at the shore.

But the longer he stared at it, the less fearful he grew, and the more beauty he saw in this seemingly infinite creation of which he had sung, this sea on which his greatest hero had wandered. How much more might he have said in his song had he only been able to first view the majesty of these waters?

At last the raucous cawing of Zeus tore his gaze away from the sea, and he looked at the land below. A small harbor town lay as if between sea and earth. Several small boats, tied at the dock and a pier jutting into the water, moved constantly above and with the swelling of the waves. The singer saw men passing along the narrow dock and in the street, and even from a distance he could admire the supple fluidity of their limbs as they walked and raised their hands in greeting to others. There was so much movement and color and life that his mind could scarcely comprehend it all.

He walked down the road toward the village, the sword in his hand forgotten. Children were playing on the hillside, and birds flew from tree to tree. An animal ran with the children, and when it barked, the singer was sure that it was a dog, as he had first suspected. The animal came bounding in his direction, and he did what he had always done when there was a dog present. He fell to his knees and embraced it, his hands still responding to the tactile contact, but his eyes now able to see it as well, its hairy face and wide, friendly eyes, its red, drooling tongue. The singer laughed as the dog licked him. It was such a funny-looking creature, so happy and eager to please.

The god-crow screamed, angry and impatient, and the dog, startled, ran back to the children.

—Yes, my lord, I'm coming . . . but there is so much to see . . .

The singer followed, wishing he had known how jolly dogs could look when he sang of old and faithful Argos. Perhaps, when his mission for Zeus was completed, he could sing some new lines about the dog, so that it not only wagged its tail and ears, but laughed to see its old master returned.

The huge black bird flew far ahead of the singer, and he saw its form drift down upon a post at the end of the narrow pier. The singer allowed himself to run again, down the hill toward the town. It was, he thought, like flying.

The wind rushed through his hair and made the cloth of his garment flap against his sides, as the trees and brush blurred past. But near the bottom he realized that he was running too fast to stop himself, and he tripped and fell, rolling over and over until he came sliding and scraping to a halt on the loose dirt.

He had fallen before, but, amazingly enough, this time he felt no pain. The flesh of his knees and elbows were not, as he had feared, ripped open, and he only laughed and pushed himself to his feet again. He felt invulnerable, almost like a god himself.

A young boy had seen the singer's tumble, and asked him if he was all right. He assured the boy that he was, then asked him what town this was. When the boy told him, the singer knew that he had been there several times before with Timaeus and his other pupils. He thanked the boy and walked on.

He saw several different people as he passed through the street. Some walked by without glancing toward him, but those who did looked at him for a long time as he smiled at them, nodded a greeting, and then strode on. He wondered if they recognized him, and were confused to see him strolling through their streets, able to see at last.

Then his smile faded, as he thought about what it was that had finally given him his sight—his own slow and painful death, and the death of Timaeus. It had been a terrible price to pay.

He was at the harbor at last, and the sun was sinking. Had he held out his arm and brought up his hand, its heel would have rested on the sea and his fingertips would have touched the fiery ball that had now darkened to a red orange. Great Zeus, the god-crow, perched on a piling halfway down the pier. At its end sat a man, his back to the singer. His hair was black and shining greasily, as if it had not been washed in many days. There was a short sword stuck through a leather strip that was tied tightly about his waist.

The great bird looked at the singer, and then at the man on the pier. The singer looked about, but saw no one else. The figures that he had seen moving earlier were all gone, perhaps, thought the singer, at the desire of Zeus. He walked slowly down the pier, sword in hand, looking at the waves slapping against the timbers of the pier and the planking of the small boats.

There, on the pier, the sea seemed to be all around him. He smelled its salt, tasted the air in his open mouth, felt the ocean breezes play at his hair and ripple his garment. But now, for the first time in his life, he *saw* it, and all his senses reeled at his proximity to something so huge and powerful. The might of Zeus seemed as nothing compared to the natural power of this kingdom of Poseidon.

As the wind whirled about the singer, the man at the end of the pier seemed to sense that someone was standing behind him. He straightened, and then slowly turned until he was looking at the singer. His mouth opened, dully and stupidly, as though he could not believe what he was seeing, and he staggered to his feet, his gaze still fixed on the singer.

—Have you come back from Hades to torment me? Isn't it enough that my comrades have stolen what we were to share and sailed away? Must the gods now send *ghosts* against me?

The singer felt an icy chill as he heard the man's voice. This was the one who had taken Timaeus, and who had laughed and grunted like a pig in the taking. He felt rage surge within him, waves of it, like the waves that he saw crashing on the nearby rocks. He knew what he was to do, and yet he could not. He told himself that he had to be sure, that it would displease Zeus to make a mistake, ignoring the fact that it was the god-crow himself who had brought the singer to this place, this man.

—Do you know me?

—Yes, I know you. You have your hands back, and you see! What trickery is this? Are you a twin?

The greasy-haired man tugged his sword from his belt.

—If you are, I can kill you as I killed your brother!

He ran toward the singer, the fall of his feet making the pier tremble even more than the lash of the sea. His sword was raised above his head, and the singer looked on in wonder, seeing for the first time a man charging into battle, ready to slay and feed Ares. He could not help but admire the man's economy of motion, the way he held his weapon and balanced his body and closed the gap between them. The singer imagined thousands of men like this, closing the gap between the Trojans and his countrymen hundreds of years before. But not even Zeus could grant him *that* sight.

The greasy-haired renegade brought down his sword, hacking at the spot where the singer's neck met his shoulder. He felt a sudden pain that shivered through his entire body, and then the man wrenched away the sword. The singer saw a streaming trail of his own blood, dark red in the dying light, follow the sword blade.

Suddenly the pain was gone, and when the singer put his hand to his shoulder he felt no wound. He was whole and unharmed, just as he had been when Zeus had brought him back from Hades.

The renegade gawked at him in disbelief, but started to raise his sword again. Then he hesitated, as though considering where to strike next. But the singer could not allow another blow. He did not want to bear the pain again.

Before he even knew what he was doing, he had brought up his own rusted weapon, swinging it so that the blade bit from underneath into the man's ribs, ripping the flesh and cracking the bones, and knocking the renegade off the pier and into the sea. Great gouts of blood and bowel trailed behind the man, and he struck the water with a heavy splash. The singer, dripping sword in hand, walked numbly to the edge and looked into the water.

The renegade was floating on his back, rocking on the surface of the water. The current had spun him about, and his head was knocking rhythmically against one of the posts of the pier. His bowels, still attached to the cavity that the singer's sword had opened, were drifting next to him, thick and ropy.

But what struck the singer most was the blood on the water. It was spreading outward from the body of the dead man like a red cloud, and had even turned to pink the bits of white froth on the edges of the waves.

He looked outward, to where the sun, now red, was sinking still, half of its rondure beneath the waters of the sea, so that all appeared blood-red, the same hue as that surrounding the body of the man the singer had killed, the man who had killed him. Oh yes, it was not a wine-red sea, but a blood-red one.

The singer looked at the corpse again and shuddered. It was ugly. All that he had seen that day, save for Timaeus's body and now the body of this man, had been beautiful.

But this was ugly, this death, this blood, this unnatural taking of life, stopping of hearts, blinding of eyes. For the man's eyes were surely blind now, staring without blinking as the sea's stinging salt washed over them.

And he, a singer of songs, teller of tales, had created this present ugliness.

The call of the crow came from behind him, and he turned and looked at it. Then he asked of it:

—Is this your will?

Zeus did not answer, neither with words nor with a grating caw. Instead it looked at him, unmoving, stared and stared with its shiny black eyes so that he moved closer to it as though it were commanding him to do so, close enough so that the faces of man and bird were only a breath away, and he could see his own reflection in the dark depths of its eyes.

And in those twin mirrors of black glass, he saw his own face, the face of a man who had lost a friend, a song, a life. He saw the face of an angry and bitter man from whom fools had taken all. He saw the face of a man who, as he had entered the land of death, had wanted vengeance more than anything else a god could give. Then the singer realized the truth, and spoke it:

—It was *my* will.

He looked away from the god-crow, back out to the darkening sea, and felt tears course over his wrinkled cheeks. They were as cold as the air, as though the eyes from which they had come had not the heat of the living. He knew then that although he saw, he saw with dead eyes, for *he* was dead, a dead man who walked, brought back to the world for the purposes for which he had wished, the dark purposes for which he must have cried out for Zeus to grant him.

—It was for this, oh lord, wasn't it?

He looked at the crow and pointed down at the dead man floating in the sea. But the crow gave no answer. It did not have to.

Then it rose lazily and flapped into the air, flying along the coast heading north, seeking, the singer knew, the other men, the two who still lived and walked. The singer followed. He had no choice.

He walked through the night, feeling no need to stop to rest or drink or eat. Other roads turned off the one he was on, but whenever there was a fork, he would see the god-crow flying ahead of him, black against the starry sky, and follow it.

The singer moved slowly, so slowly that the bird often grew impatient, and would come flying about his ears, screeching at him to quicken his pace. But the beauties of the night were as new to him as were those of the day, and he hastened reluctantly.

The sky was a constant source of marvels. There was only a crescent moon far down against the horizon, a yellow sliver that allowed the countless stars to gleam brightly. There were the patterns of which he had been told, and which Timaeus had once set out for him with pebbles so that he might, by feeling the relative distance between them, know what lay overhead. He found the great bear and the warrior and the bull, and behind him he thought he could see, on the southern horizon, the great dog leaping out of the sea.

The golden curve of the moon held his attention most strongly, however. Though his new eyes were sharp enough to behold the hazy jewel in the dagger at the warrior's hip, he could not follow the stars as they slowly passed between the horns of the moon. One by one they winked out, and the singer wondered if the moon ate them, and then spat them out again behind him.

There were many such questions he would have liked to contemplate, but the god-crow hurried him on. Instead of sitting on a rock and watching how the sea mirrored the moon in its waters, he was forced to rush toward the fate of this first choosing, that fate for which Zeus had returned him.

He walked tirelessly all night, the sword in his hand, watching in fascination as the moon rose higher in the sky and then vanished beneath the sea, and the stars slowly wheeled through their arcs against the great sphere of blackness overhead. At last the darkness began to brighten in the east over the hills, and for the first time in his life he beheld the rose-fingered dawn of which he had sung for years, and was overjoyed to see that his words were true, free of hyperbole.

The growing light brought more and more to the singer's eyes, and he rejoiced in the sights of field and forest, of the rocks between land and sea, of the birds flitting and creatures scurrying about to begin their day. The world seemed filled with glory, until the sight of the man made him remember his errand.

The man sat on a fallen tree, far ahead. At first the singer thought that he was one of the two remaining renegades, but as he drew nearer he could see that the man was young, his aspect was gentle, and he bore no sword. The god-crow flew past him, continuing down the road, but the singer paused, looking into the youth's smiling face.

The youth greeted him and said that his name was Creophylus. The singer told him his name, and Creophylus stood, his smile replaced by a look which the singer could not identify, even though he was fascinated by the way the youth's face moved as he spoke, the play of flesh and muscles and eyes.

—I too am a singer. I have heard of you. And your songs. They are like no other's.

The singer smiled at this unexpected praise.

—But I had heard that you were without sight.

—The gods . . . are good.

So at least he hoped. Creophylus then spoke with ardor.

—May I go with you?

—I don't know where I'm going. I'm following that great crow.

—It doesn't matter. I only wish to walk and speak with you, if you will allow me.

So they walked on, the young Creophylus keeping up handily with the singer's rapid stride.

—Why are you following the crow?

—Because he is divine, and he takes me to my fate. I know little more than that.

He would not tell the youth of his death and rebirth. He did not know how he would act were he to know he was walking with a living dead man.

So they spoke of the singer's songs, and Creophylus recited parts of them. The singer was, as always, glad to know that his words would live after him. At least *some* of his words, he corrected himself. The song of striving had died.

Or had it?

—I have composed a new song, of aspiration and striving, on the life of Heracles. May I sing it for you as we walk?

From the way Creophylus's face beamed, the singer knew he was about to answer yes, but he did not have the chance. The god-crow darted back toward them, at first, the singer supposed, to harry him onward, but instead Zeus's incarnation drifted away from the road, down toward the sea.

The singer turned off the path and trotted down toward the water, Creophylus at his heels. The first thing he saw was the wreckage of a small boat that must have been broken on the many rocks lying off the shore. The next was the bodies of two men lying on the strand.

They were still alive, pulling themselves up the strand and away from the lapping water, moving slowly and sinuously, like snakes in the cold. The rocks had torn their flesh, and they were leaving trails of blood upon the pebbles of the shore. If they had had swords, they must have tossed them away when they entered the water, lest the weight of the iron help to drag them down.

The first thing that came into the singer's mind was to aid them, and he ran to the closest man with the intention of pulling him up the strand and then seeing to his injuries. But when the nearly drowned man looked up and saw the singer, he gave a squeal and cried out:

—I am drowned after all and in Hades! And here is a ghost to torture me!

The singer knew the voice, and knew why the man said what he did. These were the other two men who had slain him and Timaeus. The god-crow had not led him on an errand of mercy, but on one of death.

The second man looked up at the singer then and said nothing, only whimpered, stopped crawling, and let his head fall heavily onto the pebbles of the strand. He was sobbing, his salt tears the heavy tide of his guilt.

The sword felt huge and unwieldy in the singer's hands. But the time had come, the time to kill again, to destroy, to make more ugliness in this beautiful world.

And was that not just? He had sung, and gloried in the singing, of the great battlefields where men threw away their lives for vanity, or for the motives of kings that meant nothing to them. His most terrible songs had been of the scores of dead and their hacked-off heads and limbs, of rivers of blood pouring across the plains of war. And having sung all these death-songs, could he not take the lives of two swine who robbed and killed, not understanding the great gifts they had been given, those gifts of life and eyes with which to see the world? He had justly slain once, so could he not do so twice and thrice? Could he not butcher these pigs, destroy these unworthy lives?

The god-crow circled overhead, cawing, cawing, its cries a shriek riding above the roar of the sea.

And the singer took the sword and drew it back, and flung it out, out over the waters, farther than the strength of any living man could have thrown it, and it entered the blood-red sea and sank beneath its waves.

The god-crow hovered in the air close to him, as if floating on the wind, and although the singer did not speak aloud, he knew that Zeus heard his thoughts:

—*I am a creator, not a destroyer. I have sung the songs of shed blood, but I will shed no more. If I must suffer pain and loss throughout eternity among the shades in Hades, or in some far more terrible place intended for those who disobey the gods, then so be it. But I will not destroy. I will not defile this world.*

And without waiting to see what the great black bird might do, he turned away from it and from the struggling and fearful men, and put an arm on Creophylus's shoulder, and led him away from the beach, up the hill, and into a place where the sun's rays could touch them. Then he bade the young man join him as he sat upon a rock, and said to him:

—Now, while I still have life, I would sing to you.

And he began to sing to Creophylus the song of yearning and striving and triumph, the song of Heracles. He sang on even as the light began to fade from his eyes, and his voice began to weaken. He sang on as the cold possessed him and he no longer heard the wind among the leaves above them, and all the colors of the world darkened to a blood-red, and slowly to the blackness he had known for all his days, save for this single day and night of glory.

As death took him again, he hoped that Creophylus could remember the small portion of the song that he had sung to him, and his last thought was of how glad he was that Zeus had given him the chance to live again, and to die again.

To die singing. Creating.

*   *   *

The Taking of Oechalia (Οἰχαλίας Ἄλωσις), a poem concerning one of the exploits of Heracles, has passed to this age under the name of Creophylus. Some consider it, however, to have been the work of Homer, who was said to have been Creophylus's friend and possibly his father-in-law. The true provenance of the work, and whether it was part of a larger epic, will probably never be known.

Twice
by
Fire

Ramsey
Campbell

t's like being unable to sleep because of a fever, but it's infinitely worse. It feels as though I may never again be still. I can't tell if I'm cold as naked bones or hot as the heart of a furnace. My skin is crawling like a heap of ash on my body, which is twisted around itself as if to squeeze to death the last of my consciousness. A flickering of flames won't let my awareness take refuge in the dark. Now I'm conscious of the ache of lying on a surface as hard as my bones. The ache feels like the merest hint of worse, but it's clear I can't retreat from it. I open the charred lumps my eyes feel like and admit the light that's snatching at them.

It comes not from flames but from neon, through a gap between two black plastic bags almost as tall as a man. Several bags of garbage loll around me like a drunkard's friends, shaking their heads in a night wind. That must have been the flapping, which is the first thing I remember hearing. The bags block the alley in which I'm lying and conceal me. I've hidden here once before. The idea brings me to my feet. My body is readier than I imagined it might be, and I move to the mouth of the alley in the hope of knowing where I ought to go.

The street extends almost straight for miles. Far down it I hear microscopic shouts and screams and a tinkle of glass. A long black car crosses it, so distantly I can't tell whether its lights are on, and vanishes fast as a snake. Above the street the city jabs the sky with towers, some of them clawed or tipped with giant needles, some perforated with light. Beyond the city, on a horizon bandaged with a strip of cloud, is the silhouette of a hill. Some aspect of it fills me with loneliness, so that I feel emptier than the night. I can't make for the hill yet—I have to know why I am here. I cross the street to the bar whose neon sign brought me back to myself.

The signature of a brand of beer glows in the window. The rear edge of the glow sketches booths and tables in the unlit room. Last time I was here I hid in the alley until it was time to go into the bar. The memory feels as if my consciousness is gliding ahead of me on black wings. I close a hand around the chilly doorknob, and the door swings inward.

As I venture across the bare floorboards a silhouette jerks forward to greet me from behind the bar. It's my reflection in the long mirror against which vampire bottles rest, heads down. My face borrows light from the mirror, and gradually there I am: dark deep eyes, pale cheeks pinched hollow, thin lips weighed down at the corners. I turn away from it and see an object protruding from the shadow in the booth farthest from the door.

It could be the thumb of someone lurking in the booth, except that not only the shadow has cut it off. It's a fat half-smoked cigar—one so ostentatious it ought to have a band around it. As I pick it up, its acrid stench is overwhelmed by a memory of smells so vivid that I sway as if I've just inhaled them: carbonized wood, seared brick. Some grief I shrink from confronting is shriveling my mind into a useless lump of blackness. I stare at the cigar stub, and it tells me nothing at all. I raise my eyes and catch sight of my reflection. "What does it mean?" I hear myself pleading and see myself mouth.

Except that as I repeat the question I see my lips aren't saying it. I think they're struggling to do so until I realize they are forming other words. As they drown in the dimness under the glass they're dredging up the answer. "Look on"—I peer so hard my lips appear to blacken and wither—"the desk."

"Which desk?" Now my face mocks me by mouthing the question every time I ask it, and I'm reaching for a heavy ashtray on the bar to smash the mirror when I understand that some part of me already knows the answer. It feels like blackness and sorrow as sharp and hard as a beak, and I only have to follow where it leads. I drop the stub into a pocket of my coat, a garment so nondescript it tells me nothing about myself. I slip out of the bar and turn toward the hill.

I can't go there yet, I'm certain of that much. It sinks out of view as I leave the bar behind. Half the streetlamps as tall as the four-story blocks are shot out, and most of the properties are boarded up. Beyond more than one nailed-over window I hear sobbing or remains of voices. Some of the boards have been ripped away, and in a shop littered with smashed dusty television sets I make out several figures huddled under newspapers and sacks. A woman mumbles in her sleep, trying to fit her mouth around somebody's name. An empty bottle trundles across the floor, and a shape much smaller than the woman—a baby or a rat—retreats into the darkest corner. I'm not sorry when I reach the end of the prolonged abandoned block and cross an intersection where the prosperous stores begin.

A department store occupies most of the next block. Legs wearing shoes stand in a window, torsos without limbs expose their underwear beside an arrangement of half a dozen heads whose lidless eyes are turned inward, fixed on their nightmares. Light as pale as a mortuary, and rendered meaningless by the desertion of the street, freezes all these objects as though preserving evidence. Beside them are windows that display furniture, and I've passed several when an item snags my attention. Why am I faltering? It's just a double bed with black sheets and pillows and a paneled black headboard. Then a fragment of material rises from the foot of the bed and drifts toward me.

It settles on the inside of the plate glass and sticks there, trembling. It might be a black feather, but it looks more like a flake of oily ash—a flake of the substance to which the entire bed has been reduced. I stretch out my hands as if they can take me through the glass to ascertain the truth of what I'm seeing, and stub my fingers on the window. I'm unable to move for the notion that the bed may be about to collapse before my eyes when down the street a car starts out of a side road, howling and flashing its crown of lights.

Its cry fades along the cross street and is lost in the stone maze of the city. It has reminded me where I have to go. I move so fast I remember nothing of the blocks I leave behind except the glitter of used needles in the alleys. In no time that I'm aware of I arrive at the intersection where the car appeared. There's the police station to the left. It's where my desk is.

The long white building set back from the street glares under spotlights. Several police vehicles are parked outside the glass front doors, beyond which the duty sergeant is reading a self-help book and scratching his head. Preferring for some reason not to attract his attention, I make for the side entrance.

It can only be unlocked by typing the correct digits on a keypad. The combination must bypass my thoughts, because it seems I've hardly touched the first key when I hear the lock yield with a muffled click. I twist the icy handle and step into the bare white concrete corridor, which leads past the cells. I recall sliding back the cover of each spyhole as I passed them. One isn't quite shut, and a glance into the cell shows me that a suspect has shed all his clothes and is urinating at the door with a penis as bald and ruddy as his head. I pass by unnoticed and merge with the shadows in the office at the end of the corridor.

The large square room contains twelve desks, most of them strewn with papers. A single fluorescent tube on the far side of the room is lit, isolating a desk next to the door. I know it isn't my desk, yet my photograph is on it, propped against an hourglass whose lower half is full of red liquid. The face in the picture isn't nearly as haggard or haunted as my face was in the mirror behind the bar. I barely glimpse the difference, because the picture isn't alone on the desk. Beside it is a photograph of a young woman and her little girl.

Lisabeth and her daughter Jodie. Lisabeth's blond hair frames the depths of her brown eyes, cups her freckled cheeks and small nose, points with the end of its fringe at her delicate pink lips. Jodie has an eight-year-old's version of all these features except for her hair, which is curly and black. I want to reach out to them—them, not their images—but I can only fold myself around an ache at the center of me. I'm crouched in the darkest corner, and might as well be hiding there, when two detectives enter the room.

The swarthy sharp-faced man is Fortuna, his graceful deceptively slight partner is Chau. Neither of them sees me. They lift their coats from pegs on the wall and gaze at the photographs on Fortuna's desk. "You could take his apartment while I see if she's talking yet," he says to Chau.

I feel in danger of being torn apart by my inability to follow both of them. "Go together," I mouth.

Fortuna shrugs his shoulders into the heavy coat that's only just wide enough for them, then lifts his head as if he heard something. "Or maybe we should both check the apartment so nothing gets missed," he says.

Chau lingers over thumbing each of the buttons on his raincoat into their buttonholes and pulls his belt just exactly tight enough before he speaks. "We should go to the hospital first."

"Got you," says Fortuna, and for no reason except that's what he does at his desk, upturns the hourglass as Chau switches off the light, leaving the red fluid to drip in the dark.

As soon as they're out of sight I follow. By the time I reach the duty sergeant's desk he has grunted at them and returned to his book. He doesn't hear me pass. The doors are swinging together after the detectives, who are heading for a car. "Want to drive?" Fortuna says.

"Walk," I mouth, slipping through the gap between the doors.

"Not this time of night," says Chau to his partner. "Only time the streets are clean."

"Don't get any cleaner," Fortuna agrees, if he's agreeing, and paces Chau out of the car park.

I don't move until they're around the corner and I judge they've walked half a block. They don't seem to feel any need to look back. I trail them alongside a mile of mud-colored tenements pierced by thousands of windows not much larger than the portholes of a battleship. One street-level window hisses with bright static from a dead television channel, and in another apartment I hear a raw voice ranting at an all-night phone-in show—a voice whose owner may be talking to the presenter or only imagining he is—but otherwise there's nothing to observe except entrance after entrance repeating a view of the foot of a bare stone staircase. I'd rather let that occupy my mind than try to define my grief before I'm confronted with its source. Then an ambulance screeches out of a side road and races into the city, and the detectives turn along the road it came from.

The hospital is close to the main street that leads to the hill I can no longer see. Beyond two parked ambulances a pair of automatic doors are deferring to Fortuna and Chau. I dodge between the ambulances in time for the doors not to need to reopen themselves on my behalf. The detectives are at the reception counter across the lobby, and the receptionist doesn't have to be told what they want. "Jodie Nelson," she says. "Better hustle."

It isn't encouragement I hear in her voice. As the detectives head for the corridor leading to Intensive Care I'm close behind them. They shove each pair of fire doors wide enough to let me pass through a few paces after them. They still haven't noticed me when they veer into a short side corridor that leads to a ward. The ward sister behind her desk raises her eyes to them, and I will her not to say what her eyes are already saying—but though I may be able to make people speak, I can't silence them. "She's gone," the sister says.

"Shit," says Fortuna, and lifts an apologetic hand to his mouth.

Chau curves his little finger to wipe his left eye. "Did she ever come round?"

"No." After a pause the sister adds, "Thank God."

"Never said anything either?"

"Hardly breathed."

Fortuna breaks the silence. "Poor little bitch."

None of them is looking into the ward, but I am. Beyond a gap in the screen around the bed nearest the doors a male nurse is loading a small figure onto a trolley. His body almost blocks my view as he covers the contents of the trolley from head to foot with a sheet, but I glimpse the girl's hand. Only it isn't much of a hand anymore—it looks as though somebody has tried to make the fingers out of melted wax.

The nurse eases the screen open and uses the trolley to nudge the doors gently aside. He ignores me, and I feel as if he's expressing a contempt I deserve. When he wheels the trolley towards a lift I want to follow, but I need to stay with the detectives. I wait until they return to the main corridor, their backs to me. They're silent as far as the hospital entrance, outside which Fortuna says, "They must have known Lee was on to them."

"Maybe they meant to scare him off."

"Do we give a shit if that's all they meant?"

"We do not."

"Maybe we'll find something at his place to show he was investigating them."

"That wouldn't surprise me at all."

I'm Lee. They're going to lead me home. I stay well behind them as they tramp deeper into the tenement district—I feel as if the weight of my grief is slowing me down. Their footsteps are the only sounds in this part of the city, so that I wonder if the way their advance rings through the streets has driven into hiding anyone who prefers not to be observed. When they come in sight of my tenement I know it at once, though I can't see how anyone except a detective would be able to distinguish it. Fortuna is first through the doorless entrance. When I hear his and Chau's footsteps leave the stairs I follow.

The graffiti in the lobby, initials and words of one syllable, crowd halfway up the stairs, where someone has smashed the light at the corner. Concrete dust sifts down where the handrail has been wrenched almost out of the wall. Fortuna is at the top of the flight of stairs, unlocking my door. He uses another of my keys to turn off the alarm just inside, then Chau shuts the door behind himself and his partner.

I don't need a key to open it. No sooner has it admitted me than it's shut as though it hasn't moved. Bedroom, toilet, kitchen. My old colleagues have already opened those doors, exposing how little is beyond them, and are in the main room, where the television is hardly big enough for a solitary person to watch. Some chairs that don't look as if they have ever been introduced squat in front of it. Next to the chair that's sagging from use, charred cork filters without a gap between them ring a glass ashtray. Not many yards away across the threadbare carpet, three straight chairs press against a bare dining table, the only company they have apart from the photographs on a brick mantelpiece with an electric fire in its hearth.

One is a close-up of Jodie's grinning face that makes me have to struggle not to imagine how her face must look now. In the other Lisabeth is showing the camera the diamond on her ring finger. I was behind the camera, and I'm close to remembering too much too soon, more than I can bear all at once. It's a relief when the detectives start talking about me. "So this is how he ended up," Chau says.

"All he thought he could afford, maybe."

"More likely all he thought he was going to be able to."

Are they blaming Lisabeth for that? It would be so unfair that I'm about to declare myself when Fortuna says, "He was still a better cop than most."

"Too good not to leave us something if he thought he wasn't going to be able to follow it through."

"Just in case he wasn't, even," says Fortuna, staring around the room.

There's nowhere much for them to search. Chau pulls out kitchen drawers while Fortuna tries the bedroom. I watch him from the darkness of the bathroom, and as he opens the wardrobe I know what he'll find. He has only to reach in the breast pocket of the first of my very few suits to produce a photograph he bares his teeth at before calling his partner. "Like we figured," he says, and holds up the photograph as Chau joins him. "Price and Bilder."

"The old firm."

Though they sound like a partnership of architects, that's far from their trade. The photograph shows them about to dodge into the bar next to the alley where I came back to myself. The more than well-fed man in an expensive Italian suit with a cigar making his small fat mouth round is Price, and his thin swift companion thrusting his narrow-eyed face forward like a fist as if to scare off any watchers is Bilder. I see their faces for barely a moment before

Fortuna stows them in his coat pocket, but now I can't stop seeing them. "Enough for a warrant, would you say?" Chau muses.

"No point, the way they cover themselves. Maybe enough for a tap."

"Are you thinking there's a judge who might figure he owes us a favor?"

"When the whole department and some people higher up would appreciate it."

"Let's talk to the chief and then we can buy our judge the kind of breakfast he drinks."

That's too slow for me. As the detectives head back along the corridor to switch off the lights, I slip out of the door. I don't need to wait for them to lead me. I never had to: I simply followed them to prevent myself from learning too much too unbearably quickly. Now I want to finish.

I leave the street at the first intersection. Behind the tenements the buildings shrink away from one another and crouch low, dreaming of violence. In front of the lawns, which are a mass of weeds and litter, the streetlamps have lowered themselves so as to be easier to smash. Empty cartridge cases glint on a lawn, and in the darkness on the next there's a sprawled body—an animal's, I hope. Once I hear a clash of machetes, but by the time I reach the place the sound that came from there is only a trickle of blood leading into a house. All the doors will be reinforced, because the windows are—more than one is cobwebbed with the impact of a missile, and two sides of a corner house have been decorated with the spray of a machine gun. A girl too young and undernourished and scantily clad to be waiting alone in the night shivers under an intermittently lit streetlamp. A limousine with windows as black as its body and hers glides alongside her, and she stoops toward it as though she's flinching away from a whip. Seconds after its back door creeps open, she's inside.

As the car turns uphill I follow. The houses grow larger and farther apart, fending off the road with spiked railings and brick walls crested with barbed wire. I round a wide curve in time to see a pair of electrified gates meeting behind the limousine as it vanishes along a tree-lined drive. I can't pursue it, I'm not here for it. My destination is too close to ignore—the night has gathered itself overhead to point to it, spreading black wings over me. The road curves back on itself, and at the top of the curve is Price's house.

It's a turreted two-story Mediterranean castle that gleams white as a false smile. A notice on the railings that are more than twice my height says they're lethal, another warns there are dogs on the grounds. One window on the top floor is lit as if somebody has put a light in it for me. The night above me seems to shrink, to fly over the railings and perch above the window, folding its wings. Its black eyes gleam as I press the button on the left-hand granite column of the filigreed wrought-iron gates.

The camera squatting on top of the opposite column lowers its lens to peer at me as the grille above the button spits out static. "Who is it?"

Despite its metallic croaking, I recognize Bilder's voice. I turn to the camera and stretch my arms wide, and in case that isn't enough, I jam the stub of Price's abandoned cigar between my teeth. "Who does it look like?" I say through the taste of stale smoke.

The camera surveys the road before Bilder speaks again, not to me. "It's Lee. Seems to be by himself."

"How surprising," says Price across the room. "So why the hesitation, Mr. Bilder? Let him in."

Bilder starts to utter what sounds like a protest before the intercom cuts him off. A few seconds later the gates swing open with a whisper of oiled hinges. The camera keeps me in view as I move forward, and I've hardly set foot on the drive, which is so wide and devious it is clearly meant only for cars, when the gates shut again with a clang. It's answered at once by a chorus of snarling, and Dobermans run out from behind an elaborate shrubbery on either side of the drive.

There's nowhere I can flee, nor any need. As the dogs race to the gates I poise a hand above each glossy slavering head. The animals hesitate, their eyes clouding, their wet lips closing over their teeth, and then they move beneath my hands toward the house. Their claws click on the white gravel, their pelts blacken with shadows of orchids and shine like oil as they trot past lights half buried in the borders of the drive. When I reach the marble steps leading up to the front door I fling the cigar butt across the lawn as green and moist as a swamp. The dogs bolt after their prize, and I go to the door.

In less time than a breath would take I'm past it and it's shut. I'm in an extravagantly wide lobby from which a staircase of the kind a movie star would use for her grand entrance curves upward. At the foot of the banister, doing duty as a post, is a model of the Statue of Liberty, and I'm tempted to wrench off the torch-bearing arm for a weapon. I've no time, and apparently no need. My rage sends me up the stairs to find my quarry, and I haven't reached the top when I see them.

Price is reclining naked on almost half of a king-sized mahogany bed. The enormous hairy balloon of his stomach has his tiny penis for a mouth-piece. He's gazing out of the window, from which Bilder, dressed in boxer shorts twice as wide as his scrawny thighs, is watching the city. Price's penis inches out of its nest of gray hair at the sight of me—it tries to point at me as the small neat automatic in his pudgy fist is doing. "We've company, Mr. Bilder," he says in his high soft voice. "He can be thoughtless sometimes, Mr. Lee. He can get a little too full of himself."

Bilder turns only his head, and touches his temple with a finger which he then aims at me. "He's not arguing."

"Forgive our not having come down to admit you, Mr. Lee, but our door doesn't seem to have taxed your professional skills. Perhaps you'll tell us how you dealt with it after you've indulged me for a few moments. Do make yourself comfortable," Price says, and waves his free hand above the expanse of empty bed. "You're just in time to watch a spectacle arranged by Mr. Bilder."

I don't know if he's mocking me or convinced he has some power over me that's capable of persuading me to join him on the bed. I take hold of a cushioned antique stool in front of the dressing table laden with cosmetics facing the army of themselves in the extravagantly framed mirror. The stool is heavy enough to knock the gun out of Price's hand and smash his head and Bilder's, but I need to see what's about to happen so that I'll know everything. I plant the stool at the end of the bed and sit on it with my back to Price.

I can see his reflection in the window against which Bilder is pressing himself, sweat flaring on the glass around his hands. The pane shuts out the sounds of the city, and I realize how it lets Price and Bilder observe the poverty and despair and crime down there as though it's a movie being projected for their benefit, however much of it they're responsible for. Just now it seems there's nothing to watch, until Bilder closes his fingers and thumbs one by one, their sweat fading from the window as he counts off the seconds. At the moment when he makes another fist, a flame blooms in the shadow of the tenements. "Ah," says Price.

Another flame appears, and another. The windows of a house are blowing out. The blaze spreads around each of them and streams toward the roof, which starts to expose its blackened skeleton before it collapses into the box of fire the house now is. Fire engines as small and ineffectual as toys race across the city to add the blinking of their lights to the glow of the fire. "Exquisite as always, Mr. Bilder," Price says, his hand straying toward his swollen penis. As that dwindles he levels the gun almost casually at me, laying the barrel along his thigh. "Mr. Lee, we've neglected you long enough. We never expected you to honor our little shack."

The fire flickers next to the reflection of his penis, from which a molten jet of liquid appears to be arcing. "Whose house did you burn down?" I say through my teeth.

"Nobody but someone who owed us more than they were worth. I don't need to tell you what thieves are like. Are you still looking out for the underdog?" Price inquires, and gives my back a grin that squeezes out a fat tongue. "I find concern so fascinating."

"Maybe he's here because he's concerned," says Bilder.

"Is that the case, Mr. Lee? Is that your tale?"

Rage twists me as though I'm at the heart of a fire. I step back from the stool and face both men. "I've come from the hospital."

"You had the measure of him, Mr. Bilder. Concerned till the last."

"No stopping him."

"What tidings of the injured, Mr. Lee? What are you here to report?"

"She's dead," I say, so viciously that Bilder swings around from watching the engines struggle to control his fire. "Eight years old and you killed her."

"A regrettable oversight, would you accept, or shall we say a surplus of enthusiasm? Mr. Bilder has been known to express the view that a property with nobody in it is only half a fire." Price folds three fingers around his renewed erection as if to determine its length. "A craftsman ought to love his work, don't you agree?"

"Not just do a job because your father did," says Bilder.

He's talking about me. They're both gazing at me with a mixture of contempt and, even worse, of something not too far from sympathy. "Did you think that meant I'd give up?" I demand. "Did you think you'd scared me off?"

"At least that, didn't we surmise, Mr. Bilder?"

"I don't scare," I tell them, taking hold of a leg of the stool. "Let's see if you do."

"Crude, Mr. Lee. An abuse of hospitality." Price looks regretful, perhaps because his penis is drooping again, as he trains the gun on my chest. "If there's to be unpleasantness, you might have the grace to tell me first how you managed to penetrate this house."

"Nothing could have kept me out when I'm here for Jodie," I say, raising the stool with both hands. "I don't think you want to use that. You like to keep your killing away from your home."

"I believe we can rely on Mr. Bilder's talent for disposing of the unwanted."

"Good thing one of us knows how to hide stuff," says Bilder.

Is he comparing himself with Price or with me? I've no time to wonder. I'm poised to throw the stool at the gun. Even if Price fires, the upholstery will either absorb the shot or reduce its impact before it reaches me. I can take that and more: my fury that cares only for revenge has made me feel invulnerable, and so I fling—

The stool hasn't left my hands when the first bullet rips through upholstery and wood. My arms begin to shudder as the bullet thuds into my chest. The piece of furniture sags in my weakening grasp and then, somewhere far away, falls on the floor with its helpless legs in the air. It seems considerably less present than the plaintive caw of a bird that greeted the shot. How could I have heard that through the soundproofed window? Price looks as if he's considering that question, but he must be contemplating how much he has injured me, since with hardly a pause he fires twice.

A punch that thrusts deep into my body slams me against the wall. The third bullet pins me there like a dead insect. Still pointing the gun at me, Price reaches across himself to an ornate bedside table and plants a cigar between his lips. Instead of a band the cigar is wearing the diamond ring I last saw on Lisabeth's finger.

My rage is a physical force that jerks me away from the wall. I hear another caw outside, but now it's a cry of triumph. The power that has entered me focuses on the lumps of metal lodged in my body. I feel them soften and begin to trickle out of the holes they made. The pain feels like the start of a purification. "Take your best shot," I say, framing my chest with my spread hands as I advance on Price.

He fires again, and again. I scarcely feel the bullets as they pass through me, melting as they go, and spatter the wall. I move slowly only because I want him to see his death approaching. At last he shies the empty gun at me, and I bat it aside with a forearm. "Bilder," he screams.

Bilder is dashing for the stairs, and I ignore him. I'm at the service of the power within me. I stoop like a blaze in a gale and take hold of Price's feet. He shrieks, much louder as they catch fire. There's so much fuel in him that his legs and two wide swaths of the bed are ablaze in seconds. A stain spreads to meet the flames, but they acknowledge it only with a terse hiss as they merge at his crotch. As his torso squirms wildly back and forth, flailing its arms as if to beckon the eager fire, I leave him. I hear his cries give way to a bubbling as I race downstairs after Bilder.

Though the front door is open, he hasn't gotten far. He's trying to talk his way past the dogs—his running must have made them think he's an intruder. He doesn't hear me behind him; he's unaware of my presence when I lay a hand on his head. His scalp goes up at once, but I don't withdraw my blessing until more than his hair is on fire. His brain must be, for him to perform such a grotesque dance, dodging from side to side of the drive and kicking up the gravel as he clutches at his head while it and then his arms drip flames. Well after there seems to be too little of him to stand up he prances about, and then what's left of him sprawls in the middle of the drive, still kicking. As his heels exert a last convulsive shove I make for the gates.

Bilder must have opened them from the house. Once I'm through them I look back. The dogs stand over Bilder's smoldering remains, guarding them or about to tear at them. Flames pour from the bedroom window, and smoke, in a shape that appears to be pecking at the window and spreading its wings over the roof. Its outline flutters, and the sight loses its hold on me. I have to find Lisabeth and tell her I've done everything I can.

Shouldn't I be heading down toward the hospital? Instead my instincts are leading me uphill, where trees close around houses that gleam like tombs. The foliage cuts off the leaping glow of Price's house and, later, a howling of fire engines. A willow by a dormant fountain imitates the shape the water will take, a mournful statue averts her face from me and draws her marble robe about herself. The slope of the hill flattens toward the summit, the houses grow smaller. I remember thinking they're like servants' quarters for the mansions below them, except Lisabeth was never anybody's servant.

I can't see the city when I reach the house I recognize. Like its neighbors, it's a wooden bungalow. A child has painted big bright flowers on the fence—Jodie painted them, and that's her swing with a toy rabbit slumped on it in the concrete front yard, though her favorite place was a little clearing in the bushes behind the house, where she used to lie at night and watch the stars. The memories sharpen my grief, so that I know I haven't begun to deal with it, but how? I unlatch the waist-high gate and cross the yard to the lit porch.

Lisabeth is sitting in the middle of the bulky leather sofa in the front room. She's gazing at a painting propped against the wall, the only painting she ever kept for herself—the portrait of her with five-year-old Jodie hovering above her hands. I never knew if that meant she'd just thrown Jodie into the air or if she was suggesting that the child was coming down to her from somewhere else. I'm afraid to move, because there's a stillness about everything— the quiet room, Lisabeth's steady gaze and her fingertips touching her lips as if to hold in a thought or a sound, the house itself—that feels intensely vulnerable, protected only by the black wings of the night overhead. Then Lisabeth turns her head and looks at me.

The sorrow in her eyes is beyond words. I'm hopelessly unequal to it, but where can I go except to her? The door swings inward, though I'm unaware of having touched it. I move toward her and stretch out my hands, but her expression and the utter stillness halt me well short of her. "I'm sorry," I say, and my hands sag.

Precisely because her face doesn't alter I understand at least part of its message for me: my words and my grief aren't enough. I'm opening my mouth to ask what more I can do, though the words seem too stupid to utter, when I see movement in a bedroom off the main room—Jodie's bedroom. In a moment Jodie comes out and sits beside her mother and takes her hand.

There isn't a mark on her, nor on the T-shirt and jeans and sneakers she loved to wear. She gazes at me with the same wordless sorrow as her mother. They're waiting for me to understand. If she looks uninjured when I saw how she was at the hospital—if she can hold Lisabeth's hand like that—it means not just Jodie but also her mother must be . . . Only there's worse than that to grasp, and in a moment I see what I've misunderstood. Their sorrow isn't for each other. It's for me.

At last I remember why I had to come back. The knowledge wrenches my mouth as wide as it will go, but crying and grimacing won't help. I have to speak—I have to confess everything, to Lisabeth and Jodie and myself. "I hired Price and Bilder," I say in a voice that tries not to be heard. "I told them I'd leave them alone if they did this job. It was me."

Their faces don't change, though the faintest hint of red like a reminiscence of a fire glimmers in their eyes. The approach of dawn is beginning to tint the sky above the city, and some instinct tells me I've very little time. "I thought I'd made sure nobody was here. I called you, Lis. You said you were on your way out with Jodie to meet me. I shouldn't have waited so long at the restaurant. I did come to find you, but I got here too late."

The memory blinds me with itself: my fists punching through the block of fire the front door had become, my glimpse of two bodies on the sofa in the midst of the house, the entire roof collapsing as I ran to them . . . "Bilder came when you were leaving, didn't he? What did he do, tie you both up?"

I'm hardly entitled to rage at the thought of him. In the glow before dawn the bushes behind the house are starting to be visible through the wall, and through Lisabeth and Jodie. Is my slowness in owning up causing them to fade, to withdraw from me? "The insurance would have been for us," I plead. "We'd have gone across the border. I couldn't touch the money I stole. A crack dealer's money we found on a raid, and me and my partner took half. More than one dealer. It got easier after the first time, and I got careless. The department was waiting for me to go for it and they'd have had me. I must have been insane. I just wanted us to be together. I wanted you to have to come with me."

They're grieving for everything I destroyed. I've told them nothing they didn't know, but I had to recognize it. I can see the leaves of the bushes through them now, leaves red as flames. "I finished Price and Bilder," I say, "but I realize that isn't enough. What has to happen to me?"

My voice falters, because Jodie huddles closer to her mother at the thought. Lisabeth strokes her hair with a hand no more substantial than smoke and gazes at me. Her eyes brighten, perhaps only with the dawn, and her lips part. "We still—" she says, and then the dawn streams through the house, which vanishes instantly like mist, taking her and Jodie back where

they came from. I'm left standing in the midst of the sketch of a charred foundation on burned earth.

What was Lisabeth about to say? They came back, they waited for me, and mustn't that mean they still care for me, however undeserving I am? The dawn focuses itself on me, and I prepare to vanish—and then I understand what I must go through if I'm ever to have a chance of finding Lisabeth and Jodie again. Their sorrow wasn't only for my past, it was for now. I can feel the fire of which I was the vessel beginning to consume me from within.

I know what it felt like to be buried under the roof, but that was over in seconds. This fire will take all day to spread through the whole of me, as long as there's sunlight to stoke it. I crouch over the blaze at the center of myself and stumble through the scorched bushes, and fall down in Jodie's clearing. It won't protect me from the fire that's being raised within me, but perhaps it will help me think of her and Lisabeth. I draw my legs up and wrap my arms around myself and close my eyes. I taste dust and ash, singed earth, parched grass. I would try to breathe deeply for calm, but of course I have no breath. I can only wait until at last the day is over and the crow of night bears me away to rest.

Joy Divided

Douglas E. Winter

joy divided
    life like blood
    staining anointing
      love
wetter than death
    lacquered smile
    straining enjoining
      love
to tear us apart
      again
and again
    bitter wind
    darkness friend
    savior sin
    beginning end
as the crow flies
    sighs
    dies
the saddest song
    left
    unsung

he died at age eight, a girl snatched as a hostage by desperate men, and discarded when the ransom went wrong. They ruined her face to delay recognition. The knife wound that dispatched her was inept. Life left her body while her tears tracked cellophane ribbons through her half-congealed blood. The ending arrived with every hope crushed. Her lips parted. She cried out on a soundless chord of last breath for redress against those who had ruined all that she might have become. As her bruised consciousness flickered and ebbed, her pain pierced the veil of her mortality. A crow's feather, falling, intercepted the frail, parted skein of her spirit. A gateway opened through the heart of all mystery and gathered her desire unto its breast . . .

Again there was one.

The next passed in womanhood, with her traumatized toddler pulled away from her tattered, soaked clothing by the paramedics who could not save her. Her eyes by then were battered shut, blackened and swollen and repeatedly cut by the flange of a jet and diamond ring. She never saw what became of her daughter. Her memories had ended when, drunken, enraged to an animal frenzy, a husband rained blows on her inert flesh, and pummeled her bones as they shattered. The wish filled her being at the moment her heart stopped, and took incandescent flame as she lost her final foothold on life. She begged intercession for an innocence shattered, and a grief wrought too wide for expression by faltering synapses. Her anguish was heard. A crow's feather, falling, punched a hole through the stars and arrested her slow, upward spiral . . .

Once more, there were two.

The last, an old woman, bedridden and crippled, her gentle, delft eyes filmed with cataracts, and her left side gone flaccid from a stroke. She fought the pillow that crushed out her breath, the scratching protest of her right, fully functional hand not enough to win her reprieve. The arrogant strength that robbed her last dream was a son's, born of greed lest her nursing care should decimate the capital willed to him as inheritance. Bucking, thrashing, helpless in rage, she shed muffled tears for mercy denied, and the days of quiet reminiscence torn from her. Her fury found its full voice on the winds, and a crow's feather, falling, wound her in its shroud as she fought her forced transit out of life . . .

*At last, at long last, three held the balance, with the full moon
timed to rise and set the next night.*

Dawn broke with the gutters brimmed to puddled lead, and the still falling rain thin as a grease slick upon trash-strewn pavement. The gray brick facade of the deserted tenement held its burden of graffiti in sagging, dreary lines of faded color. There, the Crone sat, cowled in an army green blanket and feeding a squabbling flock of pigeons. The birds strutted and pecked. Haloed in silvered water, they flapped and scrapped through their greedy pavane of survival. The Crone tossed them crumbs. She did not look up as the crow hissed down through the needle-fine drizzle, and landed, scattering pigeons to whirring flight.

The crow disdained to hop after sodden crusts.

It cocked its jet head, its eye unblinking amber, and waited for Her to acknowledge it.

She took her time, first wrapping the bread heel in a creased plastic bag. Her hands were as fleshless as weathered old gloves, age-splotched and blued with a mapwork of veins. Yet when She looked up, Her black eyes were unclouded. Mystery rode on the thin streamer of Her breath as She addressed the winged form come before Her. "Three died swearing vengeance, all in the same hour?"

The crow fluffed, impatient.

"Very well. Very well." She extended a gnarled finger. "And so we shall see."

The crow cawed and unfolded drenched wings, and its three-feather offering crossed Her creased palm. She raised them. Her dark gaze grown piercing, She whispered a question to each one. "You have died, each in violence. Will you give over your desire for redress? Will you entrust me that power and go free?"

Wind blasted down the pavement, flapping the plastic with its captive crumbs, and unreeling strands of silver-gilt hair from under the mantling blanket. The Crone watched, unwinking. Her crow did the same, while the air danced and whispered over the talisman feathers, and three voices delivered their assent.

"So shall it be." The Crone split cracked lips in a toothless smile and clapped Her palms shut on the feathers; an explosion of light snapped the wet like actinic lightning.

"The power of redemption shall be yours once again. Act wisely and well." The Crone parted Her hands and pointed toward Her winged servant. Light jumped from Her nail, wrapped the crow in a blinding, starred pulse.

When the flash cleared, the rain fell, unrelenting, out of a sky like white porcelain. Only now it cast its misting pall over a being transformed, winged to two-legged on the breath of Her will, and the blood magic drawn from three dyings. A man stood alone, his cat-graceful contours fitted in skintight, dark clothing and a leather vest spiked with chrome studs.

Of the Crone, no sign remained. Only a stale bread crust tucked in polyethylene scuffled in the wind, tacking an unpartnered course down the weed-trammeled pavement.

The man rubbed his dampened, stubbled cheeks. He blinked eyes the same slate hue as the puddles, then rubbed the still tingling flesh of his forearms. He would walk two-legged for one day and one night; he, the chained spirit, dark instrument of Her power through the full phase of the moon. Blood would be let to answer for bloodshed. His quest was the force rebraided and reborn from the death-wishes claimed from three innocents. The servant of a power beyond primal understanding, his wrought purpose was to intercede in behalf of the city's next victim . . .

He walked. Each footstep completed on wet cement loosed a snap of rhythmic sound. Drifted leaves embraced soggy masses of litter. Squashed cans rattled in dopplered dissonance on the random force of the gusts. This quarter of the city was no haven, but a bolt-hole for the desperate, the dispossessed, and the damned. Broken dreams haunted the lightless, smashed windows, and broken glass cast its hoard of brimstone diamonds in the acidic gleam of the sodium lamps. These burned through the monochrome overcast in a sixty-cycle hum that did nothing to abate the less tangible darkness that ruled past the boundary of night. The memories of green earth and soil were forgotten, raped and made sterile by cement.

The only four-footed who dared forage here were the rats that scuttled to take refuge beneath the crushed cartons and other strayed trash, wind-harvested out of crammed Dumpsters.

A radio blared its morning spiel from the cracked-open door of a diner. The man turned his head, listening, his dark hair tinseled with rain. The prospect of food awoke no hunger in him. His body required no sustenance. He had no memory of his name, no memory of the face the dirty glass reflected back at him, straight nose and straight browline crosshatched by the greasepaint letters announcing the breakfast special. He did not remember any life of his own. Nor could he count how many times he had walked as an incarnate human, transformed from the shape of a crow.

He knew only that he had done so, many times.

The wailing female vocalist was strange to his ear; only the smells were familiar, a ubiquitous melding of coffee and used cigarette smoke.

Two school-aged children ran past, shrieking laughter. An oldster shuffled with a cane. The passing hurry of the middle-aged employed did not frequent this part of the city, where rage and violence beat an intangible tattoo, pitched for the acuity of overcranked nerves; the gut senses beyond range of sane hearing. The chill, falling rain could not quite quench remembrance of splashed blood and obliterated hope.

The man showed small dismay. He had killed as Her instrument, so many times. The imprint of that service lived in him, ingrained as the grit in the asphalt beneath his black boots.

Arms clutched to his chest, he shivered. He had speech, but no certain knowledge; and yet, he *had* been here before. He had trodden this same sidewalk in a gluey slush of snow, and also in a steamy summer heat wave. Many times.

The street corner he passed seemed like any other, heaved pavement spangled with beer tabs and torn matchbooks and the shards of a discarded pen. Someone had spray-painted a straggle of graffiti. He recalled the same characters of white and black, not in daylight, but in the searing glare of artificial light and loomed murk that passed for night in the city. There had been blood, and a woman's cries of terror, and he had sent her tormentor out of life with a broken neck.

No man, but a crow had flown from the kill, then watched from the spike of a wrought-iron fence while police closed the scene off with crime tape.

Another victim dead; and a rapist brought down by the boon of the Crone's gift of vengeance. There were other sites, he knew, many of them, where violence had grasped cruel advantage of the weak, and bloodshed had reclaimed the balance. A man's tracks had changed to the wingbeats of a crow, and come nightfall, must do so again.

The cycle had been; would be; and the fear struck from nowhere, that Her vengeance would rule him undisputed for all of eternity.

Suddenly worn, he sat on the sagged, peeling boards of a park bench, his head cradled between his spread fingers. He was not free; never had been. An agonized sadness closed in like an ache. He wished *as himself* that, this once, the full moon would pass by with no ruthless act to be visited upon someone helpless; that the age-old dance of victor and vanquished might misstep and leave his fixed destiny unrequited.

But this was the core of the metropolis. Here men built with money and bricks and steel locks, and then huddled in the illusion of safety they had made, but that in fact framed their prison of separateness. A hotbed breeding ground seeded by apathy, here despair brewed madness, and destruction found fertile outlet. No night would pass without someone's tragedy, and no morning dawned without heartbreak.

A victim would cry out. Blood would be answered with yet more let blood, and a crow would fly, forever seeking another three deaths to buy back Her power in an endless, sealed circle of redemption.

The man had lost count of his multiple incarnations. He clung to his haven on the dilapidated bench while the rain fell, and the people caught their midday buses in a jumbled display of haste, or despondency, or excitement. He watched the winos retreat into recessed doorways to nurse their paper-bag lunches, while the flickering neon on the video parlor scrawled juddering reflections in the gutter. His longing intensified. If he could have bargained for just one miracle, he would have stopped time, so that the summoning to come would not happen.

Yet wishes belonged to those who still treasured hope, not to a two-legged who lived a shadowed half-life as a crow, and who answered to an archetypal force whose existence was older than creation.

Night came, inexorable. He wandered, as he must. His purpose awaited in any random direction in the refuse-choked maze of dimmed alleys. The sodium lamps buzzed, their electric peach light broken by moving humanity. He befriended a runaway girl in the echoing, leaky court of a shopping arcade, dried her tears, and through streetwise, dispassionate listening, let her talk herself around to asking directions to a shelter. One victim less; perhaps. In the streets here, life's uncertainties painted an unstable fragility, vistas of beauty and pain shuffled one into the next like the jumbled glass patterns in a kaleidoscope; another fragment would settle to fill each new-made void, where free choice opened a vacuum.

He loitered, aimless, down a block lined with nightclubs, sex parlors, and drug dealers strutting flash clothes. An hour passed by, uneventful. His dark leather and saturnine melancholy made him a prized target for hookers.

He turned them away, unabashed for the fact that he had neither money or need. His smile held sadness as their language turned ugly. The pain they hid behind shellac nails and makeup tore his heart to limpid ribbons.

He left them to their hustling, each sorry one. Their risks were his misery. Any one of them could become the next link in the chain of hard luck misfortune for which he must kill, and rise winged.

Midnight arrived, to a throbbing invasion of motorcycles. He sat in the quiet. One pace to his left, seated over a sewer grate, a bag lady rocked and recited her breathless life story.

"I still dream of ironing the dumbfuckers' shirts, you know that?" She sighed for the days she had worked at a dry-cleaner's, then grumbled disjointed replies to her own whining questions. The cuticles on both hands were chewed to the quick, and she twitched like a dog as she dozed.

The man left her a sequined hair clip he'd found, dropped on the stair by a nightclub. He moved on, while the relentless night gave up another fugitive hour.

Two o'clock came, last call for the bars, and noisy arguments over billiards wore down into scattered, sullen epithets. The dance girls from the strip joints caught their buses in tight groups, or descended into the subways, heels clicking their no-nonsense haste. The man watched them go, quiet and unthreatening in the shadows. Relief hit like a wave for each one he saw catch her ride homeward without mishap.

Three o'clock, he peered through the locked gate of a church, and wondered if the back vestibule still sheltered the homeless. Probably not; recent vandals had shattered the stained glass window. There was a burglar's grille, now. The repair had been made with an ordinary pane, still grimed with the glazier's fingerprints.

The rain thinned and cleared off. Her full moon shone down, a punched disk of mother-of-pearl inlaid in ebony. A rising, chill wind scuttled a styrofoam cup down the pavement. The man crossed the street, limned red by the taillights of a late passing car, whose occupants tossed out a beer can. Wind toyed with the refuse. The can lodged, clanking, in a storm drain bedecked with a rhinestone sparkle of smashed bottles. A couple passed, smoking, the woman's slurred vowels made distinct by theatrical gestures.

At three twenty-five, the night's fate overtook him.

The girl was late teens, or an innocent twenty, a saucy brunette in smart heels with jaunty gold ankle chains. Her long legs were set off by a yellow slicker that glowed surreal in the off-color tint of the streetlamps. Late out of the nightclubs, she had perhaps quarreled with her date, or missed a ride home with a girlfriend. Either way, the rabbit-scared looks she cast over her shoulder marked her out. She was not at ease in the city, nor familiar with which bus might remove her to some safer neighborhood. Huddled by the barred and locked doorway of a shop front, she rummaged for change in her purse, cursing, breathless, snapping plum-colored chewing gum in her state of vibrating nerves.

Her aura of near-tearful panic could be sensed like a beacon from fifty yards away.

The man started forward, keyed by the same intuitive awareness that drew predators to prey, steel to magnet. A shadowy, half-formed desperation gripped his mind. If he reached her, his chance-met presence might somehow avert the inevitable. He might pass the night, *just this once,* without the requisite execution. Give the girl a protector, and the wolf-pack instinct for weakness might be derailed from responding.

He thrust off the curb, striding fast, but not running for fear that uncontainable urgency might alarm her.

The sleek, black Harley was faster, a chromium death angel roaring exhaust, and its rider, as botched a work of intelligence as the gut of the metropolis could spew out.

This one wore his self-hatred as bicycle chains and dark leather, black gloves, and a face starved to meanness. Hair tied into a greasy tail straggled over a painted insignia of snakes and skulls and viscera. He was on something. The strobe-lit flicker of a failing street lamp framed his already frenetic movements into jerks of stopped motion. Unable to feel, unable to suffer, he would let others do those things for him. Only then could he savor the passion that somehow eluded him. Always. They burned, that he could experience fire, and they cried, so he could match tears with a laughter that proved he had no soft place in him to weep. The cruelties that living inflicted on him would be charted, one by one, on the cringing, frightened bodies of the victim *he would not be himself, lest he crumble under the burden of denied sorrow and an agony that had jackhammered self-belief into unrecoverable pieces*.

Tears were for losers, the helpless, the conquered. The smile he turned to the girl in the raincoat was the knife that transfixed his own heart.

Running now, breathing in bursts, the man *knew* that same coil of grim truth; knew his counterpart in the lockstep exchange yet to come was as his flesh-and-blood brother.

"We are the same," he gasped, his long, lean legs sprinting over slick asphalt, but too slowly to score a changed script. That arrow of disappointment too bright to bear, he cursed the Crone. *She* had wedded him to a crow's immortality as the private tool for Her vengeance. He burned for pure rage. He would be too late to defy Her tonight.

By that fury he knew. He had fatally chosen to reject the role She had sealed in the blood and the bone of him. On those days that a triad of victimized souls let him walk two-legged, he would not serve as Her crow, shadowing death with more death in reprisal for the inhuman acts of humanity.

The man skirted a parked car, kicked through a tangle of newspaper, and reached the far curb. The Harley had already accelerated onto the sidewalk ahead of him. The racketing pulse of its engine pounded echoes through the blue curtain of exhaust that drifted from the mouth of an unlit alley. The man plunged through the bisected angle cast by the corner streetlight, and the darkness met him, and admitted him, crow-black swallowed into night blackness fused without boundary or seam.

On his groping way past, he turned the key on the bike. The engine silenced. Sounds remained. Someone's coarse, rapid panting, then the girl, gasping her pleas in that cornered state of terror her captor's freight of raw compulsion must wring out of her.

"God, please! No, please don't!" A sob choked her words.

Then the voice that Her two-legged minion *must* answer: "What's the matter? Think you're too pretty? Too rich? Too sweet for me? Oh, *baby*! Your mistake." A laugh, counterpoint to the rasp of a knife from a sheath.

The girl screamed.

"Oh, no. Not too pretty." The assailant resumed, his rapid-fire monologue driven breathless by the excitement set free through her suffering. "Not any more. Shall we mark the other cheek? Why not your little titties? Don't make so much noise. Somebody passing might try to barge in on our party."

Perhaps in her fear or her agony, she moved; or perhaps, he, in the uprush of unbridled rage, lost grip on his last thread of patience. The darkness that night kept its darkest of secrets.

Her two-legged avenger, just arrived from behind, heard the end as the fatal bite of steel into warm and vulnerable flesh.

The girl gasped, her whistling shriek cut short by the well of hot fluid. The scrape of her slicker down rain-wet brick filled her struggling, last seconds of life.

Then, with less sound than a breeze brushed over feathered wings, the hand of Her minion closed over the murderer's shoulder. Before today, he would not have noticed the trembling strung through his opponent's manic strength. Where once, his own blinding hatred sustained him, tonight he felt desolate pity. Truth forged an epiphany. The suffering which numbed the criminal from compassion had lasted more years, and reached a bleaker, more ruinous depth, than the girl's, in her minute of dying.

And yet, by Her choice, he was made the instrument to even a balance that was nothing, and had never been more than a parody. For where was the two-legged, born of the crow, when this drug-wasted reject had lost *his* child's innocence to damnation? Who had answered his cries when atrocity struck, bringing hunger, and deprivation, and dispossession? Did the Crone, with Her shriveled heart and Her steel-clad immortality, even care for semantics that held to no parity?

Nor were the girl victim and her killer any different at the end, in their doomed fight to cling to survival. The knife, turned in defense now, sliced into the man's blocking forearm. He felt no pain. Never had; the wound would transmute to whole flesh on the shape-change that sealed him back into a crow. He fended off a second blow. Adept at infighting, he knocked the weapon away, scarcely aware of his bleeding. He caught the assailant, wrestled him helpless with a strength no cocaine-starved body could outmatch and a remorseless weight of destiny that extended back through thousands of nights just like this one.

Yet another practiced twist would snap another neck, with Her justice granted satisfaction.

Then, one gasped word. "Please!" A masculine echo of the girl victim's outcry for mercy; and this one no less wrenchingly heartfelt.

Rebellion resurged, too hot and demanding for the man's proscribed will to deny.

He cast down the biker, hard enough to stun, an inadequate release for the black rage that towered inside him. "No!" he screamed. His protest reechoed in the close, predawn damp. "No! This ends here! I will not be Your instrument, nor will I answer this wrong with more wrong, and blood with more blood any longer."

"No." The voice in reply sang with the flute clarity of youth. "No end, but a remade beginning."

Expecting the Crone, the man spun in his tracks. He saw, not Her, but the Maiden, wrapped in the white flame of Her light. She advanced down the sordid throat of the alley, as displaced as a star in a setting of stained brick, and garbage and litter. "Bloodshed has never atoned for spilled blood. You have learned this, and now you are free."

Her touch met his arm.

He gasped, blinded by tears and by pain, for the wounds in his arm became reinscribed in a parchment of flesh that was mortal. *Restored.* He would walk two-legged, and feel all the tapestry that was the gift of world's life once again.

"You are free," She repeated. Her flawless raiment fluttered in the stir of the wind that had earlier banished the rainfall.

He stepped back.

On the oil-grimed concrete, side by side with his victim, the murderer lay, cringing and half stunned; *still alive.* In his state of chill terror he looked up and beheld Her, though not clothed in Her beauty as Maiden. He faced the Crone, eyes creased with age and a wisdom that burned outside time.

She extended a crooked finger. Her whisper snatched air and elements into an alignment that slapped quickened flesh to witness. "You are claimed. You are Mine." She blew out Her breath, and the begrimed, dark alley pulsed with the shock of Her power.

That crucible of force consumed dead flesh, and living.

From the fused alchemy of victim and tormentor, one crow took flight, seamless black in the moonlit mantle of night, seeking three deaths that would win the next chance of redemption . . .

The freed one remained, two-legged and human, weeping for a deliverance bought out of compassion. In the killer just spared, he resolved his own origins. Now the mortality reborn in the substance of him demanded that he *live,* young man to old sage, from the heart now reclaimed from the ageless coil of Her patience.

The Night Chough

Gene Wolfe

Silk was gone, the black bird reminded itself. There was no point in thinking about him.

No, it itself had gone.

Which was the same.

A gleaming pool caught its eye, reminding it of its thirst. It looked at the water and its margins and, seeing no danger, dropped from the threatening sky to an overhanging branch and scanned its surroundings.

Croaked. Sometimes hungry things moved when you croaked.

Nothing moved here.

Water below. Cold and still and dark. Cool. Inviting.

It fluttered across to the highest point on a half-submerged log, sharply recalling that it was hungry, too. Bent, stretching its neck, spreading dark wings to keep its balance. Its polished bill was the color of old blood, not quite straight. That bill was beautiful in its cruel way, but the bird was too accustomed to it to admire it any more—so it told itself, and turned its head to see it better, knowing, as most birds did not, that it was the bird in the water as well as the bird on the log, just as the log itself was partly in the water and partly above it.

"Good bird!" The bird pronounced judgment. "Pretty bird!" These were its own words, not words that forced themselves past its throat at times, the words it spoke that were not its own. "Good bird," it repeated. "Bird see." Speaking as humans did was an accomplishment that had earned it both food and admiration in the recent past, and it was proud of its ability. More loudly it said, "Talk good!" And stooped to drink.

There was someone else in the water, a blank and livid face that stared into its own with sightless blue eyes that looked good to eat. The bird pecked at them, but refraction disturbed its aim. Its bill stabbed soft flesh instead, flesh that at once sank deeper and vanished. The bird whistled with surprise, then drank as it had intended.

Already a third countenance was forming, a young woman's snarling face framed by floating tendrils of dark hair. This new young woman had a profusion of arms, some with two elbows and some with three—some, even, that required no elbows at all, arms without hands, as sinuous as serpents. She struggled to speak, mouthing angry phrases without sound.

"Bad bird!" It had not intended to say that, and was angry at itself for having done so. "Bad, bad! No eat!" It had not intended to say those things either.

"Bad eat!"

It had been trying to drink again, tilting back its head at the moment that the words emerged; it nearly choked. "Bad talk!" it sputtered.

Then, "Bad god! No talk!"

"Is somebody here?" A slender young man was approaching the pool, threading his way dolefully among fragrant incense willows. "Anybody besides Lily?" He carried an instrument for landing large fish, a pole topped with a sharp iron hook.

Reminded of its owner, the bird inquired, "Fish heads?"

"Who is that?" The young man looked around. "Are you making fun of me?"

"Good bird!" It was still hoping to be fed.

"I see you." For a moment, the young man almost smiled. "What are you, a crow?"

The bird repeated, "Good bird!" and flew up from the log to light on a branch nearer the young man.

"I've never seen a crow with a red topknot like that," the young man told it, "or a crow that talked, either. I guess you must be some new kind of crow they've got here." He groped the dark water with his hook, heedless of the distant rumble of thunder.

"Fish heads?"

"Yes," the young man agreed. "I'm fishing for Lily's head. I suppose you could say that." An audible swallow. "And the rest of her. I'm hoping to hook her gown, actually. This hook is sharp, and I'm afraid it may tear her face, if that's what we find."

The black bird whistled softly.

"When I heard you, I was hoping there was somebody else here, somebody who would help me pull Lily out of the water. Water lily. That's funny, isn't it?" Tears streamed down his cheeks.

"No cry," the bird urged, its usual stridency muted.

Still weeping, the young man plunged his pole into the dark water, groping its inky recesses with the hook, which he drew out from time to time bringing forth mud and tangled, rotting sticks. "She's here in this pond," he told the bird. "Serval said so."

The bird recalled its vision. "Girl here. In pond."

"She was walking into town." The young man spoke half to himself. "Walking to the fair. They stopped her. Serval did, and Bushdog and Marten. They made her go with them, and they took her here."

He paused, and there was that in his eyes that made the bird flutter nervously. At length he said, "They made her do everything they wanted. That was what he said, what Serval said, drinking last night at Kob's. He bragged about it. He boasted. I had it from Moonrat and Caracal, independently."

Suddenly, he laughed; and his merriment was more frightening than his anger. "Listen to me! Just listen! 'Independently.' I've been reading for the law, you see, dear birdie. Going to be an advocate and buy Lily furs. And pearls. And a big house of her own. All . . . all . . ."

He had begun to weep again. "All so she'd love me. But she did already." His voice rose to a frenzied scream. *She told me so!* He dropped his pole and sat down, heedless of the muddy ground, his face in his hands; the bird, who had more than a little experience of emotional outbursts, edged cautiously nearer.

At length the weeping stopped. The young man pulled something wrapped in a clean rag from a side pocket of his jacket. Unwrapping the rag revealed a thick sandwich, which he opened to inspect the meat inside. "Mother made me take this," he told the bird. "I don't really want it. Would you like a piece?"

"Bird like!"

The young man removed a slice of meat and hooked it on a twig, then sat down to reclose and rewrap his sandwich.

"Find girl?" Those words had not been the bird's own, and it shook its head angrily.

"Not yet." The young man shrugged. "Of course there's a lot of pool yet. I'll keep looking."

He returned the sandwich to his pocket. "This might not be the place. Moonrat may have gotten it wrong."

The meat was dangerously near him, in the bird's opinion; and it occurred to the bird that the situation would be much improved if the stirring of the pool with the hook and pole were resumed. "Girl here!" it declared. "Find girl." Again it recalled its vision. "Big wet. Have arms."

The young man stood up. "I don't have any," he told the bird quite calmly. "If I had arms, a slug gun or even a sword, I'd kill them for killing her, all three of them."

"Have arms!" the bird reiterated testily. "Girl wet."

"I don't," the young man protested, "and I haven't forgotten Lily. I will never forget her."

"Have arms!" Then something that it had no intention of saying, "Your hook."

"You mean this?" Wondering, the young man examined the cruel steel hook on the end of his pole; rendered bold by hunger, the bird took flight and snatched the red slice of beef he had hung on the twig.

"I wonder where he is now," the young man whispered to himself. "Serval. Bushdog. Marten. I wonder where they all are right now."

He turned away from the pool; and the bird—mindful of the sandwich still in his pocket—followed him, carrying its slice of half-raw beef in its beak, and pausing from time to time to tear at it.

It had begun to rain. In the hitherto silent pool where Lily waited beneath the water with the exemplary patience of the dead, the first big drops tore the water like shot. Thunder rumbled in the distance. By the time the young man and the bird reached the raw, new streets and hastily erected houses, it was raining hard, solid sheets of pounding silver rain that turned the streets to oozing mire—sheets that were whisked away by the wind at the very moment they arrived, replaced within a second or so by new sheets from elsewhere, more beautiful and more violent than their predecessors.

They went from house to house, the bird seeking shelter under each low, overhanging roof, only to fly frantically to the next as the young man moved on. When the young man himself stood beneath the eaves at a door or window, the bird perched upon his shoulder, bedraggled and dripping, nursing vague hopes of food and fire, and did its best to explain things. "Bad man. Go where? Bad man!"

"There's one," the young man whispered, pointing. Through the twenty-second window—or perhaps the forty-third—could be seen three men and a woman seated around a rough table on which stood three dark bottles and five cheap wineglasses among scattered playing cards.

"That's Marten. That's Locust and Lacewing with him. They're brothers. I think the woman's Gillyflower."

The bird only shook itself, spreading its sable wings and fluffing out its feathers in an effort to become, if not dry, at least some trifle less wet.

"Lacewing has a slug gun. See there in the corner? They'll all have knives, even Gillyflower. If I were to gaff Marten now, they'd come out and kill me, and—" A flash that might have revealed his tense features to those inside, if anyone had been looking toward the window, was followed by a peal of thunder that swept aside his final words.

"I was going to kill myself "—the young man's tones were unnaturally flat—"once I'd found Lily's body and seen that it had a proper burial."

"Bad, bad."

"Yes, it is—was." A smile tugged on his lips, became a broad grin. "I'd be killing the wrong person, wouldn't I? But I'm going to kill both Marten and myself tonight. You'd better get out of the way before Lacewing starts shooting, birdie."

The steel hook crashed through the window. There was just time enough for Marten to jerk his head around, half turning in his chair, before the sharp point caught him in the back of the neck.

It did not sever his spine, or either jugular vein; there was no terrifying gush of blood as there are when those—they are, in fact, arteries—are cut; but it stabbed through the thick muscles there, his gullet, and his windpipe, and emerged from the front of his throat after having destroyed his larynx.

He was jerked from his seat and pulled irresistibly toward the window. For what seemed almost an eternity, and was perhaps a full half-second in reality, he braced both his hands against the wall.

"Hook good!" the black bird exclaimed, its head bobbing.

Marten's own head and neck emerged, the latter bleeding copiously now. After them came his shoulders, softer and more pliable than would have seemed possible before the hook. His knife was in his right hand, making it appear that he had hoped—perhaps even intended—to stab the young man with it when he emerged.

Nothing of the kind remained within his power.

The young man braced his feet as well as he could in the liquefying street, and stiffened his body against the lead slug that he expected from the window or the front door, and heaved with all his might, drawing the dying Marten out beyond the overhanging thatch into the pounding rain, until his body tumbled through the window to a deafening drumroll of thunder and sprawled twitching in the mud. Scarlet streams of blood trickled from its open mouth, only to be washed away at once by a silver flood.

"And now," the young man told the black bird beneath the eaves, "now they will come out and kill me, and I will be with her."

No one came out of the front door, and the young man was unable to nerve himself sufficiently to look through the shattered window again.

At length he knelt in the mud and took the knife from Marten's flaccid hand. "This killed her," he told the bird. "I'm going to throw it into that pond." He paused, gnawing at his lower lip while his imagination showed him the knife plunging through the water until chance drove its long, keen blade into Lily's throat.

"But not till I have her out of there."

"Knife good," announced the bird, who had not in the least intended to do so. On its own, it urged nonviolence. "No cut!"

The young man gave no attention to either remark, and perhaps did not hear them. With a small pocket knife, he cut the dead Marten's belt. He himself wore none; but he thrust the knife into the sheath he had taken from Marten's, and put knife and sheath into the waistband of his soaking trousers behind his right hip.

When he had freed his hook, he straightened up. For a second or two he stood waiting, staring at the shattered window, which had gone dark. "They're not coming," he told the bird, and laughed softly. "They're more afraid of me than I am of them, for the present anyway."

He set off up the rain-swept street, walking slowly with long strides, each of which ended ankle deep in mud and water. "We're hunting Serval now," he muttered when he had left the house with the shattered window behind, thinking that the bird had accompanied him. "We were always hunting Serval, really."

Having gulped Marten's right eye, the bird was in the process of extracting the left, and paid scant attention.

I t overtook the young man outside a tavern, plunging from chimney-height to thump down wetly on his shoulder. The three drunken men whose presence in the doorway had prevented him from entering gathered around to look at the bird, and he was able to step through them, entering an atmosphere of warmth and smoke, redolent of beer.

The bird, seeing the blaze at the farther end of the room and discovering with unfeigned delight that it was no longer rained upon, exclaimed, "Good place!" and flew straight to the hearth, landing there in a small cloud of ash and spreading its wings to dry with much satisfaction.

The man behind the bar laughed aloud, as did half his patrons, and poured the young man a small beer. "Just to get you started."

The young man ignored it. His eyes were on a burly man, younger even than he, at the table in the middle of the room. Softly he said, "Bad evening, Bushdog."

Noisy as the room was, it seemed that Bushdog had heard him; for a second or two he glared, while the young man looked back at him as a cat watches a mousehole.

The black bird's voice sounded from the chimneypiece, "Bad man! Cut girl!" and Bushdog shouted, "Get that out of here," and threw his glass at the bird.

It smashed against the stones of the chimney, showering the bird with broken glass. For a heartbeat, the room was noisy no longer. Then the young man picked up the small beer he had been given a moment before and threw it at Bushdog.

"*Get out!*" It was Kob, and as he spoke he motioned to a pair of big men nursing beers at a table in the back. They rose as one.

Resting the hooked gaff against his shoulder, the young man raised both his hands. "You don't have to throw me out. I agree completely. I am leaving." As he went out the door, the bird flew to his shoulder.

T ogether, they waited in the rain, he leaning on the pole, the black bird perched dismally upon the hook that had killed Marten. "No fair," something in the bird that was not the bird muttered urgently to the young man, and the bird repeated it again and again. "No fair! No fair!"

From within the tavern came a snarl of angry voices, followed by the double smack of two blows struck so quickly they might almost have been one.

"Here. Take it. You'll need it." The object was a slug gun, thrust at the young man by somebody as damp as he who had stepped from a shadow.

"Moonrat? Is that you?"

The light spilling from the tavern's doorway was blocked by the bulky bodies of Bushdog and another man who shoved Bushdog out and slammed the door; holding a finger to his lips, Moonrat retreated down the street.

The young man thrust his pole into the mud and leveled the slug gun he had been given, and the bird flew to the shelter of the eaves, perching upon a windowsill from which it repeated, "Watch out! No fair!"

The young man's index finger had located the trigger. He had never fired a slug gun and was not particularly eager to begin.

Slowly, Bushdog put up his hands. "You going to take me in, Starling?"

The young man shook his head. "You killed Lily yesterday, and I—"

"I didn't! It was Serval, Pas's my witness."

"—am going to kill you tonight." There was supposed to be a safety catch somewhere that had to be released with the thumb; he recalled that from a conversation years ago, and his thumb groped for the button, or lever, or whatever that catch was.

"Perhaps it was Serval. I don't know or care. If it was, you helped him, which is enough for me." He tried to tighten his finger on the trigger and discovered that he could not.

"They'll get you." Bushdog's voice was thick with brandy. "They'll get you, and you'll get a slug in the belly, just like me."

The young man hesitated. Was there a cartridge ready to fire? Slug guns, he knew, were often carried without one—only the magazine was loaded. You were supposed to move the handle in front to make the gun ready. He tried, tugging it with his left hand; it would not budge.

"You can't just kill me in cold blood."

He swallowed. "All right, I won't. I won't if you do as I tell you. You've got a knife. Get it out."

"No fair," the bird muttered from the eaves. And again, "No fair!"

"So you can shoot me soon as I've got it in my hand?"

"No," the young man said. "Get it out. I won't shoot you unless you attack me."

Rain heavier than any he had yet seen lashed the street, rain so hard that for an instant he lost sight of Bushdog altogether. Because of that, perhaps, he was suddenly aware that the window of the tavern was full of faces, as a bowl or a basket may be full of cherries.

"I got it." Bushdog displayed his knife.

"Throw it away."

Bushdog shook his head.

His thumb had found the safety. He pushed it, unable to hear the click in the pounding rain, and unsure of what he had done. "Throw it away." He struggled to keep his uncertainty out of his voice. "Or this will be over very, very soon. Now!" His finger tightened on the trigger, but there was no shot. He had applied the safety, in that case—assuming that there was a cartridge in line with the barrel.

As Bushdog's knife flew off into the blind night, the young man returned the safety to its original position. "I'm taking out mine," he said. "I've got to take my hand away from the trigger to do it, so if you think you can rush me, now's the time."

Bushdog shook his head again. "In this shaggy mud?" He spat in the young man's direction, but his spittle was drowned by the rain almost before it left his lips.

He was swaying a little, the young man noticed; probably swaying quite a lot, in fact, for it to be visible in such small light as spilled through the tavern's window. The young man wondered vaguely whether that would make it better or worse as he pulled Marten's knife from the sheath, displayed it, and flung it behind him.

"No fair!" the bird croaked urgently.

"He's right, it isn't—not as long as I've got this." The young man held up the slug gun. "So I'm going to lean it against the wall. I won't try to get it— or my gaff—if you don't. Do I have your word?"

For a moment Bushdog stared. He nodded.

"I've killed your friend Marten already tonight. Did you know that?"

Bushdog said nothing.

"I gave him no chance at all, which is to say I gave him the same chance that you and he and Serval gave Lily. I feel bad about that, so I'm giving you more chance than I should—"

"No fair! Shoot! Shoot!" the bird urged.

"—to make up for that. I'm going to fight you on even terms, and I warn you that if I beat you I'm going to kill you. If you beat me, I expect you to kill me as well. But of course that's up to you."

"I got it."

Pointing his slug gun at the ground between them, the young man pulled the trigger. The booming report was louder than he had expected. The gun jumped in his grasp like a live thing, and a geyser of mud leaped into the air. Stepping to his left, he propped the gun next to the window.

Bushdog was on him in an instant, knocking him off his feet, big hands closing on his throat.

Something in him exploded, and he was on top of Bushdog, hammering Bushdog's face with his fists, driving it down into the water and the liquid mud. As if that moment had never been, Bushdog was astride him, biting at some dark thing that was abruptly a knife. It plunged toward him; with a convulsive effort, he wrenched away.

There was a wild cry as the black bird struck furiously at Bushdog's face, vanishing as quickly as it had come. At once the knife was gone, and both of Bushdog's hands were at the socket of his right eye. He roared with pain and shouted for help before the muddy water filled his nose and mouth and his solid, muscular body ceased to struggle, stiffened . . . And relaxed.

"Good," the bird croaked, and returned to the eaves. "Good, good!"

It is, the young man thought. He would have wiped his mouth if he could, but both his hands were still locked around Bushdog's throat, although Bushdog was limp and unresisting. It shouldn't be good to take the life of another human being, the young man told himself, yet it is. I'll never feel rain, or hear thunder, without thinking about this and being glad.

Moonrat caught up with the young man as he was scouring the town for Serval. *"Starling! Starling! Wait up!"* Moonrat was running, his feet splashing mud and water. "How's that gun I gave you, Starling? It work all right for you?"

"It was fine," the young man told him. "I haven't put a fresh cartridge into place—is that how you say it?"

"Into the chamber."

"Into the chamber, then. I haven't done that, because I thought it was safer this way. But I will."

"You're right. Wait till you're ready to shoot. Is Bushdog dead?"

From the young man's shoulder, the black bird muttered, "Bad man," and "Watch out."

"Yes," the young man said. His voice was flat.

"Good! That's wonderful, Starling."

"But Serval's really the one, isn't he? The one who put Marten and Bushdog up to it. I've seen him around town pretty often—more than I liked, in fact. But I have no idea where he lives."

"I thought you were going there." Moonrat glanced at the houses on the left side of the street.

"No. I was just hoping to find someone who would tell me where he might be."

"Well, you've found him." Moonrat edged closer. "Listen, Starling . . ."

"Yes?"

"I—I want to help you. I mean, I already did. I loaned you my slug gun."

The young man, who had it slung behind his right shoulder, unslung it and offered it to its owner. "Do you want it back? Here it is."

"No, you keep it." Moonrat backed away. "You may need it worse than I do. I've got my knife."

The bird muttered, "Watch out."

"Are you joining me?" The young man hesitated, torn between caution and hope. "In a way you already have. I realize that. You told me what Serval's been saying and gave me this. But are you willing to help me kill him?"

"That's it. That's it exactly." Moonrat moved to his left until he stood beneath the overhanging roof of a lightless house. "Won't you come over here, so we don't have to stand in the rain?"

"If you like." The young man joined him. "It doesn't bother me. Not tonight. It's as though I had a fire in me. The bird complains about it, though."

"Good bird." It shook itself, and aired out its feathers as all birds do when they wish to be warmer.

"Can I ask you something?" Hesitantly, Moonrat took the young man by the sleeve.

"If I may ask a question of my own in return."

"I—I've been following you. Not ever since I gave you my gun, I went away then. I didn't want him to see me. But I started back when I heard the shot."

"I understand."

"You were gone by then, and your bird was pecking at Bushdog's . . . at his face. So I was sure you were going to Serval's, so I ran down the street to catch up to you. Maybe you didn't hear me, because of the storm."

"I didn't," the young man said.

"Then your bird flew past and lit on your shoulder, and a girl was with you, walking beside you. The—your bird had brought her. That was what it seemed like."

"Lily's ghost?" The young man was silent, pensive.

"I don't think so." Moonrat's voice quavered. "I've seen Lily, you know? Around town sometimes with you. It didn't look like her. Not—not at all like Lily."

"I wish I'd seen her." The young man might not have heard him.

"You had to. She was right beside you. In the, you know, the lightning flashes I could see her better than I can see you right now. I wanted to ask who she was."

"*Scylla.*" That was the bird. And not the bird.

"I didn't see her," the young man declared, "and in fact, I don't believe you. She was beside me, when the bird was on my shoulder, and you were running up behind us?"

He sensed rather than saw Moonrat's nod.

"Well, what happened to her?"

"I don't know. She wasn't with you when I got to you."

The young man shook himself, perhaps from cold, possibly in unconscious imitation of the bird. "We're wasting time. Where does Serval live? I want to get this over."

"I'll show you." Moonrat stepped out into the rain once more. "I'm going to go with you, and—and help out, if that's all right."

They pounded on the door; and when Serval answered it, the young man put his hook around Serval's neck and jerked him out into the storm, then knocked him down with the steel back of it. A woman screamed inside. A moment after Moonrat had closed the door, they heard the clank of a heavy bar dropped into place.

"You killed Lily," the young man told Serval. "You raped her, and then you killed her." He had passed his gaff to Moonrat, and he held Moonrat's slug gun so that Serval could see the pit of oblivion that was its muzzle.

"Shoot," Moonrat whispered, and the bird took up the word, croaking, "Shoot! Shoot!"

Serval himself said nothing, wiping mud from his eyes and cheeks, then rising slowly and cautiously. He had been holding a poker when the young man's hook had caught him, but that had vanished into the mud.

"Since you killed her," the young man said, "I think it only fitting that you help me give her a proper burial. If you do it, I suppose it's conceivable that I may not be able to bring myself to kill you."

Serval cleared his throat and spat, taking a half step backward toward the door, as if he expected it to open behind him.

"Shoot!" the bird urged, and lightning lit the street. Serval looked at Moonrat, whose gray steel blade seemed almost to glow in the flash.

"Refuse," the young man urged him as the thunder died away. "Why don't you refuse and make it easy for me?"

"I got to go in and get my clothes." Save for mud that the rain was quickly washing from his body, Serval was naked.

"No." The young man shook his head. "Do you refuse?"

"I'll do it. What do I have to do?"

"How did you dispose of Lily's body? You seem to have told the rest of the town, so tell me."

"There's a pond in the woods." Serval's voice was husky, his eyes upon the muzzle of the slug gun, though it was almost invisible in the dark and the rain. "We threw it in, then we threw rocks and stuff at it till it sank."

"Take us there," the young man said.

"If I do—"

"Take us!"

When the town was behind them, and the roar of countless raindrops upon uncounted millions of leaves filled their ears, Serval said, "I didn't kill her. You know?"

The young man said nothing.

"You know?" Serval repeated. "I didn't have her neither."

"You said you did last night in the Keg and Barrel."

"In the cock and bull, you mean." Serval actually sounded chastened. "I couldn't say I didn't, you know?"

"Bad man!" the bird declared damply, and clacked its bill for emphasis.

The young man remained silent; so did Moonrat.

"Listen. If I'd had her, would I pay that little slut Foxglove tonight? That was who it was with me back there in my place. You must have heard her."

Moonrat urged Serval forward with the butt of the young man's gaff.

"I tried, all right? I tried, and I held one leg for the other culls. But she was about dead already, 'cause somebody'd put his knife in her, you know? So I couldn't. It wasn't, you know, fun no more."

"Had it ever been fun for Lily?" the young man asked him. "Say yes, and die."

Serval did not.

"Who were those others? You said you held one of her legs for them. Who were they?"

Moonrat said loudly, "You might as well tell him. They're already dead, both of them. He killed them."

Lightning showed the rain-whipped pool gleaming like a mirror through the trees.

"Why do I have to tell him, then? He knows."

"Yes," the young man said. "I know." He fingered the cracked fore-end of the slug gun. "Give him my gaff, Moonrat."

Moonrat passed the pole and its cruel-looking hook to Serval, saying, "Here. This did for Marten."

The young man nodded. "Go to the water. You threw Lily into it. Now you can fish her out."

Serval went, and the bird flew after him, alighting upon the half-submerged log it remembered. The rain was no longer quite so violent, it decided; still it longed for the heat and cheer of the tavern fire, and the dry and smoky room with food on half a dozen tables. "Here girl," it told Serval loudly. "Girl wet."

Serval looked at it incredulously, then returned to groping with the hooked gaff in a part of the pool far from its perch.

"Girl here!" the bird insisted. "Wet girl!" Its bill snapped with impatience. "Here! Here! Bird say!"

Stepping into the shallows, the young man poked Serval's back with the muzzle of the slug gun. "Go over there and have a look."

Sullenly, Serval waded out to the bird's half-submerged log.

"Good! Good!" Excited, the bird flapped its wings, hopping up from the log itself to a stub that protruded from it. "Girl here!"

The steel hook splashed, and the pole stirred the black waters of the pool. For the young man waiting upon the bank, the seconds plodded past like so many dripping pack-mules, laboring mules carrying the universe to eternity, bit by bit.

By a final effort of the dying storm, lightning struck a dead tree on the far side of the pool, exploding it like a bomb and setting its ruins ablaze; and Serval screamed, turned, and fled, splashing through the shallows and slipping in the mud, but virtually invisible to all but the bird, who squawked and whistled, and whooped, "Man run! Bad man! Shoot! Shoot!"

The young man jerked back the slide of the slug gun, pulling harder than necessary because of his inexperience, then ramming it forward again, hearing the bolt thud and snick into place as it pushed a fresh cartridge into the chamber and locked up.

As if by the gun's own volition, the butt was tight against the hollow of his shoulder. He fired at a shadow and a sound, the flash from the muzzle lighting up the rain-dotted pool as the lightning had, and vanishing as quickly.

Serval shrieked with pain, and the young man nodded to himself, cycling the slide once more while he wondered vaguely just how many cartridges a slug gun held, and how many had been in this one when Moonrat had given it to him.

"You got him!" Moonrat slapped him on the back.

"I doubt that he's dead," the young man said. "I couldn't see him that well. In fact, I couldn't see him very well at all."

"Bird see!"

The young man nodded to the bird as though it were a person. "No doubt you did. Your eyes are much better than my own, I'm sure."

"Eyes good!"

"He eats them," the young man told Moonrat conversationally. "He ate Marten's, I believe, and from what you said, I would imagine that he ate Bushdog's too."

Moonrat said, "I wonder what got into him. Into Serval, I mean."

"See girl," the bird informed them. "Arm girl."

The young man nodded, mostly to himself. "Lily's body is there. It has to be. He must have brought it to the surface just as the lightning struck. It was too much for his nerves."

"I don't think you killed him either." Moonrat's knife was out. "If you didn't, I'll finish him for you."

"Wait just a moment." The young man caught him by the elbow.

"You better let me go, Starling." Moonrat tried to shake free of his grasp. "He may not be dead."

"I'm sure he's not." Smoky flames from the burning tree illuminated a smiling face in which nothing at all could be read. "If he were dead the bird would know, and it would have gone for his eyes."

"No dead," the bird confirmed.

"But he's unarmed and wounded, and he's seen her face, down there in the water. I'll get him tomorrow. Or the day after that, or perhaps the day after that. Possibly Lily's brothers may get him first. Her brothers or her father. He'll realize that, when he's had time to think. He'll run, or barricade himself in his house with a slug gun. But we'll get him."

"I'll get him now," Moonrat declared.

"No." The young man released Moonrat's arm and held out his hand. "Give me your knife."

Moonrat hesitated.

"Give it to me. I want to see it."

Reluctantly, Moonrat handed it over. A flip of the young man's hand sent it spinning away to raise a splash in the middle of the pool.

"Now I want you to find Lily and bring her out," the young man said. "I think he dropped my gaff. The weight of the hook will have sunk it, but the handle will be standing straight up in the water, or nearly. It shouldn't be hard to find."

"Wet girl," the bird explained.

Moonrat started to speak, bit it back, and substituted, "All right if I take off my boots?"

Leveling the slug gun, the young man shook his head.

"Have knife," the bird announced. It had not intended to announce that; but it was true, and the bird was glad afterward that it had said it.

"In his boot." The young man nodded and smiled, smelling the rain and the wood smoke from the burning tree, and still practically unaware of the scene this combination of odors would invariably summon from memory as the years passed.

"In boot!"

"It may remain there. Go get her, Moonrat." The young man's finger tightened on the trigger. "Go now."

Moonrat waded out, ankle deep, knee deep, and at last waist deep in the pool. After half a minute he found the gaff and held it up for the young man to see. By that time it had nearly stopped raining, although the sky was still dark.

"Moonrat."

"What is it?" Moonrat's voice was sullen, his face expressionless.

"The end of the hook is very sharp. Try not to stab her with it, please."

If Moonrat nodded, it was too small and slight a nod to be seen.

When Lily's body lay on the sodden leaves, the young man ordered Moonrat back into the pool, leaned his slug gun against a white willow, and covered Lily with his tunic. She had been small, and his tunic reached—mercifully—from the top of her forehead to a point just below her naked loins.

When the young man picked up Moonrat's slug gun again, Moonrat asked, "Can I get out of here now?"

The young man said nothing, wondering again whether there was a cartridge in the chamber. He pressed the slide lock and opened the action a little, but the faint light from the east was not sufficient to let him see the cartridge, if there was one. His fingertips found it, and he closed the action again.

"I won't go after Serval if you don't want me to." Moonrat took a tentative step toward the still-smoldering tree.

"I thought you might want to tell me about it," the young man said. His tone was almost conversational.

"What?"

"About raping Lily, and about killing her."

Moonrat said nothing.

"Bad man!" the bird announced virtuously.

"You couldn't be convicted in court unless Serval talks, and that may be the chief reason I'm going to kill you here and now. It may be. I can't be sure."

"I didn't."

There had been a tremor in Moonrat's voice, and something in the young man sang at the sound of it. "There were four of you. There had to be, because neither Marten nor Bushdog had scratched faces. Shall I tell you about that?"

The bird urged, "Man talk!"

"All right, I will. Serval said that he held a leg while the others raped her. Someone else, clearly, held her other leg, and there must also have been a third man holding her hands. Otherwise there would have been scratches, as I said. I got a good look at Marten when he was sitting at a table with a candle on it, and an even better look at Bushdog in the tavern. And neither of them had scratches or bruises. So there were four of you. At least four. Now do you want to tell me about it?"

Moonrat said, "No."

"I'm not going to let you pray or plead, or anything of that foolish kind. But if you'll confess—if you'll tell me in detail, and truthfully, just what you and the rest did and why you did it—you'll have those added minutes of life."

"No," Moonrat repeated.

"Man talk!" This time the bird was addressing Moonrat.

"Someone might come by while you're talking. You might be saved. You should think about that."

Moonrat was silent, possibly thinking.

"You were very, very anxious to help me—"

"I'm your friend!"

The young man shrugged and raised his slug gun, squinting down the barrel at the front sight and a trifle surprised to discover that there was light enough for him to see it. "You're an acquaintance. You came to me—so did Caracal—to tell me that Serval had been boasting about . . . about what you did. But you knew a lot more than Caracal did, or at least a lot more than he told me." The young man lowered the slug gun. Not yet.

"I said what Serval'd said." Moonrat sounded less than confident.

"Bad man!" The bird was cocksure. "Shoot! Shoot!"

"Soon," the young man promised, and spoke to Moonrat again. "Caracal only said that he had boasted of doing it. You said he had named Marten and Bushdog, and you even knew where they had disposed of Lily's body, and were able to tell me accurately enough for me to find the place—this pond. Do you want to hear some more?"

Moonrat shook his head, and the young man noted with some slight surprise that he stood shoulder deep in the water—if indeed he were standing.

"Well, I do. I'm marshaling all my arguments, you see, so I can pardon myself afterward for having killed you, even though I've killed Marten and Bushdog already. Or perhaps I'm merely looking for a reason to let you run like Serval. You're planning to duck under the water when I'm about to fire, aren't you?"

Moonrat shook his head.

"No. Of course not. Well, we'll soon find out. Where was I?"

"Say name," the bird prompted him; and it seemed to Moonrat, although only very briefly, that the woman of many arms whom he had seen earlier was standing in the water beside the log upon which the bird perched.

"I had finished with that." The young man was silent for a moment, thinking. "When I looked through the window of the house where I found Marten, I saw Lacewing and his brother Locust, and Lacewing's girl Gillyflower. They were sitting around a table talking to Marten, or perhaps playing some gambling game. There was a slug gun with a cracked fore-end in a corner. I assumed that was Lacewing's, and even imagined him coming out and killing me with it. He didn't, but later you gave me that same gun, so that I would kill Bushdog."

"I was trying to help you," Moonrat muttered, "so that doesn't prove anything."

"I didn't say I could prove anything," the young man replied. His tones were reasonable, his eyes wholly insane. "But then I don't have to prove, do I? I know." He sighted along the barrel. The pool was awash in gray light now, and tendrils of mist snaked upward from its surface.

"I wanted to be friends," Moonrat repeated stubbornly.

"You wanted someone else to commit your murders," the young man told him, "and you found me. Serval was talking, and even if he hadn't named you—or Marten or Bushdog—you knew that Lily's brothers would beat your name out of him. Then you would die. So you gave me their names and told me where her body was, thus establishing what we pettifoggers call a presumption of innocence. Where were you when I hooked Marten? Relieving yourself?"

"Watch out," the bird muttered, and snapped its bill. More forcefully it repeated, *"Watch out!"* Moonrat was straightening up or standing up, his torso emerging from the water until the ripples were scarcely higher than his waist.

"Before I killed Bushdog he cried out for help," the young man said. "Kob's tavern was full because of the fair, and I thought he was calling on the drinkers in there. But you were watching, at least in the beginning, and he had seen you and was calling to you, pleading for you to help him before I took his life. You'd been his friend, and he thought you'd come to his rescue. On whom will you call, Moonrat?"

Moonrat's hand and Moonrat's knife leaped from the water like fish, and the slug gun boomed.

The knife flashed past the young man's ear to thud against a tree behind him.

Moonrat's throw continued, his arm preceding his face, until he lay, as it

were, upon the dark, mist-shrouded water, his legs still sunk by the weight of his boots. The bird left its log to fly out to the corpse and perch upon the back of its head, claws gripping its hair.

"No eyes for you," the young man said. "Get off there."

"All right." The bird regarded him with an intelligence that seemed almost human and flew to the overhanging limb of a threadwood tree. "No eat."

Recalling his sandwich, the young man took it from his pocket and unwrapped it again. The bread was torn and crumbled, but the meat remained largely intact. "Here, you can have this. But no eyes, understand?"

"Good, good!"

The bird was eyeing the sandwich, and the young man stepped away from it. "Take it and go. Take whatever you want—but after that you have to go back to wherever it is you come from, or keep on going to wherever you were going when you saw me. Understand?"

"Like bird?"

"Yes, I do." The young man hesitated. "But I'm going to have to leave Lily here while I go to tell her father and her mother, and I won't leave her with you. Not as long as you're alive."

"Take meat?"

"Yes. You may take it and eat it, but then you must go. Don't come back, I warn you."

The bird dove toward the meat and snatched it up, rising in circles, higher and higher, with the meat still clamped in its bill. At length it found a favoring wind and flew northwest, apparently following the coast.

The young man watched it go, a winged dot of black against the morning sky, until wings and dot vanished. Then he propped Moonrat's slug gun against the bole of the tree Moonrat's knife had struck and began to walk, wondering as he walked just how much of the life he had known might be salvaged, and how much, in addition to Lily, was gone forever.

Hot Animal Machine

Henry Rollins

Where I smash myself into a million pieces
Grow scar tissue
Stronger than ever
Doomed to endure and prevail

Every minute I spend alone I get stronger
Every time I keep my mouth shut
Every time I masturbate instead of touch a woman
I do a good thing for myself
When I stop resisting reality
When I see clearly
I must feed myself to myself
I cannot be destroyed by outside forces
I must keep the blade sharp
I must be hard on myself
I must remain one
Nothing matters except
The uncompromising will to destroy
The forward roll of the square wheel
I reach deep inside myself
I rip out a handful of bleeding crackling wires
I squeeze the juice out
I burn them out
I want to see where the truth lies
I want to see where it all breaks down
I walk down the mouth of every beast I can find
So I can see what's at the end
That's the only part that interests me
The end
The rest is all getting there

Shuttlecock

Edward Bryant

JOBARR '98

1. My Unfunny Valentine

Well, shoot, he thought.

And did.

Mitchell Valentine jerked the trigger. *That was the mistake,* he decided later.

The muzzle blast deafened him. Fire ripped a deep furrow through his thinning hair. It seared his scalp. The .38 slug's trajectory possessed too shallow an angle to do its job properly. The soft metal caromed off Mitch's skull (Mom always said his head was just too doggoned hard) and, at a rapidly decreasing velocity, plowed into the cheap PhoneMate answering machine that held his electronic suicide note.

He decided later it was probably just as well that the phone gadget sprayed sharded plastic and electronic parts all over the echoing living room.

What if he'd succeeded and his soul went away to some remote location where he could look back on events in the physical world?

What if no one called and received his shakily recorded final words, aside from the occasional randomly dialing telemarketer who would hang up before the initial words, "If you're hearing this . . .," were uttered via microchip?

It would be too much to bear for eternity.

Actually, Mitch figured he was bound for oblivion. That's what he hoped death would be. Blessed peace, utter silence, complete darkness.

The abrupt pain of fire, flash, and bullet crease was something else again.

I'm still alive, he thought with bewildered amazement. *Goddamn.* Mitch stared down at the smoking pistol in his numbed hand. He had a nearly full box of ammunition in the kitchen. This mishap need only be a minor setback. Another shell, another decision, another chance to erase all his miseries.

He tapped the hot barrel against his temple. The feeling was no longer romantic at all. He brushed his lips with the muzzle. Nope. All of a sudden, he hated the idea of his head exploding with an exit wound that would do justice to the special effects in a David Cronenberg movie.

Someone was pounding on the door of his apartment, he realized. He heard a familiar voice—his upstairs neighbor.

"Yo, Mitchell, m'man. You okay?"

He staggered over to the door. He felt the blood dripping freely from his ear to his shoulder and figured maybe he shouldn't open the door. "Yeah," he called. "Cleaning my gun. Had a little accident. Sorry. I'm okay."

"You wanna open the door and let me in to make sure you're all right?"

"Really," he said. "Truly I am. Hope I didn't do anything to your apartment."

"Don't think so," said the voice, "Nobody's bleeding or nothing. I would have noticed."

Mitch heard distant sirens. "You call the cops?"

"Figured I had to, man. But you're okay?"

"Yeah."

"Well, I can't *un-call* 911. Guess you'll have to deal with it."

Shit, he thought. *I can't deal with this.* "Okay," he said. "I'll deal with it."

"Good man," said the voice. "You're okay, I'm going back to see the end of my show. You take care now."

"Yeah," he said. "Thanks."

"Think nothing of it."

Mitch heard steps retreat up the stairs, listened as his neighbor's door squeaked shut. So where were his other neighbors? Nobody was showing up. Well, that was part of the point.

The sirens neared.

Mitch thought about the cops, the interview, the ride to the hospital, the psych evaluation, the overnight observation, and the rest of what he figured would happen. Didn't sound like much fun.

It took him thirty seconds to pack what he expected he'd need into a nylon backpack. Then it was out the window and down the fire escape. As he descended, he heard louder, more insistent pounding on his door.

He shook his head and wished he hadn't. His brain felt like it had swelled two sizes larger than its container. *This is my own affair,* he thought. Mitch tried not to let his boot heels clang on the metal treads. *Nobody else's business.*

Once he was away from this neighborhood, he wondered, maybe he should find a pay phone and call Carri Ann, let her know what he had done tonight. Let her know *exactly*.

No. This time he remembered not to mirror the thought with a head shake. Mitch wanted her to regret his passing. If his bad luck continued to carry through, she probably wouldn't shed a tear.

So what was the point?

He had to drop the last ten feet to the hard alley floor. Mitch twisted his ankle when he hit. He tried to roll, but one shoulder led his head in smacking the brick. Damn. Everything hurt even worse.

He realized he *could* have broken his neck in that last drop.

Mitch hadn't. It was that kind of a night.

2. Dorothy Parker Redux

Mitch sat in a back booth in the kind of all-night diner where the help didn't actually care if a customer's head was smeared with dried blood, so long as he looked good for the check. He drank a lot of coffee.

Guns were out. He thought about other ways to kill himself.

Something came back to him from the last time he'd seriously considered the topic. He remembered Dorothy Parker's ditty about suicide. Gas, poison, all that—he sort of agreed with the old lady. Except for the conclusion.

He didn't *want* to might as well live!

"More of my hot java?"

The waitress was a young thing, becalmed somewhere in her early twenties, too much dark eye shadow for Mitch's taste, a slight lisp from the gleaming tongue stud. He liked her hair, though, the auburn so deep red it shimmered like liquid metal in the fluorescents.

She'd flirted with him outrageously since he'd come in.

Mitch didn't think he had responded, though, to tell the truth, she was the sort of pick-up he'd once have grabbed in a hot moment. He guessed tonight he wasn't in the mood.

He reckoned he'd turned off his dick when he'd loaded the presumed fatal bullet in the pistol. So was he horny again now that he'd survived? He didn't think so.

"Where you going from here?" said the waitress, elbows on the booth divider at Mitch's shoulder, outlined nipples suggesting the coffee shop was colder than he thought it was.

Philosophically? Mitch thought, stifling the impulse to dissolve into helpless laughter. Naw, she probably had a narrower focus. He had a sudden idea. It was brilliant, he thought modestly. No, it wasn't brilliant. It was far more stupid than the pistol inspiration. But the charm of it just about made him giggle aloud.

"I'm going to City Park," he said.

"At midnight? Park's closed," she said.

"It'll be quieter. I can do some thinking."

"If you don't get mugged," said the waitress. She looked like she was thinking aloud. "Drink some more coffee. Hold on 'til two. That's when I get off. I'll go along with you."

Mitch turned and looked up into her face. Makeup and piercings aside, she was so *innocent*. "Thanks," he said. "You're a sweetie."

"Silver-tongued devil," she said, smiling brilliantly, metal flashing.

That fatal charm never goes away, Mitch thought, not altogether happily.

A few minutes later, the waitress went back into the kitchen. Mitchell Valentine got up, left a twenty beneath his water glass, and bolted for the door. No one called after him.

3. The Island of Dr. Morose

Mitch used exact change and took the Colfax bus east to a stop two blocks north of City Park. Except for the nice old lady who looked like she'd be cadging transfers from the tolerant driver and spending the night on the bus, he was the only passenger. When he exited at Fillmore Street, the nice old lady flashed him a grin and ostentatiously licked her lips. Mitch touched the brim of his cap with a two-fingered salute.

Old, young, hot, retired, it's over, he thought. But what the hell, he was still polite.

At this time of night, it was no problem entering the park—that was a matter of crossing a final street. The new moon helped. The park was nominally closed. Automobile traffic was forbidden after ten at night. Mitch simply hiked in, ducking behind a huge elm once when headlights from a cruising cop car slid past.

The zoo fence was more of a challenge. Mitch committed himself by tossing the pack ahead and over. Then he scrambled up the storm fence, a little disappointed that it wasn't electrified, and dropped to the other side. The impact sent sharp nauseating pain through his ankle and sucked away his breath. He hunkered, doubled nearly over, until that breath came back. *Haven't I been through this before?* Mitch heard the harsh cries of disturbed birds from the branches above. Fine, so long as they couldn't dial 911.

Then he followed his memory route to Monkey Island. He supposed he could have simply vaulted over the protective fence into the environment where the polar bear troop frolicked during warm days, but Mitch didn't feel as though he wanted to be ripped apart by disinterested carnivores.

No, he'd worked out a plan for something more instantaneous and, he hoped, painless. Maybe. As he knew from earlier that night, nothing was a slam dunk.

The terrain was as he recalled it. The city's high tension lines crossed the north shore of the small lake surrounding Monkey Island. The power company kept promising to reroute the lines; so far, they hadn't. *Fine,* Mitch thought, *this ought to convince them.*

He stood beneath the humming lines, estimating the height of the lowest, vividly remembering the dead raptors he'd seen littering the prairie below

power lines when he was a boy. His father had briefed his curious son about the intricacies of completed circuits. The birds were fine, until they incautiously bridged a circuit that would ground them and send the liquid fire crisping through them and into the earth.

"But it's quick." His father had shrugged. "They never feel a thing."

Mitch wasn't quite so sure about that. But he did agree that the process was most likely fast.

For a moment, he looked out over the calm water toward the small, forested island where the monkey colony lived. The image that flashed in his brain was him as an ape, dressed in human business garb, trying to cozy up to Carri Ann. Was that how she saw him? Probably so. Or she certainly would see him that way now.

He sighed, extracted a coil of tough nylon rope from the backpack, bent down, and immersed it in the cold zoo lake water. He let it stew for a few minutes. Then he stood, coiled rope dripping, as he tied one end around the ballpeen hammer he'd taken from his toolbox. He tilted his head back, looking speculatively at the nearly invisible lines. He'd better do it before he suffered a crisis of nerve.

Mitch paid out a little rope, then gently started the weighted end in a whispering circle through the hushed night. He'd seen any number of National Geographic specials in which Argentine gauchos had spun, thrown, and connected with their bolos.

It didn't look *that* hard!

He released the rope and let it sigh through his fingers.

Everything worked perfectly. The ballpeen-weighted end wrapped eighteen inches of rope around the lowest of the power lines. Mitch stood there, tugging experimentally, feeling the give as the rope and the man pulling it barely bowed the heavy line overhead.

Nothing happened. No lightning.

Mitch shook his head. "Kee-rist on a crutch!" This was working out no better than the experiment with the pistol.

He stared at the power line, at the rope, then down and ahead of him at the Monkey Island lake. He decided to go with instinct. And desperation. Mitch looped the line twice around his right hand, turned his back to the lake, then ran like hell. As the rope tautened, he lifted his knees, feeling his body starting to rotate at the bottom of the new pendulum.

Then gravity did its job.

Mitch kept his legs folded up like landing gear until he was swinging back over the lake. Once he was above the mirrored water surface, he extended his legs and loosened his grip on the rope.

Line hissed through his fingers and yes, it burned. But he still clung to the wet rope as his feet skated along the lake surface.

Water sprayed. Then—

Sparks, flame, all electrical hell broke loose.

Mitch thought he saw ball lightning zinging down in a dotted ethereal line from the power tower.

It was hot and it was loud.

About goddamn time, he thought, and that was the last coherent thing that wrote any dialog on his brain.

The world exploded. *Mitch* exploded.

Witnesses later reported seeing the flash from the zoo lake reflecting off the foothills west of the city. That may have been a slight exaggeration. Maybe not.

Denver Public Service personnel had picked that night to perform all manner of routine maintenance. They should have opted for a different evening. On the precautionary safety side, not many failsafes worked as they should.

Half of Denver went black for a day.

All of Mitchell Valentine finally went black. For good.

Or so he thought at the time. He still heard the damned birds angrily screaming.

4. *Psychopomp and Circumstance*

Wherever Mitchell Valentine was now, it wasn't Kansas. Nor was it Colorado, New Mexico, Utah, or any other location in which he'd recently rented crummy apartments and cheap motel rooms, contract-baled alfalfa, or worked at minimum wage construction.

He stared around at the tall dark trunks and the all-enveloping tree canopy. The light sneaked through from above; a sun glowed there, but filtered.

Could this be Southern California? The thought was fleeting.

No. The air did not *feel* right. He didn't think he had ever breathed air so damp and heavy, so rich with decay, so hot it seemed to film his skin to slickness. It was like breathing rough-trade sex.

Mitch sat on the rain forest floor, his back against a tree he guessed extended better than a hundred meters up before it initiated an elaborate ritual of intricate branching. He was naked, rivulets of sweat dripping along his ribs, pooling down into his crotch. He glanced even further down and tensed, staring. A single file of startling crimson ants, stretching as far to the right as he could see, marched in lock step up over his feet, dropped again to the forest floor, then eventually vanished to the distant left. Their feathery antennae tickled. Their chitinous feet scratched his skin. Each ant was the size of his thumb, and Mitch had big hands.

He yelped and drew up his knees, pulling his feet further back. The ants kept tromping along.

Instinctively he raised one bare foot, muscles tensing, ready to deliver a killing blow with his heel.

Don't, said a voice laden with such malevolence he automatically froze in position.

"I hate ants," he said. Mitch looked around wildly. Whoever was speaking, Mitch couldn't spot him. "All bugs make me nuts."

They don't hate you, said the voice. *But if you trouble or molest or bother them in any way, they will invade, disjoint, and devour you. They will flense your hide from the inside out.*

He didn't like the sound of this. "I won't do anything to them," said Mitch. "I promise."

Good.

Mitch hesitated. "Who are you?"

He heard something in his head that might have been an exasperated sigh. The voice said, *You might think of me as your ticket home.*

"This isn't home?" As soon as he said the words aloud, he knew this tropic stew of sexuality and danger could not possibly be any home he'd ever inhabited.

The voice paused before speaking in his head. *Well . . . you could call this home under normal circumstances . . . home for a good long while. But you used to live in a different place. Somebody there wants to see you. I've no idea why, but they wish to reclaim you very, very badly.* The voice seemed to smile. Mitch sensed an image of sharp, chattery edges. He shuddered. *In the worst way, my boy. That's how they want you.*

"I don't get it," Mitch said. The moment the words exited his lips, he *knew* he shouldn't have said that.

You will.

From nothingness, the voice seemed to take form around him, forest shadow made manifest as first a cloak of fog, then as the slow beating of tremendous wings.

Two eyes black as the space between stars regarded him. He couldn't make out the rest of the face, if face indeed it was. He had the sudden sensation of a form somehow birdlike, but larger than any bird he'd ever seen. *Feathers,* he thought. *Yes, those are feathers, black and glossy with serrated edges.*

He saw the beak, long, sharp, gleaming, scimitarlike.

The beak opened, snapped shut. Words appeared in his mind.

You are called, Mitchell Valentine. In the forward progress of things, you were barely running in place. Now you're going to lose some ground. You're going back.

Things clicked together in his mind. It made a crazy sense. His lips parted, gawped, then fashioned the words he wanted. "I think I get it," he said. "All the birds screaming at the lake. The fire and everything. I died, didn't I? I'm someplace else now, but I'm not alive."

You talk too much, said the voice.

"You're not a real bird, are you? I mean not a mortal one. You're like those whatchacallums, those sparrows in that Stephen King novel, *The Dark Half?*"

No sparrows here, said the voice, sounding almost amused. *Psychopomps. That's the word you're looking for. The bearers of souls.*

"Cool job," said Mitch.

Not quite. It would be if we didn't have to deal with mortals.

"But if you didn't have us mortal souls, you wouldn't have a job."

You're a scurvy lot, said the voice.

"Thanks," said Mitch.

We're late, said the voice. *Let's go.*

"Actually," said Mitch, "I don't want to go back. It wasn't by accident I got here."

Too bad. Not my concern. Somebody wants you back bad.

The wind of huge pinions funneled around him. Feathers beat within a fractional inch of his skin. Musk filled his nostrils. "Who?" he yelled above the noise of the wind. "Who wants me back? Who cares that much?"

No one and nothing answered.

"Carri Ann?" Mitch called. "Is it her?"

Too many questions, said the voice. *You'll find out soon enough.*

"Is it Carri Ann? Does she care after all?" Mitch looked inward to see if his heart leaped with the news. He was having a hard time breathing. That was all.

Blackness whirled around him. He could see nothing, and could feel only a whirling, rushing sensation of infinite speed.

The voice, apparently faint from distance, said, *Rachel. That's who.*

The hell, he thought. "Rachel?" Mitch yelled. "This is a mistake! I don't *know* any Rachel."

And then the blackness consumed him utterly.

5. The Comfort of Carri Ann

When the bird dropped him near his old apartment, it really *dropped* him. From about twenty feet up. Mitch felt the sick vertigo as he noticed he was poised in the air above the apartment building's scrubby-grassed parking strip just like the Coyote in a Roadrunner cartoon. And like the lop-eared C-dude, Mitch registered he was suspended above a hellacious drop. Coyote went straight down. So did Mitch.

He tried hard to roll when he hit, an effort that met only partial success. His hip hit, then the right shoulder; finally his skull bounced soundly off the tough turf. The air *whuffed* with enormous enthusiasm out of his lungs.

Damn lucky I'm dead, he thought.

Lucky, indeed, echoed the voice of the bird who'd conveyed him here. *But now things are a little more ambivalent.*

The pain racketing through his bones suggested death was not a completely anesthetized state. But he also realized he was once again clothed. He even wore his familiar Warner Bros. Coyote wristwatch. God bless Chuck Jones.

So you're back for sure, said the voice. *She wants you a lot. Go do something to justify it.*

"Sure 'nuff, Boss," said Mitch. "What'd Carri Ann have to pony up for this? Her soul?"

The voice sounded a touch confused. *That dog don't hunt, I think you'd say. I'm talking about Rachel.*

Mitch experimented with getting to his feet. The knees pulsed, his legs wobbled, but he made it. He figured he had at least half his lung capacity back. "Who the hell's Rachel?"

The voice sounded confused again. *I'm an emissary, not a records clerk. Maybe Carri Ann is a pet name for your Rachel.*

Mitch started to shake his head, but changed his mind quickly as the nausea clawed at him. "No way. I had a pet name for Carri Ann, all right, but it wasn't anything as biblical as Rachel. I still think maybe you got the wrong corpse."

The voice of the bird said, *One thing we don't do, that's make errors.*

"Humble as all get out," said Mitch. "So I'm no mistake." This time he *did* shake his head, sick-making pain be damned. "I'm flattered."

Skip the sarcasm, said the voice. *You've got business to attend back here. Sooner you get to it, sooner you'll earn some eternal peace.*

"So do I get a microcassette recorder like in that old TV series, you know, the Tom Cruise movie? What kind of mission is this?"

No answer.

"Bird? Goddammit, answer me."

It started to rain. An elderly couple with a leashed elderly dog stared at him oddly and edged by, as close to the other side of the concrete sidewalk as they could manage.

"Bird?" No suggestions, no orders, no criticism, nothing at all. Only a silence in his head. Actually, Mitch realized, he didn't mind that. It had been exhausting carrying on a fruitful dialogue with a huge black supernatural bird. And he hadn't backed down, even when the creature inspected him dourly, eying him as though Mitch were an edible, but not otherwise terribly attractive bug.

Mitch realized he was shivering. The night was damned *cold*. It seemed far too chilly for mid-July. He ransacked his pockets and found a fused lump of silver alloy that had apparently been pocket change. No good.

Mitch raised his head and charged after the elderly couple. "Hey!" he called. "You look like terrific grandparents and generally nice old folks. Could you give me a quarter for the phone?"

The two old people stopped at the corner, exchanging apprehensive glances. The dog started to growl, then coughed itself into silence.

"How about a quarter?" said Mitch. "Please?"

The old man fumbled out his wallet and extracted a dollar bill.

Mitch shook his head in exasperation. "I don't need food or a drink, Pops. I need to make a phone call. Only a quarter."

The old woman extracted a twenty-five cent piece from her change purse and held it out to him.

He snatched it with gratitude. "Thanks, lady. Now you both have a great night."

He turned and started searching for a pay phone. He had to walk ten blocks before finding a phone that worked. Mitch dialed the number from memory. It was automatic.

She picked up on the first ring. The low contralto said, "Yes?"

"It's me," said Mitch. "I'm back."

Carri Ann barely missed a beat, but she did hesitate the smallest bit. "Mitch?"

"None other."

"You are dead, you know."

"I know." His turn to hesitate. "How long's it been?"

Electronic crackling scrubbed out Carri Ann's words. She repeated without prompting. "It's been three months. It's almost Halloween."

That explained the cold night. But he didn't remember killing three months in . . . wherever he'd gone.

"So you're back from Paradise?" said Carri Ann.

"*I* wouldn't call it that," said Mitch. "It was warm, but it had ants."

"Poor baby."

Mitch tried to concentrate on the phone. Was this a conversation suitable for celebrating a return from the dead? "At any rate, I'm back," he said. "Can I see you?"

She hesitated. "What kind of shape are you in?"

He stared down at his hands. "I'm not a horror movie walking corpse, if that's what you mean. I look pretty much like me."

"That's good enough," she said. "Where are you?"

He squinted, read off the street names at the corner.

"Twenty minutes," said Carri Ann. "Maybe a little less if I hurry."

"I'm not going anywhere. By the way," he said, "thanks for bringing me back."

She let out a long, mournful breath. "Don't thank me, Mitch. I'm not your savior."

"What the hell do you mean?" he said. "*Somebody* cared enough to bring me back."

"You want me to be brutally honest?"

"Sure," he said. He suspected he'd regret that. It was *never* a good idea to say yes when a woman asked that particular question.

"I'm the woman who sent you to hell," said Carri Ann." You still want me to pick you up?"

After a few moments, he nodded, then realized she couldn't see the motion. "Why the hell not? We've got a lot to catch up on." He set the outdoor phone in its cradle.

Mitch leaned against the cold weathered brick beside the phone kiosk and folded his chilled fingers under his arms.

Who *was* Rachel?

6. *The Hollies Never Met Her*

Carri Ann was there in fourteen minutes. That was the sort of thing she did. Mitch guessed his Coyote watch was absolutely accurate.

Her decade-old VW Cabriolet zoomed up with the top down. Apparently the October cold didn't matter. No doubt she found the increasingly frigid air bracing. Carri Ann wheeled the convertible into a U-turn and pulled over to the curb in front of Mitch. In the mercury vapor haze, the red paint looked black as blood.

She opened her door and stepped out. "Hey, cowboy," she said, standing a foot away, looking up at him. Hair short and blacker than the night, the skin around her eyes crinkling slightly as she grinned. The expression was a little lopsided. Her teeth gleamed white. "Hard trip?"

"Let's say it wasn't any weekend in Cabo."

"So." She reached up, put those slender muscular fingers around the sides of his face, drew him down toward her. Generous lips fractionally separated from his, Carri Ann said, "Glad to see me?"

Not kissing her wasn't so difficult as he'd once have imagined it. She bulldozed aside his hesitation by lifting herself on her toes. Her mouth was hot enough against his, he suddenly didn't notice the October chill. "No enthusiasm from you, lover?" she said.

Fuck it, he thought. He gave her some enthusiasm.

"Better," she whispered. She wrapped her arms around the back of his neck. Her right leg curled around the back of his knees.

Mitch pulled his mouth away for a moment. "I gotta ask," he said. "What did you mean about sending me to hell?"

"Mmh," she said. "Damn. I was afraid you'd remember. It's what I get for speaking without thinking."

"Not as much as what I get for kissing you again without asking."

"Point," she said, voice amused. "Get in the car. We're going to my place. Or yours."

"I doubt I've *got* a place," he said.

"It's settled." She grabbed his hand and led him to the passenger door.

Obviously no longer in quite such a hurry, it took Carri Ann twenty minutes to wheel the Cabriolet into the curving, tree-lined drive sweeping up to her neo-Victorian in Highlands Ranch. Instead of pulling the convertible into the garage, she pulled it up to the curb by the front double doors.

Carri Ann hadn't wanted to raise the car's top for the drive home, so conversation had languished in the rush of wind. Instead, driver and passenger had taken turns punching the radio button presets and cranking the volume. She preferred punk and classical; he gravitated toward country and jazz.

When they entered the front door, the lights faded up and the sound system swelled with the Hollies' "Carrie-Anne."

Mitch had to raise his voice to be heard. "Cute," he said. "You do this even if you come home alone?"

Carri Ann snapped her fingers and the audio faded to background noise. The familiar cocked head, hipshot stance, and grin. "It's a harmless indulgence, cutie. Makes me feel welcome, *especially* when I'm alone. Come on. I'll get you a drink."

"Coffee," he said. "I don't think I've had any caffeine in three months."

"You *know* I can out-steam Starbucks." She grabbed his hand and tugged him toward the kitchen.

One entire tiled counter held an espresso maker that resembled the laboratory set in a '30s Universal Frankenstein flick. Carri Ann set to work with zeal while Mitch took a seat on one of the breakfast nook stools. She clattered coffee implements about with gusto as steam hissed and bled.

She glanced at him as she talked. "You should be dead, Mitch. I guess you know that. Three months ago, you screwed up a nice, neat auto-da-fé and sat there like a complete doofus. Then you exercised some imagination, found your way to the Monkey Island Lake in City Park, and managed to shut down the city for a whole rush hour."

"I had no idea," he said in some confusion.

"Well, you did. And now you're back. It wasn't me, lover. 'Forget the dead you've left.' Remember *that* song? I thought I'd forgotten you but good." Her amiability seemed to slip. "Now you're here again and I'm trying to figure out why." She poured the steaming coffee into a black mug and handed it to him.

Mitch lifted it to his lips. "Nice," he said, "if I could taste it."

She raised dark knife-edged eyebrows. "Want an ice cube?"

He shook his head. "I want to know what you meant about sending me to hell."

She contemplated him silently for a moment or two. "Here's the deal. Do you consider yourself the suicidal type?"

He thought about that, then shook his head again. "It sure never was a problem before three months ago."

"There's a reason," she said. "Long as I've known you, you've had a disgusting optimism about life. I don't think you wanted to die—not ever. You didn't want to miss anything."

"I'll agree. But I did kill myself. I remember that."

A touch of asperity crept into her voice. "Haven't you questioned that, you self-assured asshole?"

"Nope." He sipped the cooling coffee. "Good brew."

Carri Ann took a stool across the table from him and contemplated him silently. Finally she said, "You infuriated me live; death hasn't improved your effect."

"I guess that's not a compliment," he said.

"I guess it isn't. Did you ever ask yourself why I let you pick me up back when?"

"My sense of humor?" Mitch said. "I sometimes wondered whether it was actually *you* picking *me* up."

"Point," she said. "Let me take a different tack. Was it the money?"

He shook his head. The money hadn't hurt. He recalled the first time he'd seen this lavish house, utterly incongruous in the surrounding bland bedroom community. How she'd obtained the covenant variance for constructing a home of soaring Gothic curves and Victorian gingerbread was always a mystery. But he thought he'd uncovered a clue when he examined the blown-up photocopy of a lottery ticket matted and framed in her office. It was the replica of a Powerball ticket, dated ten years before. Mitch remembered the story of the drawing. A young woman had bought a single ticket at a U-Totem in Raton, New Mexico, and claimed a cash payout of 62 million dollars after taxes.

The winner had beaten 50-million-to-one odds. Three million to one was the odds for freezing to death. Five thousand to one was the actuarial likelihood of dying in an auto accident. Mitch had examined the replica ticket more than once, looking for a clue. He'd finally marked for future consideration that two of the specifically chosen ticket numbers were 6 and 66. The Powerball number itself was 13.

He'd joked about that with Carri Ann. "The fortunes of the Antichrist?" he'd said. "The luck of the damned?" She'd smiled and then laughed and agreed with him. Months later, Mitch wondered if perhaps he shouldn't have laughed so heartily.

"It wasn't the money," he said.

She shook her head. "Well, I'll tell you one of *my* reasons for putting up with you. You were one of the few guys I ever knew who could have a good time with me without hourly cell calls to their therapist or feeding a lavish Viagra habit."

He recalled her remarkably appointed basement. "Shoot, Carri Ann, I guess you could simply say I loved you."

Her expression flickered mercurially. "Then why did you betray me?"

Mitch didn't know how to defuse the moment any more than he had a few months before. He felt a tide sweep across him, a lassitude, as though all the adrenaline was gone and his journey from death to new life was catching up with him. He examined his palms; the lines told him absolutely nothing. "I still don't have an answer, Carri Ann. I made a mistake. I screwed up. I'm sorry."

"I was sorry too, Mitchell." Her voice started to rise. "I was so damned sorry I decided to make sure you'd never do anything like that to me or any other woman again."

"I figured you'd just leave me," he said.

"If I didn't have more money and power than a seated President of the

U.S., I probably would have. Or more likely, I would have shot you myself that first night, killed you, and then served some hard time."

Mitch decided it wise not to comment.

"I was pissed, Mitch. Irritated enough to hire some good help. Smart enough to use a smorgasbord of psychoactives, classified behavioral psych techniques—oh yeah, and classical voodoo. You didn't have a chance, buckaroo." She virtually spat the last. "Anyhow, it worked, or so I thought. Even if you felt compelled to exit as theatrically as you could, you still got dispatched into the great black yonder." She slapped her palms down on the table and said almost sorrowfully, "And now what the hell am I gonna do with you?"

Mitch realized he was neither surprised at her anger nor by her confession. Not that he was delighted by what she had evidently done. And he was a pragmatist. Love no longer seemed to be an issue here. Still . . . dammit, he cared for her. At least he thought he did.

"I could apologize again," he said quietly. "Maybe we could figure out how to be friends."

"Not in my lifetime," she said. "And *especially* not in yours."

They both started as someone rapped crisply on the front door. "I'm gonna show you what I mean," said Carri Ann, rising to her feet. "Come on." He followed her through the dining room and into the front hall.

Carri Ann flung open the front doors, revealing three competent-looking men wearing leather jackets and ski masks. Two held silenced pistols in their hands. The third hefted a shotgun with a bore that looked to Mitch like the exhaust header on a '58 Chevy half-ton.

"I called them before I left to pick you up," said Carri Ann. "Lord knows, I tried subtlety. Gosh, I hate to do this. They're gonna shoot you, Mitch. And then, after I clean the hall, I'm going to go through a whole book of new magicks to make sure neither body nor soul comes back from whatever perdition you wind up in."

"Carri Ann," said Mitch. "I said I'd apologize. I'm really, really sorry."

"Even another *really* wouldn't do it," Carri Ann said. She nodded to the men in the doorway.

He didn't know what to say, but he opened his mouth to try. Too late.

Fire chuffed toward him from the cylindrical muzzles. Dead or not, it hurt like a bitch.

It was déjà vu all over again.

7. A Shrike in Crow's Plumage

This time when Mitch Valentine woke, he decided instantly he missed the rain forest. It could have been the Gobi Desert, or maybe the Kalahari. Whichever, it was sandy and hot as hell. Naked again, he sat perched on the crest of a sandy dune. It appeared to be higher than its surrounding mates, but the vantage didn't help. The serried ranks of piled sand marched away into the distance. He thought he saw what might be clouds at what he guessed to be the western horizon. Overhead the sun blazed in an otherwise empty sky the color of cobalt glass.

A breeze fanned his cheeks—all of them—but the effect was not one of cooling. He felt like a roast being basted with tickling wisps of steam.

Mitch remembered his last image of the men in Carri Ann's doorway. He glanced down, lightly touched his chest, his midsection. No holes. No scars. He stretched experimentally. It hurt, but not as much as he remembered in his final moments at Carri Ann's.

Things did not go well. The voice he could not see articulated the words not as a question, but as a declarative sentence.

Mitch agreed silently.

The wind rose a bit. *And so you're back again.*

"I think I could use the rest," said Mitch.

Not for long, the voice said, a slight tone of impatience leavened with weariness tingeing the words.

Mitch waited silently, fearing the worst.

There are rules, said the voice. *There are any number of things I'm not supposed to tell you. But enough time passes, I find myself getting a touch impatient.*

"I imagine so," Mitch said, wondering what the hell it was talking about. He thought he caught movement in his peripheral vision. When he twisted to look over his right shoulder, he caught a glimpse of what might be the rippling black feathers of a giant wing. That was all he saw.

Don't patronize, said the voice warningly.

"Sorry." He scooched around in the sand. There was nothing on the opposite side of the dune other than more sand. The fine dust that coated his body blew into his eyes and he blinked.

I do sometimes get a little irritated, said the voice. *And when I do . . .* The voice broke off for a few seconds. *Are you familiar with my cousin, the shrike?*

"We're talking about birds, right?" said Mitch.

The voice apparently ignored his evident obtuseness. *The mortal term is the family Laniidae. Their voice is terrible, and their appetite worse. Carnivores. They screech and chuckle before tearing their food apart. And the prey . . . the prey* they often keep for later use by impaling it live on thorns or fence barbs. The shrikes were quite taken with the American ranchers whose innovation was the introduction of barbed wire.

"Fascinating," said Mitch. "And your point?"

A point, a very sharp *point, is where you're going to end up if you don't keep silent a moment.*

The words were edged. An image flashed unbidden into Mitch's mental theatre: he was dropped from a great height above a sunwashed clay-brick city. He plummeted with excruciating deliberation into what apparently was the market square. Faces both bearded and surrounded by swaths of brightly dyed fabric gawked up at him. Mouths of men and women opened, but he could hear nothing. For no apparent reason, a sharpened wooden pole stood erect in the center of the square. He knew where he was headed. His body rotated around the vertical axis but he still fell face down. It would get him in the belly, the pole would. He could feel the point push into his skin, the tissue stretching, attempting to resist, then tearing, allowing the stake to force its way through ropey muscle, soft gut, pulsating organs. He felt all that, though the stake still was no larger in his vision than a knitting needle. He fell in dream time.

Mitch shut up and waited.

We're all of us oscines, Mitch, the shrike and me. No one in much of the mortal world thinks of us as songbirds, but we are. Songbirds with highly evolved voices. Oscines. Since time immemorial, we've delivered omens with those voices. The voice paused before the man could say anything. *I grow weary of the constant circumlocution of omens. In some age, I should delight in the rhetoric of the direct, speaking absolutely straight from the shoulder.*

"I can go along with that," said Mitch. "I'm listening. Shoot."

I struggle, but rules still bind me. Let me try.

Mitch thought it wise at this point to keep his own counsel.

Here's the first thing, Mitchell Valentine. This is not your first journey to and from the land of the dead.

"Well, I know that," said Mitch. "I just got back from the land of the living. Again. Remember? Believe me, *I* remember."

But you don't recall the other times. You do not remember all the occasions I erased the traces.

Mitch mentally reeled. *All the other times?* he thought. *Cripes, I'm exhausted from getting killed twice.*

You have no idea, said the voice. *Your deaths have been many and varied. Some have been astonishingly grotesque, even by mortal standards.*

"Don't tell me," said Mitch. "I don't think I want to know."

It's enough to tell you that you have lived and died many times, that you have practically been what mortals would term a commuter between life and death.

He pondered that for about half a millisecond. "I don't remember any of that."

You wouldn't. That's part of your learning process.

Mitch suddenly identified with Captain Kirk attempting to out-dialogue a crazed computer in any number of old *Star Trek* reruns. "What am I learning?"

It doesn't matter. I don't think you have *been learning. Therefore it wouldn't do any good to tell you.*

"But you brought this whole thing up in the first place," Mitch said, exasperated. The wind was getting worse. Grit spattered his back and chest.

I know, I know. It was out of frustration.

He let the voice stew for a time.

Finally it said, *Your wristwatch.*

Instinctively he glanced at his bare wrist. At the same time, he realized the sun didn't seem to have moved since his arrival in the desert. "I got it at the Warner Bros. store. I love Chuck Jones cartoons. The Coyote's my favorite character."

It sounded like the voice cawed. *Coyote, Mitch. He's your favorite character, all right.*

"So?"

Coyote, Loki, the trickster, he's been around a long, long time and gotten into considerable mischief.

"I saw the movie." He hadn't, he realized, but the glib words came out without conscious volition.

Coyote's pissed off a lot of powerful forces in his time. Betrayed many confidences, betrayed even more relationships. Stuck to his accustomed behavior, though. He seems to have a learning curve that's about vertical. He can't seem ever to quite scale it.

"I'm still confused," said Mitch. He almost said, Give me a clue. Instead he actually said, "Give me an omen."

The chain can be broken.

"Yes?" he said, expecting more. "That's it?"

You're going back, Mitch. One more time.

"I just got here." The wind began to shriek. A tendril of sand lashed into his open mouth. Trying to spit it out, he choked.

Shut up and listen. After what I told you, this may be the last time. Make my own risk worth it.

Black wings beating. The flash of eye and beak. The wind swept Mitch up like the twister snatching Dorothy. It all happened too quickly for him to ask his next question.

Another special request for your presence, Mitch.

As he whirled in the cyclonic cloud, he thought, *Christ, Carri Ann* again?

Amusement darkly tinged the voice. *Now* there's *a piece of work I would welcome impaling on a rusty barb.*

The wind lessened. He glimpsed city lights rushing down toward him. His stomach flip-flopped.

No, Mitch. Patient now. *Not Carri Ann.*

He crazily wondered if he was plunging toward a hand-honed impalement stake. "Then who?"

Rachel.

Mitch still stared into swirling darkness, but he felt a stone curbing beneath him. At least he wasn't impaled. He opened his eyes. The nausea began to abate. He could think of other things.

"Who's Rachel?" he said weakly.

The voice from behind him said, "That would be me."

8. Your Kohl, Kohl Heart

Mitch slowly turned his head, his vision focusing with the inevitability of fate. He stared at the young woman looking back down at him. "You?" he said. "*You!* Rachel?"

She grinned. "Me. Rachel. You speak pigeon fluently?"

"Wrong bird," said Mitch. He tried to figure this all out. "What's the matter—my double sawbuck tip wasn't enough? You had to call me back from the dead for another ten percent?"

"The twenty was great," Rachel said. "Thanks. I was told you were an asshole who'd make a joke and miss the point."

"Let me guess," said Mitch, struggling to get up to his knees and elbows. Rachel hunkered down to help him. "You've been talking to my travel agent."

"You got it." Rachel draped his arm around her shoulders and tried to lever him erect. Uncertainly wound together, they both staggered upright.

Mitch abruptly registered how good she smelled. Crisp, fresh, like clean sheets or a new car. Like newly cut grass after a rain. *For crying out loud,* he told himself silently. *Put a brake on it. Don't fall in love.* Then he couldn't help himself as he buried his face in that glorious cataract of almost luminescent auburn hair, that vivid electric red that belonged to no palette of nature in this world. The hair smelled just as good as her skin.

"Ah, sweetie," she murmured, striving mightily to keep him from listing.

Rachel turned her face far enough to kiss the side of his neck. He felt heat burn up into his face, filling every cell with a clear radiance.

After a time, he felt steady enough to practice balancing by himself, and took a step back. Her lips quirked as she cocked her head. Some of the dark makeup around her eyes had smeared, giving her the beginnings of a distinct Pagliacci look.

His eye was caught by something glinting in the streetlight. "You, um, got a new piercing. Very cool." It was a tiny gold stud in her left nostril.

"Thank you," she said. "That's the newest. It makes an even dozen."

Ears, he thought. Lip and tongue. That'd make five. An even dozen? His mind ran riot.

"You look a little the worse for wear," she said. "How about some tea? We're a block from home."

"Done," he said. "I think I can walk that." Even so, he was grateful she put her arm around his waist as they negotiated the nighttime street. Flakes of snow began to drift down in the fuzzed auras of the mercury vapor lamps.

"What's the date?" he said.

"December twenty-first," she said. "Winter's here."

At the opposite end of the block, they crossed the deserted street and entered the equally desolate foyer of an old brick apartment block. Four flights later, they were in Rachel's apartment. It was spartan and clean, though cluttered with a variety of things: exercise equipment, stacked books, tools and supplies for fashioning stained glass, two haughty black Siamese cats, neon tubes for light sculpting, a computer desk holding an aged Mac with a full graphics package (which Rachel pointed out proudly), scattered CD albums, and matted and framed posters of a variety of musicians Mitch didn't recognize.

"What do you think?" she said, putting water onto a kitchen gas burner to heat.

He gazed into her kohl-rimmed eyes, looking this late hour much like a raccoon suffering sleep deprivation. "I haven't figured out the patterns of your life," he said, "but I like the clues I see."

Rachel smiled as she hauled out a wooden chest of Celestial Seasonings. Mitch opted for a pair of Morning Thunder bags; she chose a single Sleepytime. The tea steeped and they waited.

"Why?" he said. They both knew the referent.

She shrugged her shoulders, slender, sharp, almost fragile bones poking at the silky moire pattern of her shirt. "I usually have good instincts," she said. "You generate some real chemistry."

"You figured that from serving a few coffee refills?"

Rachel nodded. "You were troubled, you were in pain, you were vulnerable. I wanted to help you, mother you, take you home and protect you." Her face shifted subtly. "Probably I would have screwed your brains out."

"Thank you," he said simply. "I guess I had no idea."

"Your thoughts were elsewhere. That all came home to me after I found out in the papers why the lights had gone out. They didn't use a photo—you were too messed up. But the description fit. I knew it was you."

"Most people," he said, "would have shed a tear or two and let it go."

"I'm not most people." Rachel set down her cup and moved over in front of him. Carefully she lowered herself astride his thighs, facing him. Her face was close to his; he could feel the sweet tickle of her breath. "I've learned to go after what I decide is important."

"Even a dead guy?" He felt his eyebrows rise.

She nodded vigorously. Her hair whipped, brushing his face. "I found out I have a supernatural ally."

"Is it big and black and has wings?" he said.

"Sounds like a riddle." She nodded again. "It doesn't tell me its name. I think of it as the bird familiar."

You clever critter, he thought at the creature he figured was lurking nearby.

I've had time to practice a little subtlety and guile, said the voice.

This woman can't bring me back, can she? he thought.

No, but her desire petitions me. Given the urgency of her soul, I've tried to accommodate.

Mitch shook his head in wonder and admiration.

"What is it?" Rachel said.

"I used to think I was sometimes a little devious." The Morning Thunder was finally cool enough to drink. He swallowed a respectable slug and imagined he felt the caffeine sheeting through his body like some uncontrolled isotope.

"That was the idea *I* got," she said.

Mitch grinned. "Now I suspect I'm maybe the least of the wheels turning within other wheels. The rest of you would do justice to the homeboys at Olympus, Valhalla, Uluru, Place-of-Elders, or Sunken R'lyeh."

Rachel assessed him quizzically.

"Don't mind me," he said. "I read too much."

She placed his right hand on her thigh; moved her own hand so that the fingertips barely brushed his. To Mitch, it felt like water rushing, an unignorable mountain river current.

"You feel it, don't you?" she whispered.

He nodded, suddenly not trusting himself to speak.

"Wait." She stood and walked away from him, passing beneath the lintel of what he took to be her bedroom. He heard the whisper of fabric, as well as other sounds he could not identify. *Feminine mysteries,* he thought.

When Rachel reappeared, she wore an unadorned white gown that cascaded from shoulders to ankles. Her feet were bare. She carried a lit candle in a carved holder. She flipped the light switch, set the candle down on the kitchen table, then took her seat opposite him.

Her eyes found his and held his gaze for many seconds. Or perhaps minutes. Hours. "I would give myself to you," she said, the tone almost formal. "But I will not travel where I am not wanted."

Mitch took a long, slow breath. "Do you know how many times I've taken people?" he said.

"The bird creature gave me some idea."

He shook his head. "In a weird way, I think I've been sort of like my brother rolling the rock up the hill and having it always tumble back over him before the summit. Only I had a hell of a lot more fun." Mitch smiled. "But it's a chain and I've gotta break it someday." He felt the smile vanish and seriousness assert itself. "Maybe now."

Mitch stared at her face, her eyes, all her features, so close now to his. That generous mouth smiled and he caught the candlelit gleam on Rachel's tongue stud. The metal in her one nostril, the ring through her lip, the hand-wrought jewelry depending from the lobes of her ears, it all seemed to glow with an ancient, almost barbaric splendor. Her eyes were fresh and young; the look they projected toward him was old beyond measure.

"I think it's about time for you," Rachel said, extending both arms toward him. He thought he saw St. Elmo's fire dance faintly across her dark sapphire nails. "I love you." Her tone was measured as an invocation, passionate with the natural heat of fresh magma.

I can make this decision, Mitch thought then. *I can, and I can make it true.* He extended his own arms toward her. "I—" he started to say.

That's when the door of Rachel's apartment blew inward with a concussion that knocked them both from their chairs in the kitchen. Light blinded him. Mitch couldn't finish what he was going to say because the fast-burning fire sucked all the oxygen from his lungs.

He couldn't curse. He could not protest. He could not beg.

He couldn't even scream.

9. Okey Dokey, Mr. Loki

Mitch knew who was committing mischief even before the glare light frayed and he could again see. It was no surprise when he saw the familiar guys in the jackets and ski masks moving purposefully through Rachel's apartment. Two of the big ones secured Rachel's arms and moved her against the far wall, away from the windows. Two even larger men grabbed Mitch and pulled him upright.

Three more positioned themselves strategically, all holding stubby, ugly automatic weapons. Mitch noticed that nobody this time seemed particularly inclined to utilize silencers. Apparently Carri Ann felt more secure in her actions this particular holiday season.

But for crying out loud, they'd blown down the door with a concussion grenade or something similar. Where were the sirens? Soon, he assumed. He craned his neck around toward Rachel. Her head fell forward, chin at her chest. "Rachel!" he called. She didn't respond. She didn't even move. He assumed she was alive since the intruders were still supporting her upright.

"Season's greetings, cowboy." He knew that voice. Mitch turned back toward the ragged, smoking doorway as Carri Ann entered. Unsurprisingly, she was wearing one of her Emma Peel outfits tonight. Mitch had always wondered how anything that tight could be comfortable. The answer was doubtless that it wasn't comfortable. For Carri Ann, sometimes style was all.

Mitch croaked something unintelligible when he tried to form a reply. He swallowed with difficulty, and had to settle for, "What the hell do you think you're doing? Leave the girl alone. Your beef's with me." It took about four tries to get that all out; Carri Ann waited patiently.

"Done?" she said. "Good." She nodded imperiously toward the men holding up Rachel. "You do your thing. The rest of you, let's go." Face up close to Mitch's, she mimed a kiss and said, "I know this is going to sound insufferably melodramatic, lover, but you and I are going for a ride in the country."

Mitch decided it wouldn't do much good to fire a smartass rejoinder. He concentrated on collecting his breath as the large men gripping each upper arm hustled him out of the apartment.

No VW Cabriolet this time. Carri Ann had a white limo with festive white running lights waiting outside at the curb. Mitch noticed that no one in the neighborhood seemed to be collecting out of curiosity.

The limo pulled smoothly away with its complement of the driver, the men bracketing Mitch, Carri Ann, and her captive. She snapped her fingers and one of the guards clicked shining steel cuffs onto his wrists.

"Don't get too excited," she said. "These are utilitarian."

"I'm restraining my enthusiasm," he said.

"Good." Carri Ann's smile seemed glazed in place, teeth looking more feral than hospitable. "May I offer you a drink or anything else while we travel?"

He shook his head. Expending a bit of rubber, the driver horsed the limo at speed onto the entrance ramp for the Sixth Avenue freeway and accelerated west toward the mountains.

"How'd you find me so quickly?" said Mitch. "I only got in an hour ago."

The woman spread her hands, palms up, in what appeared to be a gesture of satisfaction. "I figured you'd be back. I didn't know when or precisely where. That's where magicks come in extremely handy." She laughed. "Beats hell out of my old career."

"Torturing animals as a small child?" said Mitch.

"Ha ha," she said, expression betraying what she actually thought of the gibe. "Selling advertising for a heavy metal FM radio station."

"Well," said Mitch, "sort of the same thing."

"You've got more lives than a cat," Carri Ann observed seriously. "But there was never a cat I couldn't kill."

"You never told me about that hobby," he said.

"Never figured I had to. I didn't think you'd find it a turn on."

"Sound judgment," said Mitch.

They both were silent for a time. The limo turned onto I-70 for a few miles, then veered off onto a two-lane blacktop that eventually degraded to hard-packed dirt and gravel.

"So what's the plan?" said Mitch after the large vehicle had slid perilously close to an evergreen verge overlooking a long rocky drop. "Gonna tie me to a spruce and let the restored Canadian wolfpacks chomp me?"

"That's tempting." She stared out her window, apparently attempting to pierce the mountain darkness. "But I know you'd somehow return from that. I've been reading some new sources, practicing up on rituals that haven't been used since the Tunguska meteor strike."

"Sounds promising," Mitch said.

"I've been starting to think even acute physical pain won't compromise your bravado." There was a nasty undertone in Carri Ann's voice he didn't think he liked.

"Do your worst," he said.

"Believe me, I will."

The limo slid to a stop. Mitch couldn't see what exactly was outside. The dark and the dust were both too thick.

The two large guards pulled Mitch out the limo's door and frog-marched him out of the swirling dust. His eyes started to adapt to the mountain midnight. They all stood in a clearing in the forest. In front of him, Mitch saw a ring of fist-sized stones about three meters in diameter. He blinked, squinted, trying to ascertain if what he thought he was seeing was genuinely there. The bare ground inside the ring glowed a low, dusky red. Bare ground? No, now the surface looked more like smooth water.

"No beating or stabbing or shooting for you, bucko," said Carri Ann. "I've been choreographing this routine for a while. Remember I told you last time I'd sent you to hell? This time I for sure am. Literally."

His captors walked him over to the edge of the stone circle. What was inside glowed brighter, as if responding to his presence.

"Well, okay then," Mitch said. "Hell it is. You want me to jump?"

"Don't trouble yourself," said Carri Ann, walking over to stand close beside him. "It'll be our pleasure."

"Why do you keep doing this to yourself?" The question was suddenly very serious to Mitch. He knew that reflected in his voice.

Carri Ann stared at him steadily for a few moments. "I guess I've got an ego, too, lover. And I knew better. But I never wanted to be another Mitch bitch. You know?"

"I'm sorry," he said, knowing this time how much he meant the words. "I was wrong." He lowered his head and found her lips with his own. She didn't recoil. The kiss he gave her was long and sweet and sorrowful.

When she finally drew away, Carri Ann said, "One final thing I want you to know. I'm not completely ignorant. I realize your friend Rachel's been instrumental in bringing you back. I don't want you back again. So you know what I'm going to do."

"No," he said, mouth falling open. "Carri Ann, *no*. Please."

"Not even with brown sugar on it." She nodded at the guards. They lifted him like a child's doll and dropped him into the crimson-glowing circle.

Mitch felt no pain. What he did perceive was that the sensation of falling down a chute to hell was more like being trapped in a mutant combination of Space Mountain and a wind tunnel.

He cried out, a despairing shriek of anger and rage that was not for himself. All sound vanished as soon as it left his lips. His fall picked up speed, accelerating until the wind began to rip away bits of his flesh. Apparently there was no terminal velocity. His skin began to strip from the bone. It didn't matter, he thought.

Nothing mattered.

Until something huge and swift, something feral and black, matched velocities with him.

10. Enfolded by Her Wings

It left him back in the city. It was the same night he had departed. *You need to see this*, said the voice. There was no cruelty in the words. There did not need to be.

Mitch Valentine limped back to Rachel's apartment. There were no police cars parked outside, no bright yellow crime scene tape. Nobody even seemed awake for miles.

He climbed the stairs, forcing himself to ignore the growing dread tugging at his heels like the hounds that had once pursued him in another land, another time. Mitch hesitated at the gaping entrance to the apartment.

You've seen worse, the voice said quietly.

But he hadn't. At least not that he recalled.

Very little of the flesh and bone was any aspect of her body he could identify. It was easier to concentrate on the occasional glints of rings and studs.

The stench and the universality of the blood did not desensitize him. He heard familiar meowing. Looking a bit the worse for wear, but both clearly alive, the twin Siamese twined around his ankles. Mitch stood in the center of the room with eyes open, head bowed. He raised his head. "I love you," he said to the departed Rachel.

Carri Ann wanted to make sure this woman would not be returning, said the voice.

Mitch didn't allow hope to kindle the dimmest spark. But— "Can she?" He thought about the possibilities. "She'll never make it," he said with anguish. "She'll never get through the metal detector."

That's why I love you, Mitch. Time ticked past.

Finally, the voice said, *Something this terrible—none of us will rest. There is a chance the sadness can be redressed. But if it can, it will happen only if you mean what you have said.*

Mitch looked blank.

The part about love. About taking responsibility for yourself.

Without hesitation, Mitch said, "I mean it."

Then I will attempt a final transit . . . for both of you. We'll all see. No omens. We're past that.

Mitch realized he was attempting to assign a face to the words. "Who were you once?" he asked insistently. "A goddess? Something like that? Weren't you a woman?"

The voice paused a long, long time. Mitch sensed it would have been an extended wait even in the worldly realm. *I was . . . female.*

"I thought so," said Mitch. "You have the grace, that power, that utter sensuality. You're pretty sexy, ma'am."

Charmer.

Mitch shook his head slightly. "I call it like I see it."

And that's one of the reasons you're not consigned as dogmeat for the demons.

"Uh, thanks. I guess."

The voice betrayed a wry acceptance. *We'd better get moving, Mitch. You've still got a long distance to travel.*

"Give me any clues on the destination?"

It will unfold, my shuttlecock darling. The voice held a weary smile. *One more volley, friend. At least one more. I cannot tell you much, but I can pretty much guarantee you'll clear the net.*

Then Mitch Valentine was enfolded by her wings. The beating of mighty pinions, the rising of a dark wind enveloped his soul. *How is it these games are scored?*

Mitch tried to concentrate in the chaos. "Point, match, love."

I think that's tennis you're thinking of.

"Whatever. I may be godlike but I'm sure as hell not omniscient. Tennis or badminton, I always liked the vocabulary."

Yes, said the voice. *Game. Match. Love.*

Harmonics rose majestically around man and bird. In the midst of violence and pain, hope.

It was a good note on which to ascend.

VARIATIONS

ON A
THEME

NANCY A. COLLINS

When you keep the hours that I do, you often find yourself in other people's stories.

Sometimes the stories are funny, sometimes they're weird, sometimes they're scary. Mostly, though, they're stupid, violent, or pathetic—often all three. Over the years I've come to see a marked similarity between these stories—as if all human lives are merely variations on a theme.

Occasionally I come in at the very beginning, while other times I make an entrance during the denouement. Every so often I'm a part of the plot, if no more than a peculiar *deus ex machina*. For the most part, however, my role—if there is one—is to serve as an abbreviated Greek chorus, doomed to observe the human suffering before me, yet helpless to change its outcome.

I couldn't begin to tell you how many rapes I've interrupted over the years—be they straight, gay, one-on-one, or gang bang. Ditto the muggings and back-alley bashings. Not that I'm bloody Spiderman or Bat Girl, mind you. If I happen across a bunch of thugs tangling over turf or a couple of no-neck knuckle-draggers laying into each other with pool cues and broken bottles, I sit back and let Darwin sort it out.

On any given night I'm more likely to find a junkie sprawled, cold as clay, in some abandoned warehouse than I am to save a damsel in distress. When I come across the ODs I feel a twinge of regret, if they're young, but it's difficult to dredge up much sympathy for them. I don't understand the urge the living have to live as if they were already dead. But then, perhaps my take on such things is tempered by my situation.

Still, at least none of the junkies ever seem to have suffered overmuch, at least from the overdose, before whatever awaited them in their disposable syringe of White Tiger bore them away on the eternal nod. Judging from what I've seen—corpses with their arms tied off, works dangling from clotted veins, vomit crusted on chins and shirts—when death comes in a hot shot it's sudden, if not exactly clean.

Then there's the babies. I've found enough of them to start a nursery school over the years. Usually in the trash. They fall into two categories. The first are obvious stillbirths and miscarriages, delivered by the homeless women who huddle in the desolate squats or doss down under freeway overpasses throughout this land. Here, too, they bear a surprising similarity to one another: most are still bloody, their nostrils plugged with mucus, and their tiny, discolored faces compressed into constipated frowns, fists clenched as if outraged by the very idea of being brought, half-unmade, into a cruel, uncaring world. Usually the stillborns are bundled in newspaper, like day-old fish or a bouquet of faded roses; the only evidence of the women who birthed them a foot or so of raggedly severed umbilical cord.

I feel a small sorrow for the stillborns—the same I experience when I come across tiny fledglings that have attempted flight with unready wings—but part of me knows the poor things are better off having never taken their first breath. Good luck next time, kid—I hope.

Then there are the ones in the plastic bags. The ones that have taken that first breath, cried that first cry—and were never given a reason to stop. The ones with the bruises and the broken limbs and the black eyes and the scalding scars and the cigarette burns and the bite marks and the torn vaginas and the ruptured anuses. There's not much I can do for them besides make an anonymous phone call to the cops. I like to think the story doesn't really end there, though. Hopefully there is an end coda, of sorts. But I've learned never to hope too hard or too long for such things. It only results in breaking off another piece of what's left of my heart, and there's precious little to spare.

Of course, if I happen to *witness* the disposal of the body—well, that's a different matter entirely, and always ends with tiny victim and killer sharing the same Dumpster.

Like I said, I usually tend to stroll in after the end credits have run, the fat lady's sung, the groundskeepers have rolled the tarp over the pitching mound—choose whichever metaphor you prefer. As a result, I've tripped over more stiffs during the last twenty-five years than Cherri Vanilla.

Most came to their ends rather messily and involuntarily. Some were killed by the things I hunt, but most have been brought low by their own kind—that little ol' psychopathic naked ape called Man. I often find myself staring at their dead faces, as if I might glimpse a last fading image, echoing deep inside the brain's gray folds. Sometimes I can, if they're freshly dead.

If they're too far gone for me to scope them out telepathically, I usually check the area for signs of occult energy and to see if their recently disincorporated spirits might be wandering about, gaping at their new surroundings like tourists from Wisconsin. Such shades need a quick but gentle nudge into the afterlife if they don't want to find themselves trapped between worlds for the next decade or two. I feel it's the least I can do, given the circumstances.

I'm telling you all this so you'll understand how rare it is for me to actually witness someone else's story from start to finish. But it happens. Take this one, for instance. I didn't realize I was walking in on the opening curtain. In fact, it looked pretty damn final to me.

I was making my usual rounds, checking out the dark alleys, abandoned buildings, and lonely places where the things I hunt like to take their prey. The thing is, it's not just vampires who like desolate, dark locations in order to go about their dirty deeds—the human variety of monster prefers these sites as well.

I found the bodies in a blind alley in an inner-city industrial zone that would make Hell's Kitchen look like a Martha Stewart makeover. I don't know how they got there, unless they were brought from another location for a leisurely execution, because they certainly weren't the type to wander the neighborhood, especially after dark.

Both were male, although the smaller of the two was so slender and short I first mistook him for a woman. The slightly built one was an Asian male—possibly Japanese, although it was hard to tell, since his face had been reduced to pulp. It looked like someone had literally jumped up and down on him. There was also semen pooled in the coagulated blood that had leaked from his shattered mouth. Whoever had beaten the poor bastard to death—and there had been several of them—also orally raped him beforehand. He was neatly dressed, although his pressed chinos and white linen shirt were now stained by his own blood and his killers' piss. A small SILENCE=DEATH button, no larger than my thumb, was pinned to his shirt collar.

The second body was considerably larger and older than that of the first. He had been a black man with touches of gray at the temples of his neatly kept, close-cropped natural. While tall and big-boned, he hadn't been overly muscular. My impression was of a college athlete turned teacher. He wore a black navy-style swing jacket, a black turtleneck sweater, and black slacks. Although he hadn't been worked over nearly as badly as the Asian, I counted at least six stab wounds in his upper body. He'd put up a fight—no doubt while trying to protect his friend.

Judging from the bodies' state of decay, I estimated they'd been dead for at least the better part of a day. It wasn't hard for me to figure out the story that led to this sad end. These hapless lovers were the victims of the Regent Sides, a lovely collection of human flotsam that espoused white supremacy and homophobia in equal measure. Although, judging from the physical evidence, their hatred of gays didn't prevent them from getting hard-ons.

I shook my head in disgust at the death scene. At times like this it wasn't hard to understand how vampires justify their clandestine manipulation and culling of human society. My one solace was the knowledge that those responsible for such an act bore as much resemblance to the humans who compose operas and build cathedrals as baboons resemble men.

However, even when confronted by such utter barbarity, there was evidence of that which is good and pure in mankind amidst the horror and ruin. My gaze returned to the older of the pair. Despite overwhelming numbers and the certainty of physical harm, this man had died trying to protect his lover. I had to respect his bravery and devotion, although I had no way of knowing who he had been.

Or did I? I dropped to one knee beside the body and began searching for some form of identification. It was possible—although far from likely—that during the excitement the Regent Sides might have forgotten to take his wallet. I was right. I found it tucked inside the jacket's breast pocket. I flipped the worn calfskin billfold open and discovered my first guess concerning the dead man's occupation had been on target.

According to the faculty ID, the dead man sprawled before me was a history professor at the university. His name had been Clarence Sadler, and, in life, he'd borne a slight resemblance to Harry Belafonte. "What a fucking waste," I grunted, snapping the wallet shut.

Sadler's eyes flew open. I'd seen dead men open their eyes before. That much didn't surprise me. However, the sitting up part did.

Sadler rose up slow, a dazed and confused look on his face. It seemed to take him a long second to realize I was there, although he was staring right at me. He wetted his lips with a dry, blackened tongue and said, "I came back."

"Yeah. So I noticed." I was already on my feet, keeping my eye on Sadler as he clumsily regained his footing. If I hadn't seen him come back from the dead, it would be easy to mistake Sadler for a drunk as he staggered and lurched on his newly resurrected legs.

I quickly placed myself outside possible striking distance, my switchblade sliding into my hand as if it had been there all along. I automatically dropped my vision into the Pretender spectrum, scanning the dead man's aura to identify his breed, only to be further baffled.

Where the auras of vampires are usually corrupted, resembling pulsing, livid bruises, Sadler's was completely black. It was as if he wore an eclipsed sun as a halo. I'd never seen anything like it before, although it seemed to trigger some distant memory. Whatever revenant he might be, it certainly wasn't a vampire or a ghoul. I wondered, what manner of supernatural event could pull a man back from the fields of the dead?

"K-kiko?" Sadler had spotted the twisted, lifeless form of his partner amidst the trash and detritus of the alley. "Kiko—are you all right?" He dropped to his knees beside the body, reaching out with trembling hands to roll it onto its back. I didn't have to read his mind to know Sadler realized his lover was dead. There is no true hope amongst the living dead.

Sadler gave a throaty sob as he saw what was left of his lover's face and pulled him closer, pressing the ruined pulp against his breast. As he cradled Kiko's body like a broken doll, Sadler's mouth pulled itself into a rictus of grief, so that for a moment his features resembled those of a Greek tragedy mask, and a dreadful wail issued forth from deep inside him. It was a horrible, hopeless, despairing noise—the sound made by destroyed love and shattered lives. Sadler folded himself over Kiko's body, as if he could somehow warm it back to life—but his flesh was just as cold.

"Look what they did to your face—your beautiful, beautiful face!" he moaned, when he finally found words.

I drew back, feeling somewhat awkward. I had no place in this man's grief—for I had come to the conclusion that that was exactly what he was, not a ghoul, zombie, vampire, or larva. I knew from personal experience that none of those creatures was capable of such sorrow. He did not warrant extermination, from what I could see. Granted, he was one of the living dead—but then again, so am I.

Just as I was about to leave him to his mourning, Sadler lifted his head and spoke directly to me.

"He didn't deserve this."

"I know."

"He was so beautiful—you can't tell that by—by what they did, but he was the most handsome man I'd ever seen in my life. The moment I first laid eyes on him at the library I knew he was the one—the one I wanted to spend the rest of my life with." Sadler smiled at the memory and I caught a brief, mental glimpse of Kiko, alive and whole, flashing a smile as he reshelved books from a librarian's cart. The memory had that golden glow that comes from being cherished. In the immediate wake of the memory came a wave of grief so strong I found myself raising psychic shields to protect myself from Sadler's pain.

"It was his beauty and love that gave me the courage to finally come out, to my family, my associates, and the school. It was hard—especially with my family—but Kiko stuck by me, and whenever I weakened, he made me strong again. I—I would have died for him. I guess I did—didn't I?" This last part was addressed to me.

"Yes. Yes, I'm afraid you did."

"I thought it might have been a dream—no, a nightmare, at first. But now I can see it wasn't. The skinheads grabbing us as we left the Tosca, bringing us here in their van, what they did to Kiko and myself, the bird—the talking skull—that all really happened."

"Uh-huh," I replied, although I had no idea what he was going on about.

Sadler looked me in the eye, his voice surprisingly level, as he tenderly laid Kiko's body to rest once more. "Am I a vampire?"

"Not hardly."

He didn't seem completely satisfied by my answer. "Are you sure?"

"Believe me, I know my suckers, and you ain't one of them," I said, flashing him a smile.

The sight of my fangs threw him for a second—he hadn't been one of the living dead long enough to override a lifetime of human behavior. "O-okay—if I'm not a vampire, then what am I?"

"I'm not sure. You said something about a bird?"

"A raven or crow of some kind . . . It talked to me. Told me that I was being given a chance to right the scales . . . There was a woman, too. At least, I think it was a woman. She had a skull instead of a face. She took her head from her shoulders and held it like a bowl. There was something—wine?—blood?—inside it. She offered the skull to me and told me to drink. Does this make any sense?"

I nodded slowly, chewing on a thumbnail. "Sorta. At least I have an idea what kind of walking dead man you are. If the stories I've heard are anything to go by, you're an avenger. You were reanimated by a force far more ancient than any name human religion has ever given it—be it Sekhmet, Kali, Fury, or Nemesis.

"It is a thing that might have been a goddess—or perhaps still is. In any case, she is a being steeped in blood, without mercy or respite. Yet she is not a demon, as the Christians have come to define the term; she is not the hand-maiden of chaos, but a shadow of order. She is the Angel of the Pit, the Punishing Mother, the Divine Scourge. Hers is the face of dark justice, and her power is that of righteous indignation and holy rage. And you—Clarence Sadler—have been made her anointed champion. You've been sent back from the land of the dead to bring those guilty of the crimes against you and your beloved not to human justice—but to immortal judgment. You are an avenging spirit, given one last chance to set right the scales of justice."

Sadler nodded his head as I spoke, as if the words were a key that had turned a lock within him. "Yes," he whispered. *"Judgment."* He looked up at me, and for a brief moment I saw something very old and very, very dangerous staring out at me through his eyes. He smiled, then—or should I say *it* smiled for him—spun on his heel, and swiftly sprinted off into the darkness.

"Hey! You're going the wrong way!" I shouted.

When he didn't reply, I started after him, although I was uncertain I really wanted to spend any more time in the revenant's company. That smile—it was not unlike that of someone who realizes that even their closest compatriot has not recognized his identity.

When I reached the end of the blind alley, Sadler was nowhere to be found, although he couldn't have had more than a two-second start on me.

"Damn," I muttered under my breath. "So *that's* how it feels!"

As I stood there scratching my head, I caught a glimpse of what appeared to be a raven silhouetted against the night sky, although they rarely, if ever, fly after dark.

I didn't see Sadler again for a couple of days.

Bear in mind, I wasn't exactly out looking for him. Since I'd determined he wasn't the kind of living dead that required my special attention, my attitude was more "live and let live." So to speak. Still, even in a city of this size, it's only natural that we'd eventually cross paths again.

I was doing my rounds of the scummier dives and rougher clubs that night when I caught up with him again. Vampires tend to prey on those who dwell on the fringes of human society, those who, should they turn up missing or myste-riously dead, no one is likely to go out of their way to solve the crime—or even recognize it as such. Prostitutes, drug dealers, trannie hookers, hustlers, junkies, crackheads, and barflies tend to make up the most reliable prey categories, so it pays me to keep tabs on the local scene.

I'd just finished checking out the Backstabber Lounge—an after-hours joint popular with Black and Latino drag queens—when I heard what sounded like screams and gunshots coming from up the street. I smartened my pace and arrived just in time to see an exodus of extremely panicked bar girls fleeing from Rackham's, a combination bar and pool hall that was a favorite with the various White Power gangs in the area. A second later a body came flying through the establishment's plate glass window and hit the sidewalk, coming to rest inches from my boots.

Since he was lying facedown, I had a clear view of the Regent Side insignia—a pink triangle with a knife stuck in it—on the back of his jacket, so it didn't take a rocket scientist to figure out who was responsible for propelling this human spitball.

Sadler came climbing through what was left of the window as calmly as you please, oblivious to the jagged glass slicing his legs and hands. The first thing I noticed was that he'd acquired both a new wardrobe and substantial armament since we'd last met. His jacket, slacks and turtleneck had been discarded in favor of khaki combat pants, midcalf combat boots, and a jungle-issue flak jacket that fairly bristled with small firearms, grenades, knives, and ammo. He carried a semiautomatic pump shotgun and there was an AK-47 slung over his shoulder. At first I thought he'd smeared cammo-stick across his face, but as he drew closer I realized it wasn't lampblack I was looking at. Sadler might be a revenant, but his mortal form was still susceptible to decay.

He glowered at me for a moment, then seemed to recognize me, nodding a curt hello.

"So—you were the one who knocked over the Army-Navy Surplus the night we met," I observed. "I wondered if it wasn't you when I heard the secu-rity door was torn off its hinges. And I suppose you're also the one that venti-lated that van full of Regent Sides lurking behind the Tosca last night." I pointed to the weapons jutting from every part of his anatomy. "You, uh, know how to use all that stuff, Prof?"

Sadler lifted his arm in way of an answer, exposing very nasty, very old scar tissue from where shrapnel had torn its way through flesh and muscle. "That's how I got the money to go to college in the first place." I thought his voice sound-ed strangely thick, then I realized his larynx was rotting along with the rest of him.

Sadler bent over and grabbed the Regent Side by the jacket collar and peeled him off the sidewalk. The basher had the same general "look" favored by his gang—pegged pants, Doc Martens with white shoelaces, a white T-shirt and red suspenders. His extremely short crew cut made him look even younger than he already was. In any case, the kid wasn't getting any older, judging from the piece of broken glass wedged in his throat.

"Damn!" Sadler spat, letting the dead skinhead drop like a sack of wet laundry. "I was planning on using this one to find out where their leader is hiding!"

"Is that all? Hell, I can tell you that!"

"You know where the Regent Sides are?"

"I make it a point to know where all the scumbags in this part of town go to ground." The sound of approaching police sirens caused me to step back, casting my gaze skyward. "I'll take you to their hideout, if that's what you want. But there's no way we'll be able to approach them from the ground with you tricked out like Rambo."

"What do you suggest we do, then?"

"Follow me."

I ducked down a nearby alley, Sadler at my heels. I motioned to the metal fire escape a story above our heads. Sadler nodded his understanding, sliding his shotgun into a holster strapped across his back. I jumped up and snagged the railing, boosting myself onto the landing. Sadler was right behind me, showing a great deal of grace for a man I knew had to be feeling the effects of being dead three days.

By the time the police cars fishtailed to a halt outside Rackham's, Sadler and I were three buildings away, headed in the direction of the Regent Sides' headquarters. Once I was certain we had not been spotted from the ground, I gestured for a halt. I leaned out over the top of the tenement's Victorian-era facade and looked back up the street at the flashing lights from the assembled squad cars. The cops were standing around scratching their heads, talking to a few shaken pool players, and examining the dead Regent Side. I cast a glance over my shoulder at Sadler, who was standing behind me, as silent and solemn as a shadow.

"You realize you've stirred up all different colors of shit, don't you?" I asked. "When you whacked that van full of no-necks, the Regent Sides assumed Los Locos did it. So they hit 'em back. Took out most of the gang while they were hanging out at Taco Mundo. Now there's all kinds of payback going down. And a lot of the other gangs are fighting for the territory opening up."

"My heart bleeds piss for them."

"Yeah, that's what I figured you'd say. Can't say my attitude's any different. I'm just letting you know what kind of fresh hell's going on." I nodded in the direction of the gang's hideout. "Just bear in mind, the Regent Sides might not be expecting *you,* but they're gonna be expecting *someone.* A whole *lot* of someone, to be exact. And they're gonna be armed."

Sadler shrugged, his lips pulled into a bitter smile. "What's the worst they can they do? *Kill* me?"

I laughed and shook my head. For a dead guy, I had to admit Sadler was okay. I could tell he was studying me in return. After a long moment he asked what they always do.

"Are all vampires like you?"

It was my turn to smile bitterly now. "No. Afraid not. I'm something of a fluke. I don't prey on humans—at least, I try not to. Not the innocent ones, anyhow. I hunt vampires."

"Why?"

"Why do you feel compelled to destroy the Regent Sides?"

"They took everything from me: my future, my life, everything and everyone I loved. I can never have or enjoy those things again."

"Bingo."

Sadler met my gaze, hidden behind the sunglasses I wear, and once again I saw the familiar darkness in his eyes looking back at me, only now I knew better than to fear it. There was a long moment of silence between us that I finally ended by moving away from the front of the building.

"C'mon," I said, clearing my throat. "Let's get going. The Regent Sides' crib is six blocks east of here."

However, two blocks from our destination, something caught my eye in the alley below. It was little more than a furtive motion in the shadows, as if a prey animal had caught wind of a predator and quickly taken cover. I paused, scanning the alley below in search of Pretender spoor. Sadler turned to scowl at me.

"What's wrong?"

"Not sure—maybe nothing."

I spotted a flash of pallid flesh amidst the darkness, a look of panicked fear glittering in ruby-colored eyes set in a milk-white face. The hairs on the back of my neck prickled and a low growl began to rumble deep in my chest. I could feel the kill-urge coming up, making my body tremble like a junkie needing a fix. I turned to speak to Sadler, all the while keeping my eyes on my prey below.

"Go on ahead without me. I'll catch up with you. The address is 605 Water Street. Corner of Regent. You'll find them there."

Sadler was gone before I'd finished the sentence, leaving me to my work.

I t couldn't have possibly taken more than ten minutes—fifteen, tops—for me to finish off the dead boy cowering in the alley, then shag it over to Water

Street. I could smell the blood from two blocks away and glimpsed the flames a block later. The bastard sure worked fast.

The decrepit row house where the Regent Sides had their so-called head-quarters was little more than a squat with plumbing and electricity, full to over-flowing with junked furniture and empty pizza boxes, which probably had a lot to do with the speed at which the flames were devouring it.

There were bodies scattered along the sidewalk leading to the burning building that looked like they'd gotten up-close-and-personal with the business end of Sadler's shotgun. I shook my head in silent admiration. Sadler was def-initely a class act in the mayhem department. I glanced around, looking for a sign of the walking dead man, but didn't spot him. Then I heard the screams coming from inside 605 Water.

At first all I saw was a beautiful and deadly curtain of orange and yellow flame; then, the figure of a man emerged from the inferno's heart. Although the screams were growing louder and closer, the figure moved with an unhurried, yet purposeful stride. As Sadler exited the burning building and headed down the steps to the street, I saw the source of the screams was the man he was drag-ging behind him by a pair of bloodred suspenders.

Less than fifteen minutes earlier, the leader of the Regent Sides had been a young, relatively decent-looking white man. Now he looked like 180 pounds of barbecued kielbasa. Except that barbecued kielbasas usually don't scream at the top of their lungs. It was clear that Sadler was in even worse shape than the pathet-ic little neo-Nazi he was towing behind him like a demented pull toy. Big chunks of flesh were missing from his face, chest, and arms. What I first mistook as sweat running down his forehead and dripping from his face was actually human fat, and his hair was burned right down to his skull. The intense heat had caused his gums to shrivel, exposing the teeth in his mouth all the way to the root and giving him a decided death's-head appearance when he smiled in my direction.

"Looks like you've got things in hand here," I observed, nudging one of the Regent Sides splattered across the pavement. "So—is it over?"

"Not yet," he replied, a burp of smoke escaping his lips as he spoke. Sadler hurled the hideously burned skinhead into the gutter. The Regent Sides' leader looked like a giant blister in a sooty white T-shirt and red suspenders. He lifted his seared hands, whether to beg forgiveness or block out the sight of his neme-sis was unclear. His eyes—although now without lashes or brows, they were still startlingly blue, especially in contrast to the lobster-red ruin of what was once his face—flickered to where I stood.

"Help me, lady," he pleaded. "This nigger's a fucking monster!"

I had to chuckle at that one. The look of horror on the skinhead's face when he saw my teeth made me laugh even harder. He began to shriek again—

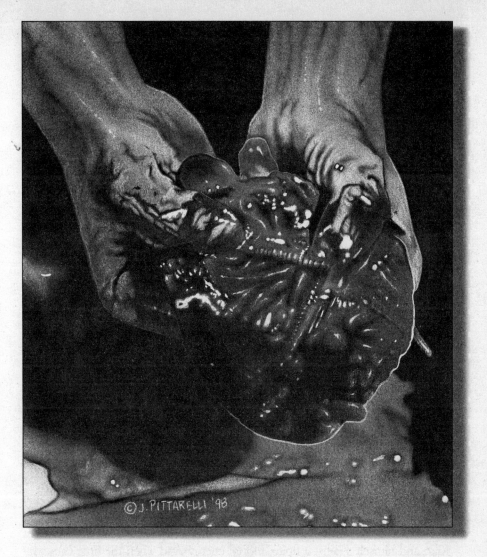

only this time out of fear, not pain. It was the scream of a man who's finally realized that he's dead, even though he's still breathing.

"You stole our lives, scum." Sadler's voice was almost unrecognizable now. It sounded more like the very pits themselves had been given voice. "And now I'm going to send you to hell for the heartless bastard you are."

Sadler pulled a six-inch serrated combat knife from a sheath strapped to his calf and plunged it into the Regent Side's chest, causing blood to erupt from the skinhead's nose and mouth in a crimson gout. Despite the gravity of his wounds, it took the punk a good two minutes to die. The last thing he saw was Sadler removing his still-beating heart from its cage of bone.

As the life, if not the horror, in the skinhead's eyes drained away, Sadler blinked and staggered slightly, like a man coming out from under hypnosis. When he saw the bloody hunk of muscle in his hand he gave a short cough of disgust and hurled it into the gutter, alongside its original owner. He lifted a trembling, crimson hand to his ruined face, grimacing as his fingers encountered exposed bone.

I gently touched him on the shoulder and he jerked like a startled sleep-walker. He stared at me for a long moment before he finally recognized me.

"What next?" I asked.

He frowned as if I'd spoken to him in Mongolian. "Next? There is no next. It's over."

"Uh-huh. I figured as much. So now what?"

Sadler shook his head, pulling a pistol out of his pocket as he straightened up. "It's *over*." He said it as if I should have understood what it meant. And maybe I did, but I didn't want to. I'd come to enjoy his company.

"Sadler—Clarence—"

"Have they found him?"

"Yeah. I called the cops after you disappeared. His body's at the morgue."

Sadler nodded. The information seemed to put him at ease. "Thank you— I'm sorry—I don't even know your name."

"Sonja."

"Thank you, Sonja." He smiled, took a giant step backward and brought the gun up to his head. Then he said, "Kiko," and pulled the trigger, spraying congealed blood and putrefying brains onto the sidewalk. And his story ended just like that—as suddenly as it had begun.

I stared at his truly lifeless body for a long moment before leaving. As I turned away, I caught sight of a large crow perched atop a nearby streetlight, watching me with that same dark, familiar intelligence I'd glimpsed in the dead man's eyes.

I envied Sadler the simplicity of his vengeance. All he had to do was avenge Kiko and himself against a finite, mortal enemy. And when the time came, he knew if his job was well and truly finished. In those last moments Sadler had known no lingering rage, no doubt, and most of all, no fear of whatever awaits on the other side.

I wondered what it would be like to surrender the cold thrill of vendetta; to be one not only with myself, but with what I have become; have to succumb to that final, unending peace. Perhaps that day will eventually come. But I know one thing—it is not coming soon.

As I said before, most of the stories I find myself entangled in prove to be no more than variations on a theme.

Including my own.

PARAGENESIS

STORM
CONSTANTINE

SCULPTURE BY LISA SNELLINGS
PHOTOGRAPHY BY RICK POPHAM

I have scars upon my left hand, but not upon my right. If I hold my hands up to the eternal sun, light shines through my flesh. But there is no flesh. I am idea, essence. I am the flash of sunlight off chrome; I am the seasons; I am the shadow beneath the eaves; I am a scrap of litter scratching across cracked asphalt. No, I am bones and blood. I am crude and heavy. I am what I am.

When I was sixteen, I ran away from my leaf-shrouded home in the enclave for the rich, about twelve miles from the city center. Perhaps it began as a suicide bid. All I did was move my limbs, without conscious volition, toward the wilderness of stone and glass that circled the city itself like a plague. It was the hinterland of decay, spreading both outward and inward, threatening city core and enclave alike. People could lose themselves there, and I wanted to be lost.

I remember that day. She was standing at the kitchen sink with her back to me. She could always sense when I walked into the room. I'd see her spine tense beneath its dress of cotton, its caul of skin. How cruel had Mother Nature been to make her spawn a child she could only fear? Blessed was the day when she no longer had to touch me; when I could feed and bathe myself, tie my own laces, rub my own hurts. I could not despise her, for I shared her bewilderment, her bitterness. When I'd been born, no doubt she'd decided to make the best of it. I was a beautiful child, but for those hidden abnormalities. Later, she probably realized that even monsters could be beautiful. My father was a nonentity, consumed by work. We rarely saw him. Our home always seemed empty when she and I were in it together. The spaces between us were too great, and as I grew older, they became gulfs.

On that final day, I could not bear to see that stiffening spine any longer. She had birthed me and raised me; now her responsibility was over. I turned around and walked away; out of the shady house into the sunlight; past the bike lying on the tarmac, where a few red leaves had drifted down; past the rope that hung from the old willow, still swinging and where I never played. The street was devoid of children: empty. Empty. This had never been my home.

On the horizon, a gray green cloud hung above the city. It was a walk of about four hours to reach it along the main highway. Sometimes, a bus might come, rattling and armored, but not very often. People with eyes like pebbles rode the bus; not coming from anywhere, going nowhere, just riding. Perhaps they thought time would stop for them in that way. I would not ride the buses, for I was afraid that if I did, I would be absorbed into that shadow community and never leave it. Another freak on the back seat.

It was midmorning when I left the enclave, and already the sun was fierce in the late summer sky. At the high metal gates, the eyes of the guards were hidden behind black glass. They stood motionless, like automatons. I passed between them, showed my ID card, and the gates slid open. A minute later, someone else might come by, and the guards would come alive. They'd touch their helmets, grin to show their white teeth, and utter a pleasantry. But not for me. After I'd gone, one would say, "That's the weird kid from Acacia," and the others would sneer.

I walked along the slip road that led to the highway. It seemed hotter beyond the enclave, and the air shimmered about me. Vigilantes had strung someone from a pole. I could see the body dangling on the other side of the road, surrounded by trees. A cloud of flies danced around it. Beneath it, someone had left some artificial flowers. Perhaps the enclave guards, high up on the gates and watchtowers, had seen it happen.

I cannot remember feeling anything then. I just walked, kicking up dust that smelled of metal and age, buffeted by the searing wind of passing vehicles. After an hour, a truck stopped to offer me a lift. The back was filled with people, crammed together like pigs on the way to a slaughterhouse. They were probably just crop-pickers, returning to the city. My feet were aching, so I hopped up into the back. Certain people always picked up on my strangeness, and this occasion was no different. My fellow travelers were like frightened animals: I saw furtive shuffling, and nervous eye movements. I didn't say anything. Eventually, one of the men offered me a cigarette and I smoked it, looking out through the truck canopy at the passing road. My mother will have missed me by now. Her relief will fill the silent house, washed by waves of shame. She will grip the edge of the sink and blink at the garden, where the sprinkler slowly turns on the lawn.

I did not resent being born different. The resentment came from other people's reactions. I was so ordinary in most respects. Dogs had never liked me; we could never keep one. Sometimes, things happened around me over which I had no control. It wasn't my fault. It was the look in her eyes. I made the saucepans fly once, but not toward her. She just screamed, her hands pressed to her face, staring at the mess on the floor. Other kids didn't like me very much, despite my parents' efforts to find me friends. I didn't mind being alone. I'd tell my mother things she thought were her private thoughts, and then her mouth would compress into two white lines. Later, I'd hear her telling my father about it. "He must *listen* to us, for God's sake! Do something!" I didn't listen. I just knew. It was like she told me things herself without words.

It was the doctors I hated the most. There was nothing wrong with me;

I wasn't ill. But my mother kept taking me back to that neat office that smelled of nothing, and let the white coats prod at me. I said, "Just let me be," and they would smile tolerantly, spreading my legs on the table for another look. They must have taken a hundred photographs. "It isn't Froehlich's syndrome," I heard a doctor say to my mother, "because apart from the genital abnormalities, there are no physical deformities."

Her reply—"Then what is it? Can you operate?"

"That is a decision your son will have to make for himself later on. We have counselors . . ."

She thought I should have been twins: a boy and a girl. But it wasn't that.

I got out of the truck on the outskirts of the city, in an area called Longhills. Once, it would have been a thriving neighborhood; now, a ruin and an ideal place to hide, to think, to do whatever would come next. Tall buildings with broken crowns reached toward the veil of evil cloud that always hangs above the city. I think it is the city's aura, an expression of its soul, soiled and poisonous. The people who live in that place are barely human, but then I had been taught to think that neither was I. Perhaps this was the place where I belonged. I wanted to cast off the trappings of affluence and live close to the edge of survival. Discomfort did not bother me.

I walked as best I could along the sidewalks, avoiding debris, bundles of cloth that may have been corpses, and the smoldering remains of fires. What did people burn here? Sometimes, it seemed they burned their own possessions. I saw fragments of books, jewelry, and crockery blackened among the embers. The smoke was toxic. Someone had burned a wasps' nest. A substance like syrup leaked from its collapsed mass. I saw few people. They kept out of the sun during the day. They slept then. Welfare trucks occasionally slid across an intersection ahead of me. They might contain bodies or miscreants or supplies. Perhaps all three at once.

At three o'clock in the afternoon, when the sun was at its most vehement, I stood in the center of a street and looked up at the sky. Buildings loomed over me, derelict and rotting. I wondered what the point of it all was. Why do we continue to live? What drives us to survive in an environment so hostile to life, an environment we have made for ourselves? Civilization was a Leviathan whose limbs were too weak to support it. Now it sank to its knees, bones cracking beneath its weight. And all who rode the Leviathan were tumbling down, their screams thin, like those of insects. My difference was just one more symptom of this fall. Our purity was mangled and dysfunctional. In those moments I saw myself as the avatar of the world's destruction, a cruel joke in the distorted form of the primal human. I could do as I pleased, for it did not matter what would happen to me.

Soon, I began to feel hungry, but willed the pangs away. I could see no way to feed myself. It was cleansing to be able to step aside from human needs. I felt excoriated, but also renewed. For a while, I sat inside a broken building, where the walls were black. I listened for sounds: the faraway throb of rotor blades, the occasional human cry, cut off short, and once the distant bark of a dog. I watched the sun slide down behind the splintered towers, and thought how in the enclave, the day would be drawing to a close. Men would be emerging from the units in the nearby industrial park. They would climb into their sleek transporters, hail a manly good-night to the guards on the wall, and drive the short distance up the tower studded avenue to the gates of the enclave. Here, wives who sought to enact the rituals of a past Golden Age would be waiting in kitchens that were devoid of stain. The women wore aprons and smiled at their children, keeping back the pain, the fear, the utter chaos that massed on the horizon of their fantasy world. None of it was real, but then I had never really conspired in my parents' dream. My very existence cracked its fragile shell.

At dusk, a gang of girls stole in through the windows of my sanctuary. They saw me crouching in the rubble, which I quickly realized was *their* rubble, and began to snarl at me and utter strange ululating cries, their bodies dipping and rising like snakes. Their leader rushed at me a couple of times, brandishing a knife near my body, but I sat as still as I could, looking at her face. Presently, she came to a decision and gestured for her minions to get on with their business. They unfolded loot from tattered sacks, and set about dividing it amongst themselves. The leader flicked glances at me occasionally. I recognized something within her that later I identified as the indomitable human spirit. Society no longer existed for her, yet she continued to thrive, albeit in a debased fashion. The girls ate and laughed together, handing round a plastic bottle of murky liquid. After an hour or so, their leader offered it to me. It was a vile, base alcohol that left a trail of fire in my throat and tasted only of chemicals. The girls asked me nothing about myself, even though they must have made judgments about my cleanliness, my neat clothes. They were separatist females who hated men. They could have killed me, perhaps, but it seemed they recognized something within me they felt comfortable with and could accept. I ran with them for a week or so, raking over the ruins, pillaging the debris. They seemed to repel rival male gangs by the strength of their voices alone, using a repertoire of chilling screams and cries. Boys would lope away from them like chastened dogs. Often, the leader would climb to the highest, most precarious point around and stand there with arms outflung, uttering a world-filling shriek of anger. They did not know about despair. I envied them.

In the asphalt wilderness of Longhills, there were few adults. Perhaps they had wisely moved away, or else been killed. Sometimes, choppers would drone over the streets and emit a stinging spray, which the girls told me was supposed to kill disease. Why would the city authorities bother? I didn't believe it. The spray probably just killed fertility.

I felt more at one with the desperadoes of the wilderness than with any of the people who hid within the enclave. It was because these outsiders expected nothing and gave little in return. They did not make demands upon one another. Coexistence, and therefore a certain amount of cooperation, were the only remaining aspects of community. Pleasure was without contrivance: a good find among the rubbish; a chance meeting with a group who had something to barter; a basement found untouched, like an unopened tomb full of treasure; an abandoned welfare truck still laden with vitamin-enriched gruel. We were grave robbers, really, for most of humanity had already died in that place. But I liked the simplicity and honesty of their lives, the fact they did not judge me.

One day, one of the gang was shot by a sniper and the leader told us we would have to move to another area. A sixth sense told her this was the beginning of something bad. So we gathered up what little we had and left Longhills behind, burrowing off through the darkness and into another decayed sector called Coldwater Valley. It must have been an industrial complex at one time, and here the survivors were older and hostile to strangers. We prowled carefully between the arching metal structures that were now smothered with tendrils of quick-growing vines. Echoes were strangely muffled by the vegetation. Any human group we came across yelled and threw things to repel us; we were not welcome. Finally, one group, crazier than the rest, directed a fire cannon on us and killed all but five of us. Our leader was among the fallen; a blackened crisp in the road. How quickly life can be expunged. It seemed inconceivable that what was left of our companions had ever housed souls. We, the survivors, went back the way we had come, but it was the end of our group. We split up, and I went alone deeper into the madness of the ruined land that surrounded the desperate core of the shrinking metropolis. Its towers seemed to have huddled together, as if in fear.

There was much activity in the air nearer to the city core. Choppers roared through the skies, and once I saw one crash. People emerged from the jumbled ruins like cockroaches and swarmed all over the wreckage, picking it clean. I did not look like an enclave boy any longer. My head was thatched with lice-infested hair, my clothes were tatters to which I was forever adding more layers, whatever I could find. I had learned to snarl in the way that meant "stay away if you value your health." I also learned much about myself. Because the convenient utensils of life were no longer available, I was forced to live on my wits, and in this way discovered that the boundaries of my difference were much further than I had imagined. It began this way. I'd been going through the belongings of a dead man on the street, who had died of a sickness rather than murder. He had many treasures, which I was greedily transferring to my own pockets. Then a group of tearaways came slinking along the spiky walls around me, uttering low, hooting cries. Their message was for me to leave, to abandon my find. I do not think they would have attacked me if I'd simply obeyed this request. But there was too much for me to leave. I growled back. They must have thought I was mad; there were at least seven of them. Their leader dropped down from the wall and sauntered toward me, looking to either side all the time. I remained hunkered down beside the corpse, my hands dangling between my knees. I did not feel afraid at all. It was as if there was someone else inside me, far wiser than I knew; someone fierce and confident. An arrow of indignation flew out of me, and somehow touched the crumbling substance of the wall behind the gang leader. There was an explosion, a gust of dust and rocky debris, and then my would-be attacker was on his hands and knees before me, his head hanging down. He shook his hair and drops of bright blood flew out. At once, I jumped to my feet and snarled. My eyes felt full of sparks that I could shoot like bullets from a gun. The gang just melted away, dragging their fallen leader with them. After this incident, I felt so much stronger, safer.

Perhaps I overestimated my strength.

Some days later, I found a hole for myself deep beneath an old department store. It had been cleaned out thoroughly years before, but some people must have lived there for a while because I found a few mattresses, some of which had not been burned. Rags had been hung from metal beams in what remained of the ceiling. It was a musty labyrinth full of silent ghosts. I imagined it had once been home to a whole community, who had either been smoked out or died from some contagious infection. There were no bones about as evidence, but the wilderness scavengers are very thorough, so that meant little. In this place, I made myself a nest. I did not think about the future, but took simple pleasure in surviving from moment to moment. The wilderness was the garbage heap of the world, yet I learned to see beauty in it: the different colors of the sky at various times of day and how they conjured sculptures from the rubble, shining through blown out windows, making a cathedral of light of the starkest structure. The passing of civilization in itself was a wondrous thing. I would walk the cracked streets marveling at the way stringy vegetation was slowly reclaiming the land. Mother Earth had learned the saying that revenge is a meal best eaten cold. She was implacable, eternal, and the green tidal wave of her reclamation was evidence of humanity's frailty and insignificance. The people had regressed, but in their barbarity possessed a startling innocence. The complex rituals of life had been pared away, and if the people were dying, at least they would do so with swift dignity, rather than being hooked up to machines in a long coma of slow decay. Those who lived in the cities, the enclaves, were deluding themselves. They should give themselves up to the inevitable. I thought I, too, would soon die, and these were my last days. Each one dawned fresh and vital. I wanted to experience life through my senses to the full, and because of this, learned how my touch was death.

He was older than me, yet seemed younger. We met when he strayed into my lair, and after a few warning shots of snarls and aggressive gestures, realized we were not enemies at all. He was like me: a runaway from the theater of luxury. His mother had been a pill-head, who sometimes had not even recognized him, while his father, a scientist, had hardly ever been at home. I tingled with empathy as he described his former sterile environment: the ceaseless hum of domestic appliances, and the automata who kept the place running, while his mother lolled on the couch, living in some better world. He explained to me the phenomena of why people like us ran away. "We know it is over. Society is dead, but some of us know we can still exist beyond it. It is like a sinking ship. We have to jump overboard with faith and hope, otherwise we'll just be dragged down with the wreck and drowned. This is the age of the individual; the age of the hive has passed. We are all floating in the sea, clinging to our bits of wreckage, but eventually we'll become sea creatures ourselves and learn how to breathe its element."

How could I not love a person who spoke like that, with such passion and optimism? He did not know about my difference—especially the physical aspect. I did not want to tell him because he was my first real friend. If he knew, it would change things. He might be disgusted or, worse, full of pity.

Some girl he knew gave him a flask of alcohol. We flavored it with the remains of a bag of sugar substitute we'd found in our basement, and one night sat across from one another and drank it. It felt shamanic, the rhythmic passing of the flask from one to the other. We both knew we wanted to be drunk, for there was business between us that the barriers of a sober mind inhibited. I was acutely aware that before the night was over he would know about me. I felt nauseated with nerves, eager for the intoxication that would free my tongue and allow me to speak the words that must be spoken.

He began to talk about the future again, rambling on about some faraway utopia that could be constructed from hopes and dreams.

Something about his vision made me uncomfortable, and I said, "This is the end, not change. We are dying."

He crawled over to me then and put an arm around me. "No, no, you are wrong. This not death at all. You are living in the past. Look forward, not back. Don't let the past become your future."

I wanted to believe, and partly did, unaware of how he spoke the most ultimate of truths. He put his head against my hair and said, "I have to ask you something. Don't answer if you don't want to but . . . are you really a girl?"

I laughed a little, more out of embarrassment than amusement. What could I say? The answer was neither yes nor no. "What makes you think that?" I asked.

I could tell he wished he'd never spoken. "I don't know. The way you walk and talk. Just body language, I guess. I'm sorry. You must think this is just an excuse to . . ."

I touched his arm to silence him. "I am what you say."

He grinned in relief. "I knew it. You want people to think you're a boy because people will leave you alone then." He paused. "I'm sorry. That sounded patronizing."

I shook my head. "No, don't apologize. The thing is, I'm male, too."

He frowned. "In your heart, your head?"

"No. In some ways, that would be more simple."

"Then what *do* you mean?" The puzzlement had swept back; the tide of delight and anticipation had receded.

"It would be easier to show you," I said, and stood up.

The only light came in from outside, but then we of the wilderness rarely craved artificial light at night, other than a fire for protection. I peeled away all the layers of my tattered clothes, feeling as if each discarded item represented a year of my life. It was all being sloughed away. When finally I stood naked before him, he sat with his chin in his hands and said, "You look male to me."

I squatted before him and took one of his hands in mine, guiding him to the truth of the matter. He didn't say anything then, but kissed me. I felt his fingers digging into my shoulders like spikes. I could feel his heart racing. He'd wanted to do this for some time, and now felt he had been given sanction. I welcomed it, too, but some part of me became annoyed that he looked upon me as a female and took it for granted that I must be dominated. Did women ever feel this way? It might sound like justification, but I feel that he was partly to blame for what happened to him. We should have come together as equals, but then I didn't know he was not equal to me. I was stronger than he was and forced him into submission. It was only a game, I swear. I just wanted him to realize what we were, or could be.

It took him a day to die. I was helpless. I tried everything, but whatever mutant substance lived in me was poison to him. Not all the water in the world could wash away what I had done to him. My essence ate into him like acid, devoured his being. The only blessing was that he did not realize what was happening to him. With my hands, I was able to stroke away most of the pain. With my thoughts I willed his mind to a far place, that idyll he had spoken of, and there he died.

I set fire to our home and emerged from it into the night against a backdrop of flames. I had been right and he wrong. Humanity was dying and I was one of nature's weapons. I could never love, for to love me was to die. Could anything be more cruel than that?

If only I had known the truth then. He could still be here now. The one who discovered that truth with me was a pale spark to his radiant sun, but perhaps that was all part of it, the great lesson I had to learn.

For days, perhaps weeks, I roamed the wilderness, feeling more drunk than I had on that hideous night. I truly wanted to die, and even climbed the high, broken towers to think about throwing myself over, but even in my grief I was too afraid of being broken, dying slowly. I kept seeing his face, hearing his laughter, and then an image of his death would come to me, the terrible writhing, the whimpers. I was more of a monster than even my mother had imagined.

I came to an area that had been inexpertly flattened; a plain of rubble, from which rusting spikes rose like the bones of dinosaurs. Here, I collapsed and stared up at the sky, watching the colors change and the stars reveal themselves. I could move no farther. Here, it would end. I felt strangely at peace, and numb. I could not feel my body.

When I saw the stooped shadow gliding toward me over the stones, I barely raised my head. Death had come for me. It loomed over me, breathing heavily, and dark greasy hair brushed my face. I saw a glint of metal and heard muttered words. "Be still, my pretty. Do not fear. I shall come to you without pain."

I did not know he meant to eat me. I just thought of sex and murder, but he opened a vein in my arm and began to drink, nibbling the flesh at the edge of the cut. He was a modern vampire, human and reeking, not at all the romantic vision I'd seen in old movies. As I lay there, feeling the pull as my blood pulsed into his diseased mouth, I was not sickened or afraid, but amused. It is not easy to find food in the wilderness, and some will do anything to live. If my death meant the life of a debased creature like this, then so be it. There was some justice in it, I thought.

But I did not die. I found myself awake with raw morning light falling down upon me. Beside me was a wretched creature who squirmed upon the ground, clutching his belly. His hair had come out in clumps and lay upon the stones. I felt weak, but also vital. As I looked at him, I laughed. Not only was my touch death, but it seemed I was also very difficult to kill. Part of my new

role, I decided, was to stay with my victims until they found peace in death. I would do what I could to ease their agony.

Unlike my beloved, this one did not die after the first day. Sometimes, he was raving and hallucinating and became violent with a preterhuman strength. At other times, he wept and mumbled about his childhood, his fingers over his face. His body was hot and bloated. He must be strong. How long would it take him to die? After two days, it began to rain, and I dragged him into a ruined office block. The rain itself can be toxic. Here, I built a small fire, and then went foraging, killing four bedraggled pigeons. I came back with two birds, and some welfare rice I'd haggled for with a band of oldsters I'd come across. My attacker, my victim, could not eat, but I cooked the pigeons and watched him as I fed. There was no feeling within me, merely a faint sense of curiosity. His skin was peeling.

On the morning of the third day, I woke up and found myself alone. I thought my companion must have died in the night, and some scavenger had come in and taken the body. Then I heard the words, "What am I?" and turned to see an angel in the doorway. As his skin had peeled, so had all the filth. He stood before me, holding out his arms, looking at his smooth flesh. I could not give him answers. There were none. I felt that I had made him into something more and above me. He shared my difference. I had birthed a daughter-son.

I had thought him the most degenerate of beings, yet I quickly learned that he blazed with vitality and intelligence. Perhaps this was just another aspect of the change he had undergone. He asked me questions constantly and experimented with the force of his being. Unlike me, he was curious about the way he could affect reality: make inanimate objects move, heal pain, hear the whisper of others' thoughts. He was proud of what he'd become, and did not hide it, but the shadow community to which he'd once belonged were now afraid of him. They did not want his healing power, his radiance. They saw not an angel, but a freak.

Unperturbed, he became almost evangelistic about our condition. "We must make more like us," he said.

I was appalled and shook my head. "No. You are a fluke. It is not meant to be this way."

"How do you know?"

We were not easy companions, yet our similarities, and the fact that I had made him the way he was, kept us together. He had changed so much from the wretch he'd been. We lived in the office block where he'd undergone his transformation. One evening, he made me climb a nearby hydro tower with him, where the rusting shell harbored clear water. He took off his clothes and dived in, summoning me to join him. "We are not part of the filth now." He sluiced my hair and rubbed the grime from my skin. "I want the grief to run from your body with this water. You must be renewed, like I am."

I think the transformation had affected his mind. He needed a religion to run.

"How did you do it?" he asked. "Tell me. Tell me."

"I don't know. It just happened. You were trying to devour me."

The light in his eyes was like that of the stars: cold and distant. "Yes," he murmured. "Yes."

I should have known he'd act independently. One day, he took me to a building near our lair, and here revealed to me his twisting litter of children. I was horrified, yet also amazed. Twelve people, both male and female, shivered and whimpered at my feet; all of them infected with his blood. I had seen myself as an avatar of death, but remote and accidental. Here was someone who was an active instrument of it, only he did not realize the fact. He thought he was a god, with a god's powers. If I'd done something to end it then, what would the world have been like now?

Of the twelve, only four survived, and all of them male. We tried to soothe the agony of the others with the healing power in our hands, but the experience was harrowing. "I think this process cannot be conducted with females," my companion said, with scientific detachment. "But we must try it with others."

"No!" My protest went unheard.

I would not help him, other than attend to his victims as they suffered. I didn't even think about killing him, or trying to stop it any other way. At the time, it just didn't enter my mind, but now I think it was because part of me knew that what was happening was preordained. My companion saw it as a cleansing ritual for the world. He loved the creatures he made, marveling at their beauty. I saw them as perverted homunculi; as lovely as the angels of hell. Yet, despite this, they were also part of me and I was part of them.

I underestimated the regard my companion had for me. He did not set himself up as a leader of our developing clan of beautiful monsters. That privilege he reserved for me, even though I shunned it. "It is your responsibility," he told me. "You began this."

"Only because you were hungry," I reminded him.

"Can't you see the potential here?" he demanded. "This is the beginning of something. It is what comes next."

I could only look down at the corpses of those who had not survived. The cost of the selection process was too high. "This is murder," I said.

He nodded. "You are right. We should give people the choice." As an inducement, he now had seven successful transformations to parade before the eyes of the desperate.

I never became involved in his recruitment drives, and for many years no other human tasted my blood. I cannot say that I wasn't affected by my companion's enthusiasm, and grudgingly I had to accept the benefits of being part of a community, something I had never previously enjoyed, other than those few weeks of running with the girl-pack. This was different, though. With the girls, I had been a tolerated outsider. Now, I was part of a group of individuals who all shared the same attributes. It was both scary and exciting.

Although we could not effect the change in women, a few of them, through persistent entreaty, still joined us. In many ways, we had more in common with them than with men. From our sisters, we learned about the wildest excesses of adorning our bodies. We became tribal and developed our own rituals connected with the inception of newcomers, or the simple celebration of our estate. Sex became sacred, yet less taboo. There was so much to explore, and so many delights concealed in the labyrinth of our dual gender.

One night, we undertook a rite to name ourselves, opening up our minds with the effects of narcotic fungi. My companion became Orien; a name he felt held power. As for me, I wandered the star-gleam avenues of my mind, until I came to a place where a white shrine glimmered against a backdrop of stars. It stood upon the primal mound of creation, guarded by two pillars, and surrounded by the waters of life. Here, I learned my true name, the person I was to become. I am Thiede. The first of all. And the name we took for ourselves as a group was Wraeththu; a word that held all the anger and mystery of the world. The visions told us the truth: we were no longer human and must forget all that we had been before.

We were close-knit and did not merely cooperate with one another. Laughter was spontaneous, and in our wild nights of dancing, as new recruits struggled with the process of transformation, I learned about the fulfillment that close friendship brings. I was intrigued by the way the different personalities within the group interacted with one another; the partnerships that developed, the enmities. We weren't above petty squabbling, but if anything from outside threatened our group, the ranks would close and seal as tight as a steel door. We were not afraid to kill to protect ourselves, and sometimes that was necessary. Various human clans and groups heard about us, and some were afraid, and thought we should be eradicated. We were seen as vampires, as predators, who stole people away in the night. In fact, that was not true. We hadn't resorted to such measures since the first days of my companion's explorations. We had to keep on the move, but even so, humans would sniff us out and come pouring over the ruins, holding flaming brands aloft, intent on burning us alive. Then we would rise up, howling, our wild hair flying, our faces striped with the colors of the night.

We never lost a single brother in our skirmishes. In our unity, we were immensely strong.

Everything that begins in the world starts small, be it a mighty tree from a seed, or a deluge from a single drop of rain. A cell becomes a child becomes a king or queen. The greatest concepts are based upon the most fleeting of ideas. Such it was with Wraeththu, the race that I spawned from my fear, my pain, my ignorance. I stand upon the pillars of the world, and look down to see the carnage perpetrated by the human race that had been its guardian. I am amazed that humanity, with all its cruel selfishness, ever rose to prominence, and that the world itself allowed the situation to continue for so long. We are the exterminators, who will rid the palaces of the earth of all their vermin. We have no choice in this role, it had been decided for us. We are  the true messengers of the gods. The howls of slaughtered innocents rise from the ruins, the whimpers of the bereaved, the snufflings of the betrayed. I stand as a colossus above it all, looking down. There is a star in the sky that is the soul of my lost love, and my own soul has fragmented into a thousand parts, into each of my children. But I do not grow weak from it, only estranged. There is much to explore about myself, and for this I need a real wilderness, where all the devils of the earth and the angels of the air can come to tempt me and teach me. I cannot make the inward journey here in the city debris.

Last night, Orien came to me, worried that some of our brethren had split off to form a separate group. I tried to assuage his fears. "This is the way it will go," I said. "We were the catalysts, nothing more. We must not interfere with the growth of our child."

He thought I was mad, or damaged, and spoke softly. "The time will come, soon, for us to move toward the city core."

I nodded. "I know," I said. "You will."

He touched my shoulder. "*We* will. You cannot deny us, Thiede."

And I smiled at him to reassure him, knowing that already I had left them.

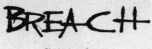

BREACH

Christine Crow

Just like that time you lost your shoe and I took your arm to steady you,
I think that last indignity of dying was something of a concession:
breach of that rigorous control that kept you wary of emotional excess.
How often now, lying alone here, watching the shadows,
I feel your strange body reflower into nothingness,
gaze with attention at your slow disappearance. After such distance,
it's like a peepshow, almost ecstatic, in an odd kind of way.
Tenderly now I give birth to you, no, pull you back into me
(must be a breech-birth or something played backwards)
like some crazy rescue party, some great body-stocking with me on the outside
        looking in.
Head first, courageous as you were in life,
you pass back up through me. Eyelids closed,
I feel you entering, back where you always were in fantasy,
back through my caverns, my strange vocal chambers,
my neck, my fangs, my serpent crown.
Now, like those ancient tribesmen who devoured lions for strength,
I have your courage inside me. Your shield, your winged sandals,
the little leather bag made of your skin.
You are in my mouth now, tenderly held, like a baby crocodile.
All precious separation between us banished,
you see through my eyes, move with my body, speak with my mouth.
Only from the photo on the wall do your own eyes still follow me,
familiar bee-stings full of reality, you-ness, difference,
and that old rigor which drew me to you in the first place.
Tenderly now as I pass a hundred times before it,
you reproach me for my crazed Romantic extravagance,
my intolerable breach of good taste.
The lot.

Carrion Crows

Jane Yolen and Robert Harris

T he carrion eaters circled high over the field as if they knew a battle would begin there soon enough. Dawn had not fully reached the field,
though it was already showing pink above the top of the forest.

"I hate them!" Arnoth said, shuddering visibly. "They go for the eyes
first." His hand went up to his brow in an unconscious shielding motion.

"All the fleshy parts, actually," Gadwen agreed without noticeable affect.
He saved the throbbing emotions for performances. "It's their job, lad. And
just as well."

Arnoth stared up at his master. Even for a Southlander Arnoth was short.
"Just as well?"

"Think of the smell otherwise," Gadwen said. He loved to shock his
apprentice, and it was so easy to do. "All that meat rotting on the field."

"Meat!" Arnoth shuddered again. "How can you call them that, sir?
There will be great princes fallen this day, and brave knights, and . . ."

"Save those sentiments for the songs we compose after," Gadwen said.
"But never forget that what you see here later this evening is meat. Just meat."
He smiled grimly. "It will keep you sane."

Arnoth turned away, disgusted with his mentor. But Gadwen knew the
boy would remember what was told him nonetheless. The lad had, as they say,
"ample belly for the ballad," for all that he was a short, puny thing.

"And are we not ourselves here ahead of time as well?" the older man continued to the boy's retreating back. "It isn't for naught that singers are called
carrion crows, though always—I will admit—well away from our hearing."

Arnoth turned around and stared fiercely at Gadwen, his mustache—
new and sparse as an old whore's pubes—all aquiver. "At least *we* do not go
for the eyes."

"Nay, lad, we get down to the bones quickly if we are any good at all,"
Gadwen replied. And recognizing an excellent exit line as soon as he spoke it,
Gadwen turned expertly and walked toward the trees, never looking back.

A rnoth scurried after his master, following him to the Nag's Tooth, the
inn where the singers had been quartered. Most had been still abed
when the two of them had left to inspect the battlefield. Indeed, Arnoth had
scarcely been stirring when Gadwen wakened him. But it was Gadwen's
wish to survey the field before it became cluttered with broken lances, fall-
en steeds, and dead warriors. He was—or so he told the boy—like a painter

who needed to spend time in contemplation of the blank canvas before splashing it with color.

"Preparation before poetry is what makes a poet great," he reminded Arnoth.

"Breakfast before poetry, or the poet grates," muttered Arnoth. But only to himself.

By the time they got back to the Nag's Tooth, most of their fellow singers had crawled out of their beds. Even the laggards, heads aching from the inn's bad wines, were shuffling into the commodious dining room. No one, it seemed, wanted to miss any detail of the day. There was not a poet worth his lines who did not remember the last ferocious battle of the Fifty Years' War, when the singer Calladen had slept through the death of the Frangonian king and no one had thought to tell him. So his verses at the evening's celebration lacked any mention of the event. He had been laughed out of court and ended his days as a teller of tales in the nurseries of the Far East. No, a racketing head was one thing, but a missed war something else again.

There was a general hullabalooing at the dining hall door. Serving wenches, their skirts kirtled above their knees, scurried to and from the kitchen. Their trays were heaped high with wheaten rolls, seven-county cheeses, pats of butter, and flagons—of water for most, though for certain veterans, more ale and wine. Bowls of steaming porridge peppered with late berries, and slabs of salted meat were set before them. The poets dug in with the kind of gusto they ascribed to their heroes in battle.

"Eat up, lad," Gadwen said. "We'll be much too busy to eat more before nightfall." His mouth was so stuffed with food, it was all Arnoth could do to understand him.

Arnoth thought about the coming battle, his first actually. The blood as red as any wine. The black circles of carrion crows. The white of bone, the green of bile. He remembered Gadwen's comment about meat.

"Not hungry," he muttered.

On the other side of him, a dark-faced Arabanian leaned over. "Then I'll take yours as well as mine, boy. Can't sing well on a sighing belly, I always say." Expertly, he speared two chunks of cheese from Arnoth's plate.

"Leave him!" said Gadwen. "First timer."

"Ah!" The Arabanian nodded, winked, put a finger aside his nose, but not before snaring another chunk of the deep yellow cheese.

In one corner the aged bard Welloway of Caer Gwalen tuned his harp, humming a few tentative notes before he began singing. His voice no longer had the clear, lovely, innocent tones of his youth, or even the powerful resonances of his middle years. But he still knew how to couch lyrics within the tune.

King Thedric came to Barson's Hall,
Dark thunder blossomed on his brow.
His daughter slain, his castle burned,
None left alive to tell him how . . .

"Oh no, not the *Lay of King Thedric*!" complained a voice from the back of the hall.

"Yes, nobody wants to hear that old stuff anymore," called out another.

Welloway's fingers tangled in the strings. "The old stuff is still good enough for me," he said gruffly.

"Old stuff all right," called out the Arabanian next to Arnoth. "And moldy. Besides, the kings have got little enough cash for songs these days, so why sing about them?"

"Right enough!" said a balladeer across the table from Arnoth. "It's the rebel knights who are buying now. In hard cash, too."

"It's still a good song . . ." Welloway said, drawing his fingers once more across the strings. "That's what should count." He cleared his throat and began again.

King Thedric came to . . .

A fusillade of wheaten rolls rained down upon him.

"Barbarians!" he muttered sourly, and set aside his harp.

"Sir," Arnoth said, turning to Gadwen, "what do you think about that?"

"The best poetry is ageless," said Gadwen. "But the *Lay of Thedric* is Thed-drek. Forget it. Eat *something,* my boy, or you will be thinking of your belly instead of your ballad, a beginner's mistake."

Hating to be called a beginner, though he knew that was exactly what he was, Arnoth forced himself to eat two wheaten rolls, several chunks of cheese, and a bowl of porridge. But he could not stomach the breakfast meats at all.

"Outlaws—that's the future!" declared the Arabanian companionably.

"Don't be daft," said someone else. "Why should anyone listen to a song about impoverished brigands?"

"Times are changing, my friend," said the Arabanian expansively. "People are losing respect for the nobility. And as for the church!" He sniffed.

"I resent that!" boomed out a tall, poke-faced man. He stood abruptly, his hand going to a short dagger at his belt. From the badges on his cotte, it was clear that he was a cathedral poet, whose rhymes rang out within services and on holy day processionals. He was at the Nag's Tooth only because a brigade of soldiers pledged to the Alscent Cathedral were to be part of the day's fight.

"Resent all you like," said the Arabanian. "You do not have to struggle for a day's pay. You have a cushy sinecure, my friend. Passed on, father to son. But the rest of us know the only monies to be had these days is with the robber barons."

"And if those songs led to further lawlessness?" Arnoth asked in a low voice.

The Arabanian laughed. "You cannot blame the rise in crime on songs about outlaws, nor rebellion on songs about barons! I thought better of you, young man, given that Gadwen is your teacher." He looked over the boy's head at his master. "And what have you been teaching this poor lad, eh?" He stood. "Fathers go to war for money, land, or glory, and their sons learn to do likewise. It is an unending cycle of violence."

"Else," said Arnoth feelingly, "we'd be out of a job."

This was taken up by all as a great jest and Arnoth—though he had meant it with sincerity—found himself quoted round the room. He was not sure whether to be mortified or proud.

"Sir?" he said, turning to Gadwen.

"Better to be thought a wit than witless," Gadwen said with a wink. He announced to the table, "The light should be full on the field now. And the first of the soldiers already unsheathing their swords. It's a small field. If you want to see it before it is reddened by . . . dawn."

The others jumped up eagerly, but Gadwen—and Arnoth, held down by his master's massive hand—did not move. This was all according to Gadwen's plan.

One other sat still. He swallowed the last bit of the herbal brew he'd been drinking, then slowly stood, saying, "I'm off . . . to Hornsworth Castle . . . myself." He spoke slowly, in that exaggerated way Ilanders had. "That's where the . . . real action . . . is going to be. I've had a . . . talk . . . with some of the . . . generals. There'll be a . . . thousand men . . . storming Hornsworth . . . by nightfall. This thing . . . here . . . is . . ." He waved a fluttering hand. "No more than a . . . skirmish."

Several of the younger poets gathered around him trying to find out more and, still talking in his slow, deliberate drawl, he edged them to the door.

"If he's right . . ." Arnoth began.

Gadwen smiled. "Of course he's right," Gadwen said. "But wrong to be going. A big affair like that will be overchronicled." His smile got broader. "Dry as dust reportage. Leaves no room for elaboration. And what have I told you about that, eh?"

Arnoth looked down at his plate where the meat lay, bloody and uncompromising. He shuddered, trying to recall what it was Gadwen had taught him. Then he remembered and said in a rush, "That history is in the hands of the poets, not the generals. That they may make a battle but we remake it."

"And?"

Arnoth looked up at his master. "I do not know what else, sir."

Gadwen sighed. Most students were slow learners, but he'd had such hopes of this one. "The elaborated lie *becomes* the truth, boy. The public believes elaboration. They distrust a simple story. Give them a big one and it grows into history. Story . . . history. Hah!" He wiped his mouth with the edge of the tablecloth and reached over for his tankard. Slowly he savored its contents.

At the front door of the inn, the wrangle of poets thinned out till they were all gone, leaving Arnoth and his master alone in the dining hall. Gadwen's attention seemed entirely on his tankard.

While his master was thus occupied, Arnoth sneaked two sheets of parchment from his pack to study them. But poets, like generals, can watch a battle on two fronts, and Gadwen noticed the movement.

"What have you there?" he asked sharply, setting the tankard down on the table with a bang.

"It is the song I helped you compose at Sir Sauncivale's banquet last week. The one with the camelopards and . . ."

"You *wrote* it down?" There was a long silence. "What kind of an imbecile are you?" The last was said in a fierce kind of hissing whisper that Arnoth had previously only associated with dragons.

"Well," he tried to explain, "I thought . . ."

"You did *not* think!" exclaimed Gadwen. He reached out for the sheets of parchment and ripped them to tatters in a few brisk, angry movements. "If you write songs down, they can be copied and passed around so that any buffoon with a smattering of letters and no memory at all can recite them by merely glancing at the paper. That would be the end of us. The end of poetry and poets."

Arnoth hung his head. He could feel his entire breakfast, all the bit and bobs of it that he'd never wanted in the first place, roiling about in his belly. "I'm sorry, sir. It won't happen again."

"I do not expect it shall," said Gadwen. He stood and nodded at one of the serving wenches who was hovering by the door. "Come, lad. I have forgotten my anger. It is time for us to be gone." He kissed his hand at the wench and pulled Arnoth out the door.

When they got outside, expecting that the crowd would have already gone off to the battlefield, Gadwen was annoyed to find the Pelmerrian army was just coming into view.

"Pah!" he said, spitting expertly to one side. "I hate late arrivals. You'd think they'd get *that* part right, even if the rest of the day goes wrong."

But his bad humor was not shared with the rest of the onlookers, who cheered the marching soldiers, what few of them there were. It was, Gadwen explained sourly to his apprentice, a very small troop. No more than a hundred footmen and two score cavalry.

"Duke Fagnar will have twice that number. Catapults, too, I warrant. Won't be a battle but a slaughter. Hard to put a good face on that, even for a skilled poet."

"But *you* will be able to do it," Arnoth said. There was both hope and admiration in the sentence.

"Of course *I* will be able." Gadwen smiled. "But these scavengers," and he gestured to the poets who were clustering by a stone wall, "will be thrown back onto the old tropes for their inspiration. You know what I mean—'brief candles in the wind' and 'riding into the valley of death' and that sort of rot. However, you and I will rise to the occasion."

You and I. Arnoth suddenly felt ten feet taller. *You and I.* He was about to say something back, something heartfelt and grateful, when Gadwen spat again.

"Yoiks! Not him!"

One of the knights had dismounted to accept a goblet of watered wine from a serving wench. She curtsied and simpered and fluttered her lashes at the man, who chucked her under her not inconsiderable chin.

"See that?" Gadwen said.

"The girl?"

"No, not her. She's a victim of too many romantic ballads. A poke in the hay and a pig in her pot is all she'll get from Sir Gimmemore there. No, *him*."

"Him?"

"Sir Ereboin of Mount Pastille. The champion bore of three kingdoms. No, lad, don't look straight on him. It only encourages . . . oh, blast! He's coming this way. Whenever he opens his mouth, my art drains away like wine from a leaky bottle. He's always pestering me to make him the subject of a heroic romance. Not doing so has been one of the small satisfactions of my life."

Gadwen waved languidly at the knight, who came over and clapped him on the shoulder.

"Gadwen, good fellow, how's the ballad business?"

"Nice to see you, too, Sir Ereboin," Gadwen replied.

"Had a deuced exciting exploit the other day," the knight announced. His weak chin, with its wobble of flesh beneath, reminded Arnoth of a chicken's.

"Wonderful," said Gadwen in a tone that clearly said it was nothing of the sort.

"Rather thought you'd think so. Maybe put it in one of your little rhymes."

"Little. Rhymes." Gadwen did well not to splutter.

"Riding through the Forest of Tuss. You know, green as grass, green as . . . well, you know. And I heard a damsel scream. Or yell. Or call. You'll know how to put it best. Well, I put my spurs to my steed and rode with speed. Ah— there's the rhyme already for you. Steed, speed. Won't pay you for what you don't come up with yourself, of course. And . . ."

"Sir Ereboin," Arnoth interrupted, "your army has left you."

"Left, bereft," pointed out Gadwen with satisfaction.

Sir Ereboin looked around, saw he was truly at the back of his troop, and remounted his horse. "We'll have to continue after the battle, then, Gadwen."

"Assuming you survive," muttered Gadwen as he waved to Sir Ereboin's disappearing back.

"I didn't mean to interrupt," Arnoth said apologetically.

"No, no, lad, you were truly heroic," said Gadwen. "With your help, we dodged that arrow successfully, though he was an arrow without a point!" It was another good exit line, Gadwen thought, and without further conversation, they walked briskly after the troops.

They managed to get back to the field without too much trouble, except for the large amount of horse droppings along the way.

"Seasoned war horses learn to empty their bowels before a battle," Gadwen explained to his apprentice.

"Then these are particularly well-seasoned steeds," Arnoth replied.

"Good lad! Keeping your wit about you! That's fabulous."

Arnoth glowed under his master's praise. But he kept his further thought—about how well-seasoned a meal the carrion crows would be getting—to himself. He didn't want to have to think too much about that.

By the time they reached the battle site proper the rebel army of Duke Fagnar was well situated at the opposite end of the field. Arnoth could see not one but two catapults.

"You were right, sir," Arnoth said. "About the catapults."

"Did you doubt?" Gadwen was smiling. "Though two is rather excessive."

"Duke Fagnar doesn't think so," said Arnoth.

"Duke Fagnar is not composing the verse. Though, with luck, he may be decomposing at the end of it!" Gadwen chuckled.

Arnoth chuckled as well, but it was to cover up the sound of his roiling stomach. "It looks like it's going to be nothing but a slaughter, sir, not a battle. Perhaps we should have gone with the others to Hornsworth Castle."

Gadwen let out an exasperated sigh. "Missing the point, lad. We are the ones who decide the importance of a battle, not the *historiographers*." He pronounced the word with venom. "You recall, I assume, the Ambush at Perystalle?"

"Who has not, sir," Arnoth replied. "It is one of the greatest and most glorious . . ."

"Yes, yes," said Gadwen. "Facts?"

"The emperor's favorite nephew, the bold Count Regnault, slew a hundred Saracens before being overwhelmed and killed and . . ." He closed his eyes and started to chant the great epic.

The vale was dark, the night had clenched
The noble band in frigid grip,
Saracen eyes gleamed like black coals
As . . .

"Don't recite the whole damned thing at me. I composed it myself. And a fine job I did, too, given the circumstances," Gadwen said.

"Circumstances?" Arnoth opened his eyes. He saw Duke Fagnar's army, which was even then positioning the two catapults.

"There were scarcely more than a dozen Saracens and most of them died in a landslide that the din of their battle horns had brought down on them. Regnault actually spent more time tending their wounded than fighting them.

"Then how did he die?" Arnoth was interested, but he was also wary of the war unfolding in the field before him. He could see out of the corner of his eye that the catapults were being loaded with huge, jagged rocks, each the size of a full-grown pig.

"He didn't die at all," said Gadwen. "He's still alive."

"Alive?" Arnoth almost choked. He turned from the battlefield to stare at his master.

"Yes, and living in a hidden chamber in his father's castle. The family and servants have been sworn to secrecy, but I have a second cousin who is an underfootman there, and he was in bed sick the day the swearing was done. Poor Regnault doesn't get out much these days. After all, he's got a reputation to uphold as one of the great heroes of Christendom. My cousin reckons the Count counts it worth the inconvenience to maintain the legend. And it does raise property values enormously."

The first of the catapults let go its heavy burden, which went whistling through the air with deadly accuracy. There was a loud *splat* as ten foot soldiers and one screaming battle horse went down in a rain of blood.

"Oh, dear Lord!" cried Arnoth, turning back to watch the battle. He crossed himself three times and tried desperately not to think of the crows.

"Let's see," said Gadwen, "better call it five thousand men per side here. You really can't get away with fewer than that and still expect to hold anyone's interest."

The second lethal bombardment fell on another ten men. This time two horses went down, their riders thrown clear, but having landed facedown in the mud with their heavy armor, neither of the men could get up before choking to death.

"Mother of God," whispered Arnoth, falling to his knees.

"Probably be a good touch," Gadwen said, "to leave out the catapults altogether. Hardly sporting, after all."

The first catapult had been reloaded by then and this time it took down a dozen foot soldiers, another knight, and Sir Ereboin himself, who landed on his back and could not seem to rise. This final disaster tore the heart from the small Pelmerrian army, and they took to their heels, throwing aside what armor and arms they had in their haste to quit the field. Galloping after the foot soldiers came their own knights. And behind them, for a few yards at least, pursued Duke Fagnar's men.

Moments into the chase, Duke Fagnar's army quit. They slumped onto the ground and loosened the straps of their mail. It was a hot day and steam rose from their sweaty bodies like mist from the surface of a lake.

Arnoth stared at the field where thirty-two foot soldiers, three horses, three knights, and Sir Ereboin lay shattered. Duke Fagnar's army was already starting to pack up and go home. "Is that it?" he asked. When Gadwen didn't answer, Arnoth took a deep breath. "Didn't take very long."

"It usually doesn't," his master said. "When you can see the way a battle is going, why stick around? Most of the foot soldiers are fighting for two meals a day and a tot of rum. It's hard to eat or drink when you've been decapitated. And the knights are only in it for the glory. But never mind, by the time we have worked our magic, they'll have been pummeling one another for three days and three nights of shining valor and unceasing brutality."

But Arnoth was no longer listening. Instead he and the ground were making a closer acquaintance as the morning's breakfast rose out of his roiling belly to spill out onto the dark earth.

Gadwen waited until the boy was done. He knew it often took young poets this way the first time. So he continued to talk as if what Arnoth was doing was nothing more than examining the ground. "My instincts tell me this will work better as a tragedy." He nod- ded as Arnoth stood, wiping his mouth. "Let's have a look at what's left of the losers."

Arnoth started toward the slaughtered foot sol- diers, but Gadwen pulled him up sharply. "Nobody's interested in them," he said. "The nobles are who they want us to sing about."

The two knights who had choked in mud could not be interviewed, of course, but Gadwen led his apprentice expertly across the field to where the third knight lay staring into the merciless sun.

"What is your name, brave knight?" Gadwen asked, standing over in such a way that his shadow gave the man some respite.

"Hunwald," croaked the knight.

"Of Cantivar or Bellrancor?"

"Cant . . . Cantivar." The man grimaced, but Gadwen took it as a smile of recognition. "You wouldn't . . . have any water?"

"Sorry. Left it at the inn," said Gadwen, and when Arnoth lifted a finger as if to offer to find some, shook his head. "So how did it feel when the arrow struck?"

"Damned stones," the knight said. "Not arrows."

"Well, it will be arrows when I tell it," said Gadwen. "So how did it feel?"

"Feel?" The knight was fading fast.

"When you got your deathblow," said Gadwen.

"Bloody awful!" said the knight. The effort seemed to have exhausted him and he lapsed into unconsciousness.

"Well, that can certainly be tidied up," Gadwen announced. "They rarely say anything of interest at the end, but I always hope. Now—where's his sword?"

Arnoth found it in the mud and held it up mutely to his master.

"Good," said Gadwen. "Excellent. It has the look of a sword forged by Wayland himself and passed through generations of ill-fated heroes."

"But it has Marco of Monmouth's mark on it," Arnoth pointed out.

Gadwen ignored him. "No doubt it has slain a hundred foes and has itself been the cause of not a few wars. This is merely the latest tragic episode in its illustrious history. But it's going to need a name." He looked meaningfully at Arnoth. "Here's your chance, boy."

"Marco?" Arnoth said.

Gadwen shook his head.

"Monmouth?" the boy ventured.

Gadwen shook his head again. "Think poetry!" he demanded. "You've been with me these past six months. Haven't you learned anything?"

"Calimbara!" said Arnoth. He'd had a dog of that name once.

"Calimbara. I like that. Good boy!" Gadwen said. "Now where's that pesky Ereboin?"

Arnoth pointed behind him. "There, I think. But I fear he's dead."

They walked over to the body and gazed down. Ereboin's face was twisted in its death throes. His weak chin looked even weaker in the glare of the sun. He had two hairs coated with blood sticking out of his nose. His sword was still in his hand.

Arnoth felt his empty stomach roil.

"Good!" said Gadwen.

"Good? I do not understand, sir," Arnoth said. "I know you said he was a bore, but . . ."

"We can blame the whole business on him. I'll make him the arch-traitor who betrayed his own side. He always wanted to star in an epic. Now's his chance!"

"That's a bit hard just for being boring, sir," Arnoth said.

Gadwen looked at his apprentice. "You never had to suffer through innumerable retellings of the time he slew that wild pig that was running loose in the Utterwent Marshes. One bore about another boar. Believe me, death alone is too good for him."

"Foul villain!" Ereboin opened one eye unexpectedly. "Thou shalt not gain glory from this disaster." And so saying he made a weak but skillful upward thrust with his sword. It sliced through Gadwen's not unprodigious gut.

The poet, with a surprised look on his face, fell to the ground, the sword like a pigsticker still in his stomach.

"Master!" Arnoth cried. For a moment he couldn't think what to do.

Gadwen's lips tried to form words but he didn't seem to have the breath

to blow them out. So Arnoth knelt by his side and put his ear right down by the old poet's mouth.

> Brave Gadwen of the poets' band,
> Undone by a poxy traitor's hand . . .

Gadwen's eyelids fluttered. "You'll have to do the rest yourself, lad."

"But, sir, how can I compose without you?" Arnoth's voice whined and his eyes brimmed over with tears. "You've been like a father to me. T'was you showed me versification. Your hand guided, your tongue led, your . . ."

Gadwen grabbed the boy's jerkin and yanked him closer till they were nose to nose.

"Save it for the song, you bloody fool," he hissed, and died.

Arnoth stood up and saw how the carrion eaters already commanded half the field. He knew what poem he would write. It would bring him, he guessed, little fame. But truth, he thought, had been the loser in rhymes for too long a time. It would be his task to redress that crime. Someone, he was sure, would listen.

> Where comes our meat? the raven cries
> And all too soon pecks out the eyes
> Of soldiers on a field of glory
> Who die to live again in story.

It was a start, he thought, as he left the crows to their feast.

Red as Jade

S. P. Somtow

I

Vampires can be your friends. No one fucks with a vampire. Even when, on the outside, he looks like a harmless little kid. I suppose that was my rationale for taking Timmy Valentine to the Golden Triangle with me. The underground jade market can be a dangerous place to hang out, and I look like an easy target—I'm a slip of a Chinese American woman, and at thirty I don't look a day over fifteen.

No one believed I would actually want to take over my father's business when he got sick. Most of our relatives believed that the Jade Emporium in San Francisco was just a laundering operation for my father's heroin smuggling, but actually it was the other way round—the drug trafficking was just a way for him to finance his consuming passion. That was how we were alike, me and Dad. Jade was my father's life . . . and mine.

It's hard to explain that to someone who doesn't share that passion. "Like explaining music to the deaf, I guess," Timmy told me, as we rode two bicycle rickshaws side by side down a banana-tree-lined dirt road.

"Or the undead to the living?" I said. The rickshaws squeaked, the hot air swimming with strange odors: dung; tropical flowers; exotic, decaying fruits. Sometimes I couldn't tell if Timmy Valentine believed his own hype, or if he was just really, really protective of his platinum-sales persona.

"Don't, Pauline," said Timmy. "I'm sensitive about vampire jokes." We rode in silence.

I don't talk much. When I was little, I didn't speak at all, then I stuttered a lot—with some people I still do. But although I hadn't known Timmy Valentine long, I trusted him; since our trip started, I hadn't stammered once.

It's true I had never seen him eat. It's true that this vampire thing got on my nerves sometimes. We'd become friends at one of my father's big mafia-cum-movie-biz dos. Both loners, I guess. Not that I saw him much, him being a busy celebrity, me constantly trying to make sense of my father's scribbled figures on old legal pads.

The market is not really underground; it's a ways past the last stilted house in the village of Doi Yok, in a mountainous country that's neither Thailand, Laos, or Myanmar; you start your journey at a five-star Hilton in Thailand, still well within shouting range of civilization, but within an hour you're in no-man's-land. It was dark when you started, and now it's misty morning in a landscape dense with teak trees and wild orchids.

Now and then there's sniping. You have to realize that this territory is being fought over by various entities—the Burmese military government, the rebels of the Shan Free State, a hill tribe or two—but a petty war is not enough to halt commerce. I think the jade trade finances all the warring parties one way or another—taxes, levies, protection money, whatever you want to call it.

I make this journey every three years for my dad; this time I had a secret mission as well.

When the path starts to wind up a hill called Doi Sawan, you see a few thatched kiosks where children or old men watch over piles of boulders, but these are the ones that have already been picked over.

"Picked over?" Timmy asked me. "But they look—"

"Just the same as the others?"

That, of course, is part of the mystique of the stone. Jade boulders come with a skin around them, a dull, dirt-colored skin. No way of knowing what's inside—a deep, oily green; a delicate lavender; the prized white—or just plain old dirt-colored to the core. And you have to bid on it before you cut it open.

I told the rickshaw pedalers to stop a moment. Just as well, with a recalcitrant elephant hogging the road ahead. I showed Timmy one of the boulders, palm-sized, asked him what he'd bid on it.

He smiled a little; yes, that million-dollar smile, so enigmatic, so—what had the *Times* said about that smile?—"joyous yet melancholy, innocent yet pregnant with the promise of an undeliverable sexuality." "Okay, I'll play," he said. "Five bucks."

I fished the money out of my pocket. Handed it to the giggling, gap-toothed vendor. Then, extracting a file from my jeans, I sawed away at a little corner of it to expose the jade's true color.

"Red," he said, and laughed. "Natural for me, I suppose."

"Not a bad color. Probably not a translucent jade, but rich, a little sinful even. Okay," I said, "now watch me."

I took a deep breath. Reached into the basket. They weren't all boulders—some were no more than pebbles—and they tinkled as they slid, making the crystal-cold music jade always makes. I have a sense of jade, inherited from Dad, I suppose. Some stones seem to sing a little. Soon my fingers were tingling. A pebble slithering away from me. They were alive to me, those stones. Pushed my arm in deeper. *Touched it!* A shock wave through my body. Yanked it out.

"Five bucks?" I said, and threw the old crone the equivalent in Thai money. She wasn't so happy this time. Maybe she only worked the bottom of the hill, but she must still have had a bit of the jade-sense.

"So tell me," said the boy who claimed to be a vampire, "what's the difference between the two pebbles?"

"I couldn't tell you," I said. "From the outside, they're equally dull. But this one sets me tingling. I don't know how they could have missed it." I took the file and exposed a corner of it. Just as I thought: creamy white, translucent . . . if only I could be sure it was that way all the way through . . . but I was pretty sure. "You really don't feel anything at all?" I asked him.

"Well," said Timmy Valentine, and he looked at me with those strange, clear eyes, "I do feel something. But not this jade-sense of yours. When your fingertips grazed that stone inside that basket, the air around us was flooded with the scent of longing. A pheromone, I guess. Charged with eroticism. People think I can't feel love, but I do know what love smells like."

Timmy Valentine is a scary guy. I mean, this was broad daylight, and you knew that the boy was probably just a victim of his own handlers, but you could see how he had become the Prince of Neo-Gothic. He looks like he's around twelve, but I think it's some kind of hormone deficiency thing, probably, and that also explains his voice, which just doesn't sound human.

"Don't be scared, Pauline," he said, "I don't bite."

"Give me a break, Timmy," I said. "This is probably the one place in the world where you won't be mobbed by screaming teenage girls . . . you can be yourself."

"I am," he said. And stared into his brown boulder with the crimson streak, fascinated . . . as though it were a living, bleeding thing.

We came to the market at last. Canvas stalls everywhere, and old men playing the bidding game in tight, silent circles. "Watch me," I told Timmy. A monkey scampered across our path. The first pavilion was the most crowded. The boulder, of good size, had an edge exposed, brilliant green, kryptonite-colored—very attractive. There were about a dozen bidders, bearded old men, a few Europeans; the auctioneer was a bushy-bearded, plump man in a paramilitary uniform . . . Uncle Chang.

"Go away, girl," he said. "You know tradition. No women."

I said, "I am my father, not myself." I showed him the white jade *bi*, three thousand years old, that hung on a gold chain around my neck. The old men muttered and glowered. I placed my hand on the boulder. The other bidders did the same. Jade had always been auctioned this way, in silence, in a secret language written with the fingertips.

Uncle Chang threw a silken cloth over the boulder and the circle of hands, the signal that the bidding was now to begin. Immediately I felt the restless drumming and scratching, the time-honored technique of bidding, the fingers dancing while the faces stayed impassive. Beneath the cloth, my hand felt snared in a nest of snakes. I looked from bidder to bidder. But I felt no tingle. Usually there's a different vibe for every color; I trace my finger along the surface, I feel the traceries, the bumps, the bubbles of lucidity; I feel the stone's soul. But no. Nothing at all. Only the pinprick sizzle of neon green where the skin had been breached. So I did not bid.

There was one other man who did not bid. I had never seen him here before. He wore a double-breasted duster—a weird affectation for this climate—and a slouch hat. He did not seem Chinese, but there wasn't much of him visible. He was draped in shapeless black, and I didn't see his eyes because he wore a pair of silver-rimmed mirror shades.

Was he gazing at me? He seemed to be. No one else paid attention. The bids were climbing sky-high. I felt the frantic wiggling, the cursive outlines of Chinese characters that spelled out names, the tap-tap-tapping of units, tens, hundreds, thousands—greenbacks, cash, the only valid currency in this borderland—and then, at last, no movement at all.

The silk was whisked away.

A fat little man was unrolling a wad of Benjamin Franklins from his chest, and smiling smugly to himself.

"Is it over?" said Timmy Valentine, who had been sitting in a corner, watching a rerun of *The Waltons* on a battered black-and-white television. A chained gibbon shrieked from its roost in the awning.

"Yes," I said. "Nothing to see here. Let's move on."

But I did not move.

Because I felt the tall man's presence. He hadn't moved either, though the bidders had all left the circle, and the auctioneer was getting ready to heft another boulder onto the stand.

At length, the tall man gestured dismissively at the successful bidder, who was sipping a quick *café filtre* by the side of the pavilion.

"He will be disappointed," he said—he had a soft voice, high-pitched; you imagine eunuchs talking this way—and looked away at last.

"I-I-I-know," I said. For the first time in a week, I was having trouble talking. Fuck! Not now, not in front of these people!

"I know who you are," said the man, "and I know why you're here. Be careful."

He took off his mirror shades and looked me straight in the face.

And his eyes were mirrors, too.

I think I would have screamed if I hadn't felt Timmy's hand on my shoulder. The tall man loped away, uphill a little further, toward the cavern of antiquities—his real destination, and mine.

"What was all that about?" said Timmy.

"H-he's after the Empress of Jade," I said.

Everyone heard me say that; the chatter went dead—the kind of silence that tells you that the gunman has entered the saloon. Uncle Chang looked at me askance. "No be so blatant!" he whispered.

"Where is she?" I asked him.

"Up the—" He looked shiftily about. "Hundred tell you where she hidden."

I uncoiled the C-note from my sleeve and dangled it before his nose. He snatched it away. "Cheap theatrics!" he scoffed. "You think this is some cheap kung fu movie?"

"M-maybe," I said. "Well, not cheap."

Uncle Chang then proceeded to whisper in my ear the words that would take me to the thing my father most longed to possess. This buying of jade boulders, seeking out the finest, sending them to the best carvers to make precious objects for the homes of the nouveau riche of Chinatown, this was only part of the Jade Emporium's business. More important to my father was the room in the attic, the room of his secret treasures . . . the room that would one day be mine.

I was so excited that I wanted to rush to the viewing location right away, but I knew I had to pace myself. I would give the tall man an apparent advantage. He would spend all day thinking he had already won the prize, and I would swoop in the next day and snatch it from him.

"Who is he, anyway?" I asked Uncle Chang, and stuffed another hundred dollars in his hand.

"Nobody know," he said. "First time here. Some people call him the White Giraffe, because he very tall, and he albino. He very good jade-sense. Some people here think your father send him, come to senses this year, marry you off properly to rich American doctor."

"My father would never send someone in my place," I said, unsure of myself suddenly. I had to keep my cool. Couldn't let it get to me—wouldn't they just love that! They'd nod their heads and murmur sagely about how a girl should never have slipped into their private little club.

So I spent the rest of the day buying up stones, and come evening we took two more bicycle rickshaws—downhill this time, so the extra weight did not entirely kill the pedalers—and trundled back down toward the village where we would get back to the Mercedes and chauffeur waiting patiently by the grove where the drivable dirt road came to an end, backtrack to the back street, and finally come to an incongruous fifteen-kilometer stretch of super-highway that would bring us back to the Hilton and the twenty-dollar hamburger deluxe and civilization.

Timmy didn't have dinner, not even a glass of wine. "I'll eat later," he told me. At midnight, when I woke up screaming, he wasn't there.

The nightmare sent me right back to childhood. It was the same one, though I hadn't had it for twenty years. I know the day it happened because it was the night before my mom died in a car crash.

It's a dark room. Here and there a shaft of cold light on a stone face. I know that I am trapped. I'm wearing a flimsy nightgown. Or maybe it's a shroud. The air is dense, putrescent.

I try to touch my face and arms and all I feel is something hard, chitinous. I try to scream but my lips are mandibles, and only a dry chittering issues forth. I crawl among the dead things. I have too many arms and legs. A burning drool oozes from my jaws. Who am I?

The dust hangs heavy. I'm here to fight someone. Who? What?

I skitter among the dead things.

There is a hall. An empty coffin. On the coffin, a crow perches. A dragon, coiled, asleep, around the tomb. And suddenly I know that it's my tomb, my bed, my place of rest, and if I can only reach it I won't be afraid any more . . . I edge closer to the sarcophagus . . . smooth and cold . . . white limestone.

If I can only slither across those glassy scales . . .

But as I graze one jeweled claw the dragon wakes. His eyes snap open with a metallic rasp, like the gates of a cemetery. And he exhales a searing, frosty fire, and in that fire's chill blue shimmering I see the faces around me, faces of sacrificial victims, women, men, children, eunuchs, dogs, horses, hecatombs of corpses overrun with rats and maggots, and the dragon lunges over the dead toward me, and all I can do is cry out, "Let me in, let me in—," and in the mirrors that are the dragon's eyes I see myself, not a human but a monstrous bug-thing—

The crow flaps its wings and shrieks, and then I scream—

In the Hilton at the edge of the country with no name, I remembered the first time I woke up from that dream.

Weeping, in my father's arms.

And I can't talk. The words don't come, "Tomb! Da-da-da-da-da—insect!" How old was I? Nine, ten? I know it was before puberty.

"Hush," said my father, "hush, my daughter; it's time for you to see the attic."

He put a terry cloth robe on me, and led me from my room, past the master bedroom where my mother lay snoring, my baby brother in her arms, past the lace and marble bathroom and the linen closet, to the door I had never seen him open. He took the big key that hung from the dragon-shaped hook, which made me shudder because it brought back the dream a little, and the door creaked open, and—never letting go of my tiny hand—he pulled me upward toward the landing where the moon shone through the round window, a circle inside a circle.

At length we reached the little treasure room. The room was legendary in our house, yet no one save my father had ever been known to set foot in it. "La, la, l-l-l-light?" I said.

"The first time," he said, "sometimes things are best viewed in the moonlight, my daughter." He spoke to me in Cantonese, which he never did in front of company, or even in front of my mother, who was Italian. "You will come here often enough by day."

For now the treasures were only glimpses—a mottled horse rearing up, an urn carved with flowers, a white dragon, the greasy luminescence of fine jade. That was when I felt the tingle for the first time. The air was electric. I knew the colors without seeing them, because I said at once, without stuttering at all, "Daddy, I thought jade was supposed to be green."

"That famous green," said my father, "comes from Burma, and they only started mining it in quantity two centuries ago . . . You must learn to appreciate other jades, too . . . celestial white . . . imperial yellow . . . bloodred." He sat me down on his knee and made me close my eyes and tell him the color of whatever he placed in my hand, and sometimes I felt laughter shake his whole potbellied frame, and sometimes I felt a tension rack him. At last he gave me an object I knew was white—even through my closed fingers it irradiated my body. "Tonight," he said, "you dreamed of the cicada. That's a very important dream. In the Han dynasty, two thousand years ago, the jade cicada was a symbol of the soul's victory over death . . . Now open your eyes . . . and your fist."

I did. It was a stylized artifact, angular, ungainly. "In those days," my father told me, "they buried you with a jade cicada on your tongue. It ensured your immortality."

I looked at the cold white thing, me a whiny little girl in an attic room in San Francisco, the cicada reaching to me from my past, and from my dream.

"You want to try it?"

"Try?"

"Open wide."

He popped the jade cicada between my lips. I felt like gagging for a moment. Hadn't this thing been in some dead person's mouth before? With all those worms. A stone bug. I thought I was going to choke. I spit it out. My father caught it. I was shaking. My father wiped the cicada and put it in a jar with half a dozen others.

"There now," he said at last, "in your dream, you were trapped in the cicada. Now you've turned the tables on that mean old insect."

He made me laugh in the end, and I didn't have the dream again for years; but lately, lately it had been coming back, and this time I wasn't a child anymore, and I couldn't sit on someone's lap; so instead I lay in my bed in a suite in a five-star hotel and watched CNN for a while, until I heard a tapping at my window, and I saw Timmy, curled up on the sill, leaning against the air conditioner.

"Don't worry," he said. "I've eaten."
He climbed in and I closed the window behind him. "You really go overboard with this method acting," I said. "I haven't seen you gag on garlic, or get burned by the sun, I mean, you're pretty damn selective when it comes to the trappings of vampirism . . ."

"Myths, Pauline," he said, wiping the blood from his lips.

Then I looked out at the parking lot. There was a large gray mass lying between two Mercedeses.

"Don't worry," said Timmy. "He was old. He asked me to release him."

"Timmy, there's a dead *elephant* in the parking lot."

"He'll be gone by morning. His mahout already knows about it; it's been in his dreams all week; before dawn, he'll be here soon, with younger elephants to help bear their comrade away. There's a tiger loose, they say." He shrugged. "But you've been dreaming, too."

It's weird. It didn't seem to matter that my companion was some kind of schizoid maniac and that I was stranded at the very edge of civilization. Somehow, I knew that Timmy would understand. His life had been stranger than mine could ever be. I knew he'd listen. I knew he wouldn't think I was crazy. I told him everything—the cicada and the dragon. I told him my secret reason for coming here this year. I told him how afraid I was, how the tall albino with the mirror shades made me almost want to turn tail and flee back to America.

And Timmy held my hand in his—his was as cold as a jade that has been in the grave for a thousand years—and said, "I'll tell you something about myself, then, Pauline Huang, and here it is: you have this uncanny jade-sense—touch the stone's skin, feel its true color; some may think it's magic, but to you it's as natural as breathing—and I have a soul-sense. When I touch the skin of a mortal, I feel that mortal's true colors—I see his soul. It's not magic for me, either. It's probably something to do with pheromones, or the subtleties of body language, or—well, you see what I'm getting at."

"What are you telling me?"

"The tall man with the mirror shades. He looked at you. Something happened. I know. My hand brushed against you at that moment and I saw inside your skin."

I was getting the creeps. Timmy has this way of totally sucking you into his vision of the world. When he speaks to you, no matter how absurd it all is, you know, at the time, that it's God's plain truth. Softly I said, trying to make light of it all, "And who did you see? Eleanor Roosevelt?"

"No, Pauline. I didn't see anyone at all."

"What?"

"You were gone, Pauline. Just for a moment. Until he turned away and walked uphill. You were empty. You were a shell. Your soul was somewhere far away."

2

All right. So what *was* my secret mission? It was an order from my father to bring back something—someone, I suppose you might say—from the cavern of antiquities in Doi Yok. The Empress of Jade.

My father is a shady man. Because of him, junkies share needles in back alleys, and kids die of AIDS. I can't help that. I love him. He has always been the best of fathers, and I am pretty dutiful and obedient, for an American— that Confucian culture runs deep in my blood. I love him, but I have a hard time telling him; it's then that the stammering comes worst of all, as though I had a big rock wedged in my throat.

My father is a bad man, but he's not without compassion. He inherited this business. He couldn't help it either. It was in *his* blood, you see.

My father has been ill for several years now, and my cousin takes care of the dirty business while I run the Jade Emporium. He won't go into a hospital, because he thinks that he'll never come back out; so he lies upstairs, in the attic, among his treasures, on a high-tech superbed with IVs, a nurse on duty 24/7, even a machine that goes *ping*. A week before this trip, he made sure the nurse was out of earshot, and he told me to open a velvet box, one he hadn't shown me before.

"Time to understand the cicada and the dragon," he said at last. "Time to face down your nightmare."

"But, Dad," I said. "I haven't had that nightmare in a long time."

"Open the box," he said.

Inside were little rectangles of jade. Not the fine jadeite from Burma, but the ancient nephrite, muddy green streaked with a dried-blood brown. They were like *mah jong* tiles . . . or like the scales of a dragon, perhaps. Each corner had a hole, and in some of the holes were scraps of gold thread.

"What are they?" said my father.

"Western Han dynasty," I said. "They're pieces from a jade burial suit."

My father nodded . . . wheezed a little . . . indicated the Demerol dispenser with his head. I gave him a little shot of the painkiller, even though the doctor had told him to go easy on it. "Good girl," he said.

"When a high-ranking person was buried," I said, knowing how he liked to hear me repeat, word-for-word, the lessons he'd taught me, "nine orifices were plugged up with jade—the cicada for the tongue, jade pigs clenched in each fist—and then the entire body was encased in a jade suit. The body and soul, the life-essence, bottled within. Immortality ensured."

For a moment I thought he was going to ask me to have one made for *him*. He could have afforded it, but I didn't think he really believed those millennial superstitions . . . did he?

"No, nothing like that," he said, reading my mind, as usual. "But what if . . . somewhere out there . . . in the undisturbed burial chambers of ancient China . . . there was an empress, preserved by the magic of the jade, the cicada still unborn upon her tongue, her body sewn into its shroud of magical stone . . . waiting through the centuries for—"

"There *is* such an empress, isn't there?" I said. "And you want her."

"Chang sent me a letter," he said. "I think I'm in love." He pulled a wrinkled color Xerox from under his pillow. "Look . . . look."

And there she was. Resting on a slab of concrete. No dragon coiled at her feet, no crow standing watch over her sarcophagus. In the background, a dirt road, a truck, a gang of peasants with shovels posing with crooked smiles. The whole scene bathed in a faceless sunlight.

"Can you bring her to me?" my father said. "Since your mother died I've been lonely . . ."

"Dad," I said, "that's morbid. Sure, a jade suit would be the crown of your collection. But with a dead woman inside—"

"With jade," he said. "there really is no death. Anyhow, I get a special feeling from this jade, even from this poor reproduction of a photograph. It was found near the ancestral village in China. It calls to us."

"If you say so, Dad." My jade-sense didn't work over distance; my father always claimed that his did, though unreliably.

"And when something calls this strongly," he added, "there is also danger."

"Danger? Either I'll bid on it, and I'll get it and bring it back . . . or someone else will. You'll set a limit . . . I know you will . . . you'll be sensible."

"You are to bring it back at any cost," said my father, with such intensity that I reached for the Demerol button, thinking he'd have another spasm. "But no, the danger is not that we'll wipe out all our bank accounts. You will see."

"Then—"

"The danger," my father said, "is in your dreams."

So there we were. The crates of raw stones all ready for shipping, and now there was only one order of business left. The cavern of antiquities was the most circuitous sector of the underground jade market. It was not just a single cavern, but a whole labyrinth.

By the front, shafts of daylight streamed in from holes in the cavern vault. Here were dealers with new objects, or objects pretending to great age. Wagonwheel-sized *bi* incised with scenes of hunting and how-to guides to sexual positions. Goddesses with sweeping robes. Amulets by the thousands, carved into good-luck calligraphies or laughing Buddhas. The vendors were mostly children or middle-aged women, some in their hill-tribe costumes, bowed by the weight of their silver ornaments.

Further in, little chambers, hollows in the rock like side chapels in a cathedral, and now the *objets d'art* were more reliably authentic, though nothing much older than Ming. Here were rows of dragons, horses, goats, and turtles, and those ornamental urns with florid reliefs, and glowering lions and fu dogs, and yes, crows, too, perched on carved branches with cunningly wrought leaves. The sellers were middle-aged, and men, mostly; no native dress here but Armani suits or, more casually, Versace jeans. Here, improbably, were credit card machines linked via cellular modems to the world of commerce beyond the no-man's-land. Prices were in the five, perhaps even six, figures here. But I had little patience for these trinkets; we had ones just as lovely back at the Emporium, made in our own workshop in darkest Palo Alto.

The directions Uncle Chang had given me were convoluted. At least once, Timmy and I found ourselves doubling back, or walking in circles. I suppose we were being tested, or something.

Presently we seemed to be descending deeper into the hillside. Not many vendors now, and we were regressing in time, to objects of Sung, Han, Zhou, Shang, or even Neolithic vintage. And the salesmen were older and more ferocious.

"This is it," I said at last. "This corner, and we should be—"

We entered through a narrow gap in the rock. A misty space, echoey, and too dark to see the size of it; here and there, a naked lightbulb swung. The stench of bat dung in our nostrils. I started to move forward—

The tall albino blocked our way.

"I'm sorry," he said, "I was here first."

"We get to look," I said. "The auction's not until tomorrow."

"I've made a preemptive bid."

I looked into his mirror shades and saw myself reflected . . . or was it me? Were those the compound eyes of a great cicada, the jointed limbs? Of course not. Letting him get to me, I thought. Can't do that.

I looked past him. Past the swinging lightbulbs . . . to the wooden board that leaned against the far wall. She was there all right. I could feel each one of the scales, dark green jade spattered with the color of dried blood . . . she was near . . . my jade-sense doesn't work over distances . . . I couldn't see her yet, but my blood was singing in my ears . . .

"Oh, Pauline," said the tall man, "I've seen her. She is perfect. Not a scale missing, not a strand of gold frayed . . . she is beautiful. And inside that suit she's there, all of her, untouched by time."

"Well, let me be the judge of that," I said, but I knew he was right.

"Let's not fight over her," said the tall man. "This is history, this is the interface of truth and legend."

"Ya, ya, y-you're not going to turn this bidding war into some mythic battle," I said, though the man was clearly suffering from an Indiana Jones complex.

"Hardly," he said. He reached into his duster and pulled out a business card. "Just doing my job." He tossed it to me.

The card read:

DAVID S. COLEMAN, PH.D.,
DEPARTMENT OF ACQUISITIONS,
THE SAN FRANCISCO MUSEUM OF ANCIENT CIVILIZATION

"You're from a museum?"

"What did you think—that I'm some vengeful demon out of time, come to hound the old lady beyond the grave?"

"You do come across that way," I said.

"Well look, little lady," said Coleman, "this treasure's meant to be seen by millions, not locked up in some drug dealer's attic. So go home and let's not have a bidding war. I've got a resource you can never outbid—the tax dollars of John Q. Public."

This wasn't the battle I'd been expecting. There stood this man, as outlandish-looking as a comic-book villain, surely some ancient nemesis of my father's who had nurtured a grudge since some childhood spat and now was prepared for some mythic catharsis . . . but no. He was making himself look like the forces of feel-good liberalism, and me like the villain. That threw me off guard.

It was Timmy who stepped in. "Pauline," he said, "there's something wrong here."

"Get out!" Coleman screamed. "You were never part of this equation!"

Well, I had come twelve thousand miles and then some, and suffered nightmares and wormed through this labyrinth, and I wasn't going to leave without at least touching the Empress of Jade. I could see her clearer now, getting more used to the dark, and my jade-sense was jangling in my veins, in my brain, making me feel almost superhuman. I started forward, tried to shove Coleman out of my way even though he was a foot taller than me, but instead he whacked me with the back of his hand, casually, across the chest, and sent me sprawling hard against jagged stone.

How could a man be that strong? Confused, I tried to sit up. The stalactites wheeled overhead. It was then that I saw Timmy Valentine transform—

Transform? He shimmered against the phosphorescence of the limestone. Arms flapped into dark wings. Lips tightened to a beak. *I'm dreaming!* I thought, and kept hearing my father's voice: *The danger is your dreams in your dreams your dreams—*

Timmy cried out . . . and his cry was the harsh caw of the raven . . . and his eyes were amber yellow, and feral, and fire-bright . . . the naked bulbs swayed, and through the crisscross beams he flew, arrowing at the tall man's heart—

Coleman leaped up . . . suddenly he was on a ledge, ten feet overhead, like a demon in a kung fu movie. Timmy spiraled higher, shrieking. What was going on? Hadn't I seen crows in my dream, stone crows guarding the sarcophagus?

"Oh no," said the tall man, "no, you don't. You're not the one I'm destined to fight, you're not even supposed to be here—" He pulled a revolver from his duster and squeezed the trigger, point blank, as the crow prepared to swoop down on his shaded eyes.

I screamed.

There was no gunshot. It was a water pistol. A stream of liquid hit the bird and vaporized it. A flurry of feathers.

"Never know," said Coleman, tossing the weapon in his pocket, "when holy water's gonna prove handy." He turned his back on me and strode to where the Empress of Jade lay. I looked down at my hands and saw they were the chitinous limbs of a monstrous insect—

And suddenly I was somewhere else: in a bed at the Hilton, being tended to by Timmy. Chicken soup and cold compresses. And Timmy sitting by the bed, normal as can be, in neatly pressed Versus casuals, just your ordinary underaged neo-Gothic superstar on his day off.

"You—a crow—what did it mean?"

"When I transform," said Timmy, "I become the thing most feared. Obviously our friend believes that a crow will be his ending. But I was only an illusion . . . not his real death. I'm not the real enemy . . . am I now?" He turned to me as if I would have the answers.

"How should I know?" I said, and moaned.

"Pauline," he said softly, "are you ready to tell me who you *really* are?"

3

"Only," I said, "if you tell me who *you* are."

"Oddly enough," he said, "I've never lied to you."

"Well, I haven't lied to you either."

"But you *have* lied to yourself. Or rather, you've chosen not to see . . . certain things.

"There's another person inside Pauline Huang. A person who cries out to be avenged. A person from an ancient time. A person you fear to let out, because you're afraid you'll lose your own self."

"The holy water? What was all that about?"

"I shouldn't have let it faze me. It took me by surprise, I admit. Usually my defenses are up a lot more. Anyway, it wasn't your everyday holy water from the local church . . . it was blessed by a true believer . . . it was pretty potent. I don't understand how he managed to carry it on his person— although the water wasn't touching him directly."

"Why wouldn't he have been able to?"

"Oh, you don't get it?" said Timmy Valentine. "He's a vampire, too."

Night. Still groggy, my head still throbbing, I went with Timmy from the Hilton, into the empty town. He had insisted that I make arrangements to ship all the jade I had already bought, though normally I would never do so until just before flying home.

"Where are we going?" I wanted to know, but he didn't answer me. "We can't call a hotel limo at this hour," I said. "We can't even rouse a bicycle rickshaw. How can we go anywhere at all?"

The streets of the border town were quite, quite vacant. To call it a town was flattery; the Hilton and its support system *were* the town. One bar was open a few blocks down. Peasant music—some people call it "Country 'n' Eastern"—played from within; a whining, melancholy music. A couple of prostitutes sat outside, and an old man with a hookah puffed opium into the jasmine-scented air. In the window, a tall silhouette moved. *Coleman.*

"Ignore him," Timmy said.

We pressed on.

"He thinks you're beaten," said Timmy, "but he doesn't know that you still have a powerful connection to the past . . . your jade-sense."

We walked . . . rather, we ran, toward the hilly country. As we ran it seemed that our feet left the ground sometimes. It seemed that I was enveloped within mighty, dark wings, which held me close and were somehow comforting.

The night air was warm and moist. It rushed over me. My hair streamed.

The embrace of the vampire held me tight. I had not felt this safe since childhood, wrapped in my father's sheltering arms. I looked down. We were racing toward the jade mountain. My jade-sense was more alive than ever. The whole hillside was thrumming with it. We swerved up toward the silvery moon. We swooped. I had felt this before. I knew it. I recognized it. I had flown before. Without help. Alone.

We reached the market. Deserted now. Guards with AK-47s—soldiers of the insurgent Shan army, perhaps—stood watch, but there was a fiercer protector than they: the spirit of the mountain itself, sitting in a shrine in a niche in the naked rock, a battered wooden image covered in gold leaf and garlands of decaying jasmine. The baskets of boulders were locked away in chests. Some of them had a child or a dog sleeping next to them.

There was the entrance to the cavern of antiquities. Unnoticed, cloaked in Timmy's private darkness, we entered. There were more guards, but we flitted from shadow to shadow. Aluminum shutters covered the private stalls, and the corridors were illuminated only by an occasional cigarette.

We followed the path we had followed before . . . quicker now, since there were no distractions . . . I don't know when we ceased to fly and took on human shape . . . I think we were flitting from form to form . . . the jade-sense seized me totally . . . color and texture whirled around me . . . *she* called out to me . . . *Pauline* . . . *Pauline* . . . only it sounded like some ancient Chinese name . . . *Pui Yi* . . . *Pui Yi* . . . the Empress of Jade was speaking to me, and knew my name, because, because—

"Don't shy away from it!" Timmy cried.

We stood in the innermost cavern now, with the swinging lightbulbs and the bats, and there was the Empress, splayed out on a wooden platform, ready for shipping, and I reached out to touch the texture of the jade with my mind, felt every speck of cinnabar and scar of calcification, felt the deep green and the flecks of bloodred, knew there was real blood, too—

"Do you remember now?" Timmy demanded. "Do you feel, do you see? It wasn't any accident that you ran into me at the charity fundraiser, that you invited me to come on this trip just as I was feeling the need for a week of anonymity. There is someone else inside your skin . . . and that someone else and I have been together before, long ago, a thousand years, two thousand years ago . . . ."

Then it came to me all at once.

I remembered who I was, and why I had come. It was as clear to me as if it had only just happened . . . and in a sense, that was true, for the time spent waiting in my carapace of jade had been a time outside time, a moment that was not a moment.

4

... brightness ... I know it is bright outside because there is a chink in the wall of my litter. I am being carried through the streets of a city. I hardly dare peek through the curtains, but I know the litter bearers are husky and move in a rapid, even rhythm. Beside me sits the woman who has raised me, the woman I call Auntie Chiu.

She is dour today. She rarely smiles, and today she has not smiled at all. I am weighed down by layers of silk and ornaments of jade, bracelets carved with dragons, a ten-piece pectoral ornament that tickles as the litter bearers jog, their leader calling the beat of their running in a monotonous guttural melody. It is a hot day, and I am thirsty, but my aunt doesn't let me drink, because she doesn't want me to ruin my painted lips.

"If the Emperor chooses me—," I begin.

"He will not choose you," says Auntie Chiu, but I know that it is what she hopes for above all things. But to say so would be an ill omen.

I don't think of being chosen. Instead, I daydream about rejection, about returning to my cousin Wei, my true love, who has sworn to become a monk if I am chosen.

... brightness ... it hurts my eyes to step down from the litter, because I have been traveling in it for days, stopping only after dark to sleep in secret places, for it would be calamitous if malicious eyes were to see me. But now, all at once, I face the light ... not only the dazzling brightness of an inner garden, but also the luminescence of the high court of the Son of Heaven. I do not have time to take in the sculpted hedges, the chrysanthemum bushes, the terra-cotta statues of gods and goddesses. On a dais sits a tall, impassive presence with pale skin and white robes, so hung with white jade ornaments that I can hear him tinkling as he waves a languid arm to command that music begin, a raucous jangle of gong, fiddle, and fife. Surely, I think, the emperor. Hastily I begin to make the motions of the prostration, but my aunt, embarrassed, stops me just in time.

"You fool!" she whispers. "Do you think the Son of Heaven would condescend to show you his sacred countenance?"

She indicates a screen behind the tall man's seat, a screen of bronze, jade, and ivory. Though no one sees behind, we all know that it is thence that all power in this garden emanates. Before the screen is an empty throne whose arms are carved in a design of dragons.

I have no way of knowing that this is just a minor court ceremony, a little light entertainment to pass the emperor's time in between more important

---

duties, such as diplomacy or feeding the imperial crocodiles. I've been rigorously trained since I was six years old in case such a moment as this might one day occur. And now I see that there are other litters, too, and other young women stepping from them, and my heart sinks. All are beautiful. All, doubtless, have been trained.

Next to the throne sit a dozen court ladies, tittering, fanning themselves. One by one the tall man calls the girls to the foot of the throne. Most he dismisses in a moment or two. Many are already in tears. At last it is my turn. It is already late afternoon, and slaves are fetching torches. Humbly I inch my way toward the empty throne.

The tall man speaks. His voice is high and pure, and I realize that he is a eunuch. Of course he is . . . men would not be permitted in this inner garden . . . only the Son of Heaven himself. "Your name?" he inquires.

"Pui Yi, Excellency," I say, not daring to meet his gaze, trying to maintain the demure composure that Auntie had taught me. If he is a eunuch, he could be very important. The decision might even be entirely his, for why would the Son of Heaven concern himself with such mundane chores as choosing a bedmate for the night?

"They tell me that you sing," says the tall man.

"I've had a little training, Excellency. My master was quite distinguished in the title role of *The Daughter of the Raven*."

"Impertinence!" he says. "Don't volunteer any information. *Yes* or *no* will suffice."

"Yes, Excellency."

This is already going badly. I can imagine the shame my auntie must be feeling. But then the eunuch claps his hands and says, "We shall see how this pupil of the late Son of Heaven's favorite opera star may perform."

The sun sets. There enters a boy with a *p'ip'a*, a graceful child with luminous white skin and large, hypnotic eyes. Surely he is a slave from one of the legendary empires far to the west. He kneels before the throne and begins to strum his lute. Fascinated, I find myself staring at him . . . silence has fallen. He has done what even the celestial radiance from behind the throne could not do: he has stilled the chatter of the court ladies.

The boy beckons for me to kneel down next to him. His fingers stroke the strings of the *p'ip'a* in a way that reminds me of my many stern lessons in the sensual arts. "Don't be afraid," he says. "Follow my lead. We'll do the song together."

And so, raising his voice, he eases me into the song, which is a well-known ballad about wine, and chrysanthemums, and being drunk on love. My voice is weak, but he supports me. He doesn't seem to breathe at all, but soars effortlessly through the song's convoluted melismata, and soon I'm soaring with him. It's as though I'm being borne on great wings to an eyrie high above the world. I don't think of the Son of Heaven at all . . . only of my penniless cousin Wei, lost in his hopeless fantasy of wedding me. I know that the young boy sees this. He understands me. He, too, has lost something precious . . . which he must mourn forever.

When the last notes die away, the tall pale man seems more displeased than ever. I think to myself: good, at least there will be no more performances . . . I will be assigned some cell in the women's quarters and be forgotten, like the thousand other gifts and tributary objects the emperor receives each year . . . cataloged and shut away to gather dust forever . . .

But no. "You will ready yourself," the tall man says. "Today, fortune smiles upon you, Pui Yi. May Heaven bless your womb."

The audience is over. I am led away. I have not even seen the face of the Son of Heaven, but without uttering a word he has already taken from me my past, my life, my soul.

"More!" cried Timmy Valentine. "Try to remember all of it—"

I was shaking. My hands gripped the breasts of the Empress of Jade. Timmy *was* a vampire, and I had seen him before . . . in another existence . . . as the young musician who understood my loss. Was it a past life of mine, or was I somehow being possessed by this dead woman's spirit?

"Listen," said Timmy.

I did. There were stirrings in the cave of antiquities. I could not tell what time it was, but I knew the vendors would start to set up long before dawn.

I gazed into the thousand scales of jade, still glassy from their millennial interment, saw myself, saw the cicada's compound eyes, the flapping of the crow's wings . . .

Night. I am alone. The bridal chamber is hung with crimson silk and paper lanterns. The bed has been strewn with attar of roses, and I have been dressed, combed, rouged, and painted by a dozen faceless maids. Now I lie in the bed, alone, in a sheer robe, awaiting my fate. It is a large bed, and the reeds are fresh and fragrant.

Time passes.

Presently comes the sound of a sobbing child. Who can it be? One of the imperial children? But they all have nursemaids. The sound does not go away. I keep thinking it is only the wind, but at times there are words.

My curiosity gets the better of me. I get up from the bed. My auntie has always warned me about my curiosity, but am I not a chosen consort of the Son of Heaven? I follow the source of the sound ... opening first one door, then another, growing bolder ... a woman in black banging a jade chime to attract the attention of the Goddess of Mercy ... eunuchs lighting joss sticks ... nobody sees me, and nobody seems to hear the sound of the weeping child ... save I.

At last, sliding open a panel ornamented with a bas-relief of elephants, phoenixes, and tigers, I see the weeping child. He is almost a man, really; he is a little past puberty, but he is dwarfed by the hugeness of the chamber, and by the thronelike chair of ebony inlaid with mother-of-pearl. Sitting at his feet is the young bard with the *p'ip'a,* the boy who sang with me earlier this evening. Incense wafts through the room, which is lit by moonlight from a window that overlooks a pond; the song of frogs and cicadas fills the night air.

The boy-musician sings another song now:

Do not weep, my Lord,
for there will be many days ahead
when you will need those tears;
death, famine, war, destruction, pestilence are waiting.
Rejoice, my Lord, while time remains.

I recognize the song; it is from *The Daughter of the Raven,* and it is the song the raven's daughter sings to her father, knowing that she must sacrifice her life for his in a moving display of filial piety.

It is a strange choice for a song with which to cheer a weeping child, but in this chamber, where we are dwarfed by crimson columns and statues of beasts and bearded men, where a white jade *bi* hangs above the throne like an artificial sun, it does not seem out of place.

"This is the girl I was telling you about," says the boy singer.

"She seems very sweet, Musician," says the child.

"But she is sad, too, Little Newt," says the musician.

"There's no reason to be sad here," says the child. "Here they have everything ... picture books, flowers, delicious candies. I'm the only one who is allowed to be sad."

"My life isn't my own," I say.

"Does that pain you?"

"I am told," I say, "that I have been selected for the highest honor a woman can attain. But sometimes I think of a man I left behind, who now must enter a monastery ... Have you ever left something behind? Is there someone who weeps for what you might have been?"

"There are so many things," says Little Newt. "If only I could tell someone—"

"You can tell me if you like."

"I'm afraid. I'm only a puppet. A pale, tall man is pulling all the strings." He comes down from his throne and he embraces me . . . He kisses me gently on the lips . . . there is a disturbing sensuality to his kisses, as though I were more to him than a woman intercepted by chance on her wedding-night . . .

And now we are both sobbing disconsolately, and it dawns on me that this is no ordinary child . . . even though the musician addressed him with no honorifics . . . even though he has spoken to me as a boy might speak to an elder sister . . . yes, a pale, tall man has been pulling all our strings. He is as helpless as I! He is only a boy, and he, too, is a prisoner in a gilded cage—

"Your Majesty!" I cry out at last, and hasten to perform the proper prostration. But before my head strikes the floor—

A wild-eyed man has thrust open the door and comes running with a dagger in his hand.

"I can't bear it, Pui Yi!" he screams. "I can't let you be taken by another—"

"Cousin Wei!" I shout. He throws himself at the emperor, but instantly the chamber fills with guards. Cousin Wei does not even finish his utterance. His head lies at the emperor's feet, and blood gushes from his neck stump as his headless body flounders and collapses. We are drenched in blood, yet the entire scene of violence cannot have lasted more than a minute.

I am numb. I finish my prostration, hitting my head three times on the slippery floor. The guards are already wiping the marble clean and spiriting away the corpse . . . I barely have time to understand that this was a man who loved me, who died in a hopeless attempt to possess me.

When I look up from my kowtow, it is as though nothing has happened at all. Little Newt is still seated at the foot of his throne. But on the throne itself sits the real power . . . the tall, pale man with the empty eyes.

"General Zo," the emperor says softly. It amazes me that a eunuch may be called *general,* but no one can question his power.

"You did well, Your Imperial Majesty," he says, and I can see that his formal obsequiousness conceals an absolute disdain. "The plot to overthrow you is utterly crushed."

"There was no plot," I cry. "There was a man. He loved me. It was stupid of him. He has been killed."

"Silence, woman!" says the general. "Your kind never ceases to astound me. How long did you and that cousin of yours plot? Which of His Majesty's ousted half brothers financed your plan?"

I am trapped. I know he must have overheard my entire conversation with the emperor . . . heard me speak to him coarsely, as a girl to a younger brother . . . heard me confess of another love, another life . . . and all these things *are* treason . . . all are capital offenses.

"Your Majesty, it remains only for you to sign this." He pulls a lengthy scroll from his capacious sleeve.

"What is it?"

"The execution order for this rebel," says General Zo. He pushes me down into a posture of submission with his foot.

"Help me, Little Newt," I gasp.

The emperor clears his throat. In the moonlight, I can see fresh tears springing to his eyes. "Are you sure, General," he stutters, "that she is a rebel? Do you think she might be just . . . an innocent, lost amid things she cannot comprehend?"

The general laughs. It is the laughter of all mad villains, the laughter of pure evil. "Of course she's an innocent," he says. "How else could she have been duped into betraying you? Sign, Your Majesty."

He signs. He has no choice. We are all pawns. But, I think to myself, whose pawn is General Zo?

"I am sorry for you, Pui Yi," the general says, as he pockets the scroll and summons the guards to drag me hence. "You thought you would be an empress, didn't you? And you will be an empress, though your domain will consist only of jade."

Defiance is all I have left. I know there can be no countermanding of an emperor's signature. The will of heaven is immutable. "May you live," I scream at the general, "until I find a way back from the grave to wreak vengeance."

"What kind of a curse is that?" the general laughs. "You have just condemned me to eternal life!"

As they lead me away, I hear the musician break once more into the lament of the raven's daughter, and I know that the Son of Heaven still weeps.

It is a terrible execution. It is not an execution at all. They do not kill me. They condemn me to everlasting torment.

To still the voice that sang so seductively, they slice away my tongue. They cut me in a thousand places, with such exquisite cunning that every nerve is exposed yet the blood still runs true and I cannot lose consciousness. Then, as I lie on a marble table in the executioner's chamber, unable to scream, they begin to prepare me for living burial.

Two jade pigs they cram into my fists, and plugs of jade they stuff into all the orifices of my body. Almond-shaped jades cover my eyes. At last comes the jade cicada, symbol of rebirth . . . now it replaces my tongue, a cold hard thing that grates against my teeth and pushes the back of my throat so that my gorge rises, only I am too weak, too drained to vomit. Now, with excruciating slowness, they begin to sew the jade platelets over my body, sealing in my soul. Each sliver of jade rubs the raw flesh and makes my nerves scream out anew. Each time the needle with the spun gold stitches one jade scale to the next, the sharp edge pinches my flesh. In my mouth, the jade cicada begins to suck the life from me, a larva wriggling in its stony casing. This anguish goes on day after day . . . it is a sacred process, and ritual must be followed precisely, for though I am a traitor I cannot be summarily killed like a common criminal . . . I am also a consort of heaven, whose life and death must reenact the cycles of earth and sky.

Once set in motion, the procedures of my execution are painstakingly prescribed. Entombment, too, is a lengthy process, with interminable rituals to go through. How much better to be dead! By the time I am to be buried, I am sure that the people at court have quite forgotten me. I suppose I have already gone mad by then; so much pain, and the life-preserving quality of the jade always keeping me at the fringe of consciousness, never finding oblivion. But in the end, someone does come to visit me.

I sense his presence through the searing pain. He has brought his *p'ip'a* with him. I am already in the burial chamber—he must have funneled in through some tiny crack or chink from the world outside—but when the music begins I am in a different place. The music soothes me a little, stops me from choking on the cicada crammed into my mouth, even sets my jade suit to chiming in sympathetic vibration.

"Your curse," says the young singer, whose name I have never learned, "will come to pass. I've made sure of it. The jade will not make you immortal . . . that is a myth . . . I, who am a myth made flesh, understand above all the emptiness of myths. But your anger is stronger than jade. It may be stronger than death. Vengeance is as old as mankind itself. I know. I've heard that vengeance comes in the form of a crow . . . perhaps that is why you have learned to sing the song of the raven's daughter so poignantly. I have a power, Pui Yi . . . for you must know by now that I am no boy, but a creature of an ancient time, one who preys upon mortals . . . and I have used my power on General Zo. He will die but not die. And there will come a day when you and I will stand together, and you will battle the dragon, and the treasure you both seek will be your soul."

The musician touches the jade that envelopes my face. I know he does not weep—his kind cannot, though they can bring tears to the eyes of mortals—and he adds, "And Little Newt says he is sorry he could not say good-bye."

5

Only an instant had passed. I knew why I had come. "You made General Zo a vampire," I said to Timmy.

"Yes."

"David Coleman is General Zo."

"The secret of your resting place was well hidden, Pauline. But with all those burial grounds being dug up to make foundations for new shopping malls in China—"

"I see," I said.

I also understood why it had taken me so long to learn to speak, and why confronting Coleman brought back my childhood stammering . . .

More noise now. I took Timmy's hand, and together we merged into the nearest shadows. Uncle Chang had come into the chamber, and he had workmen with him, with tools and lumber.

"Box it all up, la," he shouted at the workmen. "San Francisco museum. Letter of credit. Finally, I retire!"

Bright lights now. Coleman was nowhere to be found. Perhaps he was more sensitive to daylight than Timmy . . . perhaps he was sleeping, gorged with the blood of some peasant prostitute, in a coffin in the basement of the Hilton.

I wanted to stop the workmen, cling to the jade suit that held my lost soul, but Timmy held me back. *There is another way,* he said. He spoke not in words but in a language of night, of the movement of ripples in the pools of shadow. He held me to him in a close and dark embrace. I understood him. I let myself meld into him. He flowed over me, and together, as a stream of shadow, we trickled toward the crate they were building around the Empress of Jade.

The coolies were pounding in the nails. We ran past them, noticed only as a momentary flicker, a sudden chill. Slid into the makeshift coffin through the micro-thin slits between the boards. In darkness now, taking up no space at all, for the Empress of Jade was the world.

"In the end," Timmy said to me, "it'll be like the last time. This is between you and the general. I'll only be able to watch."

"I know," I said.

I wrapped myself around the woman of jade. My ancient self, still trapped within, still frozen in her timeless agony, called out to me through her epidermis of chill green stone. It was time for soul and body to come together. I sank into myself and became one once again. And awoke to the echoing pain and rage.

In a corner of the packing crate, shrunk to the size of a rodent, Timmy, too, waited.

In time, I felt motion. This, then, was why Timmy had wanted me to ship everything home early. I was to go on a different journey. I made my mind very still. Now and then, I heard the lilting music of some ancient lullaby, and knew that Timmy was doing what he could to soothe my torment.

There was a journey by oxcart, I think, from the bumpiness of it and the constant lowing of cattle. Then a truck. At length, a much smoother ride—we must have reached the cross-country highways of Thailand.

Then many days of stillness. A warehouse, perhaps. Searing heat—my jade carapace sucked fire and moisture from the air, inflaming my rage and pain.

Then, finally, more motion. Eased onto another truck. Stop-and-go . . . jerky moves back and forth . . . clearly, we were now bouncing our way through the legendary traffic jams of Bangkok.

And then, finally, the pounding of hammer and crowbar, and I found myself once more on display.

6

I dreamed . . .

In my dream, I dreamed . . .

I dreamed that I woke from the nightmare, that I fled into my parents' room . . . my mother still alive then, her arms wrapped around my baby brother, never waking . . . my father holding me . . .

And Cousin Wei, too, holding me on the day they told me I was to be sent to court . . .

My father is holding me. I am the cicada bursting from the earth. I am the crow of vengeance. I am a weeping child. In my dream I cry out to him, "Dad, Dad, they tell me you're a bad man, because of you junkies die in the streets—"

My father lies on his sick bed. My hand is on the Demerol button. He groans. The IV tube sways in the wind from an open window. The walls are lined with artifacts. And suddenly there are tubes everywhere, catheters, stethoscopes, wires, and they are jerking my dad into the air and they are not medical tubes at all but puppet strings, and my father is suspended above the bed and his arms and legs are wriggling and his lips open and close to the snap of a marionette string, and he cries, "Good and evil are just parts in a play . . . we're just acting out . . . for ever and ever . . ."

And I see that what is to come was writ millennia ago, and I'm destined to act it out, no matter that I've lived a hundred lifetimes in a hundred bodies.

"Why me?" I cry. It's a question others like me have always screamed out, despairing, since the dawn of humankind.

My father's body dances. He is an empty shell of jade. He has lost his soul. And I can give it back to him . . . at the cost of my own . . . yes. Like the raven's daughter in that ancient Chinese opera.

Suddenly I see my mother's coffin flying back up from the earth and the cicada bursting from its chrysalis and above it all, wheeling, crystal-eyed, the black-winged messenger of death—

One by one the scales of the dragon shatter like—
Shards of jade and—

Neon. I hadn't expected that. I'm lying on a marble plinth, I think. The neon is overhead, flashing in garish hues of pink and turquoise. The jade skin is welded to my flesh, it has become my skin, the almond-shaped jades over my eyes are lenses through which I see level after level, rainbow-diffracted, escalators, elevators, crystal, glass . . . Jesus Christ, I think to myself, I'm in a fucking *shopping mall*.

No people, though. It's night but my senses are sharp because I perceive everything through my jade skin. The neon is flashing, and I make out words: ARMANI • VERSACE • TOWER RECORDS • CYBERCAFÉ. This is a shopping mall then. In Bangkok, a new shopping mall goes up almost every five minutes. Bangkok is the new mecca of consumer vulgarity. So this is where the Empress of Jade has ended up . . . as a centerpiece in a shopping mall! So much for Coleman's pretensions to being some kind of museum curator!

Timmy, where are you? I cry out. It's the language of night, of course. And now I see him. On a landing atop a marble stairway, seated at a white grand piano, wearing his trademark Dracula cape, the one he does his concerts in.

There's nothing I can do, Timmy responds. *I am only a watcher. This is not my dream. I'm here to complete the picture, just as I was with you when these events were set in motion.*

He starts to play. Not a piece of music, but a kind of meditation on music, different motifs weaving in and out, sometimes a burst of singing, a half-formed melodic fragment. This is not a music designed to bring me peace. It is uneasy listening. The dissonances grate on my jade scales. It's a chaotic music . . . a music pregnant with the pain of rebirth.

As the music dies away, I know that David Coleman has entered the atrium where I lie behind glass, in a recreated model of my tomb. I see him now, but I'm not yet ready to reveal myself.

I can hear his footsteps echoing on marble. He wears a black Armani suit and a yellow "power" tie. He is carrying a briefcase. I hear ticking. A bomb. I do not move. I reach out with my heightened jade-sense, and I see him through a veil of green, his eyes still shielded by mirrors. What now? Has he gone from grand vizier to museum curator to pyrotechnician? I wait.

Timmy is coming down the escalator. His cape is fluttering behind him—it must be the air-conditioning—and his hair is wild.

David Coleman holds out a crucifix.

"Not this time, General Zo," Timmy says softly. They confront one another. Timmy touches the crucifix and it shatters. "I'm prepared this time, and you know that superstitions are losing their power."

"This is none of your affair," says Coleman.

"I know," says Timmy. "I'm just a thing in Pauline's dream, a watcher, an explicator. After all, we've reached the comic-book moment when the villain must reveal his dastardly plan . . . and you need someone to reveal it to."

Coleman laughs. "It's all a big cosmic joke, isn't it?" he says. "I don't even know why we go through the motions."

"We're vampires, you and I—we can afford to take the long view. But why are you about to blow up this spanking new mall, which has its grand opening tomorrow, complete with stunning jade exhibition on its way to the San Francisco collection?"

"You know as well as I do that the jade suit must be neutralized. I've searched for almost two millennia for Pui Yi's resting place. After you made her curse come true, I've wandered the earth in torment."

"Believe me," says Timmy, "I understand. But blowing up the shopping mall?"

"Just a little side job—you know, the usual corrupt bureaucracy, crony deals with insurance companies, insider trading, stocks about to fall—all the banalities of villainy."

"All right then. I'll go back to providing the soundtrack, and leave the two of you to duke it out, good versus evil, the whole cosmic shebang."

Timmy turns, goes back up the escalator, sits back down at the keyboard, begins, improbably, a New Age rendition of "Melancholy Baby."

David Coleman unlocks the glass portal. He stands inside the mockup of my tomb. He surveys the scene with a kind of pride. As, indeed, he ought to. The simulacrum is excellent. As he sees each object, I, too, with my jade-sense, see what he sees, and it fuels my rage.

There are the terra-cotta statues of my entire family—poor Auntie Chiu never knew what hit her—all were quietly decapitated and their bodies thrown into the river, but the grave of a royal consort must contain the full complement of relatives and hangers-on, and so they are all there in miniature. There are valuable items, too, bronze vessels, an enormous jade 'tsong, a basket of carved bi, a whole menagerie of jade beasts, both real and mythical.

Coleman sets to work. He opens the briefcase, sets the timer, carefully places it beneath the marble plinth so that I will be incinerated.

"Time to die, my little concubine," he says softly.

He looks down at me. Who does he see, Sleeping Beauty?

"I wanted you," he says. "Why should Little Newt be the one to fill you with his seed?"

A song rings out from the landing above us:

Do not weep, my Lord ...
death, famine, war, destruction, pestilence are waiting.
Rejoice, my Lord, while time remains.

He puts his arms around me—scaly, anguished woman encased in stone—and with exquisite tenderness he kisses my jade lips. I feel his tongue through the sliver of cold stone, feel it vibrate against the jade cicada, feel the final surge of fury that propels me back from the shadowland—

I am changing. My flayed flesh bonds to the jade. I stretch out my arms.

"Magnificent!" says General Zo. He loosens his tie. Is he afraid of nothing? I feel his hand shoving hard against my pubic region, ripping at the frayed flaps of skin, forcing my millennial blood to well up ...

I sit up. Blood is oozing from between my scales of jade. Tears of blood are running from my blank green eyes. The general throws his jacket on the marble floor.

"If only you could sing to me," he muses. "But you can't anymore, can you?"

I want to scream but now, as in my childhood, I cannot. The cicada clamps my vocal cords tight.

He unbuckles his belt. What is he thinking of? Is he not a eunuch? How can a eunuch love any woman, let alone a corpse encased in stone?

But no. He is not about to rape me. He is changing. Growing. His teeth are lengthening. He shakes his head and his mirror shades fly across the tomb. His eyes are mirrors, too, and in those mirrors I see—

No. I, too, am changing. Black feathers are erupting from the jade. Great wings are sprouting. The general spreads his arms and he, too, has wings, leathern, scaly wings, and his forehead flattens into a reptile's, and his nose elongates and breathes out brimstone—

He rips into my side with a claw. But the jade holds firm ... The blood congeals and scabs over and binds the carapace harder.

The raven wheels above, flitting from level to level of the shopping mall, shrieking death. I fly at the dragon. I batter him with my beak. I curl into a ball as his flames roar over me. The glass that encases the exhibition melts. The odor of burning sulfur is nauseating, but I cannot vomit. The jade cicada is a lump in my throat, choking off my voice, tethering me to the land of the dead ...

A full-scale dragon now, he rears up, claws on the balcony above, pulls himself to the next floor, smashes the glass panes of a fashion store, slams his tail into a Tower Records sign, which explodes in neon sparks. I run after him ... and suddenly I am aloft, a soaring chimera of soul and stone ... I dart toward his eyes, I jab at them with my beak, a foul blue acid spurts from them and fountains over the marble floors, which fizz and hiss and dissolve . . . I, the guileless girl with the voice of an angel, I have become the avenger, returning evil for evil . . . rending the flesh from the cheekbones . . . and still he flies, higher, higher, toward the garish cupola of this cathedral of commerce, a painted sky of electric constellations that spell out SONY PANASONIC JVC . . . Blinded, he smashes against that ceiling, and the signs short out and the constellations blink and sizzle . . .

The dragon plummets, flailing. I dive after him. He smashes down on the dais where my body lay before. The statues of my ancestors shatter and dust flies up in the wind of the dragon's breath.

And finally, wounded, he speaks to me. My talons are deep in his flesh. Our blood gushes like lava, searing all it touches. "Pui Yi," he says, "why are you killing me? I *want* to die. What kind of revenge is it . . . to end my torment . . . to set me free?" I become angrier. I almost speak, but the cicada clogs my throat still.

I see my puppet father jerking up and down on his strings . . . I see the boy emperor, helpless, manipulated . . . I see myself. What kind of a choice is this? No choice at all. To avenge myself is also to fulfill my enemy's desire. My strings have been pulled. A terrible despair wells up. I will burst.

"Do you think I am a bad man?" I look into the dragon's eyes, and I don't see the enemy. I see my father. "You think I'm evil because I profit from the suffering of junkies and throwaway children?" A fuming tear rolls down his gnarly cheek, and I see that he, too, is carapaced in jade, he, too, is bound up inside an identity of stone. And the death-embrace we share is also a moment of tenderness. The coupling of lovers. The comforting hug of a father and child.

At last, the welter of emotion dislodges the cicada inside me. I feel it move, I feel it stir to life, feel the wriggling of protoplasm beneath its stone meniscus. It writhes behind my lips like an unwelcome penis. I feel its wings emerge. The insect legs gouge my cheeks and uvula. Slime oozes from the jade. At last, my lips are pried apart by the cicada's steely forelegs and my mouth rips open in a scream of unendurable anguish, and the cicada bursts forth, tearing my face wide open.

"Perhaps I came to destroy you," I say, "perhaps to release you. The cosmos is a grand eternal symphony, and good and evil are just the little dissonances and resolutions that propel the song to its end which is also its beginning. In the end it's not important which side we are on. Our destiny is to dance together, black and white, man and woman, good and evil, light and shadow, life and death. We have to believe in good and evil . . . because . . . if we start to veer from this world of absolute truths . . . then what are we? We are nothing, and where once stood God, there is only emptiness. The dance of good and evil is the magic that holds together the illusion that is reality."

This is the awful truth that I have learned, the truth in the eyes of the dragon. I am free to forgive General Zo. I am free to love my father, even though he is not a good man. I see that a vampire, child of darkness, can be a harbinger of light. The scales of jade have fallen from my eyes.

I love myself. It is a bitter love, but true.

The cicada settles on the dragon's face and methodically begins to eat away at the flesh. I have a tongue again. My voice doesn't get swallowed up in my throat like a lump of lead. I can speak. I can sing.

The dragon is dissolving as the cicada devours it, sucking in blood and flesh and scales of jade. The cicada grows with every bite, molting, shedding its crystal carapaces, growing, growing until it has engulfed the dragon and seemingly the world . . .

And, as the young musician vampire plucks the plangent melody out on his *p'ip'a,* I sing the last words of the song of the raven's daughter:

Rejoice, my father, while you still have time;
Rejoice, rejoice.

Then the bomb goes off, and the shopping mall crumbles in a flash that barely goes noticed in Bangkok's noisy neon night.

7

I watched the explosion on CNN, in my father's sick room, in San Francisco, and so I knew that I had not dreamed everything. A brand new mall had collapsed before its opening, crushing the jade exhibit smuggled in from China. No mention of a bomb, though. Faulty structure . . . complaints about the unregulated building boom . . . heads were rolling, but nobody believed they were the right heads. David Coleman, respected archaeologist, Indiana Jones sort of reputation, reportedly killed. No one else.

There was a crow perched on the window sill.

"The Empress of Jade was crushed to smithereens, Dad," I said. "This was all I could bring back."

I put the cicada in his hand. Translucent white jade, carved in that stylized, almost postmodernist style that characterized the western Han dynasty. The flawlessness of it set off my jade-sense. A shudder ran through me. A cold thing, a thing of severe, uncompromising beauty.

"I've not been a good man," my father said.

"I know," I said, and I embraced him, frail and shriveled, a ghost before dying; I wept. "It doesn't matter," I said. "No regrets now, Daddy."

"This is beautiful," my father said, holding the jade cicada up to the dying light. The crow flapped its wings. It looked at me with the eyes of a young boy. "This is absolute," my father said. "When I die, put it in my mouth. Perhaps it will speak for me in the afterworld."

"Yes."

"Now, Pauline," he said, sighing deeply, "maybe you'll bring yourself to tell me that you love me."

I did not stammer. I did not stutter. For the first time in my life, the truth did not stick in my throat.

Timmy Valentine has a hit single out. The song in the music video is "Crucify Me Twice," and it's got all the typical neo-Gothic tropes—it's Nine Inch Nails for the *latte* crowd, with whipped cream and brown sugar on top. But there's a second song, too—a bonus track—a weird, whiny Chinese melody that's supposed to be two thousand years old. I don't see much of Timmy, but he has a habit of leaving private notes in the most public places.

The Enquirer pointed out that when you play that track backwards, it says, "Pauline, Pauline." Thus, I have been "romantically linked" to Timmy, although it's bullshit, of course; vampires and humans just don't, you know.

I'll have to look him up soon. Apparently there's an underground jade market opening up in Yunnan, where a huge Neolithic burial site's turned up where they were going to put in a new stadium. Maybe Timmy will feel the need to get away again.

Vampires, after all, can be your friends . . .

Jesus Christ's Wrists

James O'Barr

I need an empty face so that I can
Paint you
   I'd put wire around my neck to
Prove my love for you
   I'd cut my arms, Valentine, yes, I'd do
That too
   I want Jesus Christ's wrists
I need to double check the lists
For any angels that are due
   I'd suffer this all for eyes
That are true
   Eyes that are blue like a
Moonrise hue
   I want Jesus Christ's wrists
I need to run down the lists
For any angels that I missed
   I need skin so white that light
Passes through
   A barbed wire crown for the
Monsters that I slew
   Iron nails in my wrists and my
Ankles, too

Sector E was by far the quietest section of the hospital. In Sector E nurses tiptoed unconsciously, physicians whispered even when they were confident—especially when they were confident—and normally boisterous janitors spoke little while keeping their Walkmans cranked to the point of pain. In Sector E there was not to be found a speck of dust, not a smidgen of smudged newsprint, not an afterthought of the casually overlooked. Sector E was pure, immaculate, unsullied. Everyone who worked there wanted it that way. Not for themselves, but for the patients who were consigned to E Sector.

That's because Sector E was the Last Stop, the Ultimo Resting Place, the Amphitheater of Final Breaths, the Terminus of the Terminal. It was where those who had sunk beyond the pale of modern medical science were brought to respire one last time. It was a zone for dying, as scrubbed and impeccable as the hospital employees could make it. There were no cigarette butts crushed into covings, no abandoned magazines disporting slickness brilliant with life, no helpless hollow gestures of machine-picked flowers slowly desiccating in cheap, throwaway vases.

There should not have been a bird there, either. But there was.

Black as the night outside. Black eyes guided it down the deserted corridor, black blood flowed through its veins, and black bird-thoughts drove it inexorably onward. It flew on wings more silent than the air they barely disturbed, and it made not a sound.

Nor did the man gliding along the overpolished floor behind it.

He was a large man, but his build was not athletic. Alive, he would have wheezed and puffed with the effort required to keep up with the bird. Dead, he moved swiftly and with a grace that had been denied him in life. All in black he was clad, with a face dusted white by the Follies-Bergere of the Afterness. Black streaks scored his cheeks and lips as if they had been scorched by flaming tears.

The crow paused briefly outside a door. It looked at the following man out of emotionless bird-eyes, then turned and flew off down the hall. Flew away, not through a window, but through a wall, and was gone.

The man, whose name in life had been Harry Harper, paused outside the door. Expecting to encounter a guard, he was pleased there was none. The omission surprised him, but he did not let his surprise overcome the other emotion that seethed through him. Instead, he imagined a tingle of presentiment coursing through his entire body. Imagined it, because he could no longer actually feel. That was good, he reflected, because it would help him in what he was about to do. At first he had not been sure he was capable of it, but the nearer he came to the desired but unsought fulfillment, the greater his anticipation had become. By now his blood would have been boiling—had he had any.

Reaching down, he pushed gently on the handle. The door opened inward, silent on heavy hinges, to reveal a private hospital room lit by a single indirect overhead fluorescent and the screens of monitoring equipment. Like so many somnolent nonhumanoid robots, these surrounded a bed. In the bed lay a patient. The tangled artificial viscera of transparent plastic tubing ran from hard bottles and limp bags and inexplicable medical devices to the lumpy shape beneath the sheets.

As soon as he saw the body lying in the bed, the last of Harry Harper's uncertainty fled. He knew now that he could do what he had been brought back to do, that he was capable of fulfilling that which had been signed upon him. In life he could never even have contemplated the act. Being dead freed not only the soul, it seemed, but the emotions. Raising his hands, which were large and heavy, he moved toward the hospital bed, silent as the wraith he had become.

He could strangle the figure, he thought. Patiently, watching its hands flail helplessly at his own, observing the bulge of the eyes as they slowly emerged from the skull. Or he could dismember it, starting with the tongue so the figure could not cry out, then removing assorted appendages and body parts, keeping the body alive as long as possible. The more he contemplated methodology, the more he found himself looking forward to it.

The shape in the bed did not move. It couldn't. He decided he would have to wake it first. He badly wanted it to see him, to recognize the face of Harry Harper come back from the dead, to know the identity of its avenging assassin. As he loomed over the bed he saw this would not be necessary. The figure was already awake. Eyes turned to stare up at him as he leaned close. His fingers twitched anxiously, expectantly.

The emaciated human outline lying in the bed was thirteen but looked nine. Muscle and flesh had wasted away, gnawed and devoured from within by an immutable avalanche of cells gone berserk. In the face of such a violent internal onslaught by a body that had chosen to cannibalize itself, medical science could only do so much.

The shade of Harry Harper hovered. Massive hands hesitated. Expecting to find himself gazing down upon the scum-sucking, obscene, sadistic visage of Carl Sipowicz, age twenty-four, noted mugger, rapist, car-jacker, child molester, and soon-to-be-convicted multiple murderer, he found himself staring instead at the wan facade of a much younger man. No, he corrected himself—a boy.

Bewildered, he moved around to the foot of the bed. The gaunt torso beneath the sheets laboriously tracked his movements with its eyes. Attached to the foot of the bed was a chart, and on the chart was a name, and information. Together they did not make an explanation.

James Wilsonia Lee. Age thirteen. Diagnosis: lymphatic cancer. Prognosis: terminal.

There was more, but given what he had already read anything else seemed superfluous in the extreme. Harper put the chart down and glanced sharply toward the door. Nothing moved there, and more importantly, nothing hovered. No black wings stirred, no obsidian eyes stared. It was impossible, and it was absurd. It was also indubitably so.

The crow had made a mistake.

"Mister?"

Harper thought purposefully. If Sipowicz was not here, then it followed that he had to be someplace else. Most likely, someplace else in the hospital. He sure as hell wasn't going anywhere soon. Not with the two bullets Harper had pumped into him before Sipowicz had blown the top of his antagonist's head off. The memory of that final confrontation slashed through Harper's thoughts like a paper cut across the brain.

Another room. Staff had moved Sipowicz to another room. That was why there had been no guard outside the door to this one. The filthy bastard was going to recover, Harper knew. It was why *he* was here. Why he had been brought back from the land of the dead. To make sure that Carl Sipowicz did not cheat his deserved rewards. To make sure that he did not recover to torment and torture anyone else.

Yes, there had been a mistake. But hardly an insoluble one. Perhaps Sipowicz lay in a bed just across the way, or down the hall. Harper would find him. The respite was momentary, that was all. He started for the door.

"Mister . . ."

The voice that floated up from the bed was less than a croak. There wasn't much left of it, just as there wasn't much left of the boy it emerged from. Harper wavered, his hands balling into fists. Revenge sucked at him, nagged at his anguished soul with insistent little teeth. He was a chariot yoked to the steeds of death, and they were pulling at him.

The enervated utterance that had risen so feebly from the bed was elevated on a sea of pain. Fighting the urgency that had brought him back, he turned toward it.

Limpid eyes gazed up at him. Like invading parasites grown bloated, tubes attached to large needles pierced the boy's neck and chest. Another thrust up one nostril, plunging down into lungs that were more like flaccid sacs than efficient bellows. Other hoses vanished none too discreetly beneath the sheets, entering the boy's body God knew where.

"They just moved you to this room, didn't they, Jimmy?"

The boy tried to speak; failed and could only nod.

"You have cancer. You're dying." Harper's voice was flat, straightforward. There was no reason for the dead to lie. "You know that, don't you?"

Again, the nod.

Harper glanced longingly toward the door. "I have to go. I'm sorry for you and your parents."

Again the voice rose from the bed, small dry lips struggling with the weight of the air. "I don't have any parents. They died last year, in a crash on the freeway."

Jesus, Harper thought tightly. Compassion squeezed him. How fair is life. Well, tough. He had another to deal with.

"Mister—thank you."

The malignant allure of the open doorway was equaled by the pull of the debilitated voice from the bed. Harper felt himself caught between life and death. Both clung to him mercilessly.

"For what?" The small, shrunken eyes were blue, Harper noted. Washed out, pale, but still blue, still flush with the guilelessness of youth.

"For talking to me. Nobody wants to talk to me anymore. They say I'll be dead by tomorrow night. I know they're right. I can feel it—inside. But I still like to talk, while I can. I like life, Mister."

"So did I, Jimmy. So did I." Rage boiled, frothed within him, leaving little room for anything else.

"What happened to you? Was it cancer, like me?"

"Yes, Jimmy. A different kind of cancer. One that walks on two legs. One that calls itself Carl Sipowicz." Again the memories, the fiery remembrances, lancing through every aspect of his being.

"He came into my house, Jimmy. Sometimes I had to work late. I'm a— I was a pharmacist. When I came home that night I saw the front door was open and I knew something was wrong. So I went back to my car and got my gun. Because of my job, I had access to things other people wanted. Medicines. Sometimes they wanted what they couldn't have, and so I thought it would be a good idea to carry a gun." His voice was tense, controlled. There was nothing he could do about what had happened except tell it.

"The house had been ransacked, torn upside down. On the stairs I found Steven. Steven was my son. He was six years old. He was lying with his feet facing up the stairs and his head facing down. His throat had been cut and all the blood had run out down the stairs. There seemed to be an awful lot of blood for such a small boy. I started to shake then, Jimmy, but I kept going.

"On top of the landing I found Melody. Melody was a little older than you, Jimmy. She was dead, too, and I won't tell you what had been done to her." Black tears coalesced in the corners of the dead man's eyes, began to spill slowly down white cheeks.

"My wife's name was Mary-Ann. She wasn't an especially pretty woman, but to me she was more beautiful than any movie star. She was on the bed, our bed, and this man, this thing, this cancer named Carl Sipowicz, was on top of her. He had a gun in one hand and a knife in the other, and he was doing—things. Doing them even though Mary-Ann was already dead. I thought her eyes were looking at me, but now I know they weren't looking at anything. They were just open.

"I must have made some kind of noise, I don't remember what, because he turned. I won't try to describe the look that was on his face. I'm not sure I could. I never was very good with words. Anyway, I shot him. I don't remember doing it, but I'm sure it was me because there was nobody else in the room. I shot him twice, but he was a very strong man, physically. He raised his gun, and he must have shot me, because I remember a quick moment of the world exploding, and then nothing. Nothing for what seemed like a long time." He lowered his eyes to the bed.

"Now I'm back, I'm here, and I'm going to kill him. With my own two hands."

The boy in the bed could not really nod, but his neck and head seemed to twitch ever so slightly. His eyes closed, as if the simple effort required to keep them open had exhausted him.

"I'm sorry for what happened to you, Mister. Thank—thank you for talking to me. I'll remember you doing it, in case it's the last time."

Expressionless, the dead man turned away. In another room nearby, Sipowicz lay sleeping. Drugged, most likely, to mute the pain while he recovered from his gunshot wounds. The wounds the agonized pharmacist had inflicted. Harper could smell him, could perceive the residence of sedated violence. When he was well enough Sipowicz would be tried, and possibly convicted, and maybe let out early for good behavior. Only that would never happen. Harper was there to make sure it never happened.

He would execute the murderer. Dispense the justice that had been delayed. Remove the cancer.

The cancer. Remove.

On the bed the boy lay silent, eyes shut, kept alive a little longer by tubes and the genetically programmed reluctance of the body to surrender to the

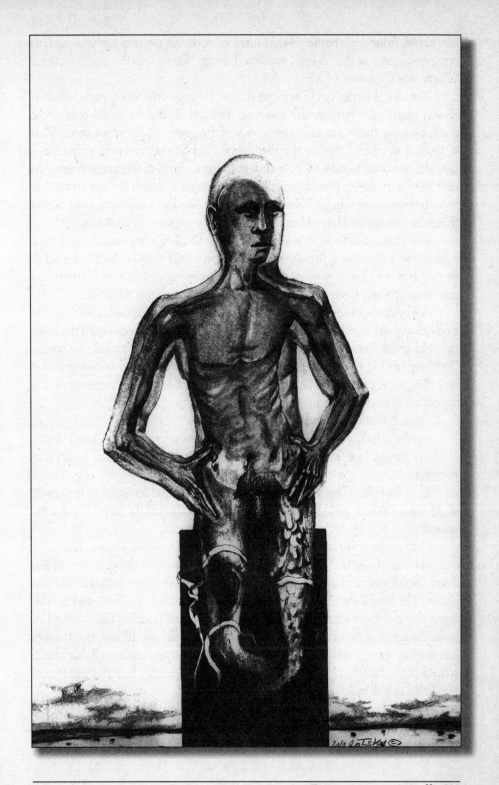

inevitable. Jimmy, his name was. Jimmy Lee. Lost his parents last year and his compensation was this. A curt, saddened dying. Where was the justice in that? Where was the sense of it?

Remove. Harper could remove things. Tongue, eyes, body parts, whatever was required, whatever the moment demanded. But he could only do so once, because there was only one who was the object of his vengeance. What if, instead of dismembering the loathsome Carl Sipowicz slowly, a piece at a time, he removed him *all*? Whole soul and entire, down to the tiniest fragments that went to make up that abominable Self? Would that not, for just an instant, leave only an empty shell? A shell that could be filled by something else? Something the specter of Harry Harper might also be capable of removing?

No. It was madness, it was insane. What kind of a life would that be for a sensitive child, for a Jimmy Lee unaware of and unexposed to the adult world? It would mean a swap from dying to a living death. He, Harper, had not been brought back to interfere or to judge, but simply to render.

And yet, there was a poetry to it, to the thought of Sipowicz trapped for a few final pain-wracked hours in the cancer-riven mass of a doomed thirteen-year-old child. Unable to move, in a few hours doubtless unable to speak. Watching his life bleed away through inert plastic tubing and knowing that it was the shade of Harry Harper that was responsible for it. A revenge most appropriate, and utterly unique.

Only, it was not his decision to make.

Softly inhaling death and decay, he leaned over the wasted form. "Jimmy? Jimmy Lee, can you hear me? If you can hear me, Jimmy Lee, open your eyes."

Lids fluttered. The boy made an effort, and the great weight of the small, slight eyelids retracted. Behind the pale blue, life still lingered. And consciousness.

"Jimmy, listen to me. I am not—an ordinary person anymore. There are certain things I can do." Dark eyes flicked calculatingly in the direction of the door. "Somewhere close to here, in another room, is the evil man I told you about. The one I shot. But not fatally. He will recover, and live, and maybe some day do more terrible things to other innocent people. That's why I'm here. To see that that doesn't happen. I came to kill him, Jimmy, but maybe, just maybe, there's something else I can do." He canted closer still, his black-scored white face hovering inches from the boy's. Jimmy Lee did not flinch. He could not if he had wanted to.

"I think I can pull him out of his body, Jimmy, and you out of yours. Pull you both out and switch you. He'll be in your body, this one, the one that's dying. And you'll be in his. It's a powerful body, Jimmy. Big, and healthy, and adult. You'll live.

"But understand, you'll live as Carl Sipowicz, accused murderer. People will look at you with hatred, and you'll see horrible things in their eyes. I don't know if that's much of a life, or even how long it will last. They don't have the death penalty in this state, but a life in prison isn't much in the way of living." Reaching down, he took the fingers of the boy's right hand in his own, shocked at how little flesh remained attached to the bone.

"It's your call, Jimmy. I can let you die, or—the other. This is up to you."

Animation flickered behind blue eyes. A life force stronger than the body that contained it. The voice was weaker than ever, but the words were unmistakable.

"Mister—I want to live. Even if it's in prison, I want to live. I haven't had enough—time." Tiny, withered fingers exerted the faintest of pressures against Harper's own.

Straightening, he nodded. "Then let's see if the thing is possible."

It did not take him long to find Sipowicz's room, four doors down the hall. A simple squeeze, a silent touch, and the police guard seated outside slumped unconscious in his chair. He would rest thus for several hours. Harper walked noiselessly past him, into the room.

Even in slumber the smirking demon looked healthy, confident, self-assured. Seeing him for the first time since the confrontation, all thoughts save revenge rushed from Harper's mind. He wanted to put his hand over the other man's mouth and wake him, watch him squirm and twist impotently as Harper took him apart, bit by bloody bit.

Only—he couldn't do that now. Couldn't do it because those bits had been promised to another. To one who deserved them.

The hospital gurney glided on silent wheels down the still-deserted sterile hallway. It cozied close enough to the bed of Jimmy Lee for Harper to stand between the two and simultaneously reach both. Tensing as he sucked in a deep, airless breath, he took the boy's right hand in his left and Sipowicz's long, powerful fingers in his right. Then he closed his eyes, and pulled. Pulled with all the prodigious, preternatural strength that was the province of the active deceased. Pulled with his mind and with his heart.

A pale white efflorescence flowed from the body on his left. It traveled not over or across but through the adumbration that was Harry Harper. At the same time, another stream of selfness emerged reluctantly from the burly bulk of Carl Sipowicz. It, too, was blanched, but tinged rose, stained red. It resisted the draw, futilely.

When the two shuddering streams of selfness crossed within Harper, his otherworldly body staggered and his head vibrated on the pole of his spine. Then the selfness of Jimmy Lee passed into and took possession of the body of Carl Sipowicz, while the sick, damaged soul that had been its former tenant was thrust into the gaunt torso of the cancer-riven thirteen-year-old.

Breathing hard even though he was breathing nothing but satisfaction, Harper leaned over the strong young figure on his right and whispered, "Jimmy?"

There was no response. No encouraging words fell from parted lips, no shuttered eyes open to turn and look at him. But fingers, slowed but not stilled by powerful morphine derivatives, gently squeezed his hand.

Harper shut his eyes, suffused with gratitude. He had forgone the kind of vengeance he had originally sought, but this was better. Much better. Straightening and turning, he stared down into pale blue eyes. They were alive, but not for much longer. Alive with recognition, and with rage. They burned, they threatened, they screamed—helplessly.

"It was a good body you had, Sipowicz, but this one suits you better. Far better. The kid needed yours. He deserved it, not you. You can have this one." Harper eyed the tubes, and the lights, and the silent, workmanlike machines that were keeping the corpus of Jimmy Lee alive for a short while longer.

"I hope you enjoy it, you sick fuck."

Boyish lips fluttered, opened, moved. What emerged was not the response of a thirteen-year-old.

"Kill . . . you."

Harper smiled down. It was the first time he had smiled since he'd died. And the last, because his work here was finished.

"I don't think so, Sipowicz. I don't think you're going to hurt anyone, ever again. Besides, I'm already dead. But you know, I don't hurt anymore."

With that he turned, and gurneyed the body, but not the self, of Carl Sipowicz back up the hall to its assigned room. Then he turned and left for the place whence he had come, anticipating his arrival there, looking forward to it, at long last content with himself.

True to the doctors' distasteful declarations, the vile murderer Carl Sipowicz recovered. Wordlessly he endured the harangues of the lawyers and the tears of the deceased's relatives, the corrupt intrusions of the cyclopean television cameras, and the sickening morbid interest of those reporters who, like so many slick used-car salesmen, puked promises in exchange for interviews.

The trial itself was mercifully swift, whereupon he found himself consigned for the rest of his natural life to a place of barren plains and blasted lives situated somewhere in the middle of the vast American heartland. Somewhere where people could not see and would hopefully forget about the existence of malformed creatures like Carl Sipowicz.

There Jimmy Lee labored in the body of the hated killer, winning over fellow inmates and guards and even a reluctant staff with a manner and ways that were unlike those of any mass murderer they had ever encountered. It did not matter. While those who sat on the parole board grew gradually sympathetic to so obviously changed a man, so heinous were the crimes for which he had been committed that any kind of release was out of the question. If nothing else, such a gesture would have been politically inexpedient.

So Jimmy Lee Sipowicz sat, and flourished in the prison library, and learned. He chose to study medicine, and before long was assisting the prison medical staff, who were astonished by his skill, disconcerted at the range of his knowledge, and more than anything else, confounded by his compassion for the afflicted.

On a frenetic and celebratory Fourth of July, some years later, the notorious mass murderer Carl Sipowicz escaped. The event incited a brief flurry of interest in the media. When he wasn't caught immediately, the story passed to the back pages of the papers and absented television entirely. Soon, except for the embarrassed and grim-faced authorities charged with recapturing him, his existence was forgotten by all.

Well, not quite by all. There was one other who heard the news, and did not forget, and kept it tucked close to him. One who could not be counted among the pursuing authorities. One individual whose interest burned brightly at the news of Carl Sipowicz's daring escape.

That individual was Carl Sipowicz.

Because contrary to everything the doctors had predicted, little Jimmy Lee did not die. He had fought back. Fought with a rage and fury and intensity even the cancer could not stand against. Additional chemotherapy was advanced, and strong radiation, and Carl Jimmy Lee sucked it all in and called for more.

His recovery from the cancer was complete. A minor miracle, the doctors called it as they shook their collective heads and wondered at the strength of spirit that had battled back from near death. But the physical damage the cancer had done remained, irreversible and daunting. The young boy could barely speak. Never particularly strong, his wasted body did not recover entirely, so that he had to take powerful medication every day of his life. Reacting to the pills, he was often nauseated, and was forced to spend long, painful spells in the hospital.

But he lived. Short on stomach and intestines, frail of heart, weak of body, he lived. Rage kept him alive, a rage he kept carefully hidden. The body he occupied was not a fit vehicle for retribution, nor even for carrying out the horrors he could only envision. He required, demanded another. But there was only one that was suitable, and it had been denied to him. Locked away, isolated, unreachable, in an inaccessible fortress on the plains.

And then it escaped.

Carl Jimmy Lee's joy knew no bounds. He rooted for the escaped murderer, cheered aloud every time the police confessed their latest failure in the newspapers. He crammed his tiny, liquor-stained, public-supported hovel of a downtown room with clippings and tear sheets, tracking the progress of the hunt while making copious notes of his own.

Having lived something of a life on the run, he could understand what was happening, could see a little of what Jimmy Lee Sipowicz might do. He could anticipate, and imagine, and plan. Oh, how he could plan!

In the makeshift infirmary in the rain forest, the doctor slowly made his rounds. It was unbearably hot, as always, and unbearably humid, as always, and as always the infirmary stank of death and rotting flesh. But the doctor did what he could, and now and then some were saved. Enough so that the reputation of the infirmary spread far, and its buildings were always crowded.

People walked, or were carried, or crawled from miles around, for it was said that in the infirmary was a man, a doctor, who cared more for the dying than for himself. A man who was not afraid of the terrible diseases and the pustulant infections, who cradled sick children in his arms as if they were his own, and who comforted the dying so that when they passed on it was without pain, and ofttimes even with a smile of contentment on their lips.

It was dark when the doctor finished his rounds for the day. He rose earlier and went to bed later than any of his assistants. They were all in awe of him, and had come to think of the big, powerful figure as invulnerable, immune to the insidious afflictions that mindlessly ravaged this part of the world.

He wasn't invulnerable, he knew. He was only a man. But he accepted their adulation because it was useful, and helped him to keep the vital stream of supplies flowing to the small infirmary from skeptical foreign donors. In the previous years he had saved many lives; certainly hundreds, perhaps thousands. Only *he* knew that soon his work must draw to a close. That was regrettable, but nothing could be done about it. Nothing was inevitable, nothing was eternal. The doctor knew that better than most.

He was sitting at his simple desk, fingering the laptop computer by lantern light, composing a request for certain specific medicines and supplies, when the shape slipped into his room. It was thin, naturally slim without being malnourished, as were so many of his patients. But it was not a patient. Nor was it one of his assistants, or one of the nurses. Turning in his chair, he squinted into the unstable, flickering glow.

"Hello. Can I help you?"

"Yes." The intruder's voice was a steely croak. "Yes, you can help me, Doctor Sipowicz. You can give me back my body."

The figure advanced, and the doctor's eyes widened as he recognized himself. Himself grown, matured into adulthood, clearly showing the ravages of the cancer that should have, but had not quite, killed him. Himself filled with enmity, and a determination that shone out of other eyes. The eyes of the murderer and sadist Carl Sipowicz.

The visitant's left hand clutched the top of a strong cane for support. His right held a silencer-equipped pistol. "Don't bother calling out. I can bring you down with a shot to the leg. But I'd rather not damage my body, you know?" A strained smile fissured the gaunt face.

"I'm going to take back my body, you fucking little creep. It's mine, and I want it. I can do it, I know, because I was conscious when that freak Harper switched us years ago. I always paid attention to details, kid, and as angry as I was, I paid attention to that. I couldn't exchange with anyone else, but you better believe I can switch with myself!" With the tip of the cane he tapped his left leg.

"I've gotten stronger over the years. Better, the doctors say. But I still heave every morning when I get up, and I still have to take a handful of fucking pills every day, and women can push me out of the way." Blue eyes glittered. "There's one or two in particular that I've marked for a little visit when I get home. In that body. Which I'll do the pushing with—and other things." He advanced.

"You could probably break me in half with that body. Don't try it. Make a move and I'll blow your foot off. Don't think I won't, man! That body minus one foot is better than this one with two. It's mine, and I want it back. You can have this one. It's yours anyway." Again the crooked, lopsided smile. "Don't you miss it? By rights it should be dead. If you were still in it, it would be, but I'm stronger than you are, than you ever were. I fixed it up a little for you. Maybe I won't even kill you. It wasn't your fault, what happened. That fat prick Harper's the one who was responsible." He waved the pistol loosely.

"Besides, there's others that need killing more than you do." Casting the cane aside, he extended his left arm and gestured with the gun. "Give me your hand, Jimmy Lee. Come on, it won't hurt. It didn't hurt the last time, did it? Give me your hand, and let's get this over with. Otherwise I'll have to shoot you, and do the thing while you're unconscious."

Dr. Jimmy Lee Sipowicz took a step backwards. "I can't do that, Carl."

"The fuck you can't."

"These people here need me. I'm the only doctor in the territory on a permanent basis. The others only visit, and then they get frightened, and leave."

"Africa," the transposed murderer muttered. "Why the hell did you have to come all the way to fucking Africa?"

"Because this is where I was needed," the doctor replied simply.

"Yeah, well, it made it rough on me. You know how many credit cards I had to rip off and go through to get here? Fortunately, you weren't hard to find once I made it this far. The famous Dr. Sipowicz. That's one for the books! Well, the famous Dr. Sipowicz is about to retire." The hand reached, and scrabbled spiderlike at the front of the doctor's sweat-stained vest. "Say good-bye to this shit-hole, Dr. Sipowicz!"

Before Jimmy Lee could move, or even think of moving, a dark, mean glow oozed out of the bony body of his deranged visitor. It forced its way into the other, pushing what existed within outside, shoving it forcibly away. That overwhelmed selfness had no choice but to flow to the only available receptacle—a thin, frail, but still living human configuration nearby.

Both bodies shuddered and twitched with the force of the exchange. The white light of selfness flickered and flared, pushing back the glow of the lantern.

And then it was done.

Blinking, old reflexes restored, Carl Sipowicz reached out and snatched the gun away from his former body. Raising his arms, he turned a slow circle while looking down at himself. The body was older, more mature, but as powerful as ever. It was him. He was back, stronger and smarter than ever.

This time he would be more careful. No brazen, thoughtless murderer in his early twenties, he was now the renowned Dr. Carl Sipowicz. He would sustain that identity. It would allow him to kill and play and torture with comparative impunity, and under cover of the new identity thoughtfully supplied by the studious Jimmy Lee, he could go on like that forever. No police, no authorities would suspect him now. He had reformed. He had a reputation to sustain him. His delighted, demented laughter echoed through the room.

Then he caught sight of Jimmy Lee, standing restored to his own body, watching him. Slowly, the younger man hobbled over to pick up the cane. Sipowicz had to grin.

"Not much of a body, is it, you little asshole. Yours, and welcome to it." He waved the gun. It felt weightless in his strong fingers. "I could kill you so easy, but this is better. Live, knowing what's happened, knowing that every day I'm catching up on my own too-long-neglected work. Knowing that no one will believe you. Oh, it's delicious!"

And then he coughed.

The smile fractured momentarily, and he coughed again, reflexively covering his mouth. When he looked down, there was blood on his palm, and on his fingers. Eyes widening, he looked up sharply at the lank figure of Jimmy Lee, who was walking toward the doorway.

"Wait a minute. What's this?" He shook his hand at the other man. "What the fuck is this?"

"The reason why no other doctors will stay here." Jimmy Lee spoke softly, quietly, with his old, damaged, but still serviceable, vocal cords. He eyed Sipowicz without rancor, spoke without malice. "You try, but working with so many of the sick, and the dying, it's difficult not to become infected. Here, as long as I've been among these people, it's almost impossible."

Sipowicz coughed again, and this time it brought him to his knees. Lee smiled sadly.

"I've tried to keep it hidden from my assistants and patients as best as I could. I didn't want them to lose confidence in me. I have—or rather, you have—Ebola H, Carl."

"Ebol-what? What the fuck is that?" Deep, hacking coughs racked the big body, and more blood spilled from his lips. Black blood.

"It's very unpleasant. I know—I've seen a lot of it this past year. First your internal organs liquefy, then you excrete the result from your body. Eventually the same thing happens to your heart, and then you die. Very unpleasantly. I thought, I hoped, that I had another week or so to help a few more of the sick. Now I see that it was only a matter of a day or two."

Using the cane, he stood straighter. His old body was still feeble, but it was improved over what it had been when he had been dying at thirteen. Considerably improved. With proper care, it should last for years, perhaps even decades. And it would receive that kind of care, from a trained physician. One who would miraculously replace the noble, honored Dr. Sipowicz. One who could even, as Jimmy Lee, return without fear of the authorities to the United States, there to work on a cure for the appalling disease and its insidious cousins.

He backed out of the room. "Good-bye, Carl. You'll have a fine funeral. The locals will throw a great feast to honor you, and you'll be interred with flowers and praises. It's far better than you deserve."

"No, wait! You little bastard. You fucking shit-faced little bastard!"

The gun came up, shakily this time, and a silenced bullet shattered the wooden post a foot to the left of Jimmy Lee's head. The second shot went into the floor, as the big body fell forward, torn by the agony of its disintegrating internal organs. Quietly, Jimmy Lee left the infirmary. Arrangements would have to be made for the disposal of the body. As Dr. Jimmy Lee, newly arrived

to assist Dr. Sipowicz, it would be his responsibility to direct them. He hobbled off into the sweltering Congo night, heading away from the infirmary.

In a small cluster of forest palms nearby, a bird with black breast and bright white wings laughed at the moon and the Fate that drifted lazily across it like mist fashioned from bloodstained chiffon. In his years in the rain forest Jimmy Lee had come to know many of the native birds, and this one was no exception. The white wings and black body were as unmistakable as its nocturnal cackle.

African crow.

THE KING OF BIRDS

Caitlín R. Kiernan

b.

*"History is a weapon, a poker you keep in your pocket
to beat the present senseless . . ."*
—Kevin Toolis, *Rebel Hearts* (1995)

Fergus has been praying all the way from Great Victoria Street, while the hijacked Ford slips along under skies as blue as steel perfect indifference, all the way from the grand fuckup outside the pub to the relative safety of Co. Armagh. First a Gaelic decade on his black rosary beads and then he just started counting them and praying in English and never mind if it's all gibberish and none of it makes sense to God or anyone else for that matter.

"For fucksake," Bernadette growls, finally, from behind the wheel. "Will ye shut him up, Gerry?"

"Just drive the bloody *car,* Bernie," Gerry MacManus growls back at her, but he tries harder not to hear Fergus.

"*Yer* man there," Bernadette says and adds an ugly sort of laugh, *yer* man so Gerry can be sure there's absolutely no doubt who's to blame for the hit going to shite, "He's gonna have a wee bit of explainin' to do, sure, when Harry catches up to us."

"Aye, Bernie," Gerry says, nothing left in his voice but exhaustion, "Aye," and he's watching the trees and the stone walls and hedges rushing past outside like every one of them might hide a soldier or UVF assassin. That they've managed to reach the IRA-controlled "Provisional Republic of South Armagh" without being blown all the way to hell and back again makes Gerry about as comfortable as Fergus's idiot prayers.

"Shut yer mouth, Fergus!" and Gerry flinches like her voice was gunfire. "Shut yer fuckin' mouth or I swear I'm leavin' yer arse in the road and ye can walk . . ."

"*Fergus!*" Gerry says loud, cutting Bernie off and turning about in his seat to face him. "Now listen, mate, everyone in Heaven *and* Hell *and* everywhere in between's heard you by now. You gotta relax," and Fergus looks at him, then, the rosary still clutched between his fingers. His eyes make Gerry want to go back to looking for prod gunmen behind the trees, eyes so bright and afraid and he thinks, *How much of you did we leave back in Belfast, Fergus Mooney?*

"I really ballsed it up, didn't I?" Fergus says and Gerry can see how hard he's trying to smile. "I really stuck me dick in it this time, didn't I?"

"Aye, ye did that, ye spotty . . ."

"Yer not helpin' matters, Bernie," and so she sighs loud, grits her teeth and stares out at an abandoned row of dryrock cottages. Thatched roofs fallen in and gardens gone to weeds and fallow earth.

"I know," Fergus mumbles, "I know, Gerry. An' I know it's my fault Padraig and John are dead. I'm so bloody sorry . . ."

"Aw, ye poor wee thing," Bernie sneers and Gerry backhands the side of her face so hard the car swerves, rubber whine of tyres and then they're right back on the road and Bernie's smiling, even though her eyes are watering and there's a thin trickle of blood from the corner of her mouth.

"They're dead and yer coddlin' that whinin' coward," she says and Gerry can see blood on her teeth.

"I'm not coddlin' anyone, Bernie. I'm *tryin'* to keep the three of us that ain't dead from gettin' that way."

"I *said* I knew it was me own doin' got 'em killed," Fergus says to the back of Bernadette's head, her hair the colour of rusted iron bars, and then he looks back down at his beads again.

"Y'know I'm not afraid of doin' what has to be done, Gerry," Bernadette says, still smiling that knife-edge gentle smile. "But by God, I'll not wind up in Castlereagh over the likes of *him*."

"She saw it, too," Fergus murmurs. "She might not admit it, but ye know she did, Gerry."

And Bernadette makes a hissing sound, then, air between her clenched teeth, like she's started boiling alive inside her skin.

"Yer talkin' a lot of ravin' shite, Mooney. All *I* saw was a Saracen fulla soldiers. All *I* saw was the bullet holes the Brits put in our fellas."

"Ah, merciful fuck . . ." Gerry moans, but this time Bernadette's determined not to be interrupted, glances back at Fergus in the rear-view mirror.

"D'ye actually think we're gonna forget all *that* if ye just keep repeatin' yer bloody rosary and all this ballacks about ghosts and fuckers with wings?"

"No, Bernie," Fergus says, nodding his head like it isn't properly attached to his shoulders, talking low like a child whispering during Mass. "I don't think ye'll forget nothin'. An' that's why I know yer lyin' about what ye saw."

"Yer fuckin' looped, Fergus," and she gives him another glance from the rear-view. And for a few minutes no one says anything else and the stolen gray Ford Escort rolls along the road to Crossmaglen. It's getting dark now, cold November twilight, and the shadows stretch out so long; Gerry holds his hands in front of the heater a moment, rubs them together but the chill seems to go bone deep.

"Ye saw him, Gerry," Fergus says from the back and this time Bernadette seems too lost in her own thoughts to bother telling him to shut up again.

"Yeh," Gerry says, jamming his hands in the pockets of his coat. "But we'll talk about it later. There'll be time enough to talk about it later."

*T*he Escort left burning at the end of an unpaved road, two cans of petrol poured out inside, soaked into the upholstery, and Bernie tossed in a flare to get it going. Gerry only looked back once, as they crossed the fields that would take them across the border into the Free State to a safe house a few kilometres past Crossmaglen. Only a faint, redorange glow still visible against the night black to mark their arson and Bernie stopped, too, and "Are ye gonna stand there all night?" she asked him.

There were five of them sent in to stiff Sergeant Colin Henderson, an off-duty member of the Ulster Defense Regiment. It should have been an easy hit. Fergus was the driver, not the torched Escort but the turquoise Honda with an English numberplate that they started out with and all they had to do was wait until Henderson crossed Great Victoria to The Crown and their man on the corner signaled that the UDR man was at the bar, settled in with a pint and his back to the street. Bernie spotted him first and she whispered from the front passenger seat, "Heads up, ladies. There's the bastard."

Gerry and a new man, Padraig Carey, were the gunmen for the hit, and after Henderson walked right by Storey, stepped between the pub's white Corinthian pillars and into The Crown Saloon, John Storey waited maybe three, four minutes, before he folded the newspaper he'd been reading and tucked it beneath one arm, nodded in the direction of the Honda.

"That's it," Bernie hissed but they were both already out of the car and moving fast, their faces hidden by black balaclavas and the adrenaline burning through Gerry like his veins were pumping pure Scotch whisky. They stepped into the pub, drew pistols from under their duffel coats and put four rounds apiece into the back of the UDR man's head before he could turn around. And then they were out again, the doors swinging shut behind them and a woman starting to scream as Henderson pitched over into his glass of Caffrey's. Fergus was waiting at the kerb, as planned, and John was already in the back.

"Come on, come on, come on . . ." Bernie was saying, over and over again, and after a second Gerry realized the car wasn't even moving and someone had come out of The Crown, was pointing toward the Honda.

"Drive on to fuck, Fergus!" John yelled, smacked Fergus hard in the back of the head, and that's when they all saw what Fergus had already seen, the armoured Land Rover rolling toward them down Great Victoria Street.

"*Oh Jesus,* now we're for it," Padraig said, pulling off his balaclava and his black hair underneath stuck up like ruffled feathers. "Will ye get us the fuck *outta* here, Fergus!"

212 X CAITLÍN R. KIERNAN

And then they were speeding backwards down the street and the RUC patrol in the Land Rover had begun shouting for them to stop, the soldiers unshouldering their rifles, fixing the Honda in their certain telescopic sights. Fergus smashed the front bumper of a car pulling out of an alley and kept going, a tinkling shard spray of chrome and broken glass and coloured plastic left on the street and the other car blaring its horn until the driver saw the RUC men and disappeared back into the alley.

"Right there, Fergus," Bernie said, "Right in there," sounding calm enough for all of them, pointing at a side street but Fergus was already past it. Then the first bullet struck the front windscreen, punched through and put a hole the size of a bloody thumbprint in John's throat. Fergus hit the brakes and the car fishtailed, squealed to a stop in the middle of the street. John didn't make a sound, slumped silently forward as if finally acknowledging defeat and bowing toward the advancing soldiers. He left a sticky scarlet smear and grainy yellowhite bits of bone all over the seat cover, all over Gerry and Padraig and the wet hole in the back of John's neck was a lot bigger than a thumbprint.

"Oh, Jesus," Padraig groaned and Gerry wanted bad to close his eyes, then, just close his eyes and wait for it to be over, for the mercy of his turn and the bullet that would take him out. If they only sat still a moment or two more the SA80s would pick them all off, one by one. But Fergus mashed the accelerator and the Honda leaped forward, toward an alley half blocked with trashcans and empty vegetable crates.

"*No,* Fergus," Bernie screamed at him. "It's a bloody dead end!" but it was already too late, even if he had heard her, even if he'd understood. The car plowed through the barricade of garbage and hurtled along between close walls of brick and plaster, bumping over broken asphalt and crumbled bits of masonry.

"Just stop the fuckin' car," Gerry said. *"Now!"* and either Fergus heard him or he saw the end of the alley rushing towards them; the car veered sharply to the right and there was a sudden, rasping scream of metal against brick and an orange shower of sparks as it scraped along the wall. The Honda screeched to a stop, jammed snug against one side of the alley and the only way out was through the passenger-side doors. By the time Gerry was able to scramble over John's body, there were already soldiers blocking their escape and Bernadette and Padraig were crouched down behind the car doors, as if the bullets wouldn't come straight through.

Then the Land Rover caught up, rolled into the entrance to the alley and sealed them in.

"I should shoot ye myself and be finished with it," Bernadette snarled at

Fergus as she popped a fresh magazine into her Beretta, dropped the empty clip, *clak,* to the ground. "But it'd be a waste of good ammo."

"Aye," Padraig said, "And ye'd be deprivin' those poor bastards there've their rightful pleasure . . ." and he stood up, one arm braced against the top of the window, getting off a full clip, wounding one or two of the soldiers, before he went down, half his face blown away.

"It's been great knowin' you arseholes," Gerry said and took Padraig's place, pausing a necessary second to aim at one of the soldiers still inside the Land Rover. The security patrol's bullets ricocheted off the alley walls like fire-crackers, ripping holes in the boot of the Honda, shattering the rear wind-screen. Gerry squeezed the trigger and the soldier in the Saracen jerked backwards, fell over, and *Ah, that's something, at least,* Gerry thought, taking aim again as the alley filled with smoke and the smell of blood and gunpowder.

"What the *fuck* . . ." Fergus cried out behind him and there was a frantic, ruffling sound then, like sheets hung to dry or the beating wings of a thousand birds, deafening loud even over the gunfire, and Gerry looked up, expecting only the vacant blue strip of sky overhead, a final glimpse of Heaven between the buildings before the rifles tore him apart. And instead, the shadow like a living curtain of midnight falling between the car and the Land Rover, and Gerry MacManus forgot about the British soldiers and the IRA and how eejit Fergus Mooney had fucked them all, and pissed himself.

*T*he safe house sits alone, abandoned at one end of a small and peatdark lough that none of them knows the name of. Gerry doubts it even has a name, and they wait together in the night, for the sound of tyres on the muddy road or helicopters in the black, moonless sky. There's a table and only two rickety chairs, but Bernadette's standing by herself at one of the windows, anyway, so that doesn't matter. There is no light, not even a candle that might give them away, that might attract unwanted attention, just the thick and musty silence of the night pooled inside the cottage.

"Maybe the oul' bastard's decided we're not even worth retrievin'," Bernie says, most of her bluster gone and her voice sounds bruised in the darkness. "Maybe we're nothin' but a liability an' Harry's just lettin' us stew a bit before he sends someone to whack us."

"You're a cheerful fucker," Gerry says, even though he's been thinking the same thing, more or less.

"I need to piss," she says back and in a moment she's gone and it's just Fergus and Gerry sitting across from each other in the rickety chairs, staring into the lightless space between them.

"Ye said we'd talk about it," Fergus says, low, like he's afraid Bernadette

will hear him. And Gerry says, "Aye, but she'll be back and I don't fancy she's in the mood."

"D'ye think I give a wee fuck *what* she thinks?"

"I think you'd piss yourself if she said 'boo,' Fergus," and Gerry moves, one leg gone to sleep and his chair creaks loud in the dark.

"Now houl' on," Fergus begins and then Bernie is back and he doesn't even finish his sentence.

"You were sayin'?" asks Gerry.

"*Nothin'*, Gerry. I wasn't sayin' nothin'."

"Fucksake," Bernie mumbles, resuming her post at the window. "Ye think I'm bloody deaf, Fergus? I heard ye. It's so quiet ye can hear the wee bloody fish fuckin' down in the lough."

Fergus sighs and Gerry can feel the tension in him, can almost believe it's the only solid thing in the night. "It's doin' me head in, Bernadette," he says. "I gotta talk or . . ."

"Then *talk*, Fergus Mooney. Sure, I'm not stoppin' ye." The tone in her voice, colder and emptier than the November night wrapped around the cottage, gives Gerry goose pimples.

Fergus is silent for a few minutes, as if maybe he doesn't really believe her, thinks Bernadette has laid some sort of trap for him and as soon as he says anything she'll be on him. When he does begin to talk, he seems almost to be speaking to himself.

"There are plenty enough things I'd rather think about, y'know," he says finally. "I can't even see me hand an inch from me bloody face and ye think I *want* to be tellin' ghost stories . . ."

"Is that it, then, Fergus?" Gerry asks him. "Is it a ghost story behind what happened back there in that alley?" His hands are shaking and he's suddenly glad for the darkness, that they can't see him and he can't see their faces, either.

"How many fuckin' slugs d'ye think they put into him, Gerry? How many did *we* put in him? An' he just *stood* there, takin' it."

And Gerry hears that sound from the alleyway again, only a memory but Jesus, that's almost as bad, bad enough. Thunder and flapping linens hung out to dry, the wings of a thousand black birds, as it settled into the alleyway between them and the patrol. And the look of it, oh, he remembers that too, and that's worse even than the sound.

"When I was a boy," Fergus says, "me Da would tell us a story about the famine and a dead man that made a deal to come back . . ." and there are sharp, clicking noises from the other side of the table and Gerry doesn't have to see to know it's the beads again, working nervously between Fergus's shaking fingers. As he talks, Gerry sits very still, not liking the way his chair creaks and cracks if he shifts his weight, and Bernie stands silent watch at the window.

She laughs her bitter, ugly Bernadette laugh and, " 'The King of Birds,' " she says, and laughs again.

"What?" Gerry asks and his chair makes a noise like an old pier in a storm. "You know what he's talkin' about?"

"Sure, but it's just an oul' fairy poem," she says. "William Yeats, y'know?" and she draws a ragged loud breath, breathes in the night through the window, and begins:

> *Hark, whispered the pale woman beneath the hill,*
> *Her eyes and mane and lips hoar-white,*
> *Only a crow, said she, can bring the soul back across*
> *To make the wrong things right.*

And Gerry stares, amazed, across the hungry gulf of shadows separating him from Bernadette; a million years and he still would not have expected to hear poetry from this hard girl from the Falls Road. She stands as motionless as stone, silhouetted against the lighter shades of dark outside.

"That's it," Fergus says, "Da, he only knew the story part, not the poetry, but that's it, sure. I know that's it."

"Weans on the street know better than to believe old ghost stories, Fergus. Yer a fool, d'ye *know* that as well?"

"Is there any more?" Gerry asks her. "D'you know any more of it?" And he wonders why he's asking now: because he wants answers for what they saw in the entry as badly as Fergus, or just to hear the sound of rhyming words from Bernadette's mouth.

"Are ye goin' daft as Fergus there?"

But, "When did you learn that, Bernie?" Gerry asks her anyway and Bernadette's shoulders rise and fall, her weary, indifferent shrug barely visible, and "What bloody difference does it make?" she says back.

*T*wo hours later and Gerry has fallen into a shallow, uncertain sleep in the creaky chair, drifted off to the unvarying harmony of Fergus's rosary and Bernadette's silence and it's all there, waiting for him: the soldiers and the terrible sound from the entry and the gun getting hot in his hands as he shoves his last clip into the Beretta. As he stares unbelieving at the blackness slipping itself between the Land Rover and the Honda, something indigestible the sky's spit up and it pours like waves of living treacle down the walls.

"Move yer skinny arse, MacManus!" Bernadette screams but he can't possibly look away from it, from the waterdim alley light snagging in its restless folds and furrows, and the face turns toward him, then. The face that might have been human a long, long time ago, before so many wounds that he wonders there's the skin left to hold it together. An empty socket and one paincloudy eye, and then Bernadette has him by the collar, is hauling him backwards and the pistol's going off in his hand and the RUC men are still subbing away at the other end of the alley. He wonders what *they* see, as he's dragged through a doorway, as the musty dark swallows him and the Beretta clatters from his hands to hard concrete. The door hangs crooked, broken on its rusted hinges, broken as the face that watches his retreat.

"No, not *that* way!" Bernadette screams at Fergus and they run together through half light and dust, around smashed furniture pieces and graffiti scar walls.

"It's comin'," Fergus says, dread in him like a cancer, and "Jesus, it's fuckin' right *behind* us!"

"No, no it's not," Gerry promises him, but he can hear it too, impossibly loud in this maze of empty, murky rooms. The taunting lie of light somewhere ahead, boarded windows and a street beyond, surely, because he doesn't want to die here with the rats and filth.

Which hurts worse, the holdin' on, or the lettin' go? and that wasn't *his* thought, but it burns bright through his head and Gerry stumbles, strikes his knee against something sharp and hard and he's falling, hands out to take the impact that never comes. Because there's no bottom to this fall, only things he hasn't forgotten (*these are not my memories,* but he can't tell the difference) can't ever forget, even through this much time and the killings, night and day and blood, even across one hundred and forty-nine years. Ragged facts of his time on earth fingered like the corners of old playing cards, like a charm against his own elusive oblivion.

"These are not my thoughts," he says aloud to the void, "My name is Gerry MacManus and these are not my fuckin' thoughts," but his name is also Jacob Banlin and his second child Síle, died in October 1846; the black year before blacker '47. Síle, newborn girl child, pink from Eileen's womb. But he never saw her alive, never saw her dead, either. Never saw anything but the frozen mound of earth with its makeshift cross, cruel parody of Eileen's belly, another death in an earth gone slowly pregnant with death. And him off for the Board of Works and Sir Trevelyan's damning relief, making new roads no one needed, unless the dead would be up and walking soon.

His half acre of dirt spared the blight of '45, and Jacob thanked God and all the saints he knew by name that his field had not been touched. That he had food enough for Eileen and little Donncha. But the next summer had come, heavy months that prowled the country like sick and ill-tempered beasts, June, July, stifling heat and too much rain, and in August the stench of blight came to his own field, the rich and putrid reek of every potato dying underground, never mind the stalks and leaves still green, luxuriant, never mind the day before and not the slightest hint of disease.

Gerry closes his eyes, but these aren't pictures to the *eyes*, pictures to ·the soul, and knowing that nothing could possibly come of their effort but sacks of black and inedible rot, he and Eileen begin to dig, frantic hands and spades, and her clumsy with the child. Tearing the tubers from the muddy earth, potatoes still much too small, at least a month from harvest, skins bruised, most already shriveled and soft as boils. And by midday, the plants themselves are showing the tell-tale marks of infestation, wilting away around them.

"Stop," he says, finally, *"Stop,"* he screams, reaching out into the nothing rushing past, reaching out to take Eileen's hands. "Stop, Eileen. It's no good," but she struggles free of his grasp, pulls another ruined potato from the dirt.

"I'll not give up so easy as that," Bernadette growls between teeth set as firm as the fury in her eyes, on her face, muddy smears and sweatstraggling hair. "It's all we have now, *it's all we have.*"

So he lets her alone then, sits back on his ass and watches as Eileen digs for all their lives, watches the withering sea of green as it turns to black before his eyes.

And he doesn't remember an end to the fall, but he's standing now, and the blackness is only around the corners, like a seething frame for the world. Halfway across the bridge, impossible arch built not of stones and mortar but bones and wire, and Gerry steps to the edge and looks over into the cold, swirling waters a thousand feet below. Beside him, Bernadette is speaking again and he strains to hear her above the rumble and wail of the cataract.

> *Empty your heart of these futile, mortal pains,*
> *Release this terrible sadness and rest . . .*

She turns toward him and the exit wound in her forehead leaks viscous red hope and black despair. "Aye, fuckin' Yeats. But ye pay attention, Gerry," she says. "He'll not repeat this for ye again," and Gerry watches her fall until she hits the water and it greedily wipes away any trace that she ever was.

Wake the fuck up, he thinks as hard as the dry bones underfoot, but the house is *not* empty and he finds Eileen in their bed, a light dusting of snow

blown in through the open door and powdering the blankets and her auburn hair. He takes her for dead until he leans closer and feels the heat of her fever against his face, and her green eyes open, hazel-green dulled by whatever sickness burns away inside her. She doesn't smile, weakly whispers his name, a sigh that is more the shape of her lips than sound and he kneels on the strawmud floor beside her, and wipes sweat and sweat-soaked hair from her face.

"I was dreamin' about death," she murmurs, "I was dreamin' about death again last night."

"Where's Donncha?" he asks, and she closes her eyes again, whispers "I saw her at the window again, last night. She isn't frightful at all, Jacob. She told me you were comin' home."

"Eileen, where is Donncha?"

"Sleepin'," she sighs, "Just sleepin', Jacob," and almost a smile for him then, before she folds the blankets back enough that Jacob can see the dead child locked up in her arms, his face black and typhus-swollen, hands like sausages and the stench from him rising up to mingle with the heat of her. And Gerry crawls away into a corner and vomits, nothing in his stomach to lose but he dry heaves anyway.

Eileen cries out, nothing intelligible, but he turns to see, trailing spit and bile from his lips and maybe there *is* a face at the window, a blur that moves quickly away before he can see it clearly. Only the impression of hair so black and eyes dark as coal, but he doesn't go to see, doesn't want to know for certain.

Later, he takes Donncha from Eileen, and she doesn't protest, too far out of her head now, or simply no strength left in her to fight him. Jacob lays the child on the bare table in the center of the room, nothing to cover him with, but he weights the eyelids with spoons to keep them closed. Fergus is sitting there in a squeaky chair, praying, and Gerry tells him to watch the boy a bit.

And he sits with Eileen, holds her hands while she raves and the day creeps past in its own cold delirium. Sometime after sundown, no light in the cottage but the nub of one tallow candle, she begins to tremble uncontrollably, the black fever's ague, and the dark rash comes, the blood blooming beneath her skin. He holds her down while she howls in pain, swears to him she's burning alive, begs him to carry her out into the snow, *Please carry me out to the woman waiting for us in the snow.*

Before dawn, there's one lucidbrief moment when the chills and seizures release her and Eileen asks him to kill her, to not make her suffer through the long days it will take her to die like poor Donncha died.

"*Please,* Jacob," but he shakes his head, incapable of what she asks because he loves her and she's the last thing left to love, and when she's gone he'll be alone with the empty world and the *bean-sídhe* wind.

So she suffers for his fear and in the end he's alone anyway, buries them both in a shallow scrape of a grave in the frozen earth behind the cottage, buries them together, wrapped in one another's arms and the lice-ridden bed-clothes. He tucks Eileen's rosary into one of her swollen hands and uses the rosewood crucifix from over the hearth for a marker. And then he turns his back and walks away, into the wrath of the storm that has swept away his wife, his babies, ready for it to have done with him, too.

Gerry turns away from the chasm and crosses the bridge.

Bernadette's voice echoes somewhere past his footsteps, a voice grown younger now, singsong lines of poetry from the lips of a dirty Belfast child,

And sometimes a crow will bring the soul back across
To put the wrong things right.

The bridge is behind him and the realm of the King of Birds rises up around him like a shattered cathedral of twigs and shit-stained feathers, nervous beaks and claws and nests of busted, empty eggshell. A towering wide gate of white and hollow gull bones, woven sparrow shafts bleached colourless, and the Court of the King on his throne. They lead him forward, all these twittering, squawking spirits of the dead, phantomswift wings that make no sound but the velvet rustle of lost time, the memory of lost skies, and the King of Birds gazes down with golden, curious eyes.

"You're not one of mine," it says and Gerry stands in the angry, whirling center of the hurricane of fleshless, wheeling bodies. The King of Birds shifts its indefinite, wary bulk, a million eyes and a million more stabbing beaks. A ribsy murder of crows for its guard, and they watch every move that Jacob Banlin makes.

"They took me wife and child," he says. "An' the old woman on the bridge, she told me that ye can send me back, long enough to make them pay for what they've done . . ."

The King of Birds laughs at him and its laughter is a hawk's beak, hooked and digging at his resolve. Laughter that rolls like thunder across the place where a sky would be if the Heaven of Birds had a sky.

Laughter that fractures time and the dream and Gerry opens his eyes, doesn't remember closing them but now they're open and he's on the far side of the peaty, nameless lough, looking across toward the safe house and the east is stained with sunrise. The water makes a patient, fruitless sound against the stones along the shore and he knows that the man is standing behind him, the man who gave up peace for vengeance and made a deal with the King of Birds.

"I thought we might all be dead," Gerry says. "I thought maybe we never made it outta that shite-hole back in Belfast and all this was a dream, too."

"Yer not dead yet," the man says and Gerry doesn't turn around, doesn't care to see and there's a sweet, rotten smell in the air like something dead on the road.

Gerry thinks maybe he can make out the ghostpale smudge of Bernadette's face outlined against a window of the cottage, and "I don't understand," he says to the dead man at his back.

And it answers, dead tongue against dead palate, dawn air forced through dead lungs for a voice as weary and regretful as the bones of the world. "Sometimes," the man says, "a crow can bring a restless soul back from the Land of the Dead. But *only* sometimes . . . if there's a way to put things right.

"When ye hurt, things always seem simple."

Gerry doesn't speak, watches Bernadette at her window, Bernadette awake and seeing the day hauling itself slowly up over the hills.

"In Ireland, things are rarely simple, Gerry," the dead man says and "Aye," Gerry replies before the sudden, chilling gust across the water, a keening wind that touches him and crawls inside, flays his heart like a surgeon's knife.

"In Ireland, yer pain is just another fucker," and the wind folds Gerry open, folds back the blank page of the coming day and a thousand blood-stained pages underneath to flutter, wind that tastes of all the hate and killing there ever was, and still it blows as hungry as before. And in the immeasurable seconds before he opens his eyes, Gerry MacManus knows that he's alone.

*H*e wakes to the gravelcrunch of tyres on the crooked, narrow drive leading to the cottage, stiffnecked and his back aching; across the table, Bernadette is shaking Fergus awake. "They're here," she says, "Harry's sent a car," and Gerry hears the sleepstarved relief wedged in between her words. Fergus blinks stupidly at the morning light getting in through the windows.

"Are ye sure it's not a trick, Bernie," he asks and wipes a bit of drool from the corner of his mouth.

"An' how would I be sure of that?" she replies. "Ye'll be sure when they don't shoot yer arse. Now get movin'," and he does what she says, tucks the rosary he's clutched through the night into his front trouser pocket as he stands up.

"*C'mon,* Gerry," Bernie says. "Jesus, but ye look like shite this mornin'," hands him a black, plastic comb from her back pocket and starts to check the four corners of the cottage to be sure they're leaving nothing behind, no incriminating evidence of their brief presence there.

"Yeh?" Gerry says, dragging the comb through his hair. "That's just what me mouth tastes like." He passes the comb back to her, and the smallest, slippery bits of a long dream come rushing up at him: a towering bridge and Bernadette turning towards him, a sea of black feathers and a face he might have seen in a window.

And before he can speak, there are footsteps outside, and the quick and certain voices of vengeful men.

PROPHECY

Lisa Lepovetsky

Bearing needles of lightning in his beak
to stitch the night's wounds
he flies to her in the time of Chaos
flies on the black waves
raised by a million voices that cry
to quench the silence of the streets
the violence of the skies
and the cold and the darkness
that eats their souls
from the inside out.

But it is too late
he is no longer enough.
His grave revelations
drift unheeded above the din
of the cities
his truths evaporate
in winds swelling hot and cold
lost among the fetid seeds
of their fear.
He is only a winged shadow
against their night.

When she knows he won't come
when she's waited as long as she can
when the lesion in her life
spreads so that
she can no longer
close it with a needle
with a thousand million needles
she drives her taloned tongue
through her breast
ignoring the psalms
and warnings of the prophets
of the fathers
of the sons.

She tastes blood and milk,
salt red and sweet white
mingled in forbidden nectar
and she licks her blood
from each black hair of the
single knifelong feather
he left her
so many lives ago.
She drifts in ebony dreams
of the father she'll never know
of the sons she'll never bear
of the mothers.

And when she finally wakes
and understands
he cannot hear her scream
so terribly small
in the glare of the morning sun.

Off a tiny uncharted island in the Caribbean a female SEAL swims alone, purposefully, not unmindful of sharks. The waves are gentle above her and the darkness at this level is illuminated by the broken patches of dappled light from the white hot sun, burning in the vast sky of cloudless indigo.

She gently scissors her trim legs, and huge swim fins propel her upward, forward, toward the target. Her back and chest are strapped with gear. State-of-the-art SCUBA apparatus and a silent, ultraquick sea sled make this SEAL extremely mobile. The thing she carries, now cradled in her arms, makes her the equal of most predators. Then there is the matter of her skill. At what she does, the SEAL is unsurpassed.

There is a break in the blue green and a neoprene hood and goggled face streaked to blend with the sea penetrate the surface. She bobs in the gentle waves, scissoring closer toward the shoreline. When she can touch bottom she stands, removes the mask, and remains submerged to eye level as she positions herself against the motion of the ocean.

A long rifle of unusual configuration breaks the surface. The SEAL, a world-class shooter, removes the watertight muzzle cap. She glances at the dull black Xonic that dwarfs her slender wrist, then locks her left arm through the body sling that helps provide a rigid firing stance against the slap of the waves. She peers through the 20-power scope, scanning the beach and the fringe of palm trees, and awaits her target of opportunity.

Shark's Head Cay cannot be reached by sea. The tiny emergent island and the reefs that ring it looked picture-perfect, the water as richly blue green as antique blown glass; the shoreline an explosion of scarlet flamboyan', vermilion-gold jacaranda, and immortelles fringed by verdant coconut palms. Only the presence of a recumbent giant spoiled the vista.

In profile it appeared to be still, barely breathing, muted, a six-foot-nine-inch, 400-pound meat freezer on its back, supine and seemingly immobile as a beached whale. But the beast had only shifted its vital signs into neutral gear. It was reading, turning the pages of articles long-ago committed to the computer that was its mind.

It is said of Mozart that he could play entire piano sonatas at the age of four, probably before he'd had any formal training. Hear a piece once, play it back perfectly. Some gifts have no explanation in science. The beast was such a genius in its own right; a Mozart of death, one might say. Presentience, brilliance that warped the charts, raw intellect beyond measuring, eidetic recall, brute force . . . and a predilection for succulent human heart.

Daniel Edward Flowers Bunkowski died when he was nine years old, when the tattooed freak he thought of as the Snake Man pulled him from the stifling metal punishment box to use him again and again; that's when the monster inside him spawned—after the human child died.

He was born again in the seemingly innocuous milspeak of a "non-skid jacks," the jargon for a National Security Council directive to the Joint Chiefs; born again when Dr. Norman—who ran the Program—shoehorned him off of Marion Fed's death row. And he died in the covert orders of a ComUS-MACV LIMDIS NORFORN to a unit once called SAUCOG: a one-man spike team, sanctioned and deleted.

He dreams of monsters. They all look like you. Not the fanged creations of films and books, the real ones. The creature reaches for you on some level, tries to touch you with the heat of his thoughts. His desire for your extermination transcends hatred.

Growing old in a world of guard dogs, sentries, alarms, hacks, watchmen, cops, yard bulls, and pain, again and again he kills the Snake Man. Its tough-guy skin was the jailhouse armor of blue ink: serpents, lizards, dragons, skulls, geckos, spiders, scorpions, scarabs, and unspeakable images that slithered around its mean, coiled muscles, while it used the boy.

His head pulsates with the dull perpetual ache that neither aspirin, Tylenol, cocaine, Demerol, Dilaudid, morphine, animal tranq, nor Wild Turkey can completely negate. Only potassium cyanide might work and he would *never* give you assholes that much satisfaction.

He uses the poisons and pain. They fuel him. They nurture him and help galvanize him. Have you ever dreamt of such a monster? He dreams of *you*. Come glimpse a real monster's nightmare . . .

The gigantic form held under heavy restraints did not so much as blink an eye, but inside his head the powerful drug was doing its best to shatter the lock he kept on his thoughts. His peripheral vision registered an electronic latticework of cords, cables, and lines hooked to a bank of sophisticated equipment. His keen hearing picked up the steady murmur of deep throbbings, electrobeeps, sensor warnings, and the sonorous purr of various monitors.

A blurred face spoke, but wasps came buzzing out of the utterance and stung him. Somewhere far away he could hear a captured animal's roar of frustration and rage. A face put itself together out of smoke and shadow and the broken image of Dr. Norman hovered nearby.

"Daniel? How are you feeling?"

The huge man flashed on a springtime long before, and a droning, buzzing, insect-filled thicket of shrubs and bushes. He'd been hiding and near his hideaway he spotted something—a black, feathery corpse. He imagined that Dr. Norman was a black, feathery object. He reached down and picked up the sad form in his baseball mitt of a hand. Sensing the heat, it fluttered momentarily, then as if by magic took flight.

"Fine."

"Daniel, I'm trying my best to understand you," the man in white spoke in soft, ingratiating tones, "so that I can help you." He came a bit closer. "How do you know so many things, my friend? Tell me how you have learned so much."

"I know chemistry, Dr. Norman," the beast heard himself say, inside a block of ice, "math, the general sciences."

"Come now, Daniel, I am well aware of your great intellect and vast knowledge. Tell me about your brain."

"Chemistry, math, the general sciences . . ."

"Daniel," the doctor resumed, even closer now, whispering into the behemoth's misshapen right ear, "can you accept the premise that you are mentally . . . different . . . and that your difference is symptomatic of an illness?"

"Yes, Dr. Norman," the basso profundo rumbled deeply and in equally measured tones, "I realize by your standards that I am mentally ill."

Dr. Norman swallowed. His throat felt as dry as if he'd ingested the drug himself. "Daniel, if you understand that almost all human acts of violence are wrong, then why do you take lives?"

"I take lives as a political statement, Dr. Norman. Rage and pain manifest themselves in many ways. Throughout the history of mankind one sees violent politicization of outrage manifested by clergy, by the radical left and reactionary right, by liberal pro-choicers and conservative pro-lifers, by socialist democrats and fascist republicans, by every force from the Spanish Inquisition to the anti-environmentalist movement. In this regard I'm no different than the society that fears and wishes to destroy me. We kill for peace." The word WATCHERS glowed bright red against the icy blue of his mindscreen.

Dr. Norman was beside himself. History was being made!

Dream, memory, formula, and hypothesis mix in a deep, warm sleep that stinks of wormy wind-whipped rain, humus, mulch, dirt, sand, cloying frangipani, death, the end of the world: did he dream this or is he dreaming it now?

He sniffs updrafts and the smell of freshly cut green rectums of lower-tract-house lawn, driving the dead convenience store clerk's previously owned junker inland. Why do they give these stupid rides such nomenclature? This is a GT, XL, Z1, SK-something. Who is fooled? All of us. We are all fooled. The OJ-69 clatters past riding-mower heaven, the zoysia and crabgrass and fescue of decagajillion urban/sub lots piquant and cool in the night. How does he know to aim in this direction? Why doesn't he need a map? He rattles over a creek bed, a load limit sign taunting him. Yellow beam seeking same. Relatively little traffic. The clerk wore an Einstein sweatshirt with the slogan "$E=MC^2$: not just a good idea, it's the law."

The law has probably found the d.b. by now, the yellowish skin not yet blue. Again—where was the blood? The smell and taste and texture of a kill, these are things that *nurture* him, and he sensed none of those tactile components. His mindscreen scans for relevant data and he finds Dr. Norman.

"Daniel, why do you take the vic . . . the person's heart when you terminate them?" Dr. Norman senses his great and irrevocable gaffe, blanches, blushes, shimmies, and shakes with fear tremors.

"The writer David Mamet is quite wrong in his assessment of one who would devour the heart of his enemy. Dali, conversely, understood that the ultimate in gastrointestinal refinement came as a result of the act of true cannibalism, the eating of living beings. He was also wrong in insisting on cooked human meat, but his grasp of edible spirituality, of the sublime elegance of swallowing the living God, of the dioscuric and aesthetic reversible cycle of to-eat-and-be-eaten, of the limits of unlimited deliquescence, of Les Saveurs Cosmiques, of craving, of the entire corpus of gastroaestheticism was wholly logical.

"I dismiss all the business about his father and wife and Picasso, the consecrated wafer of the paternal communion and all of that, as sentimental hogwash. But when he links the funereal cannibalistic ritual to the death theme of devouring, to the orality whose occult face will be revealed by the gastrointellectual eating of the dead, he clarifies rather than obscures the curious and organic duality of the dioscuric phantasm. God says, by extension, the wish to know devours me, but I devour that wish. Dali correctly identifies the orality-death linkage.

"Have you ever studied Carlo Carra's *Funeral of the Anarchist Galli?* I once saw a picture of it in a library book." He starts to tell Dr. Norman that he tore it out and ate the picture for the same reason that he ate the hearts of some of his vic . . . persons but he was not completely sure that it was a put-on and he hated to tell them anything even remotely usable.

Outside the dream, memory, formula, hypothesis, the moon burns down bright as day, lighting the ridges and fissures of Daniel Edward Flowers Bunkowski's brain wrinkles in a golden glow. The dark clouds resemble the frontal lobe. He tries to slam the secret door closed but he is still too fat to emerge from his hollow prison. On the bright side, however, frogs have been found alive inside lumps of burning coal.

Such was the nature of the new Alpha Group II Variant Beta that he could remember neither the mainland off-loading nor the Lilliputian idiots who had physically deposited him ashore. Snatches of Dr. Norman filtered through in an empyrean cloud of buzz kickier than a Jamaican splib soaked in hash oil: "sensorimotor responses, sonic repatterning, megaplexities of pre-cognitive suggestion, programmed telekinetics, and intravenously induced something . . ." He pondered his own circulatory mechanics; the hemodynamics of his bloodstream; the puzzles of his "behavior modification," and of course understood. But understanding was nothing.

It was one thing to know that the CGS unit of magnetic induction equal to the magnetic flux density that will induce an EMF of one one-hundred-millionth of a volt in each linear centimeter of a wire moving laterally at a centimeter per second at right angles to the flux is gauss, and quite another to grab a live wire. It's simply a matter of knowledge versus understanding.

Knowledge, well . . . He knew they tranqed his ass full of drugs and put him in play like a machine. He was their killer robot. Turned loose, *sine die*, so long as it served their purpose. He was Dr. Norman's pet loose cannon. He tried to curse but his tongue was improbably thick, his lips were numb, and the roof of his mouth was unaccountably missing.

He knew he was more or less comfy behind the wheel of a '92 Buick Park Avenue. Maroon and silver and doubtless street legal. From the goodies in the glove box leased to a blind-corp out of Amarillo, Texas. A spook car. Burgundy leather. Big enough to handle a driver the size of a meat freezer. A darkened parking lot. A bright neon MOTEL sign a hundred yards away, all of it as real as stolen money. He allowed his heavy eyelids to close and let the drugs work.

They had programmed him carefully, as always: video optics and stills, audionics, olfactory input, taste and tactile impressions; sophisticated and meticulously sculpted to hook him. The lion coughed again inside his icy mind, and a flood of images engulfed him.

Shalita Jefferson they said her name was. Two of the monkeys from Clandestine Services sat facing her at a long, plain wooden table. The light was way too bright, bouncing off a silver umbrella, and natural sunlight slanted through the windows along one wall painted a bureaucrat beige.

"How are you feeling, Shalita? Are you tired?" The one across from her, facing away from the camera, was bald and combing what remained from side to side the way bald guys sometimes do. The other was just a suit.

"Huh uh."

"Just a few more questions," the bald one said. She nodded. "So you say all this stuff happened down *under* the orphanage?" The third or fourth time they'd asked her. It was getting old and she let them have a little attitude.

"Tha's right," she said, a pout starting.

"In a dungeon."

"Tha's what we called it. You can say it's a basement. Whatever. It was the dungeon."

"Then you'd go back upstairs."

"Next day. You know—after you been used. They got done with you they let you go back up till next time they wanted it."

"When you were used, for sex, how often—what was the fr—uh, was it every day or what?"

"I dunno." She shrugged. Bored. "Sometimes it was sometimes it wasn' sometimes it was. Depend."

"You're telling us you were raped and beaten and forced into prostitution for *two years* and you couldn't ever escape?" the suit asked.

"I ain't lying about it," she snapped. "You don't wanna believe me tha's your problem."

"But Shalita," the bald one said in a softer voice, "didn't you ever try?"

"You don't know them nuns. I was locked down all that time. How'm I gonna get away? I saw what they did to a couple that tried to run. They got beat *bad*. Then . . . we never see 'em again. Huh uh. I was gonna wait and when I could run I'd get away and they wouldn't catch me."

The drugs made the lions cough again as afferent stimuli shot impulses inward toward his brain.

"—escaped when they took you to the man's house in Crocker City—" Just words now. He remembered them asking her to name the kids. He saw the dossier as he heard her sigh. "—what I toll ya, before. Machelle, Timmie, Carmen, Randy, Darnell—" He saw Spike's picture. The street child the beast had befriended. His only human friend. Words.

"— the fat one we called Mutha' Superior call her that—Grace. Rat-face old bitch. Messed with us, too. The boys had to watch for Mutha' Superior. She was a big fat *strong* bitch and she like to *hurt*. Even the pries' came down and mess with us said she got too carried away. I heard him get on her case when she burn Timmie."

"How did that happen?"

"Bitch put an iron on him. She get mad at you enough you was gonna vanish, you know what I'm sayin'?"

"Tell us about this boy . . ." Spike again. The beast tried in vain to tighten the screw that would pull his brain fracture back together. It was like trying to cut paper with loose scissor halves.

Crystal Stroud and the boy called Spike had known one another in Chicago. The first time she'd seen him had been when this dirty, tough, foul-mouthed kid had come up trying to sell her stolen perfume. He had a small box full of fragrances, some expensive stuff, and the girls all tried to help him out when they could. He was so cute. Like a starving puppy. Who could say no to him?

She happened to be in a bad mood the first time he came up bothering her, and she just about bit his head off.

"Get the hell away from me," she'd snarled at him.

"Fuck *you,* bitch," the tiny boy had screamed, touching himself obscenely and daring her to chase him. The other girls had laughed and—later—when he'd gone around the corner, she broke up laughing, too. He was such a tough one, that Spike. How could you help but love him?

It would have been better if she'd never started worrying about him. She knew all too well what the streets were like. But once they came together it was as if destiny had meant them for each other. Street trash that washed up in the same Chicago gutter: Crystal—he called her "Sis"—a working girl, and Spike, a homeless street urchin. They'd become pals. The odd couple. Real damaged goods, the pair of them, an outcall hooker and a little boy, and after she'd found him sleeping with the junkies under the overpass near the turning basin, she'd sort of "adopted" him the way street people will do. They'd talked about living together one day when she got out of the life, being a real family, a brother-sister deal. Never dreaming that one day it would be a reality.

Crystal had incurred the wrath of a "boyfriend" for whom she wasn't making enough money. He'd done everything but set fire to her, and the boy found her. It was his turn to do a rescue number.

The kid, Spike, had befriended a giant—a hit man whose main number was offing pimps—and it was to the big man he turned for help. A friendship had developed between Spike and the killer. The man had even fixed him up with a single-shot .22 and taught him how to use it. Taken him to the man who time and time again had sexually molested him. He'd been there when the boy went for payback.

An "unknown assailant" had left a neat hole in the head of the freak who had been Spike's biological father, but on the street everybody was hip that the word "father" was about actions and deeds—it didn't have shit to do with biology. The man called Daniel was his *father,* if you had to go putting handles on everything. The man might not like it, he might not want to *be* it, but there it was. He'd given the kid lots of money, and a diamond ring for the girl, and sent them both away. Sis had told him that the man was a "serial" killer and a "mass murderer," but that didn't mean jack to him. The giant was more of a father than anybody else had ever been. Nobody's perfect, he told her. How many times he'd wished for the man back—just to talk—since he'd come to live with his big sister.

She'd slipped back into the life, tricking in Kentucky for a long-haired redneck prick named Joey. They'd ended up in a little burg called Oak Hills, right outside Amarillo, Texas. Some family: Sis, Joey, and Spike. Spike and Joey hated each other from jumpstreet. Spike got Sis told good for giving the big ring to Joey, "for their wedding ring," even if Joey wasn't legally wed to her.

Spike was a grown man in a little boy's wiry body. He liked Texas well enough—it was clean, there were parks and stuff, and he spent his summer days goofing off, mostly by himself, a loner by choice. At dusk he came back to the little rented house in Oak Hills, just like Sis told him to do.

"Hi, Sis," he said, slamming the door. She was in the kitchen fixing them supper.

"Hi, hon. You hungry?"

"Yeah." He flopped down at the kitchen table in the chair he always sat in. He was about to ask if they were going to eat by themselves for a change but he heard the toilet flush and the sound caused him to frown and sigh. Too bad. Pretty soon Joey came into the kitchen, putting his arms around the woman and kissing her abstractly as she chopped stuff into the salad bowl.

"Let's eat," he said. He ignored the kid and began whispering something about having to date later. Spike knew he made her go out at night—he was pimping her. She ended up with the same thing she'd run away from.

"Do I gotta go tonight, baby," she purred, "I'm really out of it and I'm hoping we could—" He cut her off.

"Two bills, goddammit. It's a done deal. Just go get it, all right?" He plopped down at the table. " 'Sup, punk?" he wised off at the boy, spoiling for a fight. A year ago this fool talked to him that way he'd have pulled a razor and used it on him, but Sis was in love with the asshole and she'd begged him not to talk back. He swallowed the insult and just shook his head. "Let's go, doll. I'm starved."

"Soup's on," she said, putting bowls of food in front of them. The big gold ring covered in diamonds winked obscenely from Joey's middle finger. Spike knew the back of the band was wrapped in tape so it would stay on. It had been a giant's pinkie ring. Spike wished he could cut the finger off and take the ring back right now.

"Get your eyes full, punk," Joey said, seeing the boy staring daggers at him. "Hey, angel, I know just what your little bro here needs. I looked into this two-week summer camp the Catholics have called Camp Retreat—gives kids a nice, healthy couple weeks in the boonies before they have to start school. They learn all kindsa shit like swimming, fishing, you know—all that crap. Keeps the little bastards out of trouble."

"Yeah?" she said, smiling. "Sounds nice. Think you'd like to go to a camp like that?"

"Hell *no*, what for?"

"Don't wise off to Crystal, punk. You're *going,* so get used to it. Be good to get you out from underfoot for two weeks. I signed him up today."

"You ain't my boss." Spike drew back but not in time; the slap knocked him out of the chair.

"Don't! Please, honey." She was over Spike, holding him protectively. The kid was doing his best not to cry, pushing her off. He still had the .22 his real father had given him. He'd *dust* this piece of white trash.

"Get him outta my face."

"Come on." Crystal took Spike into his room.

"I hate that prick," the boy said. The slap stung but he'd get over it, he thought, rubbing his face.

"Don't talk back to him, Spike. The camp wouldn't be so bad, would it—just for two weeks?" He just made a face and looked away, knowing it was a sentence, but she needed to get him out of the house, he figured. It couldn't be worse than this.

"Whatever," he sneered.

"Thanks, hon . . ." She got up. "I'll bring a tray in here, okay?"

He nodded. When she was gone a trickle of tears ran down his cheek but he brushed them away and gritted his teeth, wondering how bad Camp Retreat would be. If Joey picked it out it would have to be a class A bitch. But Spike didn't know half of it.

There wasn't much of a view from the alley where Joey was parked waiting for his connection. Some traffic and another alley, that was about it. He tapped his massive ring against the wheel, waiting.

"Bingo!" he said out loud and looked over at the little boy beside him. "Get off your butt, less' go."

Spike said nothing, sullen and sulking, but he sighed and got out of the stinking car, showing nothing in his face. They walked to the van, which was painted in scenes of idyllic mountains, waterfalls, and forests, and the legend CAMP RETREAT.

"Lou, the kid's ready to roll," Joey said.

"Good," the man said, beaming. "Hop in." He opened the back of the van.

"What about my stuff?" Spike asked.

"Oh, yeah." Joey remembered the small bag and paper sack of clothes in the back. "Wait'll the punk gets his baggage." Spike went back and got his clothes. Everything about this felt wrong. Sis should have come so she could get a look at this guy. Memorize his plates or something. Oh, well, he was a man. If the guy tried to fuck with him he'd cut his throat. He patted the heavy pocket knife that he carried everywhere he went, part of the legacy from the man he always thought of as his real father.

"Make yourself comfy," the weasel-faced man named Lou said. He got in the van and they slammed the door hard behind him.

"You sure this kid's clean?" Lou whispered, getting the money out.

"No relatives. Nothing. Nobody misses him if he drops off the planet. Guaranfuckingteed." He held out his hand for the bills.

There was no more conversation. The weasel-faced man got back in the painted van and CAMP RETREAT pulled out of the alleyway and headed right. Joey drove out and turned left. If he never thought of the punk again it would be too soon.

As usual, Chaingang the beast had overloaded on chemical rush, but as irony would have it, on a massive, unintentional self-inflicted buzz. It had appeared near Chicago's turning basin, his AO of the moment; he'd been trolling for victims. Roughing off pimps. He'd killed some hairy nitwit and taken a previously abused Econoline. In a freezer with a couple of Strohs swimming in melted ice water the beast had found a decanter of cold OJ.

He'd opened the thing, sniffed, and managed a careful, tentative swallow. Delicious. He'd lifted it to his meaty lips and tipped it down in one mighty thirst-quenching chug. Belched, and flopped his nearly quarter-ton back behind the wheel. Pulled out the ignition key and watched hairs begin to pop from his massive arms; black spikes shooting from his skin like wiry little skyrockets. He'd ingested—along with icy Minute Maid—roughly two dozen hits of blotter, some pink, and a major handful of Owsley's finest . . . orange sunshine! Chaingang had dropped LSD.

"Hey— You better haul ass!" A little voice caterwauling, jarring him loose. How long he'd been there in the alleyway beside the d.b., grappling with the hammer of the hallucinogens, was anybody's guess. "You hurt, man? Better book! Cops'll get you!" A screech like fingernails on slate. The boy running before the giant could off-load himself from behind the wheel of the van, but his warning had reopened the electrical receptors. It had saved him.

He remembered their bonding clearly. How he'd saved the boy in turn. Now *they*—Norman's people—had somehow put their killing machine back into play, by using the boy, who might or might not be in a jackpot of unknown dimensions. He tried to assess the situation and felt himself overwhelmed by the new drug. He fought it with all his strength.

One moment he was on the island, the next back on the mainland, deep in some monkey-world nightmare, a program working behind the drugs: "a

Periclesian Archdiocese maintains a safe house for pedophiles" . . . "children being forced to work as" . . . the photo of Spike. They only used him when outrageous acts of animal cruelty or child molestation would take his killing rage to an apogee. Everything was tailored to bring his fury into play. They worked him as if he were their puppet, Dr. Norman controlling the strings.

Of course, there was *his* program and the Program, *their* program, and the two were never the same. Always behind shadow, umbra, shield, there was the larger picture, the offstage handlers; the watchers. He could neither sort wheat from chaff nor fog from smoke bomb. Certain givens ruled: Spike was in danger. He felt the kid's threat level as he would have his own, even through the Beta-haze.

He was no longer in a darkened parking lot, but moving, driving through the night, guided by a pull of human heartbeat and pure instinct. Spike and the behemoth were on the same wavelength, and their neural communication could not be faked. It was on this superhuman plateau the boy screamed into the mind of Daniel Edward Flowers Bunkowski. And all the beast could see—with his full focus of resources attuned—was that image of the nun and the little boy on whom she'd performed an orchiectomy. It left him with a feeling that was the closest thing he'd ever known to fear.

Spike was nearby. He could sense the boy's presence, and the awareness of implicit peril brought his concentration to a point most humans could never comprehend: some tap dance about priests and nuns, some cockeyed Dr. Norman nonsense, it was of no relevance. He was locked, loaded, and as dangerous as a grizzly in the linen closet, moving through the door of something called Our Lady of Tender Mercies, a pipe from the duffel they'd thoughtfully provided with a full load of double-ought—the Mossberg 500, stainless steel sawed-off with heat shield, four in the sweeper, one in the chamber—a nun appearing from out of nowhere, saying some bullshit, as he wound unerringly to the left through a rectory archway, passing stained leaded glass, through a plushly carpeted foyer and straight into the office of a man of the cloth.

"Hello? May I—" and around the desk touching the priest in a way he'd never been touched, some monstrous *thing* suddenly materializing out of thin air and *manhandling* him.

"The boy. Spike. Where do you keep him? I know there are other children. Take me to them now or I will tear your heart out of your chest"—not a threat, a rumbling basso profundo with terminal halitosis as sincere as leukemia in the man's face.

"I don't—*YAAAGH!* PLEASE!" Chaingang twisting the man's chest, one of the most painful come-along holds there is.

"I'll rip your nipples off next. Believe it. Now where . . . *are* . . . they?"

"Yes." The man was starting to cry. "I'll take you to them. Please don't, please—" The priest buckling at the first hideous pain jolt. "Oh!" He was hurt.

"Move. Let's go. You can cry later. Where are they?" Moving him from behind the desk, the two of them like clumsy dancers, the priest off the floor as he tried to point.

The woman who'd asked the gigantic intruder what he wanted had heard the Father scream and ran into the doorway. She was slammed by a wall and her lights were extinguished instantly, but the wall was long gone by the time she fell.

The two of them stopped at a small door marked PRIVATE, the priest nodding through his tears of pain. He moved, did something, and Chaingang, beginning to redline, realized it was an elevator even before the door slid soundlessly open. They stepped in.

"One trick"—his rumbling whisper was a menacing thing that tasted like garlic in the priest's mouth—"and you're a dead pervert."

"Please—" Fear sweat dripped off him in waves. The priest managed to punch the bottom of a set of four buttons. The elevator sank to sublevel one and they got out, more or less together, the priest more frightened than he'd ever been in his life. They moved quickly through a large basement meeting area filled with folding chairs and long tables, entered a small utility chamber, and then a supply room beyond that.

The priest nodded toward a door. They entered. A dim light glowed. He started to say, "The door must be shut—" but the giant had already pulled it closed behind them, found the switch, and was opening the thick, sound-proofed door. It revealed a long, empty tunnel. Chaingang looked into the eyes of the priest, looking death into the man's heart. "Just across there—the other entranceway—" his voice small and scared, as he felt himself being moved, the huge beast propelling him toward the heavy wooden door. A sur-veillance slit was covered by a sliding, spring-held device and Chaingang snicked it open and peered into the darkness. Saw the light switch. Hit it. Illu-minated four small forms, apparently asleep in a large stone room.

They entered through the heavy, bolted, and locked door and two of the kids looked up. Spike and a dark-haired boy about his age, also Caucasian, a Black girl of maybe eight or nine, a female Latina child perhaps thirteen. Mouths taped with silver tape. Eyes wide with fear.

Rage poured through the giant like molten lava. He pounded the priest on top of the head with a bottom fist hard as a sledgehammer, and the man dropped like a sack.

"MMMF!" Spike doing his best to speak. Agitated. Moving all over the place in spite of being hog-tied.

He felt the threat even as Spike telepathed it. It was Mutha' Superior who had waddled out of her personal quarters on huge, bare feet so as not to make noise. She was truly massive in every way, an apparition nearly as awesome as Bunkowski himself, not as tall but wider and nearly as strong, a woman who resembled Chaingang in a nun's habit, a monstrous thing about an inch away from the back of his head with a ball bat almost to the target when the Mossberg 500 roared and she sprayed him with a nasty shpritz of dark blood, his reflexive whirl causing the bat to barely tick him as he blew her into dogshit. It was still enough to knock him from his feet.

He bounced up, shook off the pain, and concentrated on getting the kids loose. Spike was running his mouth but he paid no mind. He was half deaf from the noise of the twelve gauge and half goofy from the ball bat.

"Come on," he said, racking another shell into the mouth of the pipe and herding the kids back around the mess in the tunnel.

"—told you he'd find me—" he could hear the boy say to one of the other kids. They moved back the way he'd come, heading out of the church and toward freedom.

Too easy, almost. Where was the security? An archdiocese with that much money and clout, into *that* degree of organized child sex, and not so much as a gun-toting rent-a-cop? Were they so arrogant, or was the huge nun all they felt was necessary? Too easy, Dr. Norman, he thought. But he shrugged off the notion that he'd forgotten something and they were back in the vehicle and moving.

"How'd you *know*?" Spike asked for the third time. He tried to give the huge man at the wheel a hug in response to Chaingang's version of a shrug. "I told Trace you'd find me, man." Trace was the boy on the back seat.

"Nn." Bunkowski did his best to dismiss the kid with body language, which was a serious thing in his case, but the boy was as wild as a box of puppies and twice as friendly. "Where do each of you want to go?" he rumbled. He couldn't wait to get this pack of smelly children out of his ride.

"My grandma's house," the girl—Carmen—said. He questioned her sufficiently to determine that it sounded reasonably safe, and headed for the first cab stand he could spot. He wasn't about to run all over Texas like a fucking escort service.

"Shouldn't we call the cops?" Trace piped up.

"Don't be stupid," Spike snarled, "all they know how to do is turn your ass over to Juvey. *Never* call those assholes." He was eleven going on thirty, street smart, and Chaingang realized the boy wasn't wiggling with energy, the kid was trembling. Every kid in the vehicle looked scared shitless. Small wonder.

"Where do you want to go?" he asked Spike. "I can set you up safely wherever you say."

"I'm staying with you," the kid said with all the finality he could muster. Knowing he was going to be turned down. Blinking back tears and saying the one word Chaingang didn't want to hear, his voice choked with emotion. "Please?" Whispered like a prayer.

"What about you, boy?" he asked Trace, trying his best not to commit himself to Spike. Knowing damn well he was going to let the kid go with him.

"Please—mister—can me and Spike stay together? Can I go with you? I—"

"No, that's impos—"

"I don't have nobody wants me. I got nowhere to go." Trace blurted the words out. Chaingang could sense him trembling.

"Please, Pop, let him come with us," Spike asked.

"Goddamn . . ." Chaingang hated the feeling of helplessness that prevailed in the car, the atmosphere ripe with the smell of scared children. "I'm not your father so . . ." He shook his huge head.

"Please, he won't be no trouble. I'll personally get him with the program," the little street urchin promised. "Can he?"

Jeezus, Chaingang thought. Something about this was funny. He wanted to laugh.

"What about you, little girl?" He glanced at the small, cowering child in the backseat. "Where do you live?"

"She don't talk," Carmen told him. "We don't know where she came from."

He found a row of taxis in front of a hotel, and let the older girl out, giving her some money. He put Carmen in a cab personally, glowering at the East Indian driver and then smiling dangerously at him.

"Make sure she gets home safely, Mr. Pashwar," he threatened, reading the man's name off his license, "and with a minimum of conversation, please. She's tired." A huge, frightening, paternal smile. "All right?"

"Of course, you bet," the driver said, as Carmen got in the vehicle. Bunkowski drove away rather aimlessly, sorting options, while he looked for an out-of-the-way motel.

"Norman R. Childs" and family were pleasantly nestled all snug in their beds when the maids employed by the Live Oaks Motor Lodge and Cafe began their ritual banging and screaming at eight A.M. the next morning. Childs was awake, having awakened at precisely seven without benefit of alarm clock or telephone, but still in his king-sized bed, grossly nude and staring at the ceiling, working through various mental checklists when the shrieking of the maids penetrated the jet-engine decibel level of the Live Oaks's AC. He pulled his tonnage more or less erect, and padded on 15EEEEE splayed feet to the bathroom. There he proceeded to shower and shave, after which he defecated in the sink, wiped on the curtains, and urinated on the mattress. These, and other vile personal acts too unspeakable to detail, were standard with him, and done out of no special maliciousness. He felt it was his moral duty to behave toward the monkeys in a certain manner on principle. That was why—for example—he always turned a faucet off so hard that the washers split through; why he always shoplifted even when he could easily afford to pay; why he liked to leave certain surprises in the adult products of convenience store shelves; why he had so many unfortunate accidents—falling, crushing, tearing, breaking, manhandling—when he was in public places; why he routinely vandalized parked vehicles; why he put hideous things inside public telephones. It was good for the monkeys. It kept them alert.

He was on the phone, the drapes admitting sunlight, when the boys came in.

"Hey," Spike said. He might have tilted his head an eightieth of an inch in greeting, but otherwise did not acknowledge their intrusive presence.

"Yes—that'll be fine," he boomed into the telephone. "The keys will be at the motel office in your name, and there's a down payment in the glove compartment. The rest will be waiting for you as agreed, in your name in care of Los Angeles General Delivery . . . I'm sure there'll be no problems. Thanks and—have a safe trip." Mr. Childs hung up the phone.

"What was that all about?" Spike said, starting to sit down on the urine-soaked bed, then catching himself in time. He had the sense not to ask anything else.

Chaingang made a note and looked up as if he'd just seen the two for the first time.

"Where's the little girl?"

"Sleepin'. You want us to wake her up?"

"No. But one of you stay with her. The other one, take this—" he stretched a massive paw out and Spike took a handful of money "—and go over there to the cafe. Here is a list of what I want you to bring me. Get whatever you two want, and get a plate of bacon and eggs and some fresh orange juice for the girl. Bring me my food first then you all can eat. Make sure one of you is with the girl. I have to go out briefly. Don't let the maid in. Tell her she can come back when we've checked out. Do it."

"You stay with her," Spike ordered, taking the money. Trace nodded and the boys left. He'd put them in the adjoining room, the little girl in one bed, them in another. He called after Spike as he left.

"When you get done eating take a *shower*."

Spike waved a limp hand but he kept going, thinking to himself that he might stink but at least he didn't wet *his* bed. He was so happy to see his big pop that he smiled for the first time in a long while.

He was planning what he would have to buy for the children, whether to go for two sizes of crossbows, how much bottled water should they take, what about changes of clothing? What should he do about the girl? He trusted no one, least of all the family services and foster care system. It made him physically uncomfortable to think about having to take *three children* with him even for a short trip. Was it absolutely necessary? He knew zero about little girls and their care and this specimen did not even speak. What if it needed . . . *milk* . . . or something? He was in as close to a dither as he ever got.

He made up his mind. There was a time element at work. The children had to go but they could take hind tit if push came to shove, and if they didn't like that they could all go back to Our Lady of Tender Baseball Bats. He really didn't give a good righteous fuck at this point.

First things first. First he would *eat,* and the anticipation of a triple order of sausage and hash browns, one dozen eggs scrambled in butter, a half gallon of orange juice, ten pieces of toast, and three breakfast fillets—rare—would take the sting off the morning. He could *think* then, and see where the holes were.

He was not trying to evade anyone but he wanted a jump on his *watchers*. When the young man who'd called the Oak Hills News in answer to his ad had arrived at the newspaper office, he'd found a cleaned XXXXL-size cammo T-shirt waiting for him to try on over his own clothing, together with Chaingang's old bush hat. Yes, the shirt was a little big but it fit pretty good. He had a valid Texas Motor Vehicle and the money sounded right for the drive to California.

Bunkowski would run his other traps and as soon as the girl was up they'd depart for parts unknown, with only Bunkowski's brain implant to make anyone the wiser. His only big decision remaining was whether to make Dr. Norman get him a boat, buy one, or steal one . . . and that was no decision at all.

When he'd first gotten up that morning he'd placed his own call to a young woman in Amarillo, who'd been hired in the same way as his California man. He was going to meet this lady now and give her a handsome sum of money for almost nothing.

Three orders of sausages and hash browns later, with the three children awake and expectantly quiet, the crew loaded into a strange old station wagon and headed due south. Mr. Childs was behind the wheel in this weird cap, with what looked like a pair of Ray Charles's old shades. They were driving, windows down, toward the heat.

Money and Buick keys were waiting for a big heavyset guy at the motel office, and Mr. Childs dropped some envelopes in a corner letter box. Letters to Texas and New Mexico newspapers and sheriff's detectives about some gang of child molesters using a couple of Catholic orphanages as fronts. He'd had some time waiting for breakfast and—who knew?—they might even act on the information if he hit the right party.

He also remembered seeing a woman's name somewhere; she was a gung ho prosecutor from out East who'd been sacked because she took her work too seriously, and had moved to Albuquerque. He'd called her personally, given her a bit of the basics with as little rhetoric as he was capable, and put her on the trail of the Periclesians. She demanded more but got only a buzzing sound from AT&T. Mr. Childs, the informant, had skedaddled.

By dawn's rays they were back in two rooms of a Comfort Inn in God-knows-where geography of no further interest. He would head south till they saw water. He was aimed at the Gulf.

Time compressed, in the passage through a crumbling cityscape of forgotten architecture, the disintegrating gateway to another world. Then, through the bug-sprayed windshield of the station wagon, the Gulf lay waiting for them like a dark and boundless mystery, on the other side of a mid-sized marina. The smell of it, rich and indefinable, fish, worms, smoke, oil, diesel, mud, alcohol, camphor, detritus, nameless drift, the waste of commerce and leisure time, the smell of water flooded their senses. There was a smorgasbord of boats.

"You must be very still. Wait here together and do not speak until I return. I will be back very soon. Stay," he commanded, as one would order an overly friendly puppy to obey. He flung his poundage from behind the wheel and closed the door more quietly than usual. They watched his immense silhouette disappear into the night. He had not prepared a tranq so he hoped there would be no guard dog. His plan was simple: find the night watchman, put him to sleep, and take a boat. What could be simpler? Need a boat? Find one and take it.

Oddly enough, that is what he did. There was no guard of any kind, neither two- nor four-footed. Sometimes it worked that way. Everything from skiffs to fishing boats to big yachts rode their lines in the calm moonlit waters. He saw one that was perfect and went back to get the kids.

It was a big Challenger. Probably $350,000 back when it was new, and it handled as easily as a luxury car. They were all aboard and he had them cast off within a matter of minutes. Chaingang choked the big engines to life, touched the throttle with a huge paw, and took the helm. Momentarily they were leaving the dock behind them, slapping chop.

A pair of gulls triggered an image from left field: he flashed on two birds, perched side by side; crested finch and glossy oscine Corvus; something he'd fed his mindscreen through the Variant Beta programming. Lost now. A failed mnemonic, the only thing worse than an omen misread.

The children were all sleeping down below by the time he'd docked at their next port. No name, but a big Getty Power-Test sign and that was name enough. He topped off the tanks, woke Spike to stand guard, and paid for the gas, explaining he had to go ashore briefly.

By the time Chaingang was back aboard, the Challenger was running considerably lower in the water. The vessel was packed with cases of freeze-dried rations and MREs, seeds, a tremendous load of Charmin Ultra, ammo, arms, ordnance, gasoline; the usual necessities of life.

Bottled water and lots of it was a big part of the heavy cargo; that was one luxury he'd not deny them. There was no TV, which brought a mild protest from the boys, but there was a small gas generator that could power an ice maker. Bunkowski had missed cold water even more than fast foods.

It was a pleasant sun-baked excursion, but all of them were thrilled by the sight of land. The small, uncharted island was roughly the shape of a flat-cornered C. The opening was very small and in some of the worse terrain, thick jungle that clogged the windward side, a ragged cove that cut back into the top right corner of the C. The only place to put in or land a boat was on the gently sloping sandy stretch of beachfront that edged the opposite side.

Chaingang temporarily berthed the Challenger as far as he could at high tide, securing it to huge palms and an anchor even *he* could barely lift. The first week was spent in backbreaking labor, primarily his, as they worked to carve out a place where they could bring the boat up on land out of view of prying surveillance.

This required the crew rising at the first hint of dawn, eating—or watching the beast eat—the main meal of the day, and then trekking from where they slept on the leeward beach to the tiny cove. It could have been accomplished easier just by taking the boat around each day but he wanted a new pathway inland, so two days were spent chopping, burning brush, and battling insects. The kids ended up covered from head to toe with scratches from the jungle foliage, bug bites beyond imagining, and filth that not even a soak in the sea completely removed at the end of the day.

The little girl sat and silently watched them, usually accompanied by Chaingang's old pal the monkey, who seemed less interested in the huge man's return, or in the rowdy pair of boys, than in the little, quiet, dark-skinned girl. He chattered indecipherable advice to the boys as he and the girl watched.

The child who never spoke concerned Bunkowski to the extent that—on the third morning—he decided he'd better give her a complete examination. He told the boys what he was going to do and sent them on ahead to start work while he looked at her, as gently as he could, from stem to stern.

"I am not going to hurt you in any way," he rumbled softly, taking her in huge paws and pushing her back on the bush tarp. The expected tussle never happened. She didn't move, which was not a good sign in his view. "I have to look at you now," he said. She didn't blink an eye as he checked her physical condition, not even when he quickly and efficiently examined her privates, or pried her tiny jaws open and peered into the darkness of her little mouth with the aid of his penlight. "You're fine. No problem. Get dressed," he told her.

There was nothing unusual to be seen in the way of visible damage, but her eyes told a far different story. There was little to be done for her, he concluded. No magic petroleum jelly to smear on the abrasions the perverts had left. He got her dressed again in the jeans and torn top she wore, and the two of them set off to join the boys.

"It could just be," Chaingang said, resuming work, "that she doesn't have anything to say. Or that she's been around people who spoke too often when *they* didn't have anything to say." He whacked off a tree limb the size of a Light Antitank Weapon in one pulp-crunching swing. "I see no problem with it as a lifestyle. Perhaps we should all take a vow of silence in the girl's honor." He looked over at her. She was staring straight ahead, the identical look as when he was examining her. It was a look that said "nobody home."

By the week's end the borrowed Challenger was moored, baffled, and secure, in a tiny bite out of the island that put the big vessel out of sight from the sea. The next job was to secure it from overflight surveillance. Chaingang spent the next day issuing orders to the boys and working on the basic cammonet that would hold the foliage.

They were informed the jungle foliage would be changed at least five times a month. This was the boys' first island classroom experience, How to Camouflage, and the professor happened to be the ultimate living master of that particular art and science.

"When we have successfully hidden the boat from intruders we shall use our newfound ability on ourselves, and learn an interesting game. A very serious game that will, when you begin to absorb its complexities, be capable of protecting you.

"The two of you, myself, the girl if she wishes to, will take turns hiding. You've played hide-and-seek, I'm sure, or heard of it. But this game is played for reward or punishment. You . . . me, when it's my turn, will be given an hour to hide *anywhere*. The rest of us have an hour to find the hidden party."

"What if I climb a tree?" Trace asked, sure that his big new friend could not follow him if he climbed.

"Fine. There are no rules. Bury yourself if you can figure out how to do it. Anything goes. We'll then have an hour to find the hidden party. We will use an hourglass, but during the hiding I will also teach you how to make an inner clock that *never* fails, that always tells time, needs no maintenance, and that you can carry with you anywhere—even into a maximum security prison. This inner clock is also invisible, you need neither sun nor moonlight to operate it, and you'll learn how to construct it in one day. I assure you that it will be your *easiest* lesson, so enjoy every moment.

"If you can remain hidden for an hour, you will get *our* food for that day, to do with as you wish. If you are found, we get yours. Unless you wish to starve you will damn well learn to hide properly." He was getting worked up just thinking about the possibility of losing his food for a day. He happened to glance over at the little girl and she was ignoring him, watching the monkey, but she was sitting cross-legged.

The vocabulary their teacher used was uncompromising. He never reduced polysyllabic words when he was in an explanatory mode; the phrases spilled from his tongue direct from his mindscreen, unedited. He conveyed to them what they needed—in part—by elastic facial contortions and awesome body language.

Hide-and-seek was a semidisaster. They all nearly starved to death the first three days. He found the kids easily each time they hid, but the little ferrets went after his trail just as relentlessly and they found him the first time as well. He'd underestimated them.

This conspired to put him in one of his foulest moods, as it deprived him of his supper. The next day he was up at dawn and rudely awakened them. They would play "more seriously" this time. He hid. An hour of sand trickled through the glass. Nothing. They kept looking. Another hour. Still nothing.

"You *win*! You can come out now!" Their shouts could be heard all over the island.

"You can have our *food*! You won! Where are you?" He waited three hours. Around nine A.M. he swam toward shore and when he could stand he began walking out of the sea, his face covered in multicolored cammo net of blue, green, and earth tones.

"You never said we could hide in the *water*!" Spike protested. "Goddammit, that's fuckin' *cheating*!"

"You lose," he rumbled pleasantly.

"Bullshit." Spike wasn't having any of it. It was wrong. "That ain't fair." He was angry because he'd started to worry.

"Yeah," Trace agreed, "you changed the rules!"

"There's only one rule," he told them. "An old acquaintance of mine taught me that. The only rule is that there are no rules. Remember that."

Each day was spent in "island class," but from time to time he would give them—or himself—the day off and they wouldn't see him all day. He required resuscitation—shots of isolation to keep from exploding. Their eyes, the way they *watched* him all the time, was something he found disgusting, but he forced himself to ignore or endure it.

They, too, needed time to themselves, and occasionally the boys would wander off to play or fish, alone or as a pair. They might take the girl with them, but typically she would just sit on the beach, playing with the monkey when he would stay with her, otherwise just looking at the waves for hours on end. Never speaking. Eating when food was given to her. Drinking when she was thirsty. Performing the biological functions quickly, washing in the sea, the same rag of top and jeans turning to shreds.

"You will be our watcher," he told her, always anxious to put the kids to as much use as he could—especially for his own benefit—and he gave her a small pair of sunglasses. "If you ever see a reflection from goggles or a mask like a swimmer wears, or if you ever see someone watching us from the water, you come and tell me." Never mind that she didn't know what goggles or a mask was, or that she couldn't talk. He simply created the position and let her figure out if she cared to fill it.

He gave the boys sunglasses as well but only had them wear them during specific time periods when they would watch the sea together. He taught them how to look at quadrants, about rods, cells, visual renewal, how to look for something. Who were they looking for? A *watcher*. He would come from the sea far away, from a silent boat. Probably come in the night or early morning and would have underwater breathing gear. He would have to surface at some point, and when they saw this sparkle of glass or the oval of a camouflaged face, they were to tell Chaingang on the double.

He'd removed the big anchor from the boat and used it in a kind of shot put, and a couple of times a day, usually right before dinner time, he would throw it—tethered with both bailing wire and stout nylon kept in a perfect coil—directly at an imagined spot in the sea. The first week he only managed to throw it a few yards, but each day he was building up his strength and the massive anchor was inching farther and farther. What he was practicing for weighed far less than the anchor.

Wrapped in watertight sealed pouches and buried in a shallow sandy grave, an object waited for the hurling. The boys knew not to go near it—only a thick leather and canvas strap protruded from the place it was secreted— and they knew it was a high explosive that he called a "sah-chul charge." Buried in the sand was an MK-26 Model 0 Haversack, which contained eight 2.5-pound cast blocks of HBX. Over twenty butt-kicking pounds of hygroscopic big bang—just waiting for a surprise visitor.

Only a fool would starve on the island Bunkowski called Shark's Head Cay, as long as he found seafood palatable. "Bream entrails are good for catching turtles, which make a nourishing soup when prepared properly. Here is the proper way to catch a turtle." He took a combination of strange-looking parts from a fresh-caught bream and forced them onto his hook. "If the sea is choppy, or if you are fishing in a swift current such as a river, you need more weight. A quick way to add weight is to tie an ordinary washer onto the line with a double half hitch." His fingers dexterously threaded mono through the washer, tied it on, and he cast the line out again. Very soon this time a slight pull on the line alerted him.

"Got something." He slowly eased it out. "Turtle. Eel. Both bite bream guts." It was a large sea turtle, and he pulled it up on the sand. "Start the big pot of water boiling and we'll make soup." Trace ran to comply, but as Chaingang started to harvest the turtle with his blade Spike interrupted him.

"Look at Girl!" he said.

Chaingang looked over at the child. She was standing up with her hands in front of her, silently screaming in horror, mouth wide open, eyes huge, obviously terrorized.

"What the—"

PLEASE, she begged him. He heard it loudly inside his mind. *PLEASE!* Heard clearly as a shout.

It's all right, he tried to tell her with his mind, nodding, sheathing the blade, quickly getting the vise grip pliers and carefully flattening the barbed hook, easing it out of the turtle's mouth. *It's all right,* he repeated, sure by her expression she understood, gently carrying the large turtle back to the edge of the lapping waves. It didn't move.

"Go on," he said aloud. *ESCAPE,* he was sure he heard her say in their shared thoughts. So she and Spike could both talk to him! He did not try to communicate with her again and she and the monkey went off to play. He prepared instant freeze-dried ham and limas instead of soup. There was no sense of gratitude or affection. He didn't expect it or want it, but he was pleased that she could communicate. Perhaps in time the abilities she and Spike had could be nurtured and in some way developed.

He gave each of them a plain brown sack with their name printed on it in black Magic Marker: TRACE, SPIKE, GIRL. Presents, he called them. The boys were very excited. He'd given them small crossbows. The girl didn't touch her sack. He opened it and showed her the very sharp filet knife that had almost been used on the turtle.

"Be careful with this," he said, showing her by shaving a few huge hairs from the back of a steel-solid arm just how sharp it was. "It is dangerous. It cuts." He put it back in the sheath and reached over to untie her waist cord. She didn't flinch or move. He threaded the cord onto the sheath and retied it. "That's yours now. I will teach you how to protect yourself with it."

"Me 'n' Trace can teach her," Spike said, flipping open a blade similar to the large brass-bound jackknife Chaingang had given him in Chicago. "I'll teach her just as good as I did him." He glanced at Trace. "Watch." He threw the blade to the other boy who snapped it open easily, keeping it beside his leg sharp side up, the blade for gutting, just as Spike had been taught. "See?" Chaingang may have inclined his immense head a sixty-fourth of an inch.

There were several weapons tucked away between tissue rolls and bottled water. He had two heavier-duty crossbows and a serious combat knife put away for the kids as they grew into them, but he wanted the boys to have instant confidence in the important skill of archery. He began teaching the crossbow's use as both a direct assassination and mantrapping weapon.

He was particularly aware of such subtleties as weapon preferences among the children. The little girl sometimes wore the sheathed filet knife, sometimes she left it where she slept, but always the monkey was with her, or she with it. When it went to explore, or to find food, she generally tagged along. Chaingang noticed that her attention span was improving and although there was no communication from her, the three of them always included her in activities and conversation, to the extent that she let them.

Trace was obviously a blade man, and practiced with the folding knife constantly. Chaingang taught him rudiments and made a heavy swinging target for him to work on. He also gave the boy a set of cheap throwing knives, and taught him basics, with the admonition that at least 98 percent of the time, under field conditions, the skill was unusable for all but the exceptionally talented knife thrower. In time the kid would know if he had the gift for sharp iron.

Spike had proved himself as a shooter on more than one occasion, but while the skinny puppy was reliable Chaingang saw no further need to burden the boy with a single-shot weapon. He gave Spike his own Colt Woodsman, which he considered an inaccurate, weak flyswatter. Spike frowned; he'd heard his big pop bad-mouth the weapon.

"Yes, it's not very accurate, but neither is the stripped hush puppy. The thing's so weak a strong man can damn near catch the slugs in his teeth, and almost anything will stop a poorly aimed bullet, but you are not going to have to worry about that. You'll use this weapon the same way you used the skinny puppy, up so close you can't miss. The advantage of more than one round is obvious. But don't fill it up—the springs in these magazines are not heavy duty—I keep six rounds in it. Five in the magazine, one in the chamber. It's always cocked and locked. Ready?" He showed Spike the moving parts and handed it to him.

"Every week take it apart. Break it down. Clean it. Clean inside the magazine, too. One grain of sand anywhere in the weapon and you've got a pistol-shaped club. Five minutes of sea air and this metal starts to rust. Keep it swimming in oil. On land, wipe the oil off. Keep the cartridges oily, too, and keep everything in the rags. Put it in the plastic pouch and give me the skinny puppy back. You won't need it again."

"Could I give it to Trace? . . . I could teach him how to use it?"

Bunkowski shrugged slightly and walked away. But he was pleased. That's what he was going to do himself. The blade should have a backup weapon.

By their sixth week together the kids were going for short ocean swims, diving and quickly resurfacing in the shallow water of the leeward beach, all under Chaingang's watchful gaze. The girl took to water amazingly well, dog-paddling tirelessly, floating, splashing around like a baby seal. He began teaching the three of them breathing and she was the most adept.

"Breath control," he told them, "is the gateway to silence and total invisibility, a way to prolong your life in numerous ways, and also the first gate to the secret place inside the mind where the real magic is. Now, let's see how long you can go without breathing."

He timed them with his inner clock, saying "thirty-one" to Trace and "forty-four" to Spike, whose determination left his face bright purple.

"That is not how one holds one's breath. You are simply taking air into the lungs. It is very self-destructive to hold your breath in that manner, for any number of reasons. We'll begin with the basics, as usual, and show you how to breathe from your *pit*. That is the center of your power, the pit below the central gate to the body's life-support systems. This is a most difficult lesson, harder than anything we've tried, but within a couple of weeks you'll be holding your breath for a minute and a half easily. Until we can all hold our breath for at least two minutes we cannot be safe in the water." He looked hard at Girl, who was not taking part. She was listening, attentive, but so far had not chosen to practice with them.

"Can you hold your breath?" he asked her aloud, repeating it inside his thoughts. She said nothing, but blinked at him with dark, empty eyes. "All right." He turned back to the boys and they began studying the intricacies of deep breathing.

By the end of the second month on the island they were into basic demolition training. Simple stuff with military C-4. To the boys it was fun, and because they trusted their instructor it was like a weeklong Fourth of July, but neither kid had the flair for it and he only gave them a beginner's introduction to the complex art of demo.

Their third month was spent in a variety of disciplines and games. Each day he'd focus on something new. How to Stay Clear of the System, Molesters, Drugs, and the Cops was a two-day seminar punctuated by cleaning and oiling, a brief archery session, shallow dives, and knife sharpening without a whetstone or Carborundum. The next couple of days were a mishmash of mini-dissertations such as How to Get Free Legal Advice Over the Phone, Why Celibacy Is Overrated for Mature Males, How to Buy a Car for Two-thirds List, and things the kids wouldn't be needing for years. Still, he figured, he didn't know how long they'd all be together. Perhaps some of these lessons would stay with them and help them later.

One morning he'd begin showing them how to make a pipe bomb without buying any chemicals or explosives, but he wouldn't like the way they responded to instruction and by noon he'd change the course entirely, spending several days on How to Dumpster-Dive and Garbage-Hunt. It was one of their most important courses. He taught them some of the tricks of obtaining free and handy deep-cover legend, blackmail data, and intelligence, but the thrust of the lessons was generally about resupply and profit. A man or woman could live quite well off the garbage and discards of society, if he or she had the knack for rummaging and scrounging. It was all the more enjoyable, he taught them, because it was getting over on the monkeys whose social system had failed to protect them. He spent lots of time targeting the wealthy—made vulnerable by their trash and garbage—and business and industry that could be screwed savagely with their own computers. He promised them that this was but a syllabus to his Dumpster University post-grad course.

Each day would bring something new and mind-expanding. One morning they went to clean and oil the boat and couldn't find it. For over two hours they hunted for it. Trace spotted it finally, anchored offshore not a hundred yards, bobbing in the gentle waves. In the night he'd repainted it sandy tan, blue green, brown, black, gray, and an off-taupe; redelineating the foliage cammo in a pattern that the waves and bright sun rendered near invisible. It was a brilliant object lesson. Even after they saw it they couldn't quite understand the trickery that had hidden the object in plain sight.

Daniel Bunkowski did not emphasize with human emotions. Nor was he interested in "parenting," "nurturing," or becoming a "father figure" to the children. They had come from their own hells—each of them—and deserved some R and R. That's all this was and, to be sure, he would present a bill in due course. Benevolent was not part of his behavioristic vocabulary. He was Spike's big pop only to Spike. He had his own way of seeing these small creatures who were underfoot.

Girl developed at her own speed. She was growing. Physically healthy. Attentive when it pleased *her* to be. He watched her in the water, blossoming, opening up as the inner petals surrounding sporophyllis spread to drink in the sunlight. He would hone her sharp edges as she strengthened. He would use her.

She in turn received the protective if not loving care of three brothers—four, if one counted the hairiest one—and for a child who has survived madness and terror this is no small influence. Love, as these survivors knew to varying degrees, was defined by actions, not lip service.

Trace was increasingly adept with various blades now in his possession and Spike had taken nicely to the crossbow.

There were areas of disappointment. None of the kids was a rocket scientist: Spike had street smarts and a degree of common sense; Trace was average in overall acumen; Girl was an unknown quantity. Neither of the boys had shown any demolition abilities, and it was an art as much as science or tradecraft.

They were all rather small, wiry children and, of course, Chaingang thought of them as runts. But the island regimen—in tandem with the constant workload—had produced a pair of strong, lean, and sinewy warrior kids. Spike and Trace each had a swimmer's muscles, elongated bikes and trikes, showing some definition in the pecs and lats, with calf baseballs and decent stamina. Spike and Chaingang had ruddy complexions and Trace was nearly as dark as Girl. They were becoming soldiers.

Toward the beginning of their fourth month together Trace spotted the glint off something metal or glass—he was sure of it. Maybe seventy, eighty yards out to sea. He was so excited he forgot their action word—"Watcher"—and came caterwauling at Chaingang, shouting the first thing he could think of to articulate.

Chaingang was sitting on a log cleaning his sawed-off Mossberg, but the moment he saw the kid running at him he was moving. He heard the meaningless word with his mind before Trace's adenoidal scream reached his ears.

"STRANGER!"

That was close enough, Chaingang was off and running, the pistol-grip shotgun in one enormous hand.

"WHERE?" he shouted at the boy, just as the question was answered for him by the stab of sudden pain in his upper torso. A flechette was sticking out of his upper left quadrant and he wasted neither ammo nor time, snatching up the haversack, his tree-trunk legs still pumping, arming it, overwhelmed by warning vibes as he flung the big bag of high explosives far out to sea as the drug already began to hammer him.

"GIRL!" Spike yelled from down the beach. *"Swimmin' underwater!"* It was impossible. The one time somebody spots a watcher the kids are swimming, or perhaps that was what gave the shooter courage to swim in so close. The knowledge he could do nothing.

No hesitation. The huge, steel tree trunks propelled him down the beach and the beast left his feet in a clumsy belly flop of a dive, 300-and-some killer pounds smacking the ocean and taking him down as his eyes strained to spot the little girl's form underwater. The charge went off and it nearly took him off the count.

Like being sideswiped by a truck. The concussion brought him out of the water screaming. Somehow—the boys helping—he dragged himself onto the sand as he went out like a light. The kids and the monkey couldn't budge his dead weight, but the boys got plastic from the boat and the bunch of them pushed and pulled and horsed his bulk a few yards out of the water. He regained the edges of consciousness for a moment, saw three exhausted children and a beat-looking monkey flat on their backs beside him, gasping like fish.

"Where's Girl?" he imagined he asked, but he was looking at her, and the words never crystallized. Spike was the last thing he saw before he passed out again, the boy's wet hair *as dark as a crow's wing* . . .

A bright redbird and a blackbird were side by side, pecking at something. A cardinal and a crow, rather, pecking at carrion. His drug-induced mnemonic inserted a key into the locked door and turned it.

The most dangerous man alive, insofar as a certain cadre within Government was concerned, was neither North Korean, Iraqi, nor Libyan. He was an extraordinarily powerful religious leader, greatly beloved by the public, who knew nothing of his dark side. Behind closed doors this man had become uniquely influential; the man who orchestrated foreign policy; the man who made the kingmakers; the man who enriched political parties with gifts of both money and power; the controller, some believed, of the Vatican's secret purse: *Cardinal Crowe.*

Dr. Norman's people had programmed everything, even the post-mortem contacts, the letters, the available transport, all of it. With the room to his brain unlocked he could easily envision their spin-doctoring of the "massacre" at Our Lady of Tender Mercies. A body would, of course, be found. Media would do its part. "Police have not disclosed the identity" or, perhaps, "The notorious serial killer and mass murderer Daniel Bunkowski" would be believed to be responsible for the assassination of Timothy Cardinal Crowe, whom Chaingang had never seen, much less assassinated. So that was the mission. The kids were orchestrated cover. Spike—he didn't want to dwell on the extent to which he might have been inserted to motivate the beast—his presence would have been an obvious guarantee. Someday he would feed Dr. Norman one of his own flechettes for this, and then spend a very long time making him sorry as he ceased to exist . . . piece by piece.

That was the last thing he saw inside the room, the word ARCH—DIE—OR—CEASE taken apart with a scalpel. The syllables devoured by the hunger machine, the images vanished by the dream carrier in a dark iconographic of nightwings.

"—dead as a dog, man. Your bomb did her." The kids had thought he was fully with them again and they'd been running their mouths; a big conversation that he hadn't been part of was in progress. He blinked haze away and focused on a prone figure in a cammied wet suit. "Wait'll you check out the gun, man, it's way cool! It's made out of—" A meaty mitt stopped the boy's chatter.

"Where is Girl?" he rumbled.

"My name's not Girl," a little voice spoke into the sand. Apparently sleepy.

"What?" Chaingang looked at the small child. *"What?"*

"Name's Ronnie."

"Your name's . . . *Ronnie?"*

"Vuh—*ron*—ee—ca," she repeated, rolling over to sleep.

"Oh," Chaingang said, scowling. Pleased and still confused. He examined the dead sea creature and discovered about what he'd assumed he'd find . . . zip.

He saved the suit and, of course, the dartgun, and dragged her nude body down into the water for a burial at sea.

The little abused girl had not made a sound for over three months, but now everything she'd silently witnessed, felt, imagined, or thought was coming out in a torrent. By the end of the next day Chaingang was already wondering how they were going to get her to shut up.

The boys, Spike in particular, were on some kind of kid kick that involved lots of screaming and running around. Chaingang was not yet himself from the blast. His head and ears still ached and, uncharacteristically, he "felt funny."

Someone had once said life asks but one question of a man: are you happy? He was not. What did he want? He wanted more than simple vengeance. He wanted what he'd always wanted and nothing more. He wanted to destroy his tormentors.

Around three A.M. he was fully awake, sensors purring, back itching as if red ants had been biting him. He reached a paw back and felt the warm body of a child once again, tucked as close to his huge bulk as she could get. She'd never had a quarter of a ton roll over on her, so she had no reason to be afraid. He tried to inch away and a tiny paw held on for dear life, so he slowed his vital signs to a crawl and remained nearly motionless for the next three and a half hours. What the hell could he do? Around six-thirty the monkey joined them and that was all he could take. He lurched to his feet and stomped off in the direction of the boat.

But, while annoyed, he was impressed. She'd found him in the jungle— *in the dark*. She'd looked for him with *her mind's eye*. The petals had come open.

He slept aboard the boat, napping for a couple of hours and coming awake around midmorning. He felt so-so. He needed sustenance. He opened one of his last long rats, macaroni and cheese, mixed water and spices with the freeze-dried goodies, and proceeded to chow down. He washed it down with some Wild Turkey on ice, in honor of the kill and Veronica's vocalese. It slam-danced him down, *hosed* him silly, and in combination with the drug residue just about got him drunk.

Happier than he'd been in some time he waddled unsteadily to where the kids were playing and jiving and grabbing ass and shouted to them to listen up.

"Hey, you little pussies, let's get real." He was stoned on the Wild Turkey and drug remnants. The kids said not a word, but all six eyes were looking at him. The monkey ran, wisely, as soon as he began bellowing. "Tired of this kiddie shit, let's saddle up, goddammit." He swayed around and picked up a nearby bamboo pole. "New game, you fucks. I will give you five damn min-

utes to hide and then if I can find you I'll whip your butts. Got it? If you can cut me or shoot me first, you win and I fuckin' lose. Got that shit? Now take off, you . . ." He couldn't think of a name mean enough to call them, but the look in his eyes and the way he was swinging the bamboo was very convincing. They scampered away like baby mice. He thought it was hugely funny.

"This is going to hurt me more than it will you," he shouted, waddling toward the jungle, "but we gotta fish or cut bait, understand? You can't be pussies and survive." He was getting into it now. It wasn't a big joke anymore. He'd been coddling them, letting them sleep with him, for chrissakes, and it would get them killed out in the real shithole of a world where they'd be returning.

"You gotta harden up, goddammit. You need a cold fucking heart and a serious mind if you're going to survive. What's so fucking . . ." He couldn't remember what he was going to say and trailed off into a stupor. "Remember what they did to you. You want them to *do that again*? Fuck no! Harden up you little bastards and bitches, bunch of . . ." Where the fuck were they? He blundered around for about ten minutes really getting pissed.

"Come out and let's *get it on you little*—" He was screaming and thrashing around with his pole but the vibes still worked and he felt danger even through the drug and booze haze. He turned and saw the green and black tiger-striped faces, black as the core of hell, eyes glaring out of the foliage at him, and his fat drunken ass was in the sights of a loaded .22, a goddamn bolt-shooter that was pointed dead balls on at his heart, and—just in case all *that* missed him—his napping partner held a filet knife at her side and she was telling him in his mind to leave them alone.

He said nothing, stone sober. Too *damn* easy, he thought, the fucks ain't never gonna survive at this rate.

As he turned to walk away, a single bullet struck the huge mass at the head while a bolt sunk deep into his chest. Ronnie charged the beast as it toppled over.

S pike gunned the throttle as the boat headed for home. Their training complete, the taste of vengeance still in their throats. They were sure he'd be back—in time—and he'd be proud of what they'd have accomplished on their own. He'd trained them to kill, and they were no longer afraid. Or did he dream that part? It was, after all, a monster's nightmare.

Lament for the Gunwitch

Christopher Golden

The Firelion's hair burned in the darkness of the alley, turning the winter's first snowfall into steam around his scarred head. Doc Horror watched it in fascination for a moment. He'd seen a great many things in his life, before and after he came to Earth. Nothing shocked him anymore. But there were many things he didn't understand.

"Well, we gonna just stand here, or are we going in?" Starfish asked.

Horror watched her mouth move, her scarlet catfish lips drooping down to her chin. Her flesh was green and cool to the touch, and it clashed with her pumpkin-orange hair. Fish and frog and woman and whatever else . . . most anyone who had ever seen her had assumed she was genetically engineered by the Monster Shop. But Starfish was for real; last of a long-dead race.

"Phestus," Horror said to the Firelion, "shut it down, okay? We don't want to draw the attention of a beat cop, or the skels who usually haunt this neighborhood."

"Sure, Doc," the android replied, and the halo of fire above his head vanished with a crackle.

Horror poked his wolfish head out of the alley and studied the face of the brownstone across the street. Apartments upstairs, but in the basement was their target—McCluskey's Bar. It was closed now. Pacific City didn't let anybody serve alcohol after one A.M. But that didn't mean it was empty.

In fact, Nicodemus Horror knew that McCluskey's wasn't empty. There were at least half a dozen people inside. Four of them were human. The other two were bioengineered hybrids; escapees from the Monster Shop. He knew because he'd been tipped off. But more than that, Horror could smell them.

"Okay, showtime, boys and girls," he said, turning to the other two. "I appreciate the escort, but this is my show now. It's my fight; protecting Don Lupo one last time. I'm not going to ask you to come in."

"Come on, Doc," the Firelion said, offended. "You think after what you've done for us, we're gonna let you go in there solo? You gave us both a home, treated us like normal, decent people instead of freaks. We stick close, now. We're family."

With a nod of thanks, Horror turned to glance out of the alley again, his breath pluming in the cold December night. Inside McCluskey's, the don's life was in danger. It wasn't his job anymore to keep the old man safe, but the Old Wolf—Don Lupo Zampa—was more than a former employer, he was a friend. And if his punk son, Tony, wasn't going to watch out for the don, well, Horror couldn't not come to the rescue.

He reached into his left pocket and felt the smooth surface of the medallion that controlled his access to the Passage. He had preprogrammed it—could, in fact, have been inside McCluskey's already—but it was always a good idea to do a little recon first.

"All right," he said, and pulled a Colt nine-millimeter semiautomatic from his shoulder holster. He racked the slide, warmed by the comforting sound. "You know the drill. Let's put a good scare into 'em. Getting the don out of there in one piece is our priority, but don't splatter anyone you don't have to."

With one twist of the medallion, Horror, Starfish, and the Firelion disappeared from the alley. Doc felt the usual moment of queasiness that went with interdimensional travel, but ignored it. Even as his left hand snaked around for his other gun, the three Nocturnals reappeared in the foul-smelling basement saloon known as McCluskey's.

Gator and Kitty, refugees from the Monster Shop, sat on the mahogany bar nipping at each other's throats in that love-hate harmony so common to gangsters and their mates. Gator held a fifth of Wild Turkey in one clawed, scaly hand. As the bright light of the Passage winked out, he glanced up in surprise.

"Just give me a reason, Gator," Horror snarled.

The hybrid's eyes widened as he whispered Horror's name. Starfish and Firelion had the three paisans covered, but the fools grabbed for their weapons anyway.

"Don't do it," Gator told them, saving their lives.

"We're taking the old wolf and we're leaving," Horror said, watching Gator's eyes.

He didn't like what he saw there. Fear, yes. But a little craziness, too. A little too much craziness.

"You know I can't let you do that," Gator growled.

The hybrid let go of the whiskey bottle and reached for his gun. The bottle fell to the floorboards. Neither heard it shatter as gunfire exploded between them.

The long-snouted alligator-man who'd started to muscle in on some of the Zampa family's territory in Pacific City was quick on the draw. So quick, in fact, that if he hadn't had a bottle to drop before he could reach for his weapon, he might have got the drop on Horror.

He roared as reptile blood gouted from the holes in his scaled arm and plated chest. Went down hard, and Kitty, who'd obviously been unarmed, grabbed for Gator's gun. Horror ignored her, leaving her for the Firelion. Hephaestus had a way with the women.

The three humans in the room were two-time losers Horror recognized as thugs from other families that he'd frightened out of town while he'd been working for Don Lupo. Johnny "the Snitch" Terranova. His brother Vic. And Al "Smoker" Cataldo. Losers.

Vic Terranova was dead on the ground in a pile of his own brain salad before Horror even glanced his way. He'd been the one guarding Zampa, a gun to the side of the don's head. He must have been about to Kennedy the old man; Starfish wouldn't have shot him if she could help it.

Horror disliked the killing. But sometimes, it couldn't be avoided. Even now, Smoker Cataldo had his piece out and was squeezing off rounds in Star's direction. The room echoed with the angry bark of Smoker's Detective Special .38. To his left, the Snitch had a sawed-off pointed directly at Zampa's head.

Horror grew suddenly angry at the cowardice of these subhumans and their moronic games. Mercy disappeared with the feral twitch of his mouth, the tightening of his wrists and fingers.

"Papa Wolf is nobody's shield," Horror sneered, and gave the Snitch double-nines, shot him so many times the poor bastard wasn't even allowed to fall down until both clips were empty.

When he turned around, Smoker Cataldo was alive but bleeding all over the floor, blood mingling with peanut shells and popcorn grease. Starfish had Kitty in her sights, but the scared little hybrid girl hadn't even squeezed off a round. She pointed the gun at the Firelion, and it quivered in her furry hand.

"You killed him!" she wailed. "You killed Gator. He got me out of that hellhole, was gonna set us up nice. And you had to go an' kill him!"

She was out of it, now, freaking. Doc ratcheted new clips into his nines but held off. It was Firelion's play, for the moment. If Horror spoke up, he might just set her off.

"Listen, Kitty, I've been there, okay?" Hephaestus said. "Maybe I started human, but the Monster Shop made me something else. You don't have to die. All you have to do is give me the gun, and you can walk away. Leave town. Make a new start."

Kitty laughed at that. "Oh shit!" she cried. "What planet are you from?"

The gun came up, she squeezed off three rounds before the fire reached her, melting her bullets as it came. The light fur on her arms caught fire and she lunged for Hephaestus, claws out, but fell, mewling, to the floor. The acrid odor of her fur and flesh burning made Horror want to retch. He grabbed up a heavy jacket that had belonged to one of the wise guys and snuffed the flames with it.

"Ssshhhh," he whispered. "You'll be all right. We'll take care of you, Kitty."

"Why . . . ," she whimpered. "Why are you doing this?"

"You've been through enough," Horror told her.

When he stood, she sat against the bar, quietly singing to herself. It sounded like a lullaby, and Doc had to wonder if her mind was all there. He'd get her help if he could. The Monster Shop had twisted her body, the poor thing, but her mind might be salvageable.

Horror turned and walked to the don, pulled the gag from his mouth. The old man gasped for air, and when he'd been cut free, clutched at Horror's arm for support.

"Thanks, Doc," Don Lupo said. "Once again, I owe you my life."

From the doorway, someone began to applaud.

All three of them turned, prepared to shoot.

"Don't fire," Horror said, holding up a hand.

At the landing in front of the door, six steps up from the bar, stood Tony Zampa, the don's jackass of a son. The kid had wanted to control the family for years, but the don had given more and more power to Doc Horror. And when Horror had walked away, Tony had taken over completely.

Tony wasn't alone, either.

"About time you showed up, Tony!" Don Lupo snarled. There was still some of the hunter in the Old Wolf.

"Looks like you didn't need me," Tony replied archly.

"No, I'm just lucky I have someone else I can count on," Don Lupo said angrily. "But I shouldn't have to, Tony. Doc has done too much, already."

"I agree," Tony said. "In fact, as of this moment, Horror, I'm telling you to stay away from my father, and out of the family's business. We don't need you anymore."

"Could've fooled me," Starfish muttered.

"I've hired new help for the Zampa family," Tony went on. "As bodyguard for my father, and enforcer for me. If I were you, I wouldn't get in the way anymore."

As Tony spoke, a man emerged from the shadows as if he were growing out of them.

"Are you people always this messy?" the stranger asked.

"Tony, you can't talk to Doc like that!" Don Lupo raged.

"Father, it's time to come home. I run the family now, and you have to let it be run as I see fit. From now on, we're gonna let Hunter take care of business for us," Tony explained.

Don Lupo looked apologetically at Horror, still angry, but he let his son lead him away. Police sirens pealed in the distance, coming closer. Doc narrowed his eyes, trying to see the eyes of the newcomer. But it was as if Hunter could gather the shadows around himself, for Doc could see nothing of his face.

"Doc, we oughtta be going," Starfish urged him, and the sirens drew closer.

"Well then," Horror said, reaching into his pocket for the Passage device. "Until we meet again."

"Trust me," the man called Hunter replied, his voice almost seeming to echo through the dark room, coming from nowhere and everywhere at once. "You don't want that."

Then he melted back into the shadows, obviously following Tony and the don. Horror twisted the medallion in his pocket and the Passage shimmered into being before them. The Firelion lifted Kitty into his arms—Doc would see to her wounds at the infirmary back at the Tomb—and then they stepped through, leaving a pile of corpses behind, just as the police broke down the door to the bar.

*E*ve had tried to tell her father she'd be all right at home, in the abandoned tunnel they called the Tomb. He should have brought the Gunwitch with him. There was going to be fighting, probably shooting, and nobody was better at shooting than the Gunwitch.

It was what he was for.

She knew that her daddy had brought the Gunwitch to life to protect her. In the year or so that she and Daddy had been together again, Evening Horror had come to realize that the life he'd made in their new home was just as dangerous as the one they'd left behind. Daddy had brought the Gunwitch to life just to watch over her, to make sure that nothing ever happened to her again.

Eve was glad. She didn't want to be separated from her father again. Not ever. But since he got into trouble so much, she also thought he should keep the Gunwitch with him when he needed . . . what was it? Backup.

Besides, she had her toys.

She played with them now, on her bed, under the huge poster of Jack Howler, from the comics, that hung on the wall. Elf, Posey, the Wicked Witch Head, the Mummy Queen, and all the others. They told her things, the toys did. And came to her rescue if she needed them. They looked small, but really they were very big and strong and could be pretty nasty when they wanted to be.

But nobody saw them that way unless the toys wanted them to. It was easier for them just to look like toys. So Eve carried them around in a little plastic jack-o'-lantern, the kind kids used for trick or treat. It was the plastic pumpkin that had earned her her nickname. That and the fact that she'd been dressing in witch outfits ever since the day her daddy found her on the last day of October, the previous year.

Halloween Girl.

Halloween Girl?

Eve looked around. Nobody there but the Gunwitch, and he never talked. It wasn't a voice she was familiar with, anyway. Certainly not one of her toys. She looked more closely at the Gunwitch. Even if he wanted to talk to her, he couldn't. His mouth was all sewn shut. And whoever had done it hadn't done a very good job.

His eyes were on her, and Eve smiled at him. The Gunwitch never smiled back. Still, she *felt* him smile, just a little bit. Or at least felt that he was there, with her, watching over her. Maybe it was her imagination. Like the time she first put the big witch's hat with those crab apple–shaped balls dangling around the brim on his head. She'd picked them from a gigantic oak tree. Her daddy had told her they were made of a fungus-thingy that grew on the older trees, that when they moved they would scare away the flies and other bugs that were always hanging around the Gunwitch.

Phestus had said those little balls proved the Gunwitch couldn't think for himself. If he could, he'd've taken the silly hat off for sure. But Eve thought the Gunwitch liked the hat. That the Gunwitch had a sense of humor. The hat fit on the Gunwitch's head the way her own pumpkin pail fit in her hand.

She would have asked the toys what they thought, but they never talked about him. About the Gunwitch. Eve wondered if maybe they were jealous of her sitter. Or afraid. But the grown-ups all thought she was just being a silly little girl.

Little! And here she was, already six years old!

It was the grown-ups who were silly. Even her daddy, sometimes. Otherwise, why couldn't anybody else hear the toys?

Halloween Girl.

The voice again. She looked at the toys sprawled across her bedspread. Then she had a thought, and looked inside the plastic pumpkin. It wasn't like other pumpkins. You couldn't really see the bottom, for one thing. But this time, she could see a new toy. A toy she'd never noticed before. It was black and shiny, made of tin.

"Was that you?" she asked, pulling out the windup bird.

Nothing. She twisted the metal key on its side and set it on the spread, and the bird started to move. The grinding inside sounded a little like the flapping of big bird wings. But only a little.

And then, suddenly, the flapping sounded real. Only now, the black bird didn't look so much like a toy anymore. It looked like its real self. And she could hear the voice again.

Caw! It's a pleasure to meet you, Evening Horror, the black bird said. *I've heard a lot about you, on the other side. Caw!*

"What other side?" she asked, genuinely curious.

Caw! Inside the pumpkin, it said, as if that were an answer to everything. And, funnily enough, it was.

"It's a pleasure to meet you, too, Mr. Bird," Evening said, and offered a small curtsy as best she could manage kneeling on her bed. "I'm always happy to meet a new toy."

I can't stay long, said the black bird. *I've only come—Caw!—because I know you care for your scarecrow.*

"My . . ." She looked around at the tall witch's hat, the silly wooden balls dangling, the expressionless face and stitched mouth of the Gunwitch. "You mean him? Yes, of course I do. He's my friend."

Caw! He needs your help, my Halloween Girl, said the black bird.

"I'd do anything to help the Gunwitch," Eve replied.

Even if it—Caw!—angered your father?

That was a tough one. Eve loved her father, and knew he was a very wise man. But if the Gunwitch needed her . . .

"What would I have to do?"

Use your father's Passage to bring him somewhere—Caw!—someplace he can put an end to the sadness that keeps him here on this plane. Put an end to the suffering he's known for more than a century of death. Caw! The magic your father used to bring him back only works because the Gunwitch's soul is not at rest. If he were to have his vengeance, he would be able to move on.

"To die, you mean," Eve said doubtfully. "I don't know. My father . . ."

He's already dead, Evening. But the final peace—Caw!—eludes him. You can give him that.

"You mean, he's sad all the time?" she asked, the idea of it bringing sudden tears to her eyes.

Yes, the black bird replied, ruffled its wings. *Caw! All the time.*

"I . . ." Eve began, then burst into sobs. "I don't know what to do!"

Perhaps if I showed you what happened. If you knew who your friend was, and why he suffers so. Caw! Would you like that, Eve?

Eve sniffled. "I guess so."

Caw! He was not a good man, in his life, I'm afraid, the black bird began, and already Eve didn't like the story. She turned to look at the Gunwitch, but still, he gave no response, not even some kind of acknowledgment that the bird was there. She looked at the other toys and discovered something that frightened Halloween Girl very, very much.

She couldn't hear the toys anymore.

He was a gunfighter, actually, the bird continued. Evening had many questions, but she did not know what to ask first, so she only listened.

His name is lost to time. Caw! When he was twenty-four, past his prime for a gunfighter in those days, I'll tell you, a man named William Bonney said he was so fast, it was like magic, like he was some kind of witch with a gun. Caw! The

Gunwitch. The next day, Bonney was dead. Whether the Gunwitch killed him, only the two dead men know.

His legend grew, but only so much. Other gunfighters had died horrible or glorious deaths, had yearned for the attention of the newspapers and the dime novelists. Caw! The Gunwitch cared nothing for fame, or legend. He killed when it was necessary, or when he was paid. That was all he did.

Once a year, in Abilene, he visited a saloon girl named Cordelia. She had a little girl by the name of Molly, or so the legend goes. No one ever spoke of it, not even Cordelia, but everyone in Abilene knew the child was the daughter of the Gunwitch. Caw!

And then—Caw!—when Molly was four years old, Cordelia died of pneumonia. It was a hard winter, but the saloon owner, Harley Kane, took Molly in and cared for her like she was his own daughter.

In the springtime, the Gunwitch came for Molly. He never spoke a word, not even then. Caw! Just walked into the saloon and took her out, and even Harley Kane, who loved her dear, didn't lift a finger.

The Gunwitch disappeared after that. Never was heard from again. But his legend lived, and so did the bounty on his head. He'd sent a lot of men to Boot Hill in his life, made many enemies. Caw! Nobody's truly certain who hired the man who killed him. But then, so many wanted the Gunwitch dead that it didn't really matter.

Molly wasn't quite six when the man who had once been the Gunwitch came in from tending to the crops he'd planted the spring before and found his daughter not alone. As he watched, the killer cut his daughter's throat, but even before that— Caw! Caw!—he'd done things to her I can't speak of to one so young, though you've surely seen enough death in your short life.

He didn't have his guns. But nothing was going to stop him from tearing the life from the man who'd killed his little girl. The Gunwitch dove at the man, his hands outstretched to strangle the killer to death. Caw! He was shot in midair, the first time. After he fell to the ground, the killer shot him several more times.

Still, the Gunwitch would not die. He dragged himself to the bloody corpse of his daughter, and held her to him, and promised that he would avenge her.

And then he died, the laughter of his killer still ringing in his ears. His spirit walked the Earth, bound here by his promise to his daughter, until your father dug him up and revived him, using the rites of the homunculus to give him new flesh.

Halloween Girl was sobbing, her hands curled into claws covering her mouth, which was agape with grief and shock. She didn't understand everything the black bird had said, but she understood enough.

"I didn't know," she whispered.

Caw! Of course not. Even your father doesn't know, the black bird said.

"But what can I do?" Eve asked. "That was a real long time ago, right? I'm only six, but even I know that you can't go back in time!"

True, my dear. Caw! But the Hunter, the man who killed the Gunwitch and his little girl, Molly, has never died. He is not immortal, but his life will continue long after you are gone, and he will keep killing, unless he is stopped. Now he is here—Caw!—in Pacific City. I came to bring the Gunwitch back, to set fire to his spirit once again, and to offer him his chance at vengeance. But I found your father had already given him new life.

So instead, I offer your scarecrow a chance at final death. At peace.

"I still don't know what to do. You said I needed to use the Passage, but to where? Where do I take him?" she asked the black bird.

Behind her, in the hallway, she heard her father and the others returning. They were so deep down in the Tomb that they never worried about making noise. She had worried for her father, wished he would hurry home so she could stop being so anxious. Now she wished they'd stayed away a little longer.

Evening looked at the Gunwitch, and realized that he had turned away, eyes closed, as if he didn't want to look at her anymore. The Gunwitch had never done anything like that before.

When she turned back, the black bird was gone.

"Wait!" she shouted, grabbed up the plastic pumpkin and looked inside. She could just see the bird, but far away. Far, far away. But she seemed to hear its voice in her mind.

You'll know, it said.

And a short time later, when she heard her father and the others talking about saving Don Lupo, and about his new enforcer, some man called Hunter, she knew just what to do.

Alone in her room with the Gunwitch, Eve ran her fingers over her own Passage medallion. Her father had given it to her just a few months earlier, and she hadn't had much practice with it. But . . .

"Come down here," she told the Gunwitch.

He did as he was told, crouching so Eve could look him in the eye when she spoke to him. She studied his face, what was left of his nose, each stitch of his mouth, and the dark light glowing in each eye. The others always complained about how bad he smelled, but Evening kind of liked the smell, the same way she liked the smell of skunks or rotted trees, which even her toys thought was disgusting.

The Gunwitch's smell made her feel safe.

"Please help me," she told him. "I don't know what to do! I just wish I knew if you really know what I'm talking about!"

He knows, Eve.

She turned and saw that Elf lay on his side on the bed. She was sure she'd left the little doll in the pumpkin. But that wasn't what amazed her. What truly amazed her was that he had spoken at all. The toys never talked about the Gunwitch.

Then something occurred to her. They'd heard the story, too.

"Will you help, then, Elf?" she asked.

Yes, Elf replied, his moon-shaped head grinning at her. *We want to.*

Hunter smiled.

"Your son is an idiot, old man," he sneered.

"Who hired you?" Don Lupo asked. "I know Tony was fool enough to put you on our payroll, but who hired you to cap me?"

"Your friends in Reno," Hunter replied.

"Don Strega?" Lupo asked, incredulous. "I made him! He'd be nothing if it weren't for me! That city would still be in the hands of the coyotes and the lizards and the shitkickers if I hadn't . . . that bastard."

"Yeah," Hunter said. "It's a tough old world, I reckon."

It had been so simple. Human beings hadn't gotten any more intelligent over the decades. In fact, Hunter thought they'd gotten dumber if anything. He'd grown bored with killing for a while. Spent nearly thirty years around the world, working and living, trying to remember what it felt like to be a normal man.

He never quite got the hang of it. Kept running into people practically begging to be killed. After a while, the only sensible thing was to start getting paid for it again. Guy had to make the rent, after all. Not to mention that he'd made a deal all those years ago. A deal to give him all the things that life and all the people he'd known before he became *special* . . . all the things that had been kept from him. A deal that would also keep him alive, keep him young.

That required a little blood right there.

And Hunter sure as hell wasn't about to give up his own.

"I sure am glad that idiot Gator didn't manage to smoke you before I could," Hunter said. "It would have cost me a lot of money."

"What a pity that would have been," Don Lupo said.

Hunter stopped smiling. He pressed the blade of his hundred-year-old Bowie knife against the old man's chicken-neck, and a bit of blood welled up and started running down the blade.

"Here I am, trying to make conversation, and you're rushing me," he growled. "Killing's only interesting to me these days if I get to know the mark a little first."

"Fuck off," Lupo snarled.

Hunter heard the pistols cock, and reacted instantly. He ducked his head, grabbed Don Lupo around the chest and swung behind him, knife still to his throat. What he saw stunned him to silence. A little raven-haired girl, no more than six or seven, with a little plastic pumpkin, as though she were trick-or-treating.

Then there was the zombie with the guns. That right there took some adjusting to. It was a demon or a haint of some kind. It stood about coffin length, with its patchwork serape, the bandoliers across its chest, and the witch's hat making it look vaguely like a dead Mexican hijacker on the Day of the Dead.

Hunter tickled Don Lupo's Adam's apple with the point of his blade. "Okay, pal. Don't move or the old man dies!" he snarled.

"*Scemo!* He doesn't care, you idiot!" Lupo roared. "That's the Gunwitch!"

Hunter's mouth dropped open. The Gunwitch raised his pistols, expressionless. The little girl grabbed his left arm.

"Stop," she said. "Don't hurt Don Lupo."

The Gunwitch stopped. Hunter stared at him, at it. At the most important kill of his career.

"How . . . ," he asked.

"Hello, Papa Wolf," the little girl said. "Was this man going to hurt you?"

"*Buona sera* to you, Evening," Don Lupo replied. "And *sì*, I think he was."

Suddenly, the little girl's face darkened and Hunter found himself almost afraid of her, as if that were even possible.

"Not anymore," she said. "He's a bad man, Papa Wolf."

Hunter smiled, confidence returning. It was the first time he'd ever killed someone and had them come back. But as long as the Gunwitch listened to the little girl, it didn't change anything.

"Drop the guns, Witch," Hunter sneered. "I'll cut the old bastard's throat in a second, maybe cut him open just like I did that little girl of yours. She was a sweet thing, as I recall."

The little girl—Evening, the old man had called her—gasped and took a step forward, waving a finger at him.

"Mister," she said angrily, "you're just about the ugliest creep I ever saw! You just better shut your mouth, before I get really mad!"

Hunter laughed without looking at her. He kept his eyes on the Gunwitch's face. But there was nothing to see.

"What about this one?" he asked, nodding toward Evening. "She your replacement? She as dear to you as the other?"

Hunter watched the Gunwitch's face. Nothing. No reaction at all.

"Dammit, answer me!" Hunter screamed, unnerved by the Gunwitch's lack of emotion. "Nobody shows me that kind of disrespect! I killed you once, I can kill you again! Answer me, you dust turd!"

Hunter had lived more than one hundred and fifty years. He didn't even see the Gunwitch's hands move before the triggers were pulled. One bullet caught him in the shoulder of his knife arm, which had been sticking out from behind the old man, and the other passed right through the saggy crotch of the old man's pants and caught the killer in the knee.

Howling with pain, Hunter went down.

"*Stia attento!* What the hell's the matter with you?" Don Lupo roared.

For a moment, he was blocking the way. Hunter used that moment to call the shadows. As a boy, he had been laughed at, beaten, or ignored, and almost always been afraid. Now he could feel fear licking at what was left of his soul, and he didn't like it, not one bit.

The shadows came at his command, they curled around him, caressed him, and helped him glide along out of the room. In a moment, he was on one leg, knife in his left hand now, and he slipped into the library. The shadows licked his blood up as he passed, feeding their own hunger and hiding his trail.

A decent trade-off, actually. Especially since he was already starting to heal.

The library had two doors. He moved swiftly to the other, parallel to the hallway he'd come down. After the Gunwitch passed, tracking him somehow, despite the lack of a blood trail, Hunter reached from the shadows and grabbed the girl up with his right arm, weak from the bullet, but not useless. Not with the shadows' help.

She screamed and he pulled her close, enjoying her fear. When he looked up, the Gunwitch was there.

"Put the goddamn guns down," Hunter said.

Impassive. Expressionless. But not emotionless. Because this time, the Gunwitch did just as he was told.

The girl was choking, pulling at his arm. She struggled, dropped her plastic pumpkin, and all kinds of peculiar-looking toys and dolls rolled out.

"You're making a big mistake," Don Lupo said from the hallway.

The old man stood behind the Gunwitch, dabbing at the blood on his neck with a handkerchief.

"You must be joking!" Hunter cried. "This is more fun than I've had since the last time I killed something this bastard loved!"

Then Hunter screamed in terror as he was surrounded, suddenly, by the most horrible creatures he had ever seen. The big knife was knocked from his hand and clattered to the floor as giant goblins and squat reptilian army men pulled him off the girl. A huge alien robot and the floating head of a witch crowded in front of him. His left arm broke and he screamed again, but this time in pain.

They were going to kill him. Maybe eat him.

And then they stopped. The creatures backed away, forming a circle of protection around the little girl named after the night.

Hunter found himself shaking uncontrollably despite himself. He looked up just as the Gunwitch kicked an old Colt repeater across the wooden floor. It spun and skidded to a stop two feet in front of him. He could just bend. Bend and pick it up and shoot, and even if he took a bullet or two, the shadows would save him.

He met the Gunwitch's gaze and saw nothing there. No hatred. No vengeance. No emotion at all. But Hunter could feel it, somehow.

"Bastard!" he screamed, and he bent down to pick up the gun, prepared to dive forward, to shoot the Gunwitch from the ground.

His fingers had barely touched cold metal when the first bullet hit him. He felt his body jump again and again and again and he realized that there was just no way the Gunwitch could have that many bullets, even with a pair of Colts.

He felt the warmth of his own blood where it pooled around his face, and Hunter looked into the shadows, reaching out to them for deliverance. Tendrils of shadow snaked toward him, but withdrew before touching him, or even tasting his blood.

In the shadows, he could hear the faint sound of a child, very far away, laughing like the peal of a bell.

And he thought he saw a bird.

When Horror and the others appeared in Don Lupo's kitchen, after using the equipment in the Tomb's lab to trace Eve's use of the Passage, they found her sipping hot cocoa with the old man, the Gunwitch standing vigilantly by. After Don Lupo explained what had happened, Horror was furious, but only because he was so frightened of losing the girl again.

"How did you know this man was going to try to kill Don Lupo?" he asked his daughter.

"I didn't," Evening replied, and sipped her cocoa again.

"Eve," he said grimly, "you might have been killed. Do you realize that? I don't know what I would have done if anything happened to you, fruit bat."

She smiled at her father's use of his pet name for her, but then she grew serious again. Eve was quiet a moment, and then touched her father's hand.

"It's okay, Daddy," she said. "I've got my toys to protect me. Even if the Gunwitch goes away."

Horror didn't know what to make of that.

That night, in the Tomb, the black bird returned.

Eve was reading *Rinkitink in Oz* out loud on her bed. The Gunwitch sat

at the little table and chair set in one corner of the room. It ignored the orange plastic teacup full of water that was set before it on a little saucer. It ignored the smiling jack-o'-lantern design on the cup's side.

The toy black bird appeared at the edge of Eve's bed. This time, the bird didn't talk to Halloween Girl at all.

Caw! It is time, Gunwitch, the black bird said. *Time to move on to the next world. Time, at last, to be at peace. Molly is there—Caw!—well loved and well taken care of, and now you can be with her at last.*

The Gunwitch didn't look up. The black bird seemed angry.

We have given you your vengeance, Gunwitch. Your spirit can rest, now. Caw! Horror cannot hold you here with his spells.

Eve didn't like the way the black bird said her father's name. In fact, she realized she didn't even like the black bird. Not at all.

Come now, the black bird said. *Your daughter awaits you on the other side. She is at peace. Caw! Share that peace with her.*

Halloween Girl didn't want the Gunwitch to go. She would miss him. But she knew that it was for the best. He could be with his daughter again. He could go to a better place, where there weren't so many nasty people, and ugly things. So many monsters.

"Go on," she said, even though it hurt her to say the words.

The Gunwitch looked up, glanced at the nasty black bird, then at Eve. It took one step forward. Then another. At the third step, he stood at the edge of Eve's bed and stared at the bird, and then down into the pumpkin. Eve wondered if his body would stay behind, and imagined it would. Most of it wasn't real body anyway, but wood and metal and cloth, and some other things her father had magicked together.

The Gunwitch bent slightly, and Eve fought back tears. She would cry when it was gone. Not before. She didn't want to . . .

Then she felt its cold, dead fingers entwine in hers.

Her breathing stopped, and Eve looked up at the Gunwitch. It wasn't looking at her, though. It was still staring at the black bird.

Caw! Caw! You can't do this, the black bird said angrily. *It just isn't done.*

The Gunwitch took Eve's hand and turned away from the bird, leading her out of her room and into the Tomb. It was almost time to eat, she remembered. And it had remembered, too. That was the Gunwitch's job, to watch out for her.

Eve pulled the Gunwitch down and hugged it close, tears flowing freely now. She said nothing to her companion, because it could say nothing in return. But the Gunwitch would know what was in her heart, she thought. When she pulled away, she saw damp spots on its cheeks and for a moment she thought something so very silly. Then she touched her own face and realized it must be her own tears.

It must be.

She was so silly sometimes.

Photo Album

Alexandra Elizabeth Honigsberg

She always revealed herself
at the day's waning,
dark, wild-eyed,
arms extended
to take me in,
give and dismember.

The house felt a ruin
shrouded in life—
rose-thorns too evident,
hornets amidst the sun's own
daffodils, virgin's lilies,
one shattered tree my voice's witness.

The neighborhood, cliques and clans,
wrapped blind in picket-fence etiquette;
claws clutched a family,
holy and proper,
legacy was love-by-violence,
dark quickenings in archetypal guise.

The bedroom, pastels and shadows,
creeping tendrils
that snatch and strangle.
Her shadow, shrieks,
I struggle, wracking shudders,
break loose for flight.

Understanding finally
that there is
no answer
is blessing enough
to end one story
and start another.

Hellbent

A. A. Attanasio

"Evil does not die easily."
—Yi Jing

ILLUSTRATIONS BY JAMES O'BARR

THE UNDERSIDE OF THE ICE

Hell was cold, dark, and loud. A night of wind and shrieking ice obscured all direction. Souls flew past in tatters of mist, screaming cries of ripped metal. With no sky overhead but blackness, and the ground underfoot jagged and frozen, space held the dimensions of nightmare. A din of freaky agony overlay a constant thrumming, shrilling, pounding, screeching, sizzling of oppressive noises, explosions, and whinnying trajectories of hurtling projectiles immixed with massive groanings as of sliding volcanoes and wrenched ocean floors shouldering mountains.

Dren lay on the sharp ground, his blistered body squeezed tightly against the underside of the ice. He had crawled into this razorous niche to avoid the mad flight of the damned. As one of the demons of deception, his responsibility required him to wander through the raucousness of hell misdirecting souls. When their crawling howls reached him under the tempest of mad sounds, he felt their cravings. Most were insane for silence, light, and warmth, and he touched their ether bodies with the hope of realizing, even for an instant, their desires, and then he sent them hurtling toward the loudest, darkest, and coldest vortex of the moment.

Under the cutting ice, Dren lay still. Above him, shreds of fog blurred past—souls flying wildly through the chaos of torments. He wanted to hide from them. He wanted to lie still and feel the stillness in him. But under the ice, barbed spider mites seethed. They swarmed over him, puncturing his blisters, laying rabidly festering eggs in his sores, burning into every crevice of his body. In moments, the pain would overwhelm him, and he would crash up through the ice and rage blindly across the floor of hell, his loud misery mute in the blare of crazy sounds and ceaseless suffering.

But for an instant, Dren touched stillness.

The tumult of horror and hurt receded for one fraction of that instant. And he felt peace. So tenderly secret in this place of terror, peace opened its horizons—and vomit spewed through him. Gut acids scalded his gullet, and a cheesy, rancid stench flushed the hollows of his aching head. He burst out of the ice, bawling with distress. Suffering whipped him into a frenzy of running, as if the searing bile and putrid stink of his own maw could be outrun.

"Liar!" A greasy voice slid into him from out of the clamor of clashing boulders and scraping slates. "Liar!"

Dren whirled to a stop, recognizing the voice of a fellow demon. "Flayer!"

Out of the numbing dark, a hideous face of spidery tar-drop eyes and lobed brow incandesced, its cleft lips fibrillating like a squid's mouth. "Liar!" Leprous hands fumed with ghost light and reached for Dren. "Did you crawl under the ice again?" The warped hands seized him with an electric jolt. "Did you?"

"No, Nergal!" Dren shouted above the booming, whining frenzy, his words steaming in the frigid dark. "No!"

"Then you did!" A black, split tongue slithered across the rippling pleats of Nergal's mouth. "Good! Then, you heard them again? They spoke with you?"

"Of course they spoke with me!"

The twisted hands released him, and Nergal the Flayer stepped back, dimming to a vague, scarlet glimmer in the loud darkness. "Silence? Silence under the ice?" Only the frosted smoke of the Flayer's disappointment shone from where he stood. "They were never real then. The voices were never real. Just another torment, another echo of pain."

"Yes, more agony, more torture." Dren dropped to his knees under a pall of vomitous stink and shuddered with convulsive spasms in the cold. "The divine would never send messengers into hell. There is no way out. Not ever. Not ever."

"Oh, good! Oh, good, Dren!" Nergal loomed out of the dark, spirochetes of flame squirming from the fluted creases of his mouth and wiggling over his noseless countenance. "Then you believe the messengers *have* come—and you will hear them again!"

At that moment, a gust of souls whisked by, and Nergal's knobbed hands seized one and began to peel the wispy light from it with his mouth, all the while muttering the horrid reality of the soul's life that had earned it damnation. And though Dren could not hear the demon's voice for the mad uproar, he knew just what was said, and the words themselves did not matter, for in hell, only pain was truthful.

Pry Open the Red World

For uncountable instants of eternity, Dren reeled through the icy darkness listening to the cravings of souls—the yearning for warmth, the longing for light, the pining for silence. And he reached out and touched them with his pustuled hands. They felt soft and warm. Yet their psychotic raving for comfort forced him to shove them quickly away, instilling them with misdirection. And off they flew, believing they knew the way to a moment's relief but soon finding themselves in colder, darker depths of fetor and stunning noise.

Rarely, a soul flew through the black ranges yelling for God. The demons loved torturing these souls the most, for there was more hope to kill in these shriekers for divine intervention, and thus more distraction for the evil spirits from their own anguish, as well. In moments, flocks of demons descended, and the supplicant vanished among the tormentors. The few times that Dren had been the first to seize upon such aspiring damned, he had sent them crawling into the ice, telling them God was there. "Look! Look! God is there under the cutting edges of ice! Get down to show your humility! Be humble and crawl in there! That's it! Crawl in!"

The keen blades of ice cut, the spider mites attacked, and the soul's ether body bled pain in many colors. But, strangely, Dren had experienced a moment of stillness as he himself wedged under the honed ice plates to witness the soul's shock. Time and again after that, when none of the other demons were about, he had dared to wriggle into the narrow crevices and pry open the red world of pain. He had found traumatic spasms of suffering as the ice sliced him and the spider mites burrowed into his wounds. But also there had been instants of stillness. The ceaseless racket from above had dimmed, just for a splinter of a moment—and then pain and nausea wracked him again.

Over how many aeons did he seek out those brutal slivers of stillness? Time meant nothing in hell. Not until he heard the voices did he realize that time could touch him. And every touch in hell was torment.

Dren—why do you want the stillness?

The very sound of that voice had flung him through the panes of ice, lacerating him with shards. He had feared the voice was Satan's. Though it had been a long, long time since he had heard Satan's voice, he remembered it was as quiet and beautiful as the voice that had spoken to him in the ice. He did not want to hear Satan's voice. Those called by him were found later embedded in the ground, locked in epoxy, their bodies disfigured almost beyond recognition, yet exquisitely alive, eyeballs roving inanely in lidless sockets, small lightnings tangled in their blown-wide pupils.

Gradually, Dren had realized that the voice could not be Satan's. The grand master of hell could not remain still. His voice could not come forth from stillness, only tumult and fury. With trepidation, Dren had returned to the slicing crawl spaces under the ice and had found the stillness again before the toxin of the barbed mites twisted his insides and heaved him back into the cataclysmic darkness. Yet each time before the raging nausea defeated him, he cried to the stillness, "I want out of hell!"

Many times he had uttered that wretched cry before the voice of quiet beauty returned. *Will you atone?*

"Yes! Yes! I will atone!" he had wept. "I will atone!"

Again, throes of nausea had exploded him back into the loud cold. He had spun insanely among the rampageous noise of hell, flogged by the cold, sick with the stink of himself. And then he had stopped, struck still by the real-ization that he, Dren the Liar, had spoken truth. He had said yes. He had answered the voice truthfully. Never before in the blind pit of suffering had he been able to say anything but a lie.

After that, he had returned ever more frequently to the tight, hurting spaces under the ice, and he had mewled with utter sincerity, "Yes, I will atone! I will atone! Anything! Ask anything of me!"

But the calm voice had not returned. Only its memory remained with him, a silent thunder in the vehement roaring, a phosphorescent warmth in the bitter cold, a pearl of light in the bitter and fierce dark.

Hell's Agony Is My Temple

After finding Dren bleeding and infested with mites, shuddering under a plate of ice, Nergal had wanted to know everything, and it was impossible to withhold knowledge from the Flayer. Dren had lied furiously, yet Nergal had seen past his deceptions. Fearing that the demon would inform the others and that soon the Qlippotic masters, the archdemons themselves, would find out and punish him, Dren had hurled himself across the night-held pit of the damned and had avoided everyone but the souls he was meant to deceive.

Eventually, Nergal had found him again, and in the weltering noise and wrenching cold convinced him, "I've told no one! No one else must know—if we have any hope of escaping!"

"You will atone?" Dren had asked, stunned that another of the unholy would admit that freedom from perdition was possible. Until that moment, Dren had secretly believed he, the Liar, had been lying to himself to think he could flee damnation. "You really think we can get out of here?"

"You heard the voices!" Nergal had yelled above the swell of clashing storms.

"It is a trick of the masters!"

"You lie!" Nergal had seized Dren in his necrotic hands and shook him violently. "You lie! If the masters had done this, you would be glued to the floor of the pit by now and trampled on by behemoths and leviathans!"

That was true. There was no patience among the masters for lengthy deceptions in hell. In the blithering darkness, everything happened quickly and ceaselessly. Kingdom of Spasm, Night Realm of Convulsion, here pain came swiftly and repeatedly. Nergal's perception helped Dren believe that there was the chance of a future for him that was not a lie, a destiny for him beyond the cold, sightless racket of hell. After that, he looked forward to his chance collisions with Nergal the Flayer as they surged mindlessly through the booming void.

"Have you heard the voices?" Nergal asked when next they slammed into each other. "Have they told you how to atone?"

"I've heard no voices!" Dren shouted back and surged into the night, buffeted by titanic cymbals of rage. "No voices!"

"Liar!" Nergal seized Dren in his large and gruesome hands and dragged him to the serrated ground, painfully stabbing him into place among the spiked rocks. "Liar! You've heard *a* voice! I feel it in the pain I flay from you! I feel it! *A* voice! One voice! He speaks in the solitude! *A* voice! One voice!"

"I hear nothing!" Dren screamed, unable to control his lying.

"Crawl under the ice!" Nergal shouted against the bellowing wind. "Crawl under the sharp ice and listen! Listen!"

Metallic thunder reverberated, so loud that not even Dren could hear his own lie as he replied. Out of the screeching darkness, a slinky figure appeared glossed in slimy green fire, an eel-shape with sinuous limbs, slit eyes, adder's grin, and needle-thin teeth. "What are you two doing?" a sibilant voice asked above the piercing whistles and jackhammer crashings.

"Succoth!" Nergal yelped. "Succoth the Burner!"

"What voice are you yapping about?" Succoth slithered between them, his reek of sewage gagging their replies. "You have heard a voice? Whose voice?"

"I've heard nothing!" Dren brayed. "Nothing!"

Succoth's thousand teeth shone like pins. "What does the Liar hide, Nergal the Flayer? What voice has he heard?"

"He is a deceiver, Succoth!" Nergal slapped Dren hard to the side of the head and sent him sprawling onto the knifepoint ice. "A master's voice has spoken, he says! He lies! Liar! Liar!"

"A master's voice?" Succoth backed away, and his green glow and mal-odor dimmed within the sulfurous dark. "Which master?"

"Lucifuge—Asmodeus—Adrammelech—what does it matter?" Nergal's hunched body bowed smaller and his shining face of quivering mouth-parts and tiny, black sequin eyes swayed with denial. "He is a liar! Burn him, Succoth! Burn him to silence!"

"You take the name of the masters in vain!" Succoth roared at Dren and flared lividly out of the darkness, green flames leaping from his writhing, boneless form. "I will not have it! Hell's agony is my temple, and you dese-crate it with your lies! For that, you must burn!"

The rageful cacophony swallowed Dren's yowls of fright, his blistered face wide with terror: darkness fled before the infernal glare of the Burner, and dripping flames splashed over Dren, charring his flesh to ash and boiling his eyes in their sockets.

Where the Journey of Darkness Begins

"Succoth is gone!" Nergal yelled. "Our secret is safe!"

Under the wan glow of the Flayer's staring visage, Dren appeared as a nest of black bones. Slowly, he ate the pain that Succoth had inflicted on him, and his flesh returned to his skeleton like a miasmal haze. "You did the right thing, distracting him with rage," he lied, but his voice was inaudible in the grating din.

Nergal was not listening anyway. Wisps of ether smoke flashed past, and the Flayer lunged after those souls, intent on tearing the light from them to make room for more darkness, more pain.

When Dren had eaten enough agony to stitch his bones together again, he crawled into a crevice of the ice. Succoth's green fire still smoldered in Dren's scorched body, and he did not feel the edges of the cracked ground cutting him, nor the mites feasting on his cooked flesh. He lay stupid in the grip of the cold. And the stillness found him. And the voice returned.

Dren—listen to me. If you are sincere, if you will atone for rebelling against the Creator, then come to the Bridge of Ashes.

"The Bridge—" Dren sat up, rupturing the icy crust. He did not believe what he had heard, and he tried to creep back under the sheer plates to hear it again. But he was too excited; the stabbing stones cut too deeply, and the hurt surged him to his feet. Still too weak from Succoth's burning to charge through the darkness, he limped onward, muttering, "The Bridge! To the Bridge!"

When Nergal next found him, Dren was mumbling incoherently, "There is no atonement! No way to atone! No way at all!"

"You heard the voice again!" Nergal wailed, then gawked about in a fright to see if he had been overheard. When no figures emerged from the cold and clamorous dark, he took Dren in his big hands. "How do we atone?"

"We cannot atone!" He shook himself free, the blisters of his seared body shimmering like pearls. "There is no atonement! Not even at the Bridge of Ashes!"

"The Bridge—" Nergal staggered as if struck. "We cannot go there! The cold! The cold, Dren!"

"Stay here! Stay and flay the damned! There is no atonement at the Bridge of Ashes!"

Dren whirled into the dark, and Nergal hurried after him. "Are you certain that is what the voice said?"

"I heard nothing! Nothing!"

Under a discordant avalanche of sound, the two demons shambled blindly. All direction was uncertain in hell. By the flight of souls and the frequency with which they found their dim ether lights scurrying terrified through the darkness, they inferred the way to the Bridge of Ashes—the span across which souls first arrived. Screaming and yelling angrily at each other, they progressed by error and misdirection. "Not that way! This way!" "Liar! That way is cold! Go to the cold!"

After much blind bumbling, ever fearful of encounters with other demons, Dren and Nergal began to sense direction from the cold. They bowed their heads and shouldered into a frigid wind. The ground underfoot became ever more slick with ice and crunching frost, and the onrush of souls fleeing the opposite way assured them that they were on the path to their goal.

Wraiths of fog and swamp smoke flitting past, sang their misery in prayers and pleas to God, fleeing toward the warmer frigidity of the pit and the horde of waiting demons. Down below, such cries would swarm tormentors upon them. Yet these were souls new to hell, as yet unaware of the misery that evoking divinity earned in the abyss. Their mournful appeals for help guided the two demons ever more surely through the blustery cold, and soon thereafter a tarnished light shone ahead.

In that black silver glow, the Bridge of Ashes hove into view. A mammoth mountain of the cinders of creation, the Bridge rose from pylons of smoky glass above a gorge of black flames that radiated a keen wind of hail and sleet. "Here is where the journey of darkness begins!" Nergal cried into the brittle wind.

Beneath a corrosive sky, the freezing gusts blew ether fumes of souls down sooty slopes toward utter darkness and pandemonium. But one bright figure stood still at the summit of the colossal Bridge of Ashes. A radiant arm rose and beckoned to them.

RIVER OF MILK, RIVER OF PITY

"He is an angel!" Nergal's greasy words slid through the tremulous paps of his mouth with loud astonishment.

"An angel in hell!" Dren called against the flogging wind.

"Liar!" The Flayer held a cankerous hand against the gray light smoking from the river of burning shadows. "He stands at the crest. He will not descend among the damned."

"I am not afraid to go to him!" Dren's lie jolted out of him, wrenched by the battering cold.

Nergal bent over double in the brutal iciness. "If we are seen on the Bridge of Ashes, the masters will weld us to the floor of the pit!"

"My hands!" The Liar held his sore-pocked hands before him, the fingers frozen stiff. And when he pressed them against his chest of scars, a thumb and forefinger snapped off like icicles.

The Flayer swept Dren under his bulky arm and shoved him toward the bridge. "Hurry! Before we cannot move!"

The two demons shuffled against the wind, pieces of their bodies drizzling away in the storm force, their shapes eroding with each step. By the time they crossed the banks of gravel to the foot of the bridge, they had been whittled to skeletal caricatures of themselves. But the wind had ceased. And the cold had lifted. The dissonance of hell thrummed in the distance, so that an eerie quiet reigned upon the Bridge of Ashes. Only the grating snap and sizzle of the black flames in the gorge troubled hearing.

"We must flee this place," Dren spoke in a near whisper—a warning meant for himself, a lie he had little strength to voice.

Nergal beat the cold from his frostbitten flesh, and his stocky, charred body thickened as it warmed. "I'm going up there to speak with the angel. Are you coming?"

"I don't speak with messengers of the Nameless!" Dren flexed his hands, all his fingers intact, and led the way up the steep slope of cinders and volcanic ash. He peered at the heights and saw the bright figure had begun to descend toward them. "No angel can enter hell!"

The Flayer made no reply. His full attention was spent finding his footing in the sliding ash. The harder he scrambled, the more the loose slurry spilled away under him so that he made little progress climbing the mountain of soot. "We can't cross this bridge!"

"Not until you renounce Satan, brothers. Not until you swear to obey and love your Creator." A clear light projected the demons' shadows behind them, and they looked up in awe at a young man in silver raiment, the iridescent skin of his amiable face sequined with drops of sweat. "Even for me, this hike is a backbreaker! I've had it. I've got to sit down."

Against the glare of the angel, the demons shielded their eyes with their hands and gasped in unison. Their bodies had changed. Their mangled flesh was gone, and they stared at wholesome hands, skin devoid of sores, fingers no longer warped, nails clean and unbroken, a small moonrise in each. When they looked to each other, they fell to their haunches. Stripped of their demonic features, they had become again youths of enigmatic beauty—Nergal with oblique dark eyes in a proud face, his flesh umber hues of earth; Dren with vivid blue irises and pale features, blond curls falling like a mane across his long shoulders.

"You appear as the Creator made you—before you rebelled." The angel wiped the sweat from his brow with his dalmatic sleeve. "Listen, I can't stay here much longer. This place stinks, and I want to go get cleaned up. So stop gawking and pay attention. That's the way out." He jerked a thumb over his shoulder at the peak of the cinder mountain and a blue sky, where a stream of clouds ran like a river of milk, a river of pity.

The sight of the sky brought startled tears to their eyes. "Take us with you!" Nergal pleaded.

"Can't do that." The angel stood and frowned with gentle concern. "I don't have to tell you two why you're here. If you want out, that's the way. You stand here and you renounce Satan. Then you'll have one chance—just one chance—to prove you're sincere. Three days in the fallen world, among the living. Redeem one soul already lost to Satan, and I'll take you home." His frown deepened. "But if you fail, then you're back here. Understand?"

GOD HAS NO NAME

The angel vanished in a brief flurry of thermal draperies like the flutter of a mirage. The clear radiance disappeared with him, and the demons groaned to see themselves reduced again to their abhorrent shapes. "He taunts us!" Dren's blistered mouth sneered angrily. "He tempts us with all the wiles of Satan himself."

"Liar—liar—liar!" Nergal rocked his bulbous head with dismay at the sight of Dren in his thick medallions of sores and cankers. "You know what he said is true. You saw the clear light."

"We don't even know his name!"

"Liar, we know him as he knew us. We remember him well." Nergal lifted his cleaved face toward the pewter sky, searching for a hint of celestial blue and finding none. "That was Raziel—the angel who tutored the first ones and brought them knowledge of grains and tillage, of numbers and writing."

"I do not like Raziel!" Dren slid down the slope of ash. "He taunts us with what we've lost! He tempts us to defy our masters!"

"Deceiver!" Nergal jumped after him and took him by the scruff of the neck. "Can you not even speak the truth here on the Bridge of Ashes? Raziel offers a way out of hell. But to take it, we must risk everything. You know what failure means?"

"We cannot fail!"

"Oh yes we can, liar!" Nergal pitched Dren into the searing blast of the wind at the foot of the bridge and shouted after him, "The fallen world is given to Satan! The souls of Earth are his! I am the Flayer! I have peeled the light from many a soul! I have seen their evil cores! And I tell you, we *can* fail!"

Dren crawled out of the smiting cold and lay at Nergal's taloned feet. "I hate Raziel! He taunts us with what we cannot have! We dare not renounce Satan!"

The Flayer squatted, his fibrillous mouth twitching nervously. "Oh, we can do it. It's that or go back to the pit. But—" He pounded his big fists into the cinders. "Once we renounce Satan, he and all his archdemons will come after us! Three days! Ha! Three months! Three years is not enough time to wrest a single soul from the master's fist in his own world!"

"We must go back and forget this." Dren hugged his scabrous body with fright. "We must go back before the masters see we are gone and come for us."

"You're not going back!" Nergal's mouth flaps wagged derisively. "You saw the sky. You want to go home!"

"And you don't!"

The Flayer rested his thick head in his hands and listened to the wind's proficient suffering. "How can we be forgiven for what we've done? We fought against the Creator! Remember what our leaders told us?" He sat up taller, puffed with arrogance. " 'God has no name. He has no name, because he does not belong in his creation. What is made belongs to us, the first named. God creates but he cannot sustain. We do all the work. We should rule.' " He slumped. "And now we rule—in hell!"

"I have forgotten the past," Dren mumbled as several vaporous souls trickled down the cinder slopes. "And I fear the future."

"You remember well enough, but you won't admit it, liar!" Nergal tossed a handful of cinders after the souls that rushed past him and watched the gale loft souls and dust into the darkness. "And you're ready to renounce the grand master himself, I know it! I am the Flayer, and I know the insides of souls and demons!" His oily voice softened. "We were beautiful, though—weren't we? Beautiful in a realm of beauty, what were we to know of despair and broken dreams? Now, in hell, that is all we know—and beauty is forgotten."

"We are demons!" Dren sat up with a shout. "We belong in hell!"

"Do we?" Nergal shoved himself upright and gazed around at the sky's lowering gray clouds and the gorge's flaming shadows, gloomy fidelities to the black ranges beyond, where the wintry squall swept several more smoky wisps of souls into the pit of perpetual night. "I'm not going back! I will renounce Satan!"

"I won't join you! I am too frightened!"

"Liar!" Nergal helped Dren to his feet. "If we're going to do this, for once you'll have to speak the truth, you know."

As they turned upon the Bridge of Ashes, a ponderous voice shouted, "There you two are!" Succoth's eelish shape slithered toward them through the cutting wind, his green flames snapping.

Unclean Spirits

The force of the tremendous wind from the gorge nearly snuffed Succoth's fiery aura. But unlike both Nergal and Dren, the blast of cruel cold did not diminish the Burner. He was too strong. His serpentine body coiled out of the dark with muscular vigor, his blunt, hairless head leaning into the blow with a menacing grin that showed the many needles of his teeth. "Why are you in this place?"

Nergal snatched at a tendril of fog curling past and began to strip the light from the soul with his gruesome hands. "We wanted to be the first to welcome the damned to hell!"

"Why are *you* here, Succoth?" Dren wagged an obscene gesture at him. "I came to get away from you after you burned me in the pit."

"Is that what the Liar claims?" Succoth twisted out of the howling wind, behind a nearby boulder of pitted and weathered obsidian—and his flames flared a brighter and more lurid green. "I say you are hearing voices again! I say you've come to cross the Bridge of Ashes!"

"Nonsense, Succoth!" Nergal chucked the shredded soul in his grasp to the foot of the Bridge, and the wind snatched it away. "To flay a new fallen soul is a delight not to be had in the pit. Stay here with us and burn a few yourself."

"Get off that bridge!" Succoth commanded. "You are not here for the souls! You are here to flee!"

"What's that, Succoth?" Dren shouted. "We can't hear you!"

Succoth surged forward. Once past the shelter of the tall boulder, the storm rush buffeted his flames and staggered him sideways, and he returned to the rock shield. "You'll not deceive me into standing upon the Bridge of Ashes with you! You are deserters! You've heard voices! The angels are luring you!"

Nergal lowered his lobed head and glowered with his array of arachnid eyes. "Who are you to accuse us?"

"I heard you two in the pit shouting about a voice, one voice calling you in the solitude!" Needle teeth gleamed. "I suspected treachery then! Was I wrong? I watched you in the pit! When you disappeared, I followed you here! You came to cross the Bridge of Ashes! I knew it! And now that I've found you, I will report you!"

Nergal's thick hands flustered, groping for a reply, and he turned to his companion. But Dren had vanished. The threat of Succoth had terrified the Liar, gripping him with a ferocity that stripped away the last of his self-deceptions and surprised him with the certainty that he did indeed want to renounce Satan and flee hell. With the strength of that certitude, he dared what he had always before feared: he forced a deception upon a fellow demon as though mastering a mortal soul.

Succoth saw Dren rush past him, leering derisively and flinging obscene gestures, and the Burner lashed out without thinking. His enraged gush of fire engulfed Dren—but instead of burning, the image of the Liar blinked to nothing, an illusion filled with the terrible wind out of the gorge. The consuming flames blew back over the Burner, and with a staggering scream his torched body shriveled to a charred wick. The cyclonic gusts cast his ashes across the gravel tract and into the darkness.

Nergal whooped with amazement and saw that Dren stood at his side. The Liar had never left the bridge. "How?" asked the Flayer.

"That's a deception that will only work once on the Burner."

Hands on his hips, Nergal leaned inquisitively toward Dren. "Is that a lie? Or are you speaking the truth now?"

"My lies are finished," Dren stated, as much to himself as to Nergal. "Succoth will be back soon—and with the others. We must escape now, while we can."

Nergal reached out with his twisted hands, and when Dren clasped them with his blistered fingers their guises as unclean spirits bleared away. The clear light from the angel above covered them, and they gazed upon each other as they had appeared when they had lived in the light as angels. They were beautiful and whole in the forms they had imagined for themselves in the radiance of creation—Nergal shaped in the image of the Afric race, Dren an Aryan. Yet those appearances, too, were mere guises, illusions that had amused them as angels, and they shimmered and disappeared.

They faced each other as they were in the beginning, white space, without intentions, pure energy of infinite frequencies, the original light, without wanting, inside and out all at once, the plain truth before time, before fate.

Minerals of Sleep

Upon the Bridge of Ashes, the two demons stared back to the origin of their plight. Once, they had been energy itself. They had been replete. There were no angels or demons. There was only light.

And then, the light fell into the darkness. The mortal souls whom the demons tormented had recently begun to think of this horrible moment—when light plunged into the void—as the Big Bang. The whimsy of that name enraged the demons, who remembered that moment with despair, for they believed there was no way back to the first light, the white light of infinite energy.

The angels felt otherwise. They believed that God was the light itself, not only the light exiled in the dark, but also the original light of infinity. They believed that their nameless God would guide them back eventually to their place of radiant origin. But not all agreed. Some objected that there was no divinity in the light, only endless and meaningless expansion through the vacuum of darkness and cold. This disagreement led to a war among the angels, and those who believed God was a fantasy were cast out of the light entirely, to live with their despair in the void.

This memory sluiced like voltage through the two demons, who stood in the clear light on the Bridge of Ashes, and they shook with the rage of their history.

Dren remembered for the first time after an aeon of suffering how he had deceived himself while in the light. He had sympathized with those who questioned the sanctity of the light. He understood their objection to shaping the light into ever more complex forms, building atoms out of quarks, shaping the matrix of the vacuum to bend space-time and ignite stars, the angels' furnaces in which they cooked atoms to larger and bulkier elements.

Why? he had asked with the other objectors. The light worshippers acted on faith that the void should be defied. The faithful wanted to deny entropy, the tendency of the light to cool toward chaos. They built ever more elaborate machines—galaxies and galactic structures—hoping to establish systems that would not decay but would generate higher orders of complexifying patterns.

Dren had not been sure as an angel that he shared the faith of light's purpose. Even when entropy was finally violated with the creation of life, he wondered to what end. But now, after having existed as a demon, after epochs of helping other demons trying to destroy life, trying to restore entropy and return everything to chaos, to the darkness and the cold that the demons believed were inevitable, he realized he had fooled himself. He was not a true demon, just a questioning angel. He did not believe, like Satan and his archdemons, that the destiny of those fallen into the void was to become the void. Where the light was leading the angels and life itself, he did not know—but it was away from the void, away from the dark, the cold, and the emptiness that the demons accepted as the ultimate truth.

Even as Dren realized this about himself, Nergal perceived that he believed the opposite. His urge to flee hell had been a curiosity entranced by fear. Now that he remembered again, he felt loathing for the angels. They were so righteous in their empty faith. Where was their God? He had no form, no name. Yet by their faith in this formless, nameless entity, they dared cast out from the light the angels who did not agree with them. And the demons had accepted their defeat bravely and defiantly.

Forced to live in the frigid darkness, the demons had persevered in their struggle to end the atrocity of life. Nergal himself had worked hard to flay the souls of those mortals rejected by the angels and use their wan energy to mine the void for the minerals of sleep: silence, stillness, amnesia. Eventually the angels would fail and discover that no matter how complex they made the light and its frozen residue, matter, there was no way to return to the original light of infinity—no way to undo the Big Bang. By then, the demons would have an ample supply of forgetfulness for everyone. Angels and demons alike would partake of it, stop their struggle, and lie down in darkness to become one with the void.

"Is that what you truly believe?" Dren asked, releasing Nergal's hands. "That all this will come to nothing?"

"It is more than what I believe." Nergal stepped away from Dren. "This is what I am—what we all are—nothing. Face the truth, Dren. We have fallen into the void. We *are* the void."

THE MAD DAY'S MIRTH

The clear light over Dren and Nergal faded, and they appeared again as demons. In the black mirrors of the Flayer's clustered eyes, Dren saw himself, a creature of mottled sores with a head and face like a block of crumbling cheese. He backed away in disgust. "I've lied to myself too long."

"You're lying to yourself right now," Nergal said irately. "You think you love the light. You think you'll find your nameless God there. But look at yourself! Look at what your God has made you. You're not an angel of light. You're a Liar. Admit it!"

"I've deceived myself and others—but I'll deceive no more." Dren edged away from the larger demon who hunched angrily before him. "We

both remember now who we really are. You better get off the bridge before your masters get here."

"You're coming with me!" Nergal bounded forward, thick hands grasping. But Dren leaped up the slope, and the Flayer grabbed fistfuls of cinders. "I'm not letting you get away! I forgot who I was! I forgot why we're here in the darkness! But I remember now!"

Dren hopped precariously higher on the sliding grade of ash, the ground slipping away under him. "I'm an angel, Nergal. I don't belong in the pit!"

"Liar!" Nergal clambered frantically, digging into the mounded soot, snatching for Dren's ankles. "The angels are insane! They believe in what they cannot see! They build illusions out of the light! Worlds of illusions!"

"You think life is an illusion because you're a demon, Nergal!" Dren strove to master his panic and mount the unstable declivity with purposeful steps, only inches ahead of the Flayer's clawing hands. "But I saw myself in the clear light. I don't belong here. That's why the voice came to me. The angels are calling me home, to the light."

"You're not going to join them!" Nergal kicked hard against the black sand and propelled himself upward until he reared over Dren. "You're not going to help them create more madness! You're staying here! You're staying in the cold and the dark where we destroy illusions!" He grabbed Dren by the shoulders and shook him to a blur. "And you're going to help us fight our way back into the light! Do you hear?"

A giant voice boomed over the grappling demons, "Well said, Nergal the Flayer!" With a start, Nergal released Dren and slid to his back on the loose cinders. During his wild assault on Dren, he had not noticed the return of Succoth. Crisp as a scorched insect, the Burner stood at the foot of the Bridge of Ashes, needle teeth clenched in a scorched skull, fire-stick arms pointing with accusatory rage. But the vast voice had not come from Succoth.

The darkness of the pit towered above the Burner, a man shape with all the sky inside it. It lumbered closer, and distinct features coalesced out of the night depths: chambered eyes smirking in a shapeless, enormously swollen head malformed as a gorgon. Like some mutilated ideation of tragedy, its delirious mask of horror swung above the bridge. Corpse gas seeped from the curled corners of its cracked mouth, and where the blackened skin had split open along the brow and cheeks exposing pink bone, maggots writhed in swarms of hallucinated paisleys.

"Master Moloch!" Nergal gasped, breathless in the fetid stench of the rotting giant.

Dren wriggled free of the Flayer's grasp and feverishly crawled up the ashen slope, chanting, "I renounce Satan! I renounce Satan!"

Laughter gonged with percussive force, a massive iron bell struck underwater. "Crawl before me, Dren the Liar! You are the fool of this mad day's mirth!"

The gangrenous stink of Moloch burned Dren's open sores and numbed him like venom. The Liar's limbs thrashed convulsively but no longer pulled him forward. And he lay with his eyes bulged in their sockets, mouth full of ash, muttering inanely, "I renounce Satan. I renounce . . . I renounce . . ."

A gargantuan hand reached for him, putrefied fingers like dripping candles, bone tips showing. As it closed on him, a clear light basked the Bridge of Ashes. Moloch's enormous hand frittered to dust, and the giant tottered backward with a mighty shriek that startled flares of jet flame from the gorge. Into the absolute blackness of the pit, he toppled.

SATAN IS HUNG IN DARKNESS, LIKE THORNS ON THE TREE OF NIGHT

"Dren!" Raziel beckoned to the demon from the crest of the Bridge of Ashes. "Hurry!"

Dren scrambled to his feet, and the ash did not crumble beneath him. With churning arms and legs, he sprinted toward the angel. Near the summit, he glanced over his shoulder and saw Nergal the Flayer and Succoth the Burner far below, shaking with fury. Wasteland sprawled behind them, across a vista predicated on suffering—from a cutting floor of volcanic glass, through cinder cones of poisonous fumes, to a pumice sky of vortex clouds.

"Don't look back." Raziel put a light and warm arm across Dren's shoulders and turned him away from hell. "Look forward to your atonement—and to your return to the light."

They stepped off the Bridge of Ashes and into a deserted underground parking garage lit by fluorescents that receded along a concrete ceiling. Dren squinted against the glare—and his whole body ached with silence and warmth. The drumming, exploding, wailing noises of hell had stopped. The icy wind was gone. The taint of gasoline and engine exhaust lilted in the air like perfume. "Where are we?"

"Earth." Raziel leaned on the hood of a BMW 1035i, a cheerful smile on his brown, Hispanic face. The angel gestured at his expensive Italian jacket, silk shirt, gold neck chains, and razor-creased trousers. "We look however we wish here. No one can see us, unless we choose that they do. But choose wisely. Every choice has its consequences—all the more so in this world, where time is short."

Dren gazed down at himself. The sores and blisters were gone, replaced by pale, muscular nakedness.

"Here, look at yourself." Raziel flipped up the sideview mirror of the BMW. "You have the face you wore before you gave yourself to the demons. Change it if you like."

"Women," Dren spoke, his voice strange to him in the silence as he inspected a young, beardless face and brushed strands of yellow hair from before his pale eyes. "Why are there no women demons or angels?"

"Don't you know?" Raziel motioned to the aisle of parked cars, the fluorescent lights reflecting in the windshields and polished hoods like electric calligraphy. "There is only one God—and she is a woman. She is the light of creation cooled to matter."

Dren remembered. His memories of his first life in the light began to sift back. "One God—and many, many demons and angels."

"Like one egg and many, many sperm!" Raziel threw his head back with a glittering laugh. "Don't dwell too much on God. It's humanity you want to think about now, Dren. Three days in this city are all you have to prove you're sincere. That's the longest I can hope to distract Satan and keep you free of his clutches."

Dren glanced around at the tiered concrete slabs of the stacked garage. "Satan is here—on Earth?"

"You already know the answer to that, Dren." Raziel cocked his curly head impatiently. "When we threw Satan and his demons out of the light, they took up residence in the dark, where the light has cooled to matter. He's all around us now. Satan is hung in darkness, like thorns on the tree of night. Souls get impaled too easily in this world. As a demon, you saw the damned, weeping for the light they had lost."

"Why are they damned?"

"Well, the demons call them damned. Actually, they're just recycled." Raziel shrugged haplessly. "Selfish souls, hungry souls, furious souls, demented souls—they're waveforms of light that need to be broken down so they can be put together again better. But we're wasting time here talking about what you cannot change. Get going, Dren. You're on your own now. Like every soul in this world, your destiny is in your own hands. Go and do good."

Dren found himself staring at his smeared reflection in the car hood. The angel had departed. For a long moment, the demon just stood there, relishing the silence, the warmth, the indigent reflections of light. He marveled at the deceptions of his heart that had denied him this for so long. And as he began to walk up the concrete rampway out of the garage, he contemplated the shattered lives that had spilled their souls into hell—and wondered if he was deceiving himself again to believe that he could make whole just one damaged life and keep it from falling apart.

Above him, beyond the garage's mechanical barrier, car lights flowed through the night, and the towers and spires of the city glittered with an unguessed kinship to the stars.

Moving

Toward

the

Light

RICK R. REED

Alexander

1

There is only darkness. She blinks, trying to focus, but the black presses in: a warm presence, engulfing, suffocating. She reaches out, wondering if she is floating in a vast, starless sky . . . and her hands connect with wood. Reaches up . . . and her hands connect with wood. Hard wood, she realizes now, supports her back. She takes in a great quivering breath, wondering how much air is left for her. This is too unreal, she tells herself, and once more reaches around herself, fingers groping like subterranean insects, sensing only by touch.

The box in which she has been trapped is little bigger than she is. At best, there are only a few inches on either side of her, above her. Before the panic sets in, she touches the holes drilled in the top of the box.

But even with the assurance of an air supply, she is terrified. Bile rises up to lodge and burn in the back of her throat. Although she trembles with cold, her body is covered with a slick veneer of sweat. She swears she hears blood pounding, constricting her temples. Her chest feels tight, as if too great an intake of air might cause her heart to burst.

And then the panic takes over, the adrenaline pumping through her like an electric current and she is slamming herself from side to side, lunging upward, clawing the box's top with her fingernails. Clawing and clawing until she can feel hot points of pain at her cuticles and the warmth of blood there.

She's screaming, but she might as well be gagged. Her shrill cries carom off the box's interior, bouncing around inside. Her hot breath is sour, leaving a bad taste.

"Please!" she shrieks. "Please, you have to let me out! I can't stand this!" She kicks until her breath is ragged, until it's coming so fast she begins to hyperventilate and it's not just the box that's closing in on her, but her own lungs.

And then, and then—and this is the part where everything goes cold—she hears a key being fitted into a padlock above her. The soft clicking of the key as it turns suddenly becomes the only sound. No more cries. No more pounding heart. No more blood rushing in her ears.

Just a key being turned in a lock and then the rush of cold air as the box is slowly opened.

She scrunches up her eyes and wills her body to disappear into the wood.

No . . .

She will not look at him. Will not. Cannot. Look.

But her eyelids flutter anyway.

A dark hand draws closer, above her, closer, until nothing exists but that hand pressing down on her face.

* * *

Miranda awakened sweating, the sheets twisted in a ball next to her. The striped ticking of the mattress, with its topography of stains, looked dull in the gray light pouring in from the bedroom window.

Miranda sat up and ran a hand through her spiky red hair, another trembling hand across her cold, sweat-slicked face. Her temples throbbed, her throat was dry.

Outside, the el train rumbled by, carrying commuters south to their jobs in the Loop: downtown Chicago.

She recalled the date: just a couple days before Christmas, and the scattering images of her nightmare and the simple chronology made her tremble. Miranda reached out to the milk crate beside the mattress and shook a Marlboro out of the pack, lit it with trembling fingers.

It had been four years. Miranda stood and walked to the window. Outside, Lawrence Avenue was already bustling, the cars like insects, busy and hurrying, the buses roaring and throwing plumes of dark exhaust into a cloud-choked sky.

Four years ago. Miranda had made the papers then, so had Jimmy, War Zone, and Little T, a girl she never knew, a runaway called Julie Soldano. They had all been kidnapped by a sicko called Dwight Morris. Kidnapped and imprisoned in his basement on the west side. The dream was already growing murky, but not the memory: how she had been kept, like the rest of them, in a coffin-shaped box crafted of plywood. It had been Dwight Morris's intention to rid the world of street kids, mere children who kept his passion for them alive. By eliminating them with the cleansing tool of fire, he must have thought he could rid himself of his own personal demons.

Whatever hell Dwight Morris now rested in, she hoped it was filled with demons.

He had succeeded in taking away one of her best friends back then, Carlos Garcia, a fifteen-year-old hustler too effeminate to be anything but an object of ridicule among his peers and a utilitarian tool of men much older than himself. Carlos's blood had stained the interior of Dwight's pickup truck.

The worst, though, was that Dwight Morris had taken Jimmy away. Jimmy Fels, with his sandy hair, and tough-guy swagger, thirteen years old and already far too wise for his own good.

Miranda didn't want to think about this. But the cigarette burned in an ashtray as she stared out the window, remembering. She saw him standing down there on Lawrence, ripped jeans and Metallica T-shirt, a cigarette dangling from his little-boy lips, eyes scanning the traffic for a potential john, one who would give him the money to buy a little food, maybe a bottle of wine if he was lucky.

And then he would come home to her, where they had all once lived, an abandoned apartment building, soulless, eyeless with its boarded up windows of plywood. They would lie together on an old mattress with the stuffing seeping out, huddled down among blankets, old coats, newspapers . . . anything to keep the Chicago winds and chill at bay. Snuggle down and plan their futures, which did not include selling their bodies to get by, did not include the dangers of the Uptown streets that they knew so well.

But Jimmy was gone, and Miranda drew in a shuddering breath at the thought of him, the clear picture that remained in her mind. She would not cry. She picked up her cigarette and dragged on it, sucking in the smoke, wanting it to fill her lungs not with tar and nicotine, but oblivion.

It had been four years ago today that it had come down. A priest, Richard Grebb, had saved them. He was a tortured man Miranda had never known, but she could recall his tear-stained face as he huddled with her and the other kids outside Dwight Morris's house, as the structure went up in flames, with him inside.

Jimmy, too . . .

Oh God, why did it have to happen?

For a while, she had been a celebrity, a survivor of this twisted atrocity, a scene so sick and twisted it played itself out over and over, raining down on houses and apartments across the country.

Miranda had been recognized on the streets for months. The johns came from as far away as Joliet, Kenosha, Kankakee, just so they could fuck her, the famous one, scarred by brutality and perversion. In fucking her, they could touch fame.

And the only way Miranda could escape any of this was through alcohol. She had been drinking on a daily basis since she was twelve, and after all the shit came down, the drinking intensified, until Miranda did little more than drink, drinking in the morning, in the afternoon, until she passed out at night. More than once, she would awaken to find blood between her legs and all her money gone.

But that was then. Miranda was nineteen now. When the drinking got so bad it landed her in Cook County hospital, near death, she decided to seek help. Six months, she thought, six months without a drink.

And still, like a demon, it pursued her. She awakened each day wanting it and fell asleep each night, trying to recall the taste of the fortified wine she preferred, longing for the warmth it once filled her with.

Outside, the sky spat snow, icy rain that tapped on the cracked window of her room. Around her there were no signs of the holiday. Her room consisted of nothing more than a mattress, a crate, a card table, and two folding chairs. Her clothes were heaped in a corner.

She was due to start her shift at McDonald's in an hour.

Miranda sat suddenly on the bed, lowered her head almost to her knees, and wept. This was never how it was supposed to be. Wept more for the loss of Jimmy, who, through the years, had always seemed to her a kind of salvation. Together, she knew, the two of them could have broken the cycle of poverty in which they were trapped.

But alone . . .

Miranda wiped the tears and the snot on the back of the long-sleeved T-shirt she had worn to bed, wandered once more to the window.

A neon sign taunted her. Just across the street. So simple, so convenient.

What in hell was she thinking when she had rented this room right across the street from a liquor store?

TJ's, the hot pink neon read. Lights blinked around the big sign. The store's windows were obscured by hand-lettered signs offering this week's specials. Christmas cheer going by names like Johnnie Walker, Red Dog beer, Zima, Finlandia, Cisco.

Cisco . . . she had once conducted a passionate love affair with the fruity, fortified wine. Hell, she would blow a guy and drink his come in exchange for a bottle of the stuff.

It seemed then that everything in the city paused as one thought rang out in Miranda's sleep-clouded mind: just one drink won't hurt. Just one to get me through this day. *Jesus Christ, think of the hell I've gone through.* Not just this drab existence that now passed for a life, but the horror of four years ago: a horror no one, and most people, should never experience. She imagined herself unscrewing the cap, the sweet smell wafting up, making her mouth wet and her heart race with the mere anticipation of it. She imagined lifting the bottle to her lips, the burst of sweetness and the slight burning in the back of her throat, sweet oblivion.

Just what she needed.

Miranda dressed quickly, pulling on jeans and a sweatshirt, a pair of sneakers. She shrugged into her coat, a navy pea coat she wouldn't have been caught dead in four years ago, with sleeves that reached down to her fingertips.

Fuck McDonald's. Fuck AA. Fuck the whole grimy gray world in which she found herself trapped, not so very different from the box in which she was imprisoned four years ago.

Today she would honor Jimmy's memory by blotting it out.

Miranda headed toward her door, thinking of nothing, but anticipating, anticipating . . .

Miranda sat alone, murky light of dusk seeping into her room, making of the scattered, battered furniture monstrous shapes in the shadows. Warmth filled her and a haze had settled around her brain, like a mist surrounding the soft pink tissue.

It had been so long and the feelings were just right, perfect for this day, this anniversary of death and despair.

Miranda thought of nothing. The empty bottle of Cisco lay on the floor, near the mattress, its magic transferred, working to create an almost electric buzz in her body.

A siren wailed by and Miranda stood on shaky legs to look outside. Night encroached on the scene below, transforming the darkness into electric neon. Headlights glowed. Bar and store signs blinked, hummed in electric neon color.

Wind rattled the storm window, and the flakes of snow, dying as they met the ground all day long, were now finding refuge on the backs of cars and the trash and dead leaves in the gutter, the approach of night lengthening their life spans.

Miranda shrugged into her coat and left her room. Outside, the cold hit her all at once, cutting through her coat with the precision of a surgeon. Just west of Lawrence was a bar she knew would serve her. In her pocket, she had five or six dollars, enough to buy a couple drafts, enough to keep the buzz humming.

She began making her way west of Lawrence, to Broadway Liquors and Tap, imagining the look of surprise on Keith, the shave-headed, tattooed, and pierced bartender who had once been her friend, as she entered.

It would be a homecoming of sorts, Miranda thought and grinned, her teeth coming together too hard. Perhaps there were other things Miranda could trade for alcohol, other ways to barter with the bartender. Miranda knew these ways well.

A few more steps and she was passing through the smoked glass door into Broadway Liquors and Tap. The thump of the jukebox, playing the Rolling Stones' "Beast of Burden," the smoke-choked air, and the smell of stale beer and tobacco all seemed to her like old friends.

She couldn't wait for her first drink. She found an empty stool among the swiveling faces that turned to stare at her as she selected a seat, sat herself down, and with a righteous grin, searched in vain for Keith.

A woman with bleached blond hair and fat ass put down the glass she was drying and wandered over to Miranda, none too fast.

Her eyes, rimmed in pale blue shadow, regarded Miranda coolly. "What is it you want, honey?"

"Where's Keith? Off tonight?"

"Honey, Keith hasn't worked here for at least a couple months."

"Oh?"

"Yeah, he got fired for selling to minors."

"Shit." Miranda lit a cigarette and directed a plume of smoke toward the black-painted tin ceiling. "Bad break."

The blonde nodded. "Yeah, a guy could lose his license over shit like that."

Miranda began to know this visit, this homecoming, might not be as warm and receptive as she had anticipated.

"So what can I get you, sweetie? A Coke?" The blonde's eyes were tired; she knew what was coming.

"How about a draft?" Miranda nodded toward the taps.

"Got some ID?" The woman's face already betrayed that she knew Miranda was too young.

Miranda wondered why she was bothering to play the scenario out. But if she didn't try . . . "I left it at home."

The blonde smiled. "Well, then you better go home and get it, sweetheart."

"Oh come on, don't be a bitch. It's cold out. I'll bring it in next time. Promise."

The woman rubbed her forehead. "Next time, when you bring in your ID, honey, I'll buy you a drink."

Miranda slid from the stool, eyeing the brass beer tap, suddenly wanting the beer more than she had ever wanted anything. "Oh, fuck you."

The blonde hissed. "Get out of here, you little whore. Right now."

Miranda stood, then gripped the bar to stop the room from spinning. "Look, I'm sorry," she pleaded. "Just one drink and I'll be out of your hair."

"Door's right over there."

"I hate you," Miranda hissed.

"Stop, honey, you're breakin' my heart."

Miranda searched the room for a man, one who would save her.

But no one was paying any attention.

No one save for a middle-aged guy, good looking really, with salt-and-pepper hair and a big mustache. He wore a black leather biker jacket, tight, faded jeans, and combat boots. He stared at Miranda through a haze of cigar smoke. When their eyes met, he smiled.

She sidled up to him. "Hi. I'm Miranda."

"Tom." The man offered his hand, upon the back of which a tattooed cougar stretched out. Miranda grasped the hand and held it, staring into his eyes.

How easy, she thought, *I fall back into routine.*

And then the blonde was behind her. "I thought I told you to go."

Miranda, without letting go of Tom's hand, turned to glare at the woman. "I'm just visiting my friend Tom here."

"Fine, no skin off my ass. But if your friend Tom here tries to buy you a drink, you're both out."

"Fuck it," Miranda whispered, turned, and hurried out the door.

Snow whirled around her and, once again, she was drawn back to the time four years ago when all the shit came down. Miranda passed an alley where a rusted-out metal drum shot flames into the sky.

Miranda checked her pocket, making sure the few dollars she had were still there, and started toward the liquor store. The hell with Broadway Liquors and Tap: she would buy a bottle and have her own party, remembering Jimmy until she, too, passed into at least a temporary oblivion.

"Hey! Wait up!"

Miranda stopped. She didn't turn, but closed her eyes and lifted her face to the sky, letting the wet kisses of snow cover her face. It didn't take much imagination to know to whom the footfalls behind her belonged.

A breathless person stood behind her. Miranda took a deep breath, opened her eyes, and turned around.

Of course, it was Tom, the man from the bar. He stood shivering in front of her, a nervous grin causing his grizzled features to crinkle. She had seen the look before and wondered how much he would offer her.

"I saw what happened back there."

"Yeah? Well, she was right to refuse me. I'm not twenty-one yet."

"Fuck her. You wanna go someplace with me and have a drink?"

"Where did you have in mind?"

"I just live a few blocks down, on Winthrop." He grinned. "Got plenty to drink. We could have us a little party."

"A little party . . ." Miranda echoed. It was just what she needed, what she needed to get through this miserable day. A way to forget. Tomorrow would no longer be the anniversary. And, even though her depressing, hopeless life would remain unchanged, at least things could go back to normal. "That sounds like just what the doctor ordered."

"Or the bartender."

The two laughed. Tom slid his arm around her and they crossed the street, heading east, toward Winthrop. *What the hell,* Miranda thought, what she had already had to drink whirling around inside her, *maybe I can even make a few bucks tonight.*

2

Tom lived three blocks south, in a graystone three-flat, just like so many others in this neighborhood, all over the city, really. When they got to his front door, a piece of plywood over where the glass should have been, marred by gang graffiti, Tom turned to her. He hadn't said much along the three- or four-block walk, which was fine with Miranda, but now it seemed as though he had something to say to her.

"Um, listen, babe, I've already got a few buddies over. I hope that's okay."

Miranda knew where this was going. She had been the pass-around party-pack girl at other gatherings of this sort. She didn't mind; not tonight anyway. It was a chance to make enough to pay the rent, which was coming due in a week's time. But she wanted to make sure Tom understood that her favors did not come for free.

"That's cool." Miranda dug in her pocket for a Marlboro and lit it, expelling the smoke at Tom's expectant face. "I just want you to understand that I'm not here for just a good time."

"Oh?"

"Yeah," she said, and put on what she thought was her most alluring smile. "I'm here to make some money."

Tom snickered. "No problem. We expected that. Twenty per guy enough?"

"Make it fifty and I'm there. How many are there?"

"There's five."

Miranda calculated quickly. Two hundred and fifty dollars for a night's work. Not bad. She wondered what she was doing working at Mickey D's. "I can live with that. Just so they can all cough up fifty."

"Won't be a problem. C'mon; it's cold out here."

Miranda followed him into a marble vestibule that had definitely seen better days. The floor was littered with garbage; the mail receptacles had been burglarized many times before, the brass smashed and dented, names scratched off and rewritten a dozen times. A couple of the mailboxes hung open, their doors hanging down like metallic tongues.

She followed him upstairs. Inside, it smelled like old urine and the culinary attempts of countless residents. It was what Miranda was used to; her own hallway smelled the same.

On the third floor, Tom fished his keys from his pocket and approached the door to the left. Miranda heard the thumping bass of a stereo and male voices. When Tom fitted his key into the lock, the voices stopped.

3

Miranda entered the room behind Tom and, for just a moment, froze, wondering what she was doing here. Perhaps the wine was beginning to wear off; perhaps her common sense had rushed back in to taunt her. Turning a trick was one thing. But taking on a whole apartmentful of guys was foolhardy.

Tom stepped aside and she saw them.

"Hey guys, got us a little party favor here."

And suddenly all Miranda felt was sick. She was surprised at her own abrupt about-face. But the thumping bass of the music, some industrial-club dance-mix shit that Miranda hated: all the screaming and repetitive backbeat. The volume was so high it hurt her ears.

Just below the ceiling hung a layer of thick, blue-gray smoke. Tobacco and marijuana. The coffee table was littered with candles whose wax dripped into the marred dark wood surface, dirty magazines opened to pictures of spread-eagled women, a small mirror dusted with white powder, a razor blade next to it, aluminum foil packets, a crack pipe next to them. This was a serious party.

Four guys lolled around the room. Two were on the couch, their eyes bright with interest at her arrival. Miranda wanted to shrink back into the walls, into the grimy, colorless plaster, disappear. She wanted to just turn and run, but an absurd sense of decorum prevented that. It would be too strange. No money had been exchanged yet; she could just talk her way out of it.

The two men on the couch leaned forward. "Hey babe," one of them slurred, "How's it goin'?"

"Good," Miranda blurted out, her gaze everywhere but on the men. But the intensity of their stares brought her eyes back. The man who had spoken to her wore nothing but a pair of ripped and faded jeans. A fat, hairy belly bulged over the top; he had breasts like a woman, which hung down, crowned with large, dark nipples. His face was grizzled, like Tom's, with a three- or four-day-old growth of beard, graying. His head was shaved and he had hung a big crystal on a chain from one ear. His companion on the couch was black, and surprisingly well-dressed when compared with the rest of the group: dark, baggy slacks, a black banded-collar shirt open to reveal a thick rope of gold chain around his neck. He had a pencil-thin mustache above his full lips and his dark eyes were set close together. He nodded at her, but said nothing.

She felt Tom's hand on her back, moving slowly up and down, and Miranda did her best not to recoil from the touch, but it reminded her of bugs crawling along her back. *Don't shiver. Don't shiver.*

The two other men in the room lounged on the floor, big legs spread out before them. It was hard to make out their features in the light thrown off by the flickering candles, but Miranda could see one was very fat with dark hair and a Pancho Villa mustache, probably Hispanic. The other was his opposite: light, thinning, shoulder-length hair, a beard, and an almost skeletal body. Both men wore nothing but jeans.

She couldn't do this. None of the men was even remotely appealing.

"What did you say your name was, honey?" Tom whispered in her ear; she could smell the alcohol on his breath. The heat of his whisper caused her to shrug her shoulders.

"I didn't." She turned to look at him, seeing the surprise in his face. "Listen: I don't think I'm into this tonight."

"Oh, ho!" Tom shouted, startling her. He turned to the group. "Girlfriend here says she's not in the mood to party."

Everything happened so fast then. Miranda turned toward the door and then they were all upon her, pulling her back. She started to scream, but a hand landed hard enough on her mouth to stifle the scream and, at the same time, split her lip. She tasted the copper of her blood and panic rose up like electricity, jolting her. There were hands on her legs, her arms. In moments, she was aloft and being spirited deeper into the room.

"No," she tried to whisper through the sweaty hand at her mouth.

One of them opened the bedroom door. She heard the creak. *This isn't happening,* she told herself.

She was flung on the bed. She felt like a doll, landing amid dirty sheets, the springs squeaking beneath her. Laughter all around her.

"Listen, guys, how 'bout I just blow—"

A punch landed on her jaw, causing her teeth to slam together in a sickening crunch.

What was the term they used in the movies? Montage? That was how the rest of the night went for her: bits and flashes of horrible things happening, so fast, so fast . . . The entire encounter spinning dizzyingly out of control, like a car crash, no time to prevent the horror.

Even if her screams could be heard above the driving bass beat, which she doubted, one of the guys was thoughtful enough to slap a piece of duct tape over her mouth. To the back of the duct tape one of them had affixed a small, red ball which Miranda had no choice but to take into her mouth.

One of them, the black one she thought, although certainty had deserted her, stood above the bed and pissed on her. Strong, aromatic stuff, wetting her clothes, her hair, the stench of it rising up to assail her.

Hands groping, scratching, tugging . . . until she was naked. Fingers probing, prodding, entering her cunt, her ass, forcing themselves deeper and deeper, until her eyes watered and her face twisted up in a grimace. Fingers twisting her nipples so hard she wondered if they would be ripped from her body, arching her back to try and buck out the pain.

They mounted her, one after the other, sometimes two and three at a time, flipping her body around like a rag doll, laughing and hitting her, punches landing squarely, if she attempted to make any movement to thwart them. At one point, there were two of them inside her cunt and one up her ass. Miranda held down the bile that rose up to burn the back of her throat, sure that to let it go would mean death by suffocation.

Warm blood trickled down her thighs to pool between them, causing more laughter.

Over and over again. Come landing on her face, her chest, to liquefy and roll in fat beads like beetles, crawly over her skin.

Something shoved up inside her, cold and metallic. Miranda was beyond caring: she lay limp, unable to do anything to prevent the onslaught.

A fist landed on her face once more and with it, a sickening crunch. Had her jaw broken? Fat hairy thighs lowered themselves on her face and the crack of a hairy ass positioned itself just above her nose. Shit rained down on her face.

Hands around her throat, cutting off air.

Merciful, Miranda thought, *merciful* . . . just before everything went black. Just before all the air disappeared.

Miranda was alone. She didn't know where she was or where all the pain had gone to. She stood uncertainly, sure her legs would fail her, but they felt fine. She looked down at herself and found, surprisingly, everything intact. There were no scratches, no bruises, no scorches where they had burned her with cigarettes.

It seemed everything had healed in one miraculous moment.

She looked around her and gasped. There were no walls, no floor beneath her, no ceiling above her. All she saw was dim gray light and a mist rolling around her ankles.

A dark bird, its wings making a great shadow above her, chilling, swooped by. Then another and another, until the air above her was filled with the sound of beating wings, their blackness blotting out the dim, feeble light until Miranda found herself in darkness so deep it was palpable.

And then she felt herself being lifted, felt claws digging into her flesh. Her feet left the ground as she was taken up into this huge moving shadow, the sound of beating wings her only company.

Their beaks digging into her flesh didn't hurt. Surprisingly, there was only a comforting warmth in being among all these black, avian creatures, as if she were being swooped up and enfolded in their care and protection.

And then, dimly at first: a tiny pinprick of light. As the birds moved toward it, it grew larger, larger, at first a round ball, a tiny pewter sun, growing, growing until the white light before her became blinding, until she had to close her eyes, certain that vision would be scorched out of them by the brightness and heat.

And then it all stopped: the beating wings, the company of thousands of crows.

Miranda was alone. She stood in the bright light, feeling as if she were a deep part of it, its warmth enfolding her in its bosom. She lifted her hand to her face and saw that it was glowing; she had been transformed into a creature of light. With her other hand, she reached a finger out to touch herself and saw that the finger went easily through the palm of her hand.

Weird, yet delightful at the same time. She twirled and found that her feet connected with nothing solid. She could move up into dizzying heights and plunge downward, never connecting with anything solid.

Where was she? Where had she been? Miranda could remember so little. Even the memory of what had happened only minutes before had deserted her. All that existed now was the present.

And the present was just that: a delightful present. She had never felt warmer or more secure.

She never wanted to leave.

And then she heard him. A voice calling so dimly at first as to be nothing more than a drone, growing louder.

She knew who it was and didn't wonder how it was possible. It was just another delightful gift, needing no explanation.

Turning: he was beside her. Jimmy. Nothing had changed about him: he was still thirteen years old, still wearing the same ripped jeans and black T-shirt, emblazoned with the logo of yet another heavy metal band. But: he, too, was bathed in the heat of the white light that surrounded him.

There were no words. But Miranda knew he was delighted to see her, and she knew as well how happy he was to be reunited with her. When she embraced him, they became one and she merged into the skinny, adolescent body without even trying. The warmth here was a comfort she had never known.

A chill, a slight coldness came from somewhere within him and he was moving back away from her. A small voice, Jimmy's, whispered deep within her brain.

Too soon. Too soon. Everything's gonna be all right.

5

Her eyelids fluttered, at first taking in nothing. And then, bits and pieces. A bed, its mattress stiff beneath her, and the feel of something rubbery beneath the linen. Her eyes opened and details became difficult to take in; everything blurred. Finally, a little clearer and she could make out two metal contraptions at either side of her making of this bed in which she lay a crib. A metallic voice in the air: "Dr. Timmons, Room 354. Stat."

Above her, a plastic bag of clear liquid hung from a metal post. Miranda traced the clear tube down until she saw it entered her arm. The IV was dripping sustenance into her.

So she was in a hospital. She was not dead.

Miranda attempted to move her head, and with this tiny movement, pain came. The heat and deep bruised feeling of it cascaded through her, making a dim nausea rise up in her gut. She wanted to vomit.

In spite of the pain, she turned her head more, until she faced a window, a great square rectangle of blinding yellow light.

A crow flew by, its wingspan impossibly large.

Miranda closed her eyes to shut out the light. Closed them and fell back into oblivion.

Driving bass beat filled the car.

"What is this shit, man?" Carl, large, lanky, black, drew in on the one-hitter, held it with a snort, and watched the road.

"It's Moby. You like?" Brian-Mark took the little brass one-hitter from his friend and clamped it between his teeth. Without taking his eyes from the road, he fired up the disposable and brought it to the marijuana within the one-hitter, taking his eyes from the road for just a second to watch the little point of orange light grow as he inhaled, watch as it disappeared.

He tapped the one-hitter against the ashtray to expel the tiny ball of ash.

Carl and Brian-Mark were on Lake Shore Drive, heading south. Brian-Mark was Carl, except in white: the same lanky body, the same aquiline nose. But where Carl's hair was black, nappy, Brian-Mark's was long, stringy, and blond, so blond it was almost white.

Brian-Mark added to the cloud of pot smoke already hanging in the car. "I picked up this cassette down at Tower."

"You mean you stole it." Carl barked out a short laugh.

Brian-Mark joined him and grunted, "Five-finger discount, man. Five fuckin' finger . . . best value in town."

The two men laughed and took the curve. Across from them, the lights of the city's towers rose up, impossibly beautiful, hard to believe it was man-made.

They were heading south to the Eisenhower Expressway, which would then take them west, to their destination: Cicero. Cicero, where they could load up on crack rocks for distribution to a large and hungry clientele on

Chicago's north side: Uptown, where the crack would offer a temporary respite from the poverty and the grime.

Brian-Mark asked, "You think that bitch is dead yet?"

Carl replied, "If she ain't, that girl is one strong motherfucker."

The two men collapsed once more into giggles, remembering the young girl with the red hair, a skinny young thing, who, just hours before, had become for them the ultimate party favor: a lump of yielding flesh to mold into their own version of erotic nightmare.

"Man, you think we were too hard on the piece?"

"Only if she's still breathing," Carl said. "We don't need no accusing fingers to point us out."

"Shit, that bitch knows she better not fuckin' say anything. There's plenty more where that came from. Fuckin' put her light out before she gets a chance to say much."

"Damn right." Carl watched as Brian-Mark slid across two lanes to make his right that would lead them through the Loop and onto the Eisenhower. The car, an old yellow Electra 225, maneuvered through the lanes of traffic. Its rearview mirror reflected the tall buildings of the Loop as the pair headed west, away from the city.

The men drove on in silence. The road was slick beneath them, the thrumming of the tires inaudible over the music.

Brian-Mark glanced in the rearview mirror before attempting a lane change to the left, where the lane was clear and he knew he could gun the car up to eighty, ninety miles per hour.

They would be in Cicero in no time.

As he looked in the mirror, though, something black whooshed across, reflected in the glass. Brian-Mark gripped the steering wheel. "Fuck! Did you see that?"

"What you talkin' about, man?"

"Look in the backseat. Christ, I think some kind of bird got in the fuckin' car."

Carl swerved his head around to examine the dark, and empty, backseat. "Shit, man, how many of these fuckin' things you done?" He held up the brass bat.

"Shit. I don't hallucinate from that, for Christ's sake."

"Well, there ain't nothin' back there."

Brian-Mark winced as he felt something sharp pinch the nape of his neck. "Damn! What did you do?"

"What the fuck are you talkin' about?"

"You pinched my fuckin' neck, right?"

"Oh yeah, sure." Carl stared out the window.

Brian-Mark wondered if he was going crazy. He kept his eyes focused on the ribbon of black asphalt before him, gripping the steering wheel too hard, leaning into it.

"Man, you as tense as a motherfucker. Relax."

Brian-Mark tried to relax, tried to settle back into his seat, but it was as if someone had rammed a column of steel up his spine. He took a cautious glance back in the mirror again.

The face of a young boy smiled back at him from the glass.

Brian-Mark said nothing this time. He looked again.

The same face, except this time, the boy stuck out his tongue.

"Damn!"

Carl turned to look and saw what Brian-Mark had seen. "What the fuck?"

Brian-Mark felt a cold hand on his neck, gripping. He yanked the steering wheel hard to the right and heard the blaring of horns. The car was all over the expressway. At one point, a Nissan Sentra glanced off the front bumper and sent them into a tailspin.

Both men shrieked as they saw a semi bearing down on them, its horn sounding like the scream of a dragon. Brian-Mark applied the brakes, throwing his back into the seat behind him for leverage as he bore down on the pedal.

The grille of the truck grew impossibly large in seconds as the truck made impact. Brian-Mark, as his final act, gripped the steering wheel so hard it bent in his hands.

The truck slammed into the car, sweeping it underneath the cab. The roof of the Electra was shaved off and two heads, one white and one black, flew into the midnight sky and landed hard on the road, barely avoided by a station wagon carrying a group of teenagers on their way home from a Christmas party.

A large crow swooped out of the darkness, as if it were made from it, and pecked an eye out of the decapitated head of each man.

 7

Miranda turned in her bed, her nightmare causing her to whimper.

And then smile.

Her eyes fluttered open for a second and there was Jimmy. She reached up to touch his face, but couldn't quite reach. He moved back from Miranda, his grin never leaving, his gaze never leaving hers. Even though he was partially obscured by the IV and the pole from which it hung, Miranda could see he held up two fingers.

She smiled again and went back to sleep.

8

He had been fat all his life. No wonder. He came from a whole family of fat people. His parents, back in West Virginia, and his two sisters grew up in front of the television. To break the monotony of canned laughter, screaming car chases, and gunfire, his mother always had treats. Every night. One night it would be powdered sugar donuts out of a box, another night plastic bowls heaped high with ice cream. If his dad got ambitious, he would run over to the Burger King and they would all scarf down Whoppers and fries while seeing what Jack and Chrissie were up to on *Three's Company*.

And now, as Luis Soto sat in front of his own TV—a 36-inch Mitsubishi— his eyes bulged along with his cheeks as *Tales from the Crypt* spewed out another tale of gore, violence, and revenge.

He loved *Tales from the Crypt* the best. It was the only reason he paid extra for HBO. As he watched, stuffing his mouth with barbecued potato chips, a voodoo priestess cast a spell on a young man who had cuckolded his master, taking his wife while the master was off overseeing work in the fields of the banana plantation on which they lived.

It sure was some scary shit, Luis thought, washing down a mouthful of potato chips with Mountain Dew.

The voodoo priestess had made a likeness of the handsome young man who was a frequent visitor to the plantation owner's wife's bed. She held it up and Luis shook his head.

Couldn't these fucking TV people get anything right? The fuckin' doll looked nothing like the dude who couldn't get enough pussy. For one thing, the doll had bulges in all the wrong places. Instead of massive pecs and biceps, the doll had a big beer gut and monstrous thighs, just like his own. Instead of blond hair, the doll's hair was a mass of black strings, just like his own, and the dude in the story didn't have a mustache, but the doll did.

And so did Luis.

Wait a minute. Luis barked out a short laugh and groped in the bag for more chips. Empty. The doll looked *a lot* like him.

The priestess held the doll up high, staring up at it from the light of a hundred flickering candles. After whispering some unintelligible curse, she placed the doll back down on the rough-hewn wooden table that was the centerpiece of her shack. The camera moved in for a close-up and damn! if the doll wasn't a spitting image of Luis, he didn't know his own reflection in the mirror.

The whole thing was kind of spooky. Luis closed his eyes and looked again. Sure the action was a cliché, something he had seen before on *Tales from the Crypt,* but this was just too weird.

The doll looked the same. Shit, he'd have to write to the producers and see if he couldn't buy a replica from them. The thing would look so cool hanging on his living room wall.

Suddenly there was a crash in the kitchen and what sounded like . . . what? . . . the fluttering of wings. *Damn,* Luis thought, getting up from his chair. What was it now?

He'd been on edge ever since a couple nights ago, when he had gotten together with Tom, Carl, Brian-Mark, and Dave to do that little red-haired street trash whore. They'd been too rough and Luis feared the girl might die.

He shrugged as he headed out to the kitchen. He told himself again: they had no ties to the girl and who gave a fuck about a piece of trash like her anyway? No one had been around when they had left her lying near a Dumpster behind a high-rise on Kenmore.

But still, what the fuck was that noise? Luis kept casting glances back at the TV as he moved to the back of the apartment. He didn't want to miss anything.

The kitchen was still. Luis flipped on the light and the only thing moving were two or three cockroaches skittering away from some grease near the stove.

No windows open, no door left ajar. But wait, what was that on the floor near the door? Luis moved closer to get a better look, unable to believe that what he thought he had seen was really there.

He stood over the small mess on the linoleum. "What the fuck?" he wondered, staring down at the white smears across the grimy floor. It looked like bird shit.

Luis shrugged. He could worry about it later. No way it could be bird shit. Besides, he didn't want to miss any more of *Tales.* He snagged a bag of Fritos and removed the clip on his way into the living room.

As he settled down in his chair, he stopped with his hand in midair and dropped the corn chip he held.

That voodoo priestess was black before, wasn't she? And she *was* a priestess, not a priest, right?

It was the same outfit: the same long, flowing robe decorated with jungle flowers and birds, the same turban, fashioned from a rough black material.

But the priestess had changed from a woman to a young boy. Wisps of dirty blond hair fell out of the turban.

He was chanting and holding a big pin aloft. He stopped chanting and with that, the drumming that had accompanied his voice stopped, too.

He held the pin up and plunged it into the little doll's forehead.

Luis screamed as a sharp pain bloomed into existence behind his right eye. He dropped the corn chips to the floor, reaching up to claw at the eye, to try and somehow remove its burning torture from back there.

His hand came away bloody. "No," he whimpered.

And then the voodoo kid took another pin out, this one bigger than the last, topped with a dangling black feather, and brought it down, right into where the doll's heart would be.

And Luis groaned, not having the strength, with the sudden awful constricting pain in his chest and the numbness in his arm, to scream.

Luis collapsed in front of the TV, one spasming hand reaching out to knock over the glass of Mountain Dew on the TV tray to his left.

Luis's dead eyes stared up at the ceiling as the laugh of the Crypt Keeper carried him to death, as the laugh dissolved into the cawing of a crow.

Miranda emerged from murky nightmares: the cawing of a crow and demonic laughter. Her room had the strange faint light of dawn: everything gray, the light absorbing color, rather than illuminating.

Jimmy Fels floated above her bed, glowing. She wanted to cry out. She wanted to take her battered body up to meet and merge with him.

He held three fingers up.

Miranda drifted back into a dreamless slumber.

What a fuckin' life, he thought, as he stumbled west on Catalpa, toward the shit-hole he called home. Dave Ellis's whole body was singing with alcohol: the feet that carried him felt numb, almost as if he were drifting along on a cushion of air; the rest of his limbs felt the same. It was late enough that the streets of Uptown were quiet for once: no squealing tires, no sirens, no horns blaring, no pneumatic wheezes as buses stopped to pick up and discharge passengers. The street lights above him dissolved into an amber sodium vapor haze when he lifted his bloodshot eyes to gaze up at them.

He was in no hurry to get home. All that awaited him was his fat, hairy wife—where had the young girl he had once fucked senseless gone? When had she been replaced by this greasy, corpulent shrew? What a lousy fuckin' trick to play on a man! Barb would be asleep, mouth open to spew out the most disgusting noises, borne up into the darkened air on a stinky cloud of garlic and cigarettes.

It was no wonder he had to cheat on her. It was no wonder he got together with his buddies every so often to have a little party, where they used and abused some whore who always got just what she deserved . . . what she was looking for.

Dave Ellis felt sorry for no woman. That hole between their legs just took and took and took. No wonder men died before women in general. They stole the life force from men, sucking it out with their cunts, their assholes, their mouths. It was all a big, fuckin' conspiracy. He was sure they giggled about it when they were alone together.

He didn't give a flying fuck if things got even more out of hand with that redhead the other night. Couldn't care less that right now, she could be lying in a morgue down at Cook County.

She got what she deserved. Payback time for all her sisters stole from men.

Dave stumbled up the walk of the courtyard building, taking a right that almost sent him wobbling into the bushes. It was just past four A.M. and he was glad he wouldn't have to put up with Barb's accusations, questions, recriminations. Glad he could just drop into bed, catch a few z's, and be off again in the morning, before Barb got up for work. By the time she got down to her secretarial job in the Loop, he would already have had his first couple of beers. The bitch was good for something: keeping him in smokes and beer. He had to have some reason for keeping her around. It sure wasn't for pussy.

He attempted to fit his key in the lock and on the third try succeeded. Stumbling up the stairs, he longed for the time when he wouldn't have to take another step, when he could just drop his clothes on the bedroom floor—for Barb to pick up later—and collapse on the mattress next to her. And should she say anything to him about the lateness of his return, why, a good hard backhand to her mouth would silence her.

It had worked in the past.

Inside, the apartment smelled like grease. Barb's cigarette smoke still hung in a cloud near the living room ceiling.

Dave went into the bathroom, puked in the toilet, splashed cold water on his face, and glanced at himself in the mirror. Except for the red-shot eyes, he still looked pretty good for a dude pushing forty. The shaved head and the big crystal earring gave him a roguish look and the three-day-old beard he maintained kept him looking tough. Even if he had put a few pounds on he still looked damned good. That fuckin' Barb . . . what was wrong with her? You'd think she'd still be begging for his dick. Weren't many guys around who were real men like he was.

Dave stripped out of his clothes in the bathroom and padded naked into the bedroom. Damn, it's dark in here, darker than usual. Bitch must have closed the blinds good and tight tonight.

He stumbled over something that gave him pause, something that felt made of feathers. Fuck it. He was too tired to turn on the light.

When he lay down, the room spun only a little. He was used to it. Besides, he had a new preoccupation, one that was totally unexpected.

His dick was rock hard. What was this? He grinned and reached down to stroke himself. Perhaps he should just mount the old girl once more for old times' sake, shoot a load up inside her so she could grin all the way to work next morning.

But Barb beat him to the punch. He felt her hand on his dick, stroking it up and down. She had even had the good sense to put some spit on her hand, so the up and down motion was slippery and felt oh so good.

Dave groaned. He reached out to touch his wife and she pushed him away. "Wait," she whispered. Fuck, it didn't even sound like Barb, sounded younger somehow. Hell, Dave could get into a little fantasy action and he was too wasted to even think of becoming aggressive. Just lay back and enjoy.

Barb's shape, feeling somehow lighter, rose up in the blackness to straddle him. Again, Dave reached out to touch her and had his hand gently replaced on his chest. "Wait," she whispered again.

And then Dave really moaned. Fuck! What had gotten into her? He could tell from her positioning and finally, the feel of it, that she was sinking down on him not with her pussy, but with her ass.

Barb had never done anything like this before, and as the velvet tissue surrounded him, gripping him tightly, Dave closed his eyes, enraptured.

Barb began moving up and down, slowly at first, then quickening her tempo. Damn, this felt good. Almost too good. It was almost as if someone new had crawled into his bed. Barb had never let him fuck her up the ass before. What had gotten into her? A dark cloud moved across his alcohol-addled brain as he wondered if his question should not be what had gotten into her, but who.

Fuck it, this felt too good. Dave raised his hips upward to meet her downward thrust. Life was full of wonderful little surprises.

And then everything changed. The grip on his dick grew tighter, which felt good at first, but the pressure steadily increased until it was so hard, Dave was afraid his dick would explode. Already he could feel some blood vessels had popped: there was an additional wetness inside her he was sure was blood and a burning sensation deep within his urethra.

The gripping grew tighter and Dave screamed. It wasn't just pressure now: razor sharp teeth were cutting into him, penetrating deeper, deeper, shooting white hot spikes of pain throughout his whole body. Blood gushed; it poured down over his thighs.

"Christ!" he croaked, as he felt the sharp teeth penetrate so completely he was sure that in just a second, his dick would be torn from his body.

He reached up to grab Barb and suddenly stopped, the shock taking away, for just an instant, the pain. The body above him was smooth, hard.

There was no flab, there were no tits, only two tiny little nipples on a hard, silky chest. His hand dropped down to brush across an erect penis.

Just before he passed out, he felt the thing above him move away, taking his penis with him. The thing was laughing and the laughter merged into the cawing of a bird.

11

Miranda lay in bed, listless, tracing a hairline crack on the ceiling. In the hall: busy chattering. Visiting hours had just begun and patients' friends and families swarmed the halls, along with the nurses, doctors, and orderlies who made this resting place for the ill and dying their home.

She felt better. The pain was now little more than a dull throb and she was staying awake for longer and longer periods. Even had the strength to eat something.

A crow landed on her window ledge; its caw causing her to turn her head just in time to see it take flight.

And a small voice whispered in her ear, "Four."

12

It was Saturday night. And Tom Bauer was so hopped up on coke, he virtually tingled. The stuff hummed and throbbed in his veins. He cruised the streets of Uptown in his '67 orange Mustang, looking for prey, searching for the one with whom he could share his boundless energy, his bottomless well of depravity. Christmas Eve and the streets were as alive as he felt: crowded with last-minute holiday shoppers, revelers making the most of the holiday, knowing that tomorrow there would be no mindless jobs for them. The storefronts and bars seemed more brightly lit than usual, the neon augmented by flashing colored Christmas lights, Santas and snowmen backlit to glow.

It had been three days since he and his buddies had shared the sweet little henna-haired wench. Tom laughed as he thought of what they had done to the girl, violated every orifice with panache—the bowling trophy they had used on her was a stroke of genius he would have to thank Carl for, if he ever saw the dude again; he hadn't been around lately—and left her with a necklace of black, blue, and yellow, enough, he hoped, to end any fears he had of discovery. If the chick wasn't dead, she should at least be sensible enough to know that if she ever did talk, there would be hell to pay. Hell.

But the bitch wasn't enough to satisfy him. Tom reached down to turn the radio up. Melissa Etheridge was singing, appropriately enough, "Your Little Secret," and Tom thought about his own secret. His buddies would have been amazed, since he played the part of the stud with so much conviction.

But the truth of the matter was the girl from three night's past left him feeling empty and unsatisfied. And the truth Tom could only admit to himself was that the reason for his unquenched longing was that she didn't have the right equipment. Okay, she wasn't a boy.

Which was what Tom wanted. And alone like this was the only time he allowed himself the opportunity to satisfy the lust he had for smooth young bodies, flat chests, and cocks that rose up out of whispers of pubic hair.

And Uptown was the place to look for that, even if it was his home turf. This city was big enough for one to disappear into anonymity whenever one wished and that was just what Tom was after tonight, or more precisely, what gave him the safety to go after what he wanted.

Snow spit down, the tiny flakes dancing in the dark air, illuminated now and then by the yellow glare of a street light. Tom had seen several boys standing in storefront doorways, their poses defiant come-ons, cigarettes dangling from underage lips. But none of them had been exactly what he sought. It was still early enough in the evening—10:10 read the little, stick-on digital clock gracing his dash—to not cave in to desperation. He was still buzzed enough to believe he could find just what he wanted: the perfect Christmas present for himself.

Hell, no one else was going to buy him any gifts. All Tom had to look forward to tomorrow morning was an empty studio apartment and an enormous weariness as the coke wore off and the sleepless night took its toll.

Fuck it. No time now for such depressing fare. He was on the hunt. Tom lit a cigarette and, at the light, hooked his pinkie fingernail, which he had grown long and curving for just such a purpose, into a small brown vial and brought out a hefty little mound of another kind of snow. Before the light changed, he had snorted it down, already anticipating the delicious bitter drip at the back of his throat, which would give him the energy in the not-too-distant future to revel and rave the night away with his Christmas present to himself.

And just like the appearance of the angel to the shepherds in the field, Tom saw his own angel, standing just ahead.

The boy must have been only about thirteen. There was a casual defiance in the way he leaned against the storefront doorway, pelvis thrust out just enough to attract the interest of the cars cruising by more slowly than the others. He wore a faded jean jacket, Metallica T-shirt, pegged jeans, and Reebok pumps. His ripped T-shirt deliberately exposed a nipple and a flash of smooth white stomach. The top of the T-shirt was cut away to reveal a gold rope chain, glinting in the glow of the streetlight above him.

Perfect. Tom maneuvered the car into the far right lane, the one closest to the boy, while at the same time, managed to rummage around in the box of cassettes on the passenger side floor. He pulled out Metallica's *Black* and popped it in, cranking the volume.

Tom stopped in front of the boy. He leaned over to roll down the window. As if the boy were trained to respond to the rolled-down window, he sauntered over to the car.

Tom was all smiles. "How you doin' tonight, kid?"

"Good." The boy shrugged. "Could be better."

"Yeah?" Tom's eyes brightened. "How so?"

"I need a little spending money. My ma's sick and I need to get somethin' to eat."

Tom flicked his cigarette out the window. "I'll give you something to eat." He snickered.

The boy didn't respond.

"Let's cut the shit." Tom leaned closer, lowering his voice. "You wouldn't be standin' out here in this fuckin' cold dressed like that if you weren't sellin'."

The boy began to back away from the car.

"Just fuckin' wait! Get back here."

The boy moved closer, lowering his head to look into the dark interior. Christ, the face of an angel. Skin so pure, so white, it could have been fashioned from light. There was no way Tom Bauer was letting this one go.

"Look. I ain't a cop, I ain't a pervert. I just need to get close to you. I got money, I got a gram of coke, and back at my place, lots of beers. You wanna party? I'll make it worth your while."

The boy paused, as if considering the offer. Tom thought he needed to do that to hang on to his self-respect. He waited. And then the boy did exactly what he expected: opened the door and slid in.

"Atta boy." Tom squeezed the boy's leg, threw the car into drive, and merged into traffic.

"Be there in five. You like the tunes?"

Once they were in traffic, Tom asked the boy, "So you gotta name?"

"Jimmy," the boy said. "Jimmy Fels."

The name sounded vaguely familiar to Tom, but he couldn't get a handle on where he had heard it before. No matter. The kid was one fine piece. He and Jimmy were going to have themselves a time.

"Pleased to meet you, Jimmy. You live around here?"

"I've always lived around here."

They drove on in silence. Stopped at a light at the corner of Lawrence and Broadway, Jimmy turned to the guy and said, "Listen: I been thinkin' about this and I don't know if I got the time for what you got planned."

Tom closed his eyes to try to shut out the disappointment. Sure he could attempt to force the kid home with him, but memories of the other night intruded and he didn't know if he was ready for another scene like that. He sighed, "Suit yourself." Tom waited for the boy to exit the car.

Life was full of disappointments. Why the fuck should Christmas Eve be any different?

The boy turned to him, his face alight with a smile. "I've gotta little time, though."

Tom perked up. "Yeah?"

"Maybe we could go down to the park at the end of the street and fool around a little there. It's pretty safe. I done it lots of times."

Tom knew the cruisy lakefront park only too well. He pondered for a moment, then caved. The boy was too pretty to not take something, no matter how little. Perhaps after a while, he could find another boy to come home and do the party scene with him.

They found a spot under a tree, near Montrose, the south end of the park, where it wasn't as cruisy and they wouldn't be bothered by so much traffic. The harbor was just in front of them and beyond that, the skyline of Chicago rose up, its lights twinkling.

Tom let his hand wander to Jimmy's thigh and then up until he was rubbing the soft, worn denim covering the boy's crotch.

Jimmy removed Tom's hand.

Tom rolled his eyes. "You gotta problem?"

"Pay first."

"Jesus." Tom reached into the inside pocket of his leather jacket and took out his wallet. Before he knew what was happening, the kid had snatched the wallet and, almost simultaneously, was opening his door.

He was halfway out the door before Tom grabbed hold of his pants.

"You little prick! Get back in here!"

Tom's delight at finding the boy vanished as rage took over. Why couldn't things ever go right for him? Why did he always have to be the poor soul who never got a break? This time, he decided, things would be different.

The rage clouded his brain, like a swarm of angry bees: black, buzzing, blotting out reason. He yanked Jimmy back into the car, slamming him into the seat. His hands wrapped around the boy's throat, just as they had wrapped around the girl's the other night, and he began to squeeze, his thumbs digging into the soft flesh just beneath the boy's Adam's apple.

The boy gagged and choked, squirming, left arm flailing out to pound on Tom's back over and over. It felt like nothing and Tom increased the pressure. The boy tugged at himself, lower and lower on his leg, until Tom wondered what the hell he was doing.

He didn't have to wonder long. The glint of the switchblade in the boy's hand solved the mystery pretty quickly. There was a click as the boy exposed the blade.

Tom jumped back for an instant, the silver knife glinting in the wan light of the moon, hanging low over the lake.

The instant was enough. The boy rose up and plunged the knife into Tom's throat. His eyes widened and a gurgling noise spewed out of him, along with blood, which pumped across the steering wheel to stain the front window of his car.

And then everything went dark, the only sound in the car the beating of Tom's heart as it slowed and finally stopped.

And then he was watching himself. As if he were looking at a movie, he saw his own body slumped back against the vinyl interior of the car, his blood, coagulating in the darkness, looking like chocolate syrup, oozing down to stain the front of his shirt.

A great wind howled across the lake. The cold scooped him up, higher and higher, until the roof of the Mustang was nothing more than a tiny rectangular shape, until it faded into darkness. Tom felt himself carried across the water, staring down at the silver ribbon the moon's reflection made. A dark bird moved across his vision, casting a black shadow over the opalescence lying atop the water.

And then he was plunging downward, faster and faster, as if the churning waters were rising up to meet him. He slammed into the water, its surface hard as concrete and everything went black.

When he awakened, it was to darkness. So dark around him, all he could do was reach out to see if the darkness had boundaries.

It did. Just above his face, his hands connected with a rough wooden surface, upon which he pushed to no avail. He reached out to his sides, but could barely extend his arms because the same rough surface encased him on either side. As he squirmed, the same wood supported his back beneath him.

And then he felt the crawly sensation of tiny legs, thousands of them, moving across his body. Tom squirmed, trying to get them off, but there was nowhere for them to go, nowhere for him to go. And then they were biting: tiny stings on his legs, his arms. They marched across his face, moving up his nose, into his screaming mouth.

When had he started screaming?

When would this end?

Alexander 0'98

13

Miranda awakened ravenous. She felt miraculously better. All the pain was gone, vanished, healed while she slept, dreaming of Jimmy, ascending into the sky, until the silver light of the moon absorbed him.

And as he rose, he had called something out to her. What was it he had said? *All, all gone, Miranda. You're free.*

Miranda pressed the call button. One of these nurses ought to be able to bring her *something* to eat.

Corvix Canto

K. Ken Johnston

A keening black soul sweeps over the plain
The sky grows dark, the air thickens with rain
Her wings of sable in flight beyond time
Bring claws darkly dripping with the color of wine

Pain sings with her voice from whispers to screams
Embracing your spirit in its nightmares and dreams
She rends your soul from the moment you've met
She feeds on your desire with a tongue that's blood wet

Blood vengeance drives her, sharper than a knife
Wings cut through night's storms to purge another life
She rages through darkness, thirsting for souls
Searching for players to take tragic roles

Each soul as recompense for the blood of another
Each death retribution for the desecration of her mother

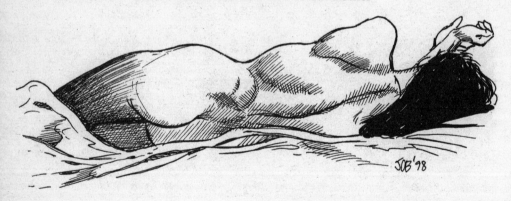

China Doll

Charles de Lint

> In theory there is free will, in practice
> everything is predetermined.
> —Ramakrishna,
> Nineteenth-century Bengali saint

The crows won't shut up. It's late, close on midnight. The junkyard's more shadow than substance and the city's asleep. The crows should be sleeping, too—roosting somewhere, doing whatever it is that crows do at night. Because you don't normally see them like this, cawing at each other, hoarse voices tearing raggedly across the yard, the birds shifting, restless on their perches, flecks of rust falling in small red clouds every time they move.

They can't sleep and they won't shut up.

Coe can't sleep either, but at least he's got an excuse.

The dead don't sleep.

He's sitting there on the hood of a junked car, three nights dead. Watching the flames lick up above the rim of an old steel barrel where he's got a trash fire burning. Waiting for China to show up. China with her weird tribal tags: the white mud dried on her face, eyes darkened with rings of soot, lips blackened with charcoal, cheeks marked with black hieroglyphic lines. He looks about the same. The two of them are like matched bookends in a chiaroscuro still life. Like they just stepped out of some old black-and-white movie, except for that red dress of hers.

He's not exactly looking forward to seeing her. First thing you know, she'll start in again on who they're supposed to kill and why, and he's no more interested in listening to her tonight than he was the day he came back.

He thinks of standing by the barrel, holding his hands up to the flames for warmth, but that's a comfort he's never going to know again. The cold's lodged too deep inside him and it's never going away, doesn't matter what China says.

Killing's not the answer. But neither's this.

"Just shut up," he tells the birds.

They don't listen to him any more than they ever do, but China comes walking out of the shadows like his voice summoned her.

"Hey, Leon," she says.

She jumps lightly up onto the hood of the car, stretches out her legs, leans back against the windshield. Her dress rides up her legs, but the sight of it doesn't do anything for him. She's too young. Hell, she could be his daughter.

Coe gives her a nod, waits for her to start in on him. She surprises him. She just sits there, quiet for a change, checking out the birds.

"What do you think they're talking about?" she asks after awhile.

"You don't know?"

Ever since they came back, it's like she knows everything. Maybe she was like that before they died. He doesn't know. First time he saw her she was in that tight red dress, running down a narrow alleyway, black combat boots clumping on the pavement. Came bursting out of the alley and ran right into him where he was just walking along, minding his own business. They fall in a tumble, and before they can get themselves untangled, there's a couple of Oriental guys there, standing over them. One's got a shotgun, the other an Uzi. For a moment, Coe thinks he's back in the jungle.

He doesn't get a chance to say a word.

The last thing he sees are the muzzles of their guns, flashing white. Last thing he hears is the sound of the shots. Last thing he feels are the bullets tearing into him. When he comes back, he's lying in a junkyard—this junkyard—and China's bending over him, wiping wet clay on his face. He starts to push her away, but she shakes her head.

"This is the way it's got to be," she says.

He doesn't know what she's talking about then. Now that he does, he wishes he didn't. He looks at her, lounging on the car, and wonders, *Was she always so bloodthirsty, or did dying bring it out in her?* Dying didn't bring it out in him and it wouldn't have had to dig far to find the capacity for violence in his soul.

She sits up, pulls her knees to her chin, gazes over them to where he's sitting on the hood.

"Look," she tells him, her voice almost apologetic. "I didn't choose for things to work out the way they did."

He doesn't reply. There's nothing to say.

"You never asked why those guys were chasing me," she says.

Coe shrugs.

"Don't you want to know why you died?"

"I know why I died," he says. "I was in the wrong place at the wrong time, end of story."

China shakes her head. "It's way more complicated than that."

It usually is, Coe thinks.

"You know anything about how the tongs run their prostitution rings?" she goes on.

Coe nods. It's an old story. The recruiters find their victims in Southeast Asia, "loaning" the girls the money they need to buy passage to North America, then make them work off the debt in brothels over here. The fact that none of their victims ever pay off that debt doesn't seem to stop the new girls from buying into it. There's always fresh blood. Some of those girls are so young they've barely hit puberty. The older ones—late teens, early twenties—make out like they're preteens, because that's where the big money is.

He gives China a considering look. Her name accentuates the Chinese cast to her features. Dark eyes the shape of almonds, black hair worn in a classic pageboy, bangs in front, the rest a sleek shoulder-length curve. He'd thought she was sixteen, seventeen. Now he's not so sure anymore.

"That what happened to you?" he asks.

She shakes her head. "I never knew a thing about it until I ran into one of their girls. According to a card she was carrying, she was the property of the Blue Circle Boys Triad—at least the card had their chop on it. She was on the run and I took her in."

"And the tong found out."

She shakes her head again. "She could barely speak a word of English, but a woman in the Thai grocery under my apartment was able to translate for us. That's how I heard about what they're doing to these girls."

There's a look in her eyes that Coe hasn't seen there before, but he recognizes it. It's like an old pain that won't go away. He knows all about old pain.

"So what put the tong onto you?" he asks, curious in spite of himself.

"I turned them in."

Coe thinks he didn't hear her right. "You what?"

"I turned them in. The cops raided their brothel and busted a couple of dozen of them. Don't you read the papers?"

Coe shook his head. "I don't—didn't—need more bad news in my life."

"Yeah, well. I've been there."

Coe's still working his head around what she did. Blowing the whistle on the Blue Circle Boys. She had to have known there'd be cops in their pocket, happy to let them know who was responsible. It was probably only dumb luck that the cop she'd brought her story to was a family man, walking the straight and narrow.

"And you didn't think the tong'd find out?" he asks.

"I didn't care," she says. She's quiet for a long moment, then adds, "I didn't think I cared. Dying kind of changes your perspective on this kind of thing."

Coe nods. "Yeah. Dying brings all kinds of changes."

"So I was out clubbing—the night they were chasing me. Feeling righteous about what I'd done. Celebrating, I guess. I was heading for home, trying to flag down a cab, when they showed up. I didn't know what to do, so I just took off and ran."

"And we know how well that turned out," Coe says.

"It wasn't like I was trying to get you killed. I liked being alive myself."

Coe shrugs. "I'm not blaming you. It's like I said. I was just in the wrong place."

"But our dying still means something. Doesn't matter if there's crooked cops, or that they rolled me over to the tong. The brothel still got shut down and the Blue Circle Boys are hurting bad. And now those girls have a chance at a better life."

"Sure. They're going to do really well once they're deported back to Thailand or Singapore or wherever they originally came from."

Anger flares in her eyes. "What are you saying?"

"That nothing's changed. The tong's had a bit of a setback, but give it a month or two and everything'll be back to business as usual. That's the way it works."

"No," she says. "This means something. Just like what we've got to do now means something."

Coe shakes his head again. "Some things you can't change. It's like the government. The most you can do is vote in another set of monkeys, but it doesn't change anything. It's always business as usual."

"Have you always been such a chickenshit?"

"I'm a pacifist. I don't believe violence solves anything."

"Same difference."

Coe looks at her. He's guessing now that she's maybe twenty, twenty-two. At least half his age. When he was younger than she is now, the government gave him a gun and taught him how to kill. He was good at it, too. Did two tours, in country, came back all in one piece and with no other skills. So they hired him on. Same work, different jungle. There was always work for a guy like him who was good at what he did, good at doing what he was told. Good at keeping his mouth shut.

Until the day an op went bad and a little girl got caught in the cross fire. After that he couldn't do it anymore. He looked at that dead kid and all he could do was put the gun down and disappear. Stopped living like a king, the best hotels, the best restaurants, limos when he wanted them, working only nine, ten times a year. He retired from it all, just like that. Vanished into the underground world of the homeless where he was just one more skel, nobody a citizen'd give a second look.

It had to be that way. The people he worked for didn't exactly have a retirement plan for their employees. At least not one that included your staying alive.

"You don't know what I am," he tells her.

He slides down from the hood of the car and starts walking.

"Leon!" she calls after him.

The crows lift up around the junkyard, filling the air with their raucous cries. It's like they think he's going to follow them, that he's going to let them lead him back to where an eye for an eye makes sense again. But it isn't going

to happen. Dying hasn't changed that. They want to take down the shooters who killed China and him, they can do it themselves.

"Leon!" China calls again.

He doesn't turn, and she doesn't follow.

He walks until he finds himself standing in front of a familiar building. Looks like any of the hundreds of other office buildings downtown, nothing special, except the people he'd worked for had a branch in it. There are lights up on the twelfth floor where they have their offices.

His gaze is drawn to the glass doors of the foyer, to the reflection he casts on their dark surfaces. He looks like he's got himself made up for Halloween, like he's wearing war paint. Back when he was a grunt, there'd been an Indian in his platoon. Joey Keams, a Black Hills Lakota. Keams used to talk about his grandfather, how the same government they were fighting for had outlawed the Ghostdance and the Sun Dances, butchered his people by the thousands, but here he was anyway, fighting for them all the same.

Keams was a marvel. It was like he had a sixth sense the way he could spot a sniper, a mine, an ambush. Handy guy to have around. Eight months into his tour, they were out on patrol and he stepped on a mine that his sixth sense hadn't bothered to warn him about. There wasn't enough left of him to ship home.

Coe glances around, but the birds are all gone. All that's left is one dark shape sitting on a lamppost, watching him.

Funny the things you forget, he thinks. Because now he remembers that Keams talked about crows, too. How some people believed they carried the souls of the dead on to wherever we go when we die. How sometimes they carried them back when they had unfinished business. He'd have got along real well with China.

"I don't have any unfinished business," he tells the bird.

It cocks its head, stares right back at him like it's listening.

Coe hasn't had anything for a long time. Once he stopped killing, he went passive. Eating at soup kitchens, sleeping under overpasses, cadging spare change that he gave away to those who needed it more than he did. He didn't drink, didn't smoke, didn't do drugs. Didn't need anything that you couldn't get as a handout.

He gives the building a last look, gaze locked on his reflection in the glass door. He looks like what he is: a bum, pushing fifty. Wearing raggedy clothes. No use to anyone. No danger to anyone. Not anymore.

The only thing that doesn't fit is the face-painting job that China did on him. Pulling out his shirt tails, he tries to wipe off the war paint, but all he does is smear the clay, make it worse. *Screw it,* he thinks. He turns away, heading up the street.

It's close to dawn and except for the odd cab that wouldn't stop for him anyway, he's pretty much got the streets to himself. Even the whores are finally asleep.

The crow leaves its perch, flies overhead, lands on the next lamppost.

"So what are you?" he asks it. "My personal guide?"

The bird caws once. Coe pauses under the lamppost, puts his head back to look at it.

"Okay," he says. "Show me what you've got."

The crow flies off again and this time he follows. He's still not bought into any of it, but he can't help being curious, now that he's heard China's story. And sure enough the bird leads him into Chinatown, up where it meets the no-man's-land of the Tombs. As far as Coe can see, there's nothing but abandoned tenements and broken-down factories and warehouses. He follows the crow across an empty lot, gravel and dirt crunching underfoot.

Used to be he could walk without a sound, like a ghost. Now that he is one, you can hear him a mile away.

He stops in the shadows of one of the factories. There are no streetlights down here. But dawn's pinking the horizon and in its vague light he can make out the graffiti chops on the walls of the building across the street that marks it as Blue Circle Boys' turf.

He hears footsteps coming up behind him, but he doesn't look. His crow is perched on the roof of an abandoned car. A moment later, it's joined by a second bird. Finally he turns around.

"You were in the trade, right?" he says to China.

She nods. "I guess you could say that. I was an exotic dancer."

"China . . ."

"Was my stage name. China Doll. Cute, huh? My real name's Susie Wong, but I can't remember the last time I answered to it."

"Why'd the cops listen to a stripper?"

"Dumb luck. Got a real family man, hungry for a righteous bust."

"And now?" Coe asks.

"We have to take them out. The ones the cops didn't pick up."

Coe doesn't say anything.

"The ones that killed us."

"The crows tell you all that?" he asks. He lifts a hand to his cheek. "Like they told you about this war paint?"

She nods.

He shakes his head. "They don't say anything to me. All I hear is their damned cawing."

"But you'll help me?" China asks. "We died together, so we have to take them out together."

More crow mumbo jumbo, Coe supposes.

"I told you," he says. "I won't buy into this Old Testament crap."

"I don't want to argue with you."

"No, you just want me to kill a few people so that we can have a happy ending and float off to our just reward."

She cocks her head and looks at him, reminding him of one of the crows.

"Is that what you're scared of?" she asks. "Of what might be waiting for you when we cross over to the other side?"

Coe hasn't even been thinking of himself, of other vengeful spirits that might be waiting for him somewhere. But now that China's brought it up, he has to wonder. Why haven't the crows brought back any of the people he's killed? And then there was the part he'd played in the death of at least one little girl who really hadn't deserved to die . . .

"It's not fear," he tells her. "It's principle."

She gives him a blank look.

Coe sighs. "We play out this eye-for-an-eye business, then we're no better than them."

"So what are you doing here?" she asks. She points at the tong's building with her chin.

He doesn't have an answer for her.

"We'd be saving lives," she says.

"By taking lives."

It's an old argument. It's how he got started in the business he fell into after his two tours in 'Nam.

China nods. "If that's what it takes. If we stop them, they won't kill anybody else."

Except it never stops. There's always one more that needs killing, just to keep things tidy. And the next thing you know, the body count keeps rising. One justification feeding the next like endless dominoes knocking against each other. It never stops anything, and it never changes anything, because evil's like kudzu. It can grow anywhere, so thick and fast that you're choking on it before you know it. The only way to eradicate it is to refuse to play its game. Play the game and you're letting it grow inside of you.

But there's no way to explain that so that she'll really understand. She'd have to see through his eyes. See how that dead little girl haunts him. How she reminds him, every day, of how she'd still be alive if he hadn't been playing the game.

The thing to aim for is to clear the playing board. If there's nothing left for evil to feed on, it'll feed on itself.

It makes sense. Believing it is what's kept him sane since that little girl died in the firefight.

"So why are you here?" China asks again.

"I'm just checking them out. That's all."

He leaves her again, crosses the street. Along the side of the building he spots a fire escape. He follows its metal rungs with his gaze, sees they'll take him right to the roof, four stories up. The two crows are already on their way.

Just checking things out, he thinks as he starts up the fire escape.

He hears China climbing up after him, but he doesn't look down. When he gets to the end of the ladder he hauls himself up and swings onto the roof. Gravel crunches underfoot. He thinks he's alone until the crows give a warning caw. He sees the shadow of a man pull away from a brick, boxlike structure with a door in it. The roof access, he figures. The man's dark-haired, wearing a long, black raincoat, motorcycle boots that come up to his knees. He's carrying an Uzi, the muzzle rising to center on Coe as he approaches.

He and Coe recognize each other at the same time.

Coe's had three days to get used to this, this business of coming back from the dead. The shooter's had no time at all, but he doesn't waste time asking questions. His eyes go wide. You can see he's shaken. So he does what men always do when they're scared of something—he takes the offense.

The first bullet hits Coe square in the chest. He feels the impact. He staggers. But he doesn't go down. Coe doesn't know which of them's more surprised—him or the shooter.

"You don't want to do this," Coe tells him.

He starts to walk forward and the shooter starts backing away. His finger takes up the slack on the Uzi's trigger and he opens it up. Round after round tears through Coe's shirt, into his chest. He feels each hit, but he's over his surprise, got his balance now, and just keeps walking forward.

And the shooter keeps backing up, keeps firing.

Coe wants to take the gun away. The sound of it, the fact that it even exists, offends him. He wants to talk to the shooter. He doesn't know what he's going to say, but he knows the man needs to get past this business of trying to kill what you don't understand.

The trouble is, the shooter sees Coe's approach through his own eyes, takes Coe's steady closing of the distance between them for a threat. He turns suddenly, misjudges where he is. Coe cries out a warning, but it's too late. The shooter hits his knees against the low wall at the edge of the roof and goes over.

Coe runs to the wall, but the shooter's already gone.

There's an awful, wet sound when the man hits the pavement four stories down. Coe's heard it before; it's not a sound you forget. The shooter's gun goes off, clatters across the asphalt. The crows are out there, riding air currents down toward the body, gliding, not even moving their wings.

"That's one down," China says.

She steps up to the wall beside him to have a look. Coe hadn't even heard her footsteps on the gravel behind him. He frowns at her, but before he can speak, they hear the roof access door bang open behind them. They turn to see a half dozen men coming out onto the gravel. They fan out into a half circle, weapons centered on the two of them. Shotguns with pistol grips, automatics. A couple more Uzis.

Coe makes the second shooter from the alleyway. The man's eyes go as wide as his partner's had, whites showing. He says something, but Coe doesn't understand the language. Chinese, maybe. Or Thai.

"Party time," China says.

"Can it," Coe tells her.

But all she does is laugh and give the men the finger.

"Hey, assholes," she yells. *"Ni deh!"*

Coe doesn't understand her, either, but the meaning's clear. He figures the men are going to open fire, but then they give way to a new figure coming out from the doorway behind them. From the deference the men give him, he's obviously their leader. The newcomer's a tall Chinese man. Coe's age, late forties. Handsome, black hair cut short, eyes dark.

Now it's Coe's turn to register shock. He doesn't see a ghost of the dead, like the shooters from the alleyway did, but it's a ghost all the same.

A ghost from Coe's past.

"Jimmy," Coe says softly. "Jimmy Chen."

Jimmy doesn't even seem surprised.

"I knew I'd be seeing you again," he says. "Sooner or later, I knew you'd surface."

"This an agency op?" Coe asks.

"What do you think?"

"I think you're flying solo."

"Wait a minute," China breaks in. "You guys *know* each other?"

Coe nods. "We have history."

Sometimes the office sent in a team, which was how Coe ended up on a rooftop with this psychopath Jimmy Chen. The target was part of a RICO investigation, star witness kept in a safe house that was crawling with feds. In a week's time he'd be up on the witness stand, rolling over on a half dozen crime bosses. Trouble was, he'd also be taking down a few congressmen and industry CEOs. The office wanted to keep the status quo so far as the politicos and moneymen were concerned.

That was where he and Jimmy Chen came in. If the witness couldn't make it into court, the attorney general'd lose his one solid connection between the various defendants and his RICO case would fall apart. The office didn't want to take any chances on this hit, so they sent in a team to make sure the job got done.

Coe wasn't one to argue, but he knew Jimmy by reputation and nothing he'd heard was good. He set up a meet with the woman who'd handed out the assignment.

"Look," he said. "I can do this on my own. Jimmy Chen's a psycho freak. You turn him loose in a downtown core like this and we're going to have a bloodbath on our hands."

"We don't have a problem with messy," the woman told him. "Not in this case. It'll make it look like a mob hit."

He should have backed out then, but he was too used to taking orders. To doing what he was told. So he found himself staking out the safe house with Jimmy. He forced himself to concentrate on the hit, and a safe route out once the target was down, to ignore the freak as best he could.

The feds played their witness close to the vest. They never took him out. No one went in unless they were part of the op. In the end, Coe and Jimmy realized they'd have to do it on the day of the trial.

They took up their positions as the feds' sedan pulled up in front of the safe house to pick up the witness. The feds had two more vehicles on the street—one parked two cars back, one halfway up the block. Coe counted six men, all told. And then there were the men inside the house with the witness. But when they brought him out, he was accompanied by a woman and a child. The witness held the child as they came down the steps—a little girl, no more than six with blond curly hair. It was impossible to get a clear shot at him.

Now what? Coe thought.

But Jimmy didn't have any problem with the situation.

"How'd you like that?" he said. "They're using a kid as a shield. Like that's going to make a difference."

Before Coe could stop him, Jimmy fired. His first bullet tore through the girl and the man holding her. His second took the woman—probably the man's wife. All Coe could do was stare at the little girl as she hit the pavement. He was barely aware of Jimmy dropping the feds as they scattered for cover. Jimmy picked off four of them before Coe's paralysis broke.

He hit Jimmy on the side of his head with the stock of his rifle. For a moment he stood over the fallen man, ready to shoot the damned freak. Then he simply dropped the weapon onto Jimmy's chest and made his retreat.

"Oh, yeah," Jimmy says. "We have history."

He laughs and Coe decides he liked the sound of the crows better. Jimmy's men give way as he moves forward.

"That's one way to put it, Leon," Jimmy goes on. "Hell, if it wasn't for you, I wouldn't even be here."

"What's that supposed to mean?" Coe asks.

But he already knows. He and Jimmy worked for the same people—men so paranoid they put conspiracy buffs to shame. When it came to that, they'd probably been on that grassy knoll in '63. Or if not them, then one of their proxies.

When Coe went underground, Jimmy must have taken the heat for it, sent him running till he ended up with the Blue Circle Boys. The fact that he's still alive says more for Jimmy's ability to survive than it does for the competence of the feds or any kindness in the hearts of their former employers. Unless Jimmy's new business *is* part of an op run by their old employers. Coe wouldn't put it past them. The Blue Circle Boys' war chest had to look good in these days of diminishing budgets, especially for an agency that didn't officially exist.

"How do you know this guy?" China asks.

"That's Leon," Jimmy says, smiling. "He always was a closemouthed bastard. Best damn wet-boy assassin to come out of 'Nam and he doesn't even confide in his girlfriend."

"She's not my girlfriend," Coe tells him. "She's got nothing to do with this."

Because now he knows why he's here. Why the crows brought him back from the dead and to this place.

Jimmy's giving China a contemplative look.

"Oh, I don't know," he says. "Can you say 'stoolie,' Leon?"

"I'm telling you—"

"But it's a funny thing," Jimmy goes on, like he was never interrupted. "She's supposed to be dead, and here she shows up with you. You did kill her, didn't you, Gary?"

He doesn't turn around, but the surviving shooter from the alleyway is starting to sweat.

"We shot them both, Mr. Chen," he says. "I swear we did. When we dumped them in the junkyard, they were both dead."

"But here they are anyway," Jimmy says softly. "Walking tall." He looks thoughtful, his gaze never leaves Coe's face. "Why now, Leon?" he asks. "After all these years, why're you sticking your nose in my business now?"

Coe shrugs. "Just bad luck, I guess."

"And it's all yours," Jimmy says, smiling again.

"Screw this," China tells them.

As she lunges forward, Coe grabs her around the waist and hauls her back. "Not like this," he says.

She struggles in his grip, but she can't break free.

"Kill them," Jimmy tells his men. "And this time do it right." He pauses for a heartbeat, then adds, "And aim for their heads. That Indian war paint's not going to be Kevlar like the flak vests they've got to be wearing."

That what you want to believe? Coe has time to think. China couldn't fit a dime under that dress of hers.

But then the men open up. The dawn fills with the rattle of gunfire. Coe's braced for it, but the impact of the bullets knocks China hard against him and like the shooter did earlier, he loses his balance. The backs of his legs hit the wall and the two of them go tumbling off the roof.

For a long moment, Jimmy watches the crows that are wheeling in the dawn air, right alongside the edge of the building where Coe and his little china doll took their fall. There have to be a couple of dozen of them, though they're making enough noise for twice that number.

Jimmy's never liked crows. It's the Japanese that think they're such good luck. Crows, any kind of black bird. They just give him the creeps.

"Somebody go clean up down there," he tells his men. "The last thing we need is for a patrol car to come by and find them."

But when his men get down to the street, there's only the body of the dead shooter lying on the pavement.

Coe and China watch them from the window of an abandoned factory nearby. The men. The crows. China runs her finger along the edge of a shard of broken glass that's still stuck in the window frame. It doesn't even break the skin. She turns from the window.

"Why'd you drag us in here?" she asks. "We could've taken them."

Coe shakes his head. "That wasn't the way."

"What are you so scared of? You saw for yourself—we can't die. Not from their guns, not from the fall."

"Maybe we only have so many lives we can use up," Coe tells her.

"But—"

"And I've got some other business to take care of first."

China gives him a long considering look.

"Was it true?" she asks. "What the guy you called Jimmy said about you being an assassin?"

"It was a long time ago. A different life."

"No wonder the crows wanted you for this gig."

Coe sighs. "If our being here's about retribution," he says, "it's got nothing to do with us. What does the universe care about some old bum and a stripper?"

"According to your friend, you're not just some—"

"That freak's not anybody's friend," Coe tells her, his voice hard.

"Okay. But—"

"This is about something else."

He tells her about the hit that went sour, the little girl that died. Tells her how Jimmy Chen shot right through her to get the job done.

China shivers. "But . . . *you* didn't kill her."

"No," Coe says. "But I might as well have. It's because of who I was, because of people like me, that she died."

China doesn't say anything for a long moment. Finally she asks, "You said something about some kind of business?"

"We're going to a bank," he tells her.

"A bank."

She lets the words sit there.

Coe nods. "So let's wash this crap off our faces or we'll give my financial adviser the willies. It'll be bad enough as it is."

"Why's that?"

"You'll see."

Coe can see the questions build up in China's eyes as he takes her into an office building that's set up snug against Cray's Gym over in Crowsea, but she keeps them to herself. The "bank" is up on the second floor, in back. A single room office with a glass door. Inside there's a desk with a laptop computer on it, a secretary's chair, a file cabinet, and a couple of straight backs for visitors. The man sitting at the desk is overweight and balding. He's wearing a cheap suit, white shirt, tie. He's got a take-out coffee sitting on his desk. Nothing about him or the office reflects the penthouse he goes home to with the security in the lobby and a view of the lake that upped the price of the place by another hundred grand.

The man looks up as they come in, his already pale skin going white with shock.

"Jesus," he says.

The hint of a smile touches Coe's lips. "Yeah, it's been awhile. China, this is Henry, my bank manager. Henry, China."

Henry gives her a nod, then returns his gaze to Coe.

"I heard you were dead," he says.

"I am."

Henry laughs, like it's a joke. *Whatever works,* Coe thinks.

"So how're my investments doing?" he asks.

Henry calls up the figures on the laptop that always travels with him between the office and home. After a while he starts to talk. When the figures start to add up into the seven digits, Coe knows that Henry's been playing fair.

In Coe's business, people disappear, sometimes for years, then they show up again out of the blue. It's the kind of situation that a regular financial institution can't cope with all that well. Which keeps men like Henry in business.

"I want to set up a trust fund," he tells Henry. "Something to help kids."

"Help them how?"

Coe shrugs. "Get them off the streets, or give them scholarships. Maybe set it up like one of those wish foundations for dying kids or something. Whatever works. Can you do it?"

"Sure."

"You'll get your usual cut," Coe tells him.

Henry doesn't bother to answer. That'd go without saying.

"And I want it named in memory of Angelica Ciccone."

Henry's eyebrows go up. "You mean Bruno's kid? The one that died with him the day he was going to testify?"

"You've got a long memory," Coe tells him.

Henry shrugs. "It's the kind of thing that sticks in your mind."

Tell me about it, Coe thinks.

"So you can do this?" he says.

"No problem."

"And we're square?"

Henry smiles. "We're square. I like this idea, Leon. Hell, I might even throw in a few thou' myself to help sweeten the pot."

"Where'd you get that kind of money?" China asks when they're back out on the street again.

Coe just looks at her. "Where do you think?"

"Oh. Right." But then she shakes her head. "You had all that money and you lived like a bum . . ."

"Blood money."

"But still . . ."

"Maybe now it can do some good. I should've thought of this sooner."

"To make up for all the people you killed?" China asks.

Coe looks down the street to where a pair of crows are playing tag around a lamppost.

"You don't make up for that kind of thing," he says. "The foundation's just to give a little hope to some kids who might not get to see it otherwise. So that they don't grow up all screwed up like me."

China's quiet for a long moment.

"Or like me," she says after a while.

Coe doesn't say anything. There's nothing he can say.

"So now what?" China asks after they've been walking for a few blocks.

Coe spies a phone booth across the street and leads her to it.

"Now we make a call," he says. "You got a watch?"

She lifts her wrist to show him the slim, knockoff Rolex she's wearing.

"Time me," he says as he drops a quarter into the slot, punches in a number. "And tell me when three minutes are up. Exactly three minutes. Starting . . ." He waits until the connection's made. "Now."

While China dutifully times the call, Coe starts talking about Jimmy Chen, the hit on Bruno Ciccone, what Jimmy's up to these days, where he can be found, how many men he's got.

"Two-fifty-eight," China says. "Two-fifty-nine."

At the three-minute mark, Coe drops the phone receiver, lets it bang against the glass wall of the booth. He grabs China's hand and runs with her, back across the street, down the block and onto the next, ducks into an alley.

"Okay," he says. "Watch."

He barely gets the words out before the first cruiser comes squealing around a corner, blocks the intersection the pair of them just crossed, cherry lights flashing. Moments later, another one pulls across the intersection at the other end of the block. They're joined by two more cruisers, an unmarked car, and then a couple of dark sedans. The feds step out of those, four of them in their dark suits, looking up and down the street.

China turns to Coe. "Jesus. That was seriously fast."

Coe's smiling. "A guy who kills as many feds as Jimmy did is going to give them a hard-on that won't go away. C'mon," he adds as the police start to fan out, heading up and down the sidewalks, checking doorways, alleys. "We're done here."

China keeps her questions in check again. She lets Coe take the lead and he slips them out of the net the police are setting up like he doesn't even have to think about it. Some skills you just don't lose.

He takes her back to the junkyard. They ease in through the gates when the old man running the place isn't looking and make their way to the rear. The dogs the old man keeps won't even come near them. But the crows follow, a thickening flock of them that settles on the junked cars and trash around them.

"That business with the phone call and the cops," China wants to know. "What was all that about?"

"We just dealt with Jimmy."

She shakes her head. "His lawyers'll have him back on the streets before the end of the day."

"Unless he resists," Coe says. "What do think, China? Think Jimmy's the kind of guy who'll go quietly and stand trial on murder-one charges for killing a half dozen cops?"

"No. I guess not. But if he gets away . . ."

"What do the crows tell you?" Coe asks.

She sits quietly for a moment, looking at them, head cocked, like she's listening. Coe doesn't hear anything except for their damned cawing. Finally she turns back to look at him.

"It's over," she says. "We're done."

Coe raps a knuckle against the fender he's sitting on. It's solid. So's he.

"How come we're still here?" he asks.

"I guess we'll cross over tonight."

Coe nods. There's a kind of symmetry to that.

"I like you better without the war paint," he says.

"Yeah? I think on you it was an improvement."

She smiles, but then she gets a serious look.

"I'm glad we did it your way, Leon," she says. "I feel better for it. Cleaner."

Coe doesn't say anything. His own soul's stained with too much killing for him to ever feel clean again. He didn't do this for himself, or because of the pacifism he's embraced since Angelica Ciccone was killed. He did it for China. He did it so she wouldn't have to carry what he does when the crows take them over to wherever it is they're going next. Into some kind of afterworld, he guesses, if there really is such a place.

He's been thinking. Maybe there is, considering the crows and how they brought the two of them back. And the thing is, if there *is* someplace else to go, he figures she deserves a shot at it with a clean slate.

Him, he'll settle for simple oblivion.

It's late at night now, close on to the anniversary hour of their dying. The crows are leading them back to where Jimmy Chen's boys shot them down. When they reach the mouth of the alley, Coe hesitates. The skin at the nape of his neck goes tight and a prickle of something walks down his spine.

"It's okay," China tells him.

The air above them's thick with crows, wheeling and cawing. Coe still can't make any kind of sense out of them.

China takes his hand.

"If you can't trust them," she says, "then trust me."

Coe nods. He doesn't know where they're going, but he knows for sure that there's nothing left for him here. So he lets her lead him out of the world, the crows flying on ahead of them, into a tunnel of light.

SPIRIT DOG

Jack Dann

My nephew Edmund McDowell came to live with us on June 6, 1862, which, coincidentally, is the same day his hero General Turner Ashby died in battle. My dear wife Rebecca Cowles McDowell and I will be eternally grateful to the Reverend Doctor A. A. H. Boyd, pastor of the Presbyterian church on Loudoun Street in Winchester, who recognized Edmund when he was found at the site of the second fire at my late brother's farm. It is due in large part to Doctor Boyd's bold efforts that Edmund was reunited with his family. He also tried to help us locate the servant Hanna, of whom Mundy seemed to be so fond. Our efforts, alas, were unsuccessful in that regard. We will always be grateful to this man of the cloth who believed so fervently in a cause diametrically opposed to our own.

But it is with extreme sadness and disappointment that I must report that Edmund left us the summer after he completed this diary. We have exhausted our resources trying to locate our nephew, to no avail—May the Lord God in His mercy protect him.

Edmund left us only the following note inserted in his diary:
"Can't wait any more. Gone back to find the spirit dog."
—Lieut. Col. Randolph Estes McDowell (Ret)
September 29, 1865
Scranton, Pennsylvania

It was around the time I saw the spirit dog and became invisible that I forgot how to talk. I can think the words in my head and write them down on paper—well, you can see that!—but when I open my mouth to try to talk, I just seem to choke. Doctor Keys had a word for it, but I forget what it was. Naming it seemed to make everybody feel better, though. That's more than I've seen most doctors do anyway—except to cut the arms and legs off soldiers. I sure as hell saw a lot of that! I think those goddamn doctors killed more soldiers than all the guns and artillery put together. But I'm getting ahead of myself here. Uncle Randolph says I'm always getting ahead of myself, but I'll tell you the whole story for whatever it's worth.

I could start anywhere, I suppose, but that would take too long, so I'll start right out on March 23, 1862. It was a Sunday, cold and miserable and cloudy.

Come to think of it, though, the only real *sunny* day I can remember around then was ten days before General Jackson pulled our army out of

Winchester because General Banks had brought his Federals down from Harper's Ferry to invade us. Not even him and Colonel Ashby's "Six Hundred" could've held out against Banks's blue-ass bucktails. Seemed like there was a million of them. And, boy, was there a commotion in Winchester! Poppa took me to town to see General Jackson, although I met him later on my own and wished I didn't. As our army started off toward the Valley Pike, all the girls and old ladies were crying and wailing that they were being left to godless tyrants, and some of the soldiers were even crying, just like their mothers, and then suddenly, the soldiers just started singing, "Yes, in the sweet by and by," and pretty soon everybody was singing it, until they left. Then the town was quiet as death, I can tell you. Well, maybe not *that* quiet, but pretty close to it. Nobody wanted to talk. Everybody just felt like crying, I guess.

But there I go digressin' away from my story . . .

Anyway, on the Sunday I originally started off talking about, the people in Winchester had damned good reason to be caterwauling and crying because that was what they now call the Battle of Kernstown, which you all know about. It was when Jackson came right back up the Pike to fight the Federals who outnumbered him two to one. And it was bad! But I'm going to write about it, no matter how much it hurts me.

Now Poppa used to insist on going to church every Sunday morning. Although he never had a church of his own, he was still a proper minister. Usually Episcopalian. And as we also had the farm and the day school, we made do well enough. We'd usually go to country churches and prayer meetings at people's houses, where Poppa could preach the skin off the snakes, as Mother used to say when he wanted her to do something. But Poppa had friends in Winchester, too, and was invited by Mr. Williams—he was the rector—to preach at the Episcopal church on Kent Street. Mother was all excited because she loved going into town and seeing everybody, especially Mrs. McSherry, who was her best friend, but I never did like Mrs. McSherry's boys. Not much, anyhow.

Of course, I wasn't going to church with them on account of the ringworm. I had the 'ruption all over my scalp, and it itched like a sonovabitch. My father attributed my malady to hanging around with the nigger kids—he would never say "nigger," even though we had two of our own before they ran away to the Federals. He only allowed us to call them "colored people" or "darkies" or "servants." Like everybody else, I called the old ones aunts and uncles, just like I did my real aunt and uncle, those I knew like family, anyway. I never understood him about that. Christ, the niggers called themselves niggers. So he thought I caught the eruption from the niggers who lived on the next farm—we'd borrow them sometimes to help with the farm work—but I reckon that I got it from David Steward's dog. David was one of Poppa's students, and his half-dead Irish setter had a terrible case of the mange, but I felt sorry for the damned thing and petted it. David had the ringworm, too, so it had to be the dog. 'Course, so did the niggers. Seemed like everyone but Mother and Poppa had it that season.

Mother didn't care how I'd caught it. She'd been doing her best to cure it by rubbing my head with silver nitrate medication that burned like fire and another potion she'd made up by dropping a copper penny into vinegar; and part of my hair fell out because of it, and hasn't grown back even yet. And as a further humiliation, I had to wear a turban around my head "so as not to scratch the worms and infect everybody else."

"I can't go out like this," I said to Poppa when he called me out of my room, expecting me to be all shined up and dressed for church. I was in my night drawers, and I left my turban off. My hair was mussed and greasy and itchy. Poppa was wearing his best black suit and a shiny cravat, and Mother was wearing her Sunday dress and a brooch and a bonnet with a white bow.

He turned to Mother and said, "If you were conspiring with him to stay home on the Lord's Day, you could have at least told me. I would have made provisions. We could have borrowed Eliza from Arthur Allen. She'd look after him while we're gone and make sure he had a decent Bible lesson." Poppa shook his head, as if he was telling somebody "No," and said, "At least his darkies didn't run off to the Yankees."

"You *know* why ours left," Mother said sharply. That stopped Poppa pretty cold, and then she looked at me and said, "And how do you suppose we'd look taking Mundy with his head looking all encrustated like that? Mr. McDowell, sometimes I wonder about—" Mother would always get started and then stop just like that. Now *she* was the one looking guilty. She talked low now, as if she was being introduced to someone important. "Mundy will be fine here alone. I've prepared his Bible lessons to study while we're at church. Everything's all laid out on your desk. You might want to approve it, of course. And we can stop at Mr. Allen's farm on the way to church. I'm sure he won't mind sending one of the servants over to look after Mundy." She looked at me and nodded, as if to say, "I told you so."

But I knew they wouldn't do any such thing. They always used to threaten me with Eliza. All she ever did though was tell me to read the "Raising of Lazarus" or "Daniel in the Lion's Den" and then she would put on all of Mom's dresses and bonnets and jewelry and twirl around like she was at a ball. But she never did steal anything.

I heard a real good blast of cannonading in the distance; and Mother got the funny look on her face that she always gets when she's concerned and said, "Perhaps we should all stay here with Mundy."

But Poppa said, "It's just the usual annoyance of the enemy," and that was that.

He limped out onto the porch to listen, though. I should have probably told you that Poppa had served in the militia as a chaplain until he got an inflammation in the bone of his leg. He almost died from the blood poisoning and brain fever, and he had to use a cane after that, and sometimes his words would get all mixed up—but never when he was preaching the skin off the snakes.

"It's just skirmishing, like yesterday, and the day before that," he said, sniffing, as if he could smell the noise. He used to do that in the schoolhouse back behind the barn, lift up his head and take a sniff, and then he'd take the switch to whoever was passing notes or whispering or not paying proper attention. "But it might just come to something. Your Colonel Ashby, God bless him, must be biting off General Shields's toes again. And I hear that Jackson's coming north. But that's all gossip. I hear the same thing most every day." He sniffed again, and sure enough the cracking of musket started, then died, and it seemed like it would just be an ordinary Sunday, except I wouldn't have to go to church.

Mother finally came out on the porch and said, "I do fear leaving Mundy alone."

"Well, I gave my solemn promise to Mr. Williams that I'd deliver a sermon, and a man's word is his bond. You can come with me or stay, as you will."

You see, Mother would always turn everything around on Poppa. And there just wasn't any way she was going to stay with me and not go to town, even if she would have to worry about me a little. We were used to the cannonading and the skirmishing. It was nothing more, I suppose, than having thunderstorms every day. Only that wasn't true. Everybody was fearful, just nobody cared to show it.

I watched my folks go off in their carriage, but I didn't know that I was only going to see them once more in my life. Or that Sunday was going to bring more than thunder.

It was going to bring the dogs right out of hell.

I listened for a while to the cannon volleys and musket fire echoing across the hills and waited for them to stop. They always did. But then they'd start right up again like rain falling hard on a tin roof. I knew something more than skirmishing was going to happen—I could *feel* it, and I knew that Mother might talk Poppa into turning the carriage around, so I went out beyond the old corn house that had burned down. I went past the garden and lumber house by the edge of the woods to check the gums, which was what Poppa called our rabbit traps. I don't know why we called them that. I'd asked Poppa about it once, and he just said that's what they're called. We used boxes about two feet long baited with pieces of apple, and they worked better than noose snares, that's for sure. Poppa wasn't much with a rifle and never had time for it, so we ate a lot of rabbit during the winter. I'd catch fifty, maybe more before summer, and that was more than enough to fill out what we had of bacon, sausage, pigs' feet, and ham. It was against the rules to kill rabbits on the Sabbath, but I usually did anyway. I'd leave them hanging in the smokehouse because it wasn't fair to leave them in the gums until Monday.

I knew I was fooling myself with all this business of going out to the woods to check the gums. I knew I was going to see about the skirmishing, but I just felt better fooling myself. Maybe I might change my mind and go back to the house and study the Bible.

I found only one rabbit; it was in the gum by our stone fence. It was a big one with brown spots; and as I grabbed its hind legs with my left hand, it shook like it was vibrating. I know how to kill rabbits quickly and efficiently, just hit it sharp on the back of the neck and drop it before it dies. Bad luck if it dies in your hands. Aunt Hanna, she was our servant who ran away to be with Uncle Isaac, told me that if an animal dies in your hands, it's bad luck and you'll surely die before your next birthday. So I always dropped them quick.

Anyway I was ready to hack this fat rabbit right behind the ears and drop it next to the gum when something strange came over me, and instead of killing it, I threw it right over the stone fence and let it escape into the woods. To this day I don't know why I did that. It wasn't like I felt sorry for the rabbit. Maybe it was because I knew I was going to break my word to Poppa and go out to watch the skirmishing. Maybe I didn't want to commit two sins right after the other. Angry with myself for being so stupid, I climbed over the fence and left the farm. But, you know, something felt different, not right, as if just then something had changed; and yet I couldn't tell you what.

It wasn't difficult to figure where the fighting was. I just had to follow my ears, which, of course, led me just about to Mr. Joseph Barton's farm. I knew this country pretty well and cut through the woods and over Sandy Ridge. No sense walking big as life through the fields and getting your foolish ass shot off. The woods were empty because the fighting was concentrated pretty much along the Pike, and it was just skirmishing, nothing much more than that from what I could tell. But I couldn't see anything much, not even from the Ridge, which is pretty high and starts to the west of Winchester and runs some six miles down to the Opequon Creek. The Pike's not far and runs along to the side of it.

I guessed that the Yankee guns were firing somewhere around Pritchard's Hill, and that our own were returning fire from Hodge Run or maybe below. If General Jackson and his army were around, they certainly weren't *here*.

'Course, soon as I figured that, I heard twigs snapping all over. Then I heard what seemed like a thousand muskets firing all around me, and there seemed to be a whirlwind of balls suddenly flying around and hissing just like snakes. I could almost feel the whomp of a minié ball as it hit a tree trunk to my right. Somebody shouted and I heard the thud of a ball hitting something soft and a noise, such like someone just had his breath knocked out of him. And then I heard a heartbreaking wailing like a mother who'd just lost her son. "Come on, boys," someone shouted in a bluebelly dialect, and more twigs cracked as men ran through the woods.

I stayed close to the ground. It was cold and damp, and I could smell the moss on the birch and, I swear, I could also smell the sour apple sweat of the soldiers even though I couldn't see much of them. I did see several men through the trees, and I thought they might have been our own, but I couldn't tell; they could just as easily have been Yankees. I crouched even harder against that birch tree as if I could squeeze myself right into the bark when the muskets started firing again. It was hard to tell where the balls were coming from. It didn't seem like there could be that many soldiers out here. Most of the Yanks were at least a half mile away. Then I heard someone stepping through the woods near me, calling and crying over and over in the most plaintive voice you ever heard, "Whey is my boys? Whey is my marsters?" And that voice sounded just like Jimmadasin, the McSherry's house servant. You couldn't miss it; he had a voice that was so high and reedy, it sounded just like a woman's. But I always thought he was having it up on all of us because when he sang his voice would suddenly get deep and full. He was responsible for minding Harry and Allan McSherry, who were eleven and fourteen respectively. I told you about them before; their mother Cornelia was my mother's best friend.

Well, the shooting stopped, and someone said, "Get the hell outa here, you crazy nigger. Yer gonna get yourself killed." That sounded like one of our boys, but I guess it didn't much matter to the nigger who it was because he just kept on walking until he was right beside me.

And just as I'd thought, it *was* Jimmadasin right there in the flesh. He was wearing the filthy felt hat he always wore, pulled down right on his forehead, and though he was old, he was no bigger than me. His face was wrinkled up like a dried prune with bushy white eyebrows, and he was shaking like he was going to have a convulsion. But he wasn't hiding or ducking down to get out of the way of those minié balls. "Lord, please, dey just chillen, bofh a dem," he whined, spreading out his arms like a preacher calling to God. "Please, marsters, don' kill dem." Then he turned and saw me, and his head nearly cracked backward with surprise. "Lord, Lord, yes indeed I foun' one a my boys, see? It's a miracle."

I didn't make a sound. I wasn't going to say a thing to this crazy nigger who seemed determined to get himself—and me—killed. But no one was paying any attention to us. Someone shouted, "Forward." There was another explosion of musket shot that just about shook the trees. There was shouting and crying and then it was just quiet except for cannon being fired near the Pike. I suddenly realized how scared I was, and I was probably shaking as much as Jimmadasin because he suddenly started hugging me and cooing like a bird and saying, "Dem soldiers gone, young marster's safe wid me," and I suppose we just sat there against the tree, rocking each other like babies until the shaking stopped and I realized that I was humiliating myself. But Jimmadasin must have read my mind, or was just thinking the same thing, because he let go of me gently and stood up, slapping at his legs, as if he was cold, and looking around, as if he were suddenly curious and impatient. "We godda get goin', more soldjers gonna be comin'."

"What're you doing here?" I asked like I had just woke up and found him standing over me, his face big as the moon.

"I thought for da minute you'se young Harry," he said, extending his hand out for me to take hold. "Das da h'nest truth. Come on now, id's dangerous here."

I let him pull me up, but before we went running off to safety, I wanted my question answered to my satisfaction. And I know this sounds crazy, what with musket exploding and soldiers running around all over here just seconds before, yet I felt safe here in the woods. There weren't any birds singing, and there were cannon and muskets firing, but right here felt sacred or something. I told you it didn't make any sense. "I ain't going noplace," I told him, "until you give me an explanation of what you're doing here."

"Whad *you* doin' here?"

"I asked *you*," I said.

"You ain' mah marster, but I'll tell you again jes like I tol' dem soldjers, I'se lookin' for mah marsters, mah chillen, an' mah mistress is jus' 'bout half crazy wid worry."

"Then Mrs. McSherry sent you," I said, and, believe me, it didn't escape my notice that he was talking in a low, deep voice now that almost was scaring me.

"*I* sen' me," Jimmadasin said and started pulling me away, but I wanted to investigate because I heard moaning not far off. "I gotta find mah marsters, an' you're goin' to help me. I goin' to save you for your folk, 'n you ain't goin' to fight me or pull away to sneak 'round dose dead 'n dyin' soldjers."

"And what are you going to do if I do," I said, feeling the humiliation burn around my ears.

"Wahmp your fuckin' arse is what I gonna do," Jimmadasin said, and when he said that in a low rumble full of meanness and menace, I felt like I was six years old again. I probably didn't mention this before, but when I was a baby, Poppa used to threaten me by saying that if I didn't do what Mother asked me to, he'd call Mrs. McSherry and have her send Jimmadasin over with his stealin' bag to steal me away and get me out of her hair. I'd seen Jimmadasin walking home once with a bag slung over his shoulder, so I knew it was true. Anyway, Poppa had turned him into the bogey monster, and I used to have dreams that Jimmadasin was coming right through my window, even though it was on the second floor, to throw me into his bag. Then he'd take me somewhere dark and dirty and when he'd pull me out of that bag, I'd be somehow turned into a girl. And I'd wake up screaming. I didn't find out until later that his real name was James Madison, after the old President. But when he talked in that low voice I'd heard him use when singing, I knew he'd do just what he said. He was my size, but everyone knew how strong he was. So I went along with him until I could escape. We kept inside the woods for a while, then went across a field with broken stone walls here and there. We were between the Cedar Creek Road and the Middle Road, and way up ahead was the tollgate and the white tents of the Yankee camp and, of course, Winchester town. The sky looked gray like it was promising to rain, and I suddenly felt the cold, maybe because I wasn't wearing any shoes, but unless there was snow on the ground that would freeze your toes off, I didn't usually wear them. I had so many calluses that I could step on stones and briars just like I was wearing shoes. I was wearing a short coat, though, which was warm enough.

Then out of the blue, after not talking, just walking, Jimmadasin said, "I 'pologize for bein' harsh. I wasn't goin' to whump ya, just potectin' ya." His voice was still soft and low and grumbly.

"I know," I said.

He nodded and said, "Den show me whey is my marsters."

"How would I know where they are?"

"You know."

"No, I don't."

"You plays wid dem."

"Only once in a while, not today."

He looked down at the ground. I could see he was disappointed. "Den I'm taking you home to be safe, an I'll find 'em myself. Don' stop here, we godda keep walkin'. The soldjers behin' us, we just saw a few a dem, but der's an army comin'." And he whispered, like under his breath, but so as I could hear, "A 'ntire fuckin' army."

"Whose?" I asked.

"Gen'l Jackson."

"Did you see him?"

"I jus' know, dat's all, now are you gonna tell me whey is my marsters, or am I gonna take you home? I should prob'ly do dat anyhow."

He took hold of my arm, gently but tightly, and I figured I'd better appease him, so I said, "I'll take you to the places I know, but it's gonna be like finding a needle in a haystack."

"We can do dat."

And so I really did try; I took him to all the places I knew around here that Harry and Allan liked best. As they always got everything they wanted, and had their own muskets, I used to go hunting with them. Of course, their muskets overshot everything, but once you got used to them, you'd have a fair chance at hitting something. Sometimes they'd let me shoot wild pigeons or doves or partridges, and I used to like their dogs that would always go along. So I took old Jimmadasin to Neil's Dam and to the woods where we always had good luck and a few other places with pretty good views, where they'd probably be if they were anywhere; and Jimmadasin started getting nervous, as he thought we were getting too close to danger, and started to talk to himself in a tiny, high voice like he was his own mother scolding him.

I asked him about that.

"You think I'se a dumb nigger fuck, don' you, but I ain't. You'se white an' don't got to worry 'bout nuthin'. If you was colored, you'd understan' quick, believe me." He laughed, but he was talking mean and quiet. "An' you also thought I mus' be a dumb, crazy fuck, Marster Mundy, whan I was lookin' for my boys in the woods. But dem soldjers ain't goin' to shoot what dey think is a dumb nigger wid a mamma's voice, now ain't dey? Nidder da 'Federate or da Yankee soldjer. I 'ready proves 'dat to you. If I was hidin', an' dey caught me, dey'd shoot Jimmadasin's ass dead. An' maybe shoot you wid me just for good measure or by mistake."

I owned that was possible.

"So maybe come a time when Marster Mundy learn dis nigger's tricks," Jimmadasin said, and we both started laughing because now we knew something nobody else did. And as we walked all over hell looking for Harry and Allan McSherry, the fighting got worse and worse, and we had to back off and keep going up toward Cedar Creek Road near where it meets the Valley Turnpike by the tollgate, which was near Abraham's Creek. I knew the creek, and so did Harry and Allan, but I knew that if they were here, they wouldn't be that far away from the fighting, which was behind us in the woods and fields between Cedar Creek Road—the lower part—and the Valley Pike near the Opequon Creek. Damned if Jimmadasin wasn't right; we saw our 'Federate boys marching across from the Pike along two routes. We were above it, but this wasn't no skirmishing; it was war. We could hear so many volleys of cannon that it just turned into one continuous roll, like the kind of thunder that seems to keep going on and getting louder after each flash of lightning. Seemed that now there were soldiers all around us, Yankee soldiers, and without saying a word we just ran, and I must admit I was glad to have Jimmadasin holding onto my hand. Everything seemed to go fast and slow at the same time. I know that sounds crazy, but that's how it was. Everything was happening inside of a second, yet it was slow, too. Ah, I don't know, that's just how it was. There was smoke everywhere like there was a fire, and I could smell powder, it was sharp and hurt my nose like I had breathed in pepper and iron filings, and there was an explosion nearby that nearly knocked us down and pieces of metal and trees were flying through the air, and Jesus Christ I thought I saw a bloody hand falling with all the dirt and debris; and there were men screaming for help and calling for their mothers and then sonovabitch if another shell didn't explode like lightning striking the same place twice, and clots of earth and leaves and branches were flying, it was like the whole world was flying up in the air, and there were more screams, probably our own, too, and I stepped on something that seemed to burst under my foot. It was part of somebody because my foot was bloody and sticky, and I remember screaming then, I don't know why because in a way I wasn't scared, it was like I was off to the distance watching Jimmadasin and myself running like fools, and everything got dark and cloudy and everyone was shouting and shooting, and Jimmadasin was pulling me along and we were both shouting, and then suddenly it was over and we just sat in a field together breathing heavy and I was so exhausted that I heaved a little before I could even catch my breath. I could still feel whatever it was that I had stepped on, and I rubbed off what I could of the blood with dirt and leaves. "Get the hell outa here, boy," shouted a Yank soldier up ahead of us, and I couldn't tell if he was yelling at me or Jimmadasin, and behind him ran a standard bearer, who didn't look like he was much older than me. I should have been fighting the Yanks, but Poppa wouldn't have none of that, and maybe I should have run away to join the militia, but I figured he would have stopped it anyway. Mother would cry that I was a baby every time I brought it up. I was old enough to be a drummer, at least. You could be twelve and be a drummer, and fourteen and be a soldier. "Move it out," someone shouted, and again, I didn't know if he was talking to the soldiers or to us, but Jimmadasin and I moved. More Yanks were moving down to meet our boys, thousands it looked like, marching down a mud road that wasn't much more than a path; and they were moving everything, including cannon. I thought we were safe hereabouts, but then we came upon a bluebelly who looked like he was asleep against a tree. One leg was stretched out straight and the other one was pulled up to his chest, which was a good comfortable way to sleep. Except he had a mess on his lap that looked like sausages.

" 'Testines," Jimmadasin said, pulling me along. "Musta been from dis mornin' 'cause dey so swollen. Big guns do dat, just 'splode all over like we seen."

I was feeling a little sick, but once we walked right through the Yankee ranks, as if we were passing them on the street in town, I felt relieved and ashamed. Relieved because I could see town people around here on the hills who came to watch General Jackson shoot the asses off these Yankee invaders. Ashamed because now we were behind Yankee lines, under the protection of General Shields, who was the enemy, and I figured that was only a coward's reason to be comfortable.

I can't remember how long we remained just standing around, as if we were lost and trying to get our direction back, but it seems that it must have been a while because I was hungry, which was probably what was making me sick all along. Still, the sound of cannon and musket echoing around the hills was a continuous roll, and I thought then that there must be thousands getting shot and blown up and killed. It wasn't that many, but I learned quick that once you've been right there with all the dead and dying soldiers, Confederate or Yank, you feel the same if it's two or two hundred. I didn't know that, then, though. I was jittery-nervous, like I was in a dream where one minute you're here and then one minute you're somewhere else, and I had a metal taste that sometimes almost choked me whenever I swallowed, and something else. Everything seemed pressed together somehow, and maybe because it was exciting, but even with all the dying and screaming I felt a strange and horrible sort of happiness.

Once I saw those people from Winchester standing around, people who I'd seen before but didn't really know, like Mr. Rosenberger, who was on the town council and knew Poppa, and Doctor Baldwin, and the dentist whose name I can't remember, I knew where we'd probably find the McSherry boys. The fighting was all going on in the woods and fields on and around Sandy Ridge, mostly where we'd been, and I pointed out some likely places to Jimmadasin. Most of them were taken up by spectators trying to get a good view, but Harry and Allan were nowhere to be found. I told Jimmadasin we had to go back down a ways closer to the fighting if we were going to find them. He said no, but went anyway—he sure as hell loved those two boys—but he scolded himself in his high, scared voice all the way back. I didn't expect to find them; I just wanted to get close to where I could see and get away from the other spectators, but we found them anyway sitting on a stone fence with a near perfect view of the Federal regiments.

"Hey, Mundy, you come to the right place to see the fight," Harry McSherry said, ignoring Jimmadasin, but looking uncomfortable nevertheless.

Jimmadasin screamed for them to come down from there because of how dangerous it was. He ran right up to both of them, pulled them down from the stone fence, nearly breaking their bones, and hugged them. They tried to escape, but, as I said, old Jimmadasin was strong; and it didn't seem that he'd ever let go of them again.

"Yo' Mamma's sick wid worry o're you, both of you."

"Lemme go," Harry said. His brother Allan didn't struggle; he just looked scared of everything. He was eleven, more than a year younger than Harry and me. "Momma knows we're watching the battle," Harry said. "We went early this morning. She gave us permission, you ken go an' ask her."

"I don' hafta ask nobody, 'cause she tole' me to bring you home safe 'n soun', dat's 'xactly what she say. An' dat's what I'm goin' to do right now." Jimmadasin started marching them around the side of the fence and turned to me, expecting me to follow, but Harry begged to stay just for a few minutes more and explained that it was safe here and Jimmadasin could see that, for there were no dead bodies here or nothing.

Jimmadasin allowed five minutes.

We could see the Federals hiding behind stone fences, and between them and General Jackson's army were trees and small brush and more fences. There were woods down a ways to the right and a ravine, but there was nothing straight ahead beyond that stone fence but empty field, and our Confederates throwing everything they had at the line of Federal soldiers. The Federals were shooting back, of course, mostly cannon somewhere off to our left, but mostly they were getting shot at and shelled. It was loud, and much of the time that we all sat there together on the fence, we couldn't hear ourselves talk. Harry was wrong about one thing, though: there were dead soldiers all around here. I could see them when I looked hard. They were covered with dirt and filth and blood that looked black, and they blended right into the ground and woods and brush, which were all torn up anyhow. Even though I don't care a wet shit about Federal soldiers, it half made me sick to see them dead and lying around all over. 'Course, I just figured they were Yanks. They could've been our own men . . .

Well, then all hell broke loose, and we almost got killed by our own 'Federate shells, which exploded in the trees right behind us; and it suddenly seemed that you couldn't be safe nowhere. A head torn right off at the neck rolled right in front of Allan's foot, as if it was a pumpkin or something; and Allan screamed. 'Course, I don't blame him for that, especially since I could swear that the lips moved. Jimmadasin made some sort of a sacred sign with his hands, then there was another explosion, and Jimmadasin and Harry and Allan McSherry were gone.

It was like I woke up and they were gone, but I remembered what happened only afterward. Jimmadasin had grabbed Harry and Allan with those big hands of his and tried to do the same with me, but I was running before

I could even think about it, not necessarily away from Jimmadasin, but running just the same, and I didn't stop until I was in a little grove of brush and young trees. There was noise all around me, and I could hear men groaning and breathing and reloading their muskets. I got to know the rattle a ramrod makes when it's pushed down into the barrel.

I had run the wrong way, and I didn't dare move, and how I wished that Jimmadasin had grabbed me, damn him, because I was right in the thick of the fighting. I could see pretty good, too, and then even more bluebellies came running into the battle, replacing the Federals who had been killed— and they were lying everywhere, like it was a game and couldn't be real, and when I didn't see pieces of flesh and smears of blood, that's the way I was thinking it was. The fire from both sides was devastating. Not even the stone wall could protect the Federals from that terrible hail of shot and shell, and I imagine our own boys were dying just the same on the other side of the wall. The were more Federals to my left, and I could see that they were the Eighty-fourth Pennsylvania. One of their officers waved his sword and shouted like he was giving a speech, "Hold your ground; stand solid; keep cool; remember your homes, and your country; don't waste your powder," and the damn fool was standing right out there in front of his men, leading them forward until someone called him to fall back because he was exposing himself unnecessarily. But he didn't pay any attention and advanced with his men right into the fire of our boys. More bluebellies were falling than advancing, it seemed; but when I saw that officer fall, even though I felt sorry for the poor bastard, I thought right then that, yes, we were going to win, that General Jackson was going to kill so many Yanks that General Banks would have to retire back to where he came from and get the hell out of Winchester for good.

I crawled forward, emboldened by the killing, I guess, although I wasn't being smart, just curious, and I've learned better since then.

Now I could see our army down below what was a hill or maybe more like a ravine, and the bluebellies were charging right down there through galling fire; and you had to hand it to the Yankees, they were determined. I watched two of their color bearers fall, and saw the flag lifted up again each time. But our guns were too much for them, and the right side of what looked like a thousand Yanks just gave way, and the bluebellies were running right back in the direction they came, but like flies around honey, more soldiers just seemed to swarm in; then the Yanks let out a terrific shout, something like a wolf howl; and Yankee and Reb were killing each other with bayonet and fighting hand to hand and getting all mixed up with each other. But the Yankees got past the stone fence, and sonova*bitch* if they didn't turn our own boys, rout them, and I remember saying to myself that this was only one little

tiny piece of the fight, that our boys were pushing the Yankee soldiers back everywhere else, but I could feel that wasn't true. I just felt sick and sort of paralyzed, and suddenly I wanted to get home, even though I would be in big trouble. If you want the truth, and I'm ashamed to admit this, but I wanted my mother. I wanted to smell rabbit stew and all the fixings. I wanted to feel the warmth of the hearth and all that. And all this would just be sort of like a dream I would forget, or just remember like you remember a good story.

I could tell by where the sun was, or the smear that was the sun behind the clouds, that it must be close to twilight. As I probably said already, everything seemed to be going fast and slow at the same time, even though I know that's impossible; and somehow the whole day had gotten swallowed up in a few minutes. But I was going home, that's all I knew; and so I just walked in the opposite direction of the fighting, back up toward where Jimmadasin and I had gone to get out of danger before. I didn't know better then, but I thought that nothing could be worse than seeing all those dead and wounded soldiers lying all around like they were dolls or something. I had to keep my eyes open and be alert, but I found I could ignore seeing the dead soldiers and the wounded ones, too; only thing I couldn't ignore was their cries, and so I gave some of them water, which they all begged for; and even now that I think of it I'm ashamed I didn't try to do more for them. But I just left them.

Well, I couldn't have done anything much for them anyway, except keep them company when they cried for their mothers and give them a little water.

I should've stayed with them.

But I wanted *my* mother.

So I pretended it was all going to be all right and took the straightest route home, not even thinking that I might step into more fighting. I just figured if I ran straight ahead, big as life like old Jimmadasin taught me, I'd get home safe and sound. Which I did. It was just before dusk when everything looks bluish and pretty, and the fields and woods were all shadowy like they were sunk in dark pools of water or something, but if you looked out at the mountains you could sometimes see parts that were sunlit, and you could sometimes see rays coming right out of the sky like a painting in the Bible. That's how it looked when I reached our farm; but even before I could see the family house, I knew something was wrong because I could smell burning and hear terrible screaming and crying, and I could tell my mother's voice, and Poppa's. Poppa was screaming more than anyone, and then he stopped and there were other voices I didn't recognize. I ran right through the woods to get to the front yard of the "Big House," as we called it, as if we had a hundred slaves like the Bartons from Springdale, who Poppa knew. But that doesn't matter, and I'm just keeping away from telling you what happened.

But I'm going to . . .

Anyway, there was our house with its big chimney, and porch with columns, and the red sandstone flags that made a pavement through the lawn between the shade trees and stopped by the board fence that Poppa and I had whitewashed. And there was the sunlight just going over the mountains. And the smell of smoke. The entire farm except for the Big House seemed like it was on fire, the barn and lumber house and schoolhouse. I was behind a big tree, and I could see every little detail of everything, it seemed, and even though I wish I couldn't, I remember it all—I remember the rotten trunk of a cherry tree that was just beside me, I remember the white fungus growing on its gray bark; and I remember the smell of the woods and the smell of the smoke, and the screaming, although as I think about it I still want to close my eyes, but I didn't, although I wish I did because two men came riding out from the back of the house; and they were hooting and shouting and laughing like they were drunk or probably crazy; and they were both wearing cheap butternut coats and pants and those funny-looking Federal hats that had enough fittings on them to make a copper kettle. One had a pine torch, and he was leaning low on the side of his horse, almost falling out of his saddle, to touch that torch to everything he fancied. The other was just riding behind him, pulling along two other horses.

"C'mon outa there," shouted the one with the torch. "Gonna get hot, an' it's our turn, ya greedy fucks."

And the house started smoking. He had started the fire in the back of the house, and suddenly I could see flames licking the roof, and I could hear terrible cracking noises like bones were being broken or something, and then someone ran out of the house and shot the horse right out from under the soldier with the torch, and someone else came out of the house, and he was pulling Mother, and she was naked and full of blood, and I wondered where was Poppa, where was Poppa, I remember thinking that over and over like a song, and I was watching when I should have been running right out there and killing them, burning them and shooting those sonovabitches, but then the soldier that had been pulling Mother just dropped her outside the door on the porch. She wasn't making any noise, but I saw her move, and then the soldier whose horse was shot out from under him ran over to the porch, and all the men started fighting with each other, and they fell right over Mother, and I heard a keening, a noise like Jimmadasin would've made, and I realized I was hearing myself, hearing the inside of my head, and I blinked, that's all it was, I blinked, and then one of the men must have dragged Mother off the porch and onto pavement, and he was on top of her and his pants were down, and another one, another one was—

Looking straight at me. I know he saw me. He must've. He just looked right at me, and I didn't move, and I didn't breathe, and then he looked away like he never saw me, and I remember thinking then that I was invisible like air or like a tree in a huge forest.

And then he was gone, as if *he* had disappeared, and so had the other men, but maybe it was me, maybe I just went blind or something because all

I remember from then on, for I don't know how long I was watching that man hurting my mother, I was remembering nice things and terrible things, as if I had escaped from that tree and the time and what I was seeing and was only seeing things in my mind.

I had to go in and save Mother, I had to find Father, for the house was burning, burning, catching fire in a hundred places, and I could feel the heat, but I was thinking remembering couldn't move touching the bark, feeling the slimy moss remembering remembering how at the start of spring Poppa and I always made piles of brush and dead leaves and vegetation, anything else burnable that we could gather in our fields. Then Poppa would check that the wind was just right, so that the fire didn't get out of control, and then with a pine torch he'd light those piles, poking them here and there with a long pole, going from one pile to another, while I ran around gathering everything that would burn to keep the hungry fires going, and I remembered and remembered so well I could see it right before me, so well that I could blank out what was happening right in front of me, and I saw me and Ishrael Moble and three of his darkie children that Poppa had borrowed from Arthur Allen who owned the next farm down the road from us, and Ishrael was ploughing a furrow around our field of broom sedge, and when he was done Poppa would light the sedge on the windward side, and it would blaze like a sonovabitch, and Ishrael and his kids and me and Poppa would beat out the fire with green cedar branches whenever it escaped over the furrow, and once it did and we lost a rail fence and burned a field and—

They were gone.

I found myself standing on the edge of the woods, holding my breath, being invisible, looking at the house burning, feeling the heat on my face like waves coming over me, and I had seen everything, I knew that I had seen what the men did, what they did to my mother, and I could see mother there yet, lying on the red sandstone flags, and I just ran across the lawn to her. It was as if I had just gotten here. Like I hadn't been watching, hadn't been invisible, hadn't held my breath for . . . how long? Five minutes? Ten minutes? Uncle Randolph says it's impossible to hold your breath longer than a minute, but I know I could have held it forever that day.

I heard that keening and knew I was making strange noises and sobbing and crying, but as soon as I knelt beside Mother I saw that she was staring off and not blinking. But it wasn't even so much that. It was like she had been turned into a doll or something. She looked like porcelain, like all the stuff had gone out of her, and I knew she was dead.

Poppa . . .

I tried to go into the house, but the fire was bad inside, and so I came out and dragged Mother away from the house, but I saw that it was hopeless, that everything was hopeless because I knew that Poppa had been in the house and was killed, too.

It was when I was guarding Mother that I saw the dog. It came running from the direction of the meat house, where I figured it had gotten in. It was the biggest dog I ever saw, more like the size of a horse, and its coat was as black and sleek and shiny as the big crow perched on top of the smoking ruins of the Big House. That dog smelled terrible of dampness and burning, and it was running right toward me with its mouth open. Its eyes were on fire. They were big as saucers and looked like balls of fire.

No one is ever going to tell me that dog wasn't real, because I saw it, and like before, when the men burned down the house, I became invisible. I kneeled there beside Mother like I was frozen. I didn't breathe. I didn't make a sound. And that dog stopped so near to me that I could smell its sour-rotten breath and its damp, sweaty fur. And I could feel the heat of it, and it seemed to just fill me up the same way Mother did when she'd pull the covers up to my chin and kiss me good-night and talk about Jesus.

It sniffed at Mother, looked at me a real long time like it was putting thoughts in my head, and then it ran off to the edge of the woods where it watched me with its eyes that were burning in the dark because it had gotten dark while I had been sitting there with Mother. It kept watching me and waiting to see what I was going to do, and I stayed with Mother while the house burned. I held her hand, which was like ice, and I felt something fill me up again like I was a bucket and hot lard was being poured into it, and I wasn't angry or sad anymore because all at once everything seemed right and perfect, and I knew exactly what I had to do. It was like I was having one of those visions Aunt Hanna was always telling me about because it came to me all of a sudden that it was up to me to kill everybody who'd killed Mother and Poppa, and that it didn't make much difference who it was. It was the spirit dog that put that thought in my head, I swear, 'cause I could feel the spirit inside me, breathing right inside my chest until I understood it all; and then when I turned around the spirit dog was still there, watching me with those burning eyes and calling me to him with my own thoughts.

Calling me to go back to Kernstown field, which was filled with muskets and caps and cartridges.

I'd gather them up to do my own killing.

For Mother.

For Poppa.

For everyone.

Until the spirit dog and me had evened things up, and then we'd just probably

Disappear.

DARKNESS AND THE SHADOW OF LIGHT

James O'Barr

I
    I feel like a statue of an armless angel
Broken; hurt
Flawed at my very core,
Rage jets thru my veins, a
Black blood poison
Hot with fury
It rolls off me like smoke, like
Sad music
    My soul rises up from the
Red sky of the west
    A fiery chariot amassed of
Iron; steel:
    Engine parts
    Bones, both human and animal
With a hideous velocity I
    Scream across the heavens,
    Washing the countryside in
A sick sweet death like some
    Monstrous plague
Anger boils over me in a
Screaming rain and
    I want to destroy everything;
If I were a god everything
    Would die a slow, horrific
    Death

II

I look at my arms.
There are spiders in my veins,
They are glossy blue-black:
The color of sin, the color
Of a waxed Porsche.
The crimson hourglasses on their backs
Shine like Christmas tree decorations
The spiders mate, they fuck
In my blood
Discharging a sick dead venom
That dozes up and down my
Arteries
Eating at the last innocence
Of my soul
To live, I must release them
With trembling fingers
I pick up a straight razor,
Its rusted serrated edge like
The fringe of a shadow
The razor needs soft flesh
Like a dozen red roses I
Give the gift of freedom to the
Spiders:
A rush of blood, down my
Forearm
An alizarin crimson curtain
Rising, like my soul, to
Signal the start of the end
Who will be the slave to
The spiders,
Now?

WINGS BURNT BLACK

JOHN SHIRLEY

PRIOR '97

"
Do not envy the Man
with the X-Ray Eyes . . .
—Blue Öyster Cult: *Heaven Forbid*

s there really any hurry about killing me, Eric?" the Murderer asked. "I mean, wouldn't you like to draw it out? Savor it?"

And the Murderer smiled a mouthful of green teeth.

" 'Smiles form the channels of a future tear,' " the Crow replied.

"The ghost quotes Byron! And how altogether Byronic you are!"

"Mockery stalls for time," said Eric, who was called the Crow, cocking his pistol, "and that's another way of pleading."

"Don't flatter yourself. I would not plead with God himself. And don't imagine that I disbelieve in God. I know better: the villain is well-known to me."

The Murderer, the object of the Crow's vengeance this night, was half reclining on a chaise longue on the balcony of his condominium on the thirteenth story of this concrete high-rise. The Murderer was nestled in an almost believable semblance of slack calm; he had a daiquiri in one hand and a Marlboro Light in the other. The Detroit night was just beginning to burn, far below. Vaporous grime watercolored the full moon a sordid gray pink. The Murderer was a slim, sunken-eyed man in leather chaps and snakeskin boots, his face angular, just a little cocaine tremor in his fingers making the ash from his cigarette shiver into the monoxide wind; the wind carried the ashes into the sky to the wheeling, raucous crow, the bird that followed Eric everywhere—and made the bird blink.

Eric was sitting on the balcony wall, rocking on the wall in a way no sane mortal would do; teetering, one leg crossed over the other, elbow propped on his knee, the gun loose in his hand but never wavering from the Murderer's forehead.

The bird settled on Eric's shoulder.

The Murderer looked at the black bird on Eric's shoulder and pulled on his cigarette, let smoke loll from his mouth and drew it back in through his nostrils, then said, "Here's another quote for you—I can't remember who said it: 'Hell is truth seen too late.' Probably is, for most people. And of course you know: the truth protects itself."

"I've heard that said." The Crow's finger tightened on the trigger . . . then eased. He simply wasn't ready to fire the gun. There was something undone here, besides killing this man, but he didn't know what it was yet.

"But I have seen the truth," said the Murderer, "and I just don't care. You see, I've been . . . well, not quite dead, but close. Enough to see through the veil." He pulled on the cigarette. "My parents were Santeria initiates, you know."

He paused as they both turned to look at a thudding police chopper tilting like a clumsy dragonfly, eddying flame-lit smoke with its blades, highlighting the murk of burning buildings with its downseeking spotlight, its bullhorn voice trying to warn the looters: the feeble, echoing voice of authority, its own self-mockery. *By order of the governor, looters can be shot. This area is surrounded by police. Do not . . . do not . . . not . . . not . . ."*

"Can you imagine being cut in half by a helicopter blade?" the Murderer asked idly.

"Yes. That'd be too quick, for you," mused the Crow, just as idly. "If I drop you from up here, you might live for a while, and your bone edges, Murderer, your splinters, would break through your skin and then I could tap them with the muzzle of my gun."

"I doubt I'd be conscious at that point. You'd be better off breaking my bones up here. I understand you're strong enough. I know I can't kill you. And you can kill me. But you cannot kill the ones who are really responsible for Shelly's death."

"Liar!" The word banged from Eric and rebounded from the concrete face of the building to pierce even the cacophony of the burning city: LIAR!

And then the Crow, in a single motion, had moved to straddle the Murderer's legs with one boot planted to either side; lividly painted face catching fire truck's cherry-top glare, flickering in and out of shadow, his premonitory eyes black as the Pit, his gun the unyielding blue of gunmetal, its muzzle now pressed to the Murderer's mouth. "If I shoot at a down angle, and miss your heart, Murderer, your jaw flies apart, and you will live to suffer, for a while, but you'll keep your foul mouth shut." His voice was like a brush-stick dragged over a snare drum. *Mouth shuhhhhhhhhhhh . . .*

But the Murderer spoke, even with a gun muzzle denting his nicotine-yellowed lips; his sunken eyes meeting Eric's, both their gazes as unwavering as the gun.

"You think you have found in me the one who ordered you attacked; the one responsible for Shelly's death. You think you pull a trigger and the deed is done. But think—and heed and check it out and I'll tell you the motherfuckin' truth!"

The Crow took a step back and said, "Raise your drinking glass."

The Murderer obeyed and the Crow quoted Byron once more, " 'Here's a sigh to those who love me, and a smile to those who hate; and whatever sky's above me, here's a heart for every fate.' " He fired the gun—fired it at the glass in the Murderer's hand, with marvelous precision, so that the shattered glass was driven into the crime lord's tendons along with the bullet.

The bird, the black crow that was Eric's familiar, settled to the concrete and began to peck at bits of flesh and spots of cocktail spattered behind the Murderer.

The Murderer managed not to scream, but a gurgling growl escaped him as he clutched the shattered, riven hand to him, sitting up, eyes hot. He didn't drop his cigarette, but drew on it deeply, shaking.

But he smiled. Green teeth.

" 'Pain is the father of truth,' " said Eric. "Now don't fucking lie to me again. I'm sure I'd already know if there were others . . ."

"There is another," said the Murderer, in a triumphant, pain-shivered growl. "The one truly responsible for Shelly's death. Listen now . . . I ordered you and your love 'done,' yes—but who am I? I am a consequence. I was raised by a man whose greatest joy was in raping very small boys, taking them from behind first and then the mouth; my earliest sharply remembered taste is of my own blood and shit. My mother was a Santeria priestess until junk made her a whore. My parents made me what I am, you see. I could have been nothing else! And if there was any margin for transcending my making, it was taken up by my genetics. My father was chromosomally a killer; my mother chromosomally an addict. *But who made them?* Their parents were at least as bad—and my father was raised in a nasty bitch of a slum. And on it goes back into the blur of time." Grimacing with pain, he paused to suck on his cigarette. "So . . . so who is to blame? I have never had the faintest inkling of a choice in the things I do. Not the faintest. None, my friend! I am a psychopath and I know it. Was Jeffrey Dahmer really given a choice? Or did he have to be what he was? He was damned from birth. So who decided his damnation? Random chance? But you are here, and you know there is a spiritual world: you are part of it. Which means that there is a spiritual agenda, a cosmic purpose—a hated purpose, to my mind, but a purpose all the same. Does that purpose stint on brutality? Does it hesitate to create Inquisitions and the Holocaust? And doesn't it just fuckin' adore creating Aztecs and Celts who butcher children for their gods? Who was it who made life brutish—and short? Who jacked up the suffering? Who made de Sade and Lizzy of Bathory? Who made Eichmann? Who decided that two-year-olds should die of AIDS and four-year-olds of cancer?" Suddenly the Murderer sprang up and flicked his cigarette at Eric, and pointed a trembling finger at him with the cigarette hand, and quoted from the Book of Job: " 'Where wast thou when I laid the foundations of the earth? . . . Who hath laid the measures thereof, if thou knowest? Or who hath stretched the line upon it? Whereupon are the foundations thereof fastened? Or who laid the cornerstone thereof . . .' "

The Crow's normal supernaturally rectified implacability was set akilter; for the first time he was unsure and his voice showed it. "It's not for me to punish blasphemy; that, others punish, later."

But the Murderer was thundering on, still quoting the Bible: " 'Hast thou entered into the springs of the sea? Or has thou walked in the search of the depth? HAVE THE GATES OF DEATH BEEN OPENED UNTO THEE?' "

"Ah," said Eric, "it was you who opened them for me." And once more he leveled the gun.

"No," said the Murderer, with a lethal quiet, dropping his hand. "He put me, like a bullet, in His gun. And He pulled the trigger, He killed you, and Shelly—I was just the instrument. I was made as I am, a murderer, and fate brought us together, you and I, and *who loads the guns of fate?*"

Eric looked at the gun in his hand, and it drooped. He looked out at the night sky: black construction paper with cheap acrylics slurred by an uncertain hand.

"I am going to inquire," Eric said. "You can run if you like, but you know it doesn't matter where you go, or how. You can go to South Africa and lock yourself in a bunker a thousand feet down a diamond mine, and I would come to you. You know that—don't you?"

"Yes." There was no guile in the Murderer now.

"Or you can stay here, and take drugs for the pain, and wrap your hand, and wait for me to answer you."

"Yes. But just remember: your mission is one of final vengeance. Don't lose sight of your goal."

The Crow stepped up onto the ledge—he spread his arms like the wings of the bird that rose to flap beside him, and dove off the ledge. He fell. He turned end over end, never changing pose as he fell spread-eagled, and when he struck the crow-black street facedown he seemed to fall through it as if it were water; the bird followed him down; and they'd vanished into the street itself. Then steam rose from a manhole cover, and there was nothing unusual in that, but this steam moved consciously, and took shape: the shape of a crow, and then another crow, these shapes becoming as real as anything is, two birds, street-black and flapping into the sky, up and up through the smoke and columns of rising heat, spiraling ever higher, to heights where no earthly bird could find air for purchase or breath to draw, and higher yet, the two of them rising like ash above the flue of the whole burning world.

And then vanishing from this world; for heaven is not above and hell is not below.

Shaped once more like a man, Eric passed into a muttering void, and he saw that his familiar was still with him, though now in the shape of . . . a conquistador.

"Is that the shape you had when you were a mortal man?" Eric asked the wraith, the dark little man with sharp beard and dull armor.

"Yes. We killed the Indians, all the Indians in the village, trying to force from them the whereabouts of El Dorado, but they didn't know, and the last to die touched me with the feather of a Crow, and said something I did not understand; thus he cursed me. Soon after, I died of typhoid; and became sometimes a man-wraith, and sometimes the bird, when I am needed. Someday perhaps I will have worked off my penance."

"And what was *my* penance? To be murdered? To have my true love murdered before my eyes? What crime was this penance for?"

"I do not know. I only know what I am commanded to do; not the why of it; never the wherefore." He drew his hand over his body, and his wraith-garment transformed, armor became soft gray cloth, and he was then clothed as a monk. "Best to dress for humility, in the higher planes . . ."

Eric shrugged and remained as he was: in black leather, face painted a livid mockery.

Still they ascended, through veils of almost-being, passing, on the way, this and that consensual fantasy of the afterlife, some decaying and some, for a time, holding fast: a glittery, musical Protestant heaven; a dour Hasidic afterlife; a roseate Hindu afterlife gyrating with blue-skinned idols; an Amerind forest of plenty; and on it went, until they'd passed from the realm of expectations and into the brighter lights, where reality became impatient and asserted itself.

Here Eric looked about for someone in authority.

The looking was a summoning: and the Guardian Entity faded up, sank upward into being: was suddenly there. To Eric in that moment the Entity looked like an emblem, like a playing-card king, almost: it had austere faces duplicated above and below, in mirror opposite; if he looked into the Entity's middle it was like looking down a reflecting corridor of mirrors into a sentient infinity. If he tried to hold the whole thing in his mind it came across like an intricately calligraphed Hebrew letter; a letter that looked back at you. Eric found that staring into the Entity was too vertiginous. He focused on the upper set of apparent "eyes" as he waited for the Entity's challenge.

The crow familiar hung about in the background, hooded head humbly

inclined as the Guardian Entity spoke. Eric stood his ground in this groundless place; he consciously remained the Crow archetype head to toe, leathers and makeup and gun; hovering in this gray but sparkling violet place, where, just on the edge of one's peripheral attention, paisley became swastikas became crucifixes became pentagrams became Stars of David became leering goat heads became enneagrams became serpents became angels . . .

"Well?" the Guardian Entity said, by way of acknowledgment. This was how the Crow heard it, anyway.

"I've come to speak to God, to demand the truth."

"You truly think you can make demands of God?"

"I was murdered; more important, my true love was murdered; it happened on the day of our wedding."

"Sounds like—you're from Earth, no?—sounds like a Scottish folk song. I'm sorry, I don't mean to jeer at you: you produce that in me yourself; I give back your own doubts. And I do know that, subjectively, suffering is its own dimension, and goes on forever; or seems to. But, as you're from Earth, have you read C. S. Lewis's *The Screwtape Letters*? 'All horrors have followed the same course, getting worse and worse and forcing you into a kind of bottleneck till, at the very moment when you thought you must be crushed, behold! you were out of the narrows and all was suddenly well. The extraction hurt more and more, then the tooth was out. The dream became a nightmare and then you woke. You die and die and then you are beyond death.' "

"Where is Shelly?" Eric suddenly felt a dizzy need to see her.

"I thought you wanted to interview God—now it's the lost love you want to see? Not that they aren't identical. But not to you, not yet. You really ought to keep your mind on your aim. Spirits quickly disintegrate, here, who flicker from one mental fantasy to another. To answer your question, Shelly is in another realm. She is caught up in her expectations. If you go there, you'll get caught up, too, and your aim will be left undone. You do intend to wreak justice, no? A reckoning?" A ripple ran through the Guardian Entity's living iconography . . .

"Yes," Eric replied. "A reckoning."

"And you know, of course, that inflicting suffering on the Bad Boys, will not really balance the scales very well."

"Yes, but it's better than nothing."

" 'It's better than nothing'—which is just exactly what God said . . ."

"It could be that you're not the servant of heaven you seem; perhaps you're a demon, sent to endlessly stall me. The way the Murderer stalled me."

"I contain shadows of course, Eric, but I am not a shadow, no. You're more shadow than I am, my boy. I see you have a gun with you."

"Yes," put in the crow familiar, "he has it. His will is in the form of a gun."

There was a shade of warning in the monkish crow's comment.

"I see it. Most impressive." His "voice" was surprisingly lacking in derision. "Quite a piece you have there. What caliber? Forty-five? A Colt, is it?"

Only then did Eric understand his own gun: it was, especially on this plane, not a mechanism of steel, except in shape; here the gun was the *embodiment of his will*.

The gun was an expression of him, as all guns will be for the user, anywhere, but on a deeper level: literally, the bullet was fashioned from his will, was compressed will itself.

As such, it was not without meaning here; it could destroy, in the higher realms.

"I will see Shelly," said Eric, "after the reckoning. Now: I have come to demand: *Who is at fault?* The Murderer has convinced me, at least to the point of reasonable doubt, that the Murderer could never have been in command of himself, really, that he was a cog moved by other cogs. Some seem to have choice in their lives—others have no choice, because of the absoluteness of their nature and, I guess, nurture. Seems like he's one of those. Unless he's lying, and I can detect lies, and he wasn't. And then there are those born demented; bad seeds, and all that: how much choice have they got in what they are? None. So who's really to blame for what they do?"

"So you're saying you should forgive everyone with equal compassion because they cannot help themselves. 'Father forgive them they know not what they do'?"

"Now you *are* mocking me. No. I exist, post death, purely to effect a reckoning; to thereby ease my suffering, and Shelly's. So our spirits can rest. There *must* be a reckoning. This is, after all, a universe in which math is king, no?"

"No, mathematics is a chancellor, merely."

"Deny it: that the Murderer is, ultimately, not responsible for his actions."

"Do you know Shakespeare? ' *'Tis true 'tis pity; And pity 'tis 'tis true.*' "

"I see."

Eric drew his gun.

"Then . . . ," said Eric, ". . . who do I kill?"

"In the land of death? Be serious."

"I'm not obtuse. This place has as much to do with being as with nonbeing and even in the land of death one can be made not to be. Who, then? Is it God?"

The Entity did not reply.

Eric thundered his demand: "Who do I kill? Who, finally, is responsible for Shelly's death? *MUST I KILL GOD?*"

Must I kill God . . . Must I kill God . . . Must I . . .

They weren't echoes, in the sonic sense, but somehow the words reverberated all through the various heavens . . .

Must I kill God . . .

He remembered the Zen saying that went: *Kill the Buddha! Kill the Buddha!*

The Guardian Entity's signatory substance opened, like a gate, and the Crow walked through it; the monkish crow familiar following. Walking through the gate of the Entity's body.

They ascended stairs that were in that moment created for him, and they passed through all spectra, from red-shift to yellow to blue to the place where waves move so frequently they mesh one into another and come to a stop, outside of time. A place where you could, if you could go there, strap galaxies onto your shoes for Roller Blades. The place that is the Sum of Suns and the Sum of Sums, at the pinpoint of the pinpoint, atop the Ray of Creation.

Here, somehow, the monk had become more his own signification; more living symbol: and glancing at him Eric saw that he had the head of a crow, big as a man's head, within a monk's robe. *Something like Horus,* Eric thought.

He was a little surprised at his ability to think at all here; surprised that this place didn't destroy his mind, as it was quite beyond human capability. But he knew, then, what protected him:

The gun.

The gun in his hand was the focal point of his will; so long as he kept the greater part of his intentionality focused there, it parted the walls of wonder for him, and kept him sane.

At length, they came to a realm where all music accorded into one recurring chord that was always the same and yet never repeated. Here an angel stood in their path, towering over them; a manlike figure of light, complete with magnificent iridescent-white wings, a tarot image that moved and spoke and carried a sword, clutched in both hands and angled downward, that seemed to stretch on forever and yet held the proportions of a sword. Eric had a sense that the sword was in relation to the subjective universe the way that a laser is in relation to a compact disc; or perhaps the way a threaded needle is in relation to the tapestry it elaborates.

"Are you the one?" Eric asked.

"Could you be more specific?" Its voice was at one with the endless chord that reverberated here. Each of its words had infinite implications. Eric focused on those that were relevant to him.

"The forger of destinies," Eric went on, with no hint of fear. "The one who decides—to be more *specific*—who is to be murdered, on my world. The one who decided that Shelly would be tortured to death. That one, I would destroy."

"Even if, in consequence, the universe tumbles apart?"

"Even if the universe tumbles apart," Eric replied, without hesitation. "Shelly *was* my world. All that was good in it."

"How did one so selfish come so far? But now I perceive: the gun. You are a kind of magician, and this gun is a kind of magical staff."

"It is the instrument of my will, which is at one with my vengeance. Who is responsible for what happened to me and Shelly? Never mind my murder: who caused Shelly to suffer as she did before she died? Was it the Devil? Is there a Satan who frustrates God's designs and takes away choice and makes a joke out of justice? Is that the deal?"

"Satan, Iblis, Shaitan, Set, whatever you care to call him, is incorporated within the total being, and is a minor functionary. Another kind of gatekeeper; a filter. A shadow. He is not responsible."

"Then who do I kill? Well? Let's have it, dammit! *MUST I KILL GOD?*"

Eric half expected the angel to make a remark about monumental, cosmic hubris; but the angel didn't. The angel knew well the power of totality of belief; of focusing absolute attention on one's Aim. How else had the created part of the universe been created in the first place?

"Yes," said the angel, not exactly lying, "I am the one responsible."

So Eric raised the gun to the place where the angel's eyes should be, to the two beacons of chaotic light set side by side, and aimed it between those fulminations, and with all that he was, made the bullet of his absolute dedication to vengeance "fire" from the "gun" and—

The angel's wings folded about him, and the bullet struck a wingtip, which exploded in white flame, and burned like the tip of a welding torch and a burned feather fell, down past the sword and into creation, and then the angel opened himself, as if he were a gate, and Eric stepped through that gate, and into the Place where God, in our terminology, can be seen.

Something like Ezekiel's Wheel turned there; something like a mandala of evanescent configuration; but Eric knew these appearances for semblance, too, and he passed through them also, with a shudder, keeping all his attention focused in his gun, and he found himself . . . strange expression, that: 'he found himself' . . . in the Presence which, to the best of Eric's capacity to see, was something like . . .

. . . *the place where plus and minus meet and incorporate one another; where positive and negative, active and passive neutralize; where two needles meet point* to infinitely sharp point, their unconditionally sharp points exactly poised one on the other; the needles—widening past the junctured points to infinitely expanding cones—turning each in the direction relatively opposite the other. And pinned between these points is consciousness, present tense: the first circle of consciousness, the stone dropped in the pond; between these point-on-point spikes is crucified this: the unspeakable suffering of God.

And radiating from this suffering: the ineffable mercy of God.

An Eye. There was, to the best of his capacity for seeing it, an Eye there, an Eye that spoke . . .

The lame and inadequate phrase "the best of all possible worlds" came into Eric's mind. The word "possible" was like a key opening up a Pandora's box of answers to his spoken and unspoken questions. The Eye spoke to Eric and he heard it this way: *"I am an outgrowth of the necessity of Being. I create, and am myself created by the Must Be. I am trying to retrieve Time and thus end suffering; I can do only that which I can do. Pull your trigger, and complete my crucifixion."*

Eric pulled the trigger, with a despairing sense of inevitability.

The bullet struck where the two infinite needles met and a void opened there and inexorably Eric was drawn into the void, and was *not*: he no longer existed: and then he was and . . .

. . . and found himself . . .

. . . spinning there, between the needles, in all possible directions, looking out at looking in . . .

Shelly . . .

Remembering her directed the part of God that had always been Eric to an interior orientation, back to the grip of time, and he was, then, back on the Earth . . .

The mortal world. Standing on the rim of a balcony. In Detroit, Michigan, on a certain October 31.

"Oh," he said, sighing. "I see."

"You really went?" the Murderer asked, with real curiosity, as he whoofed up another hit of cocaine from a little metal bottle, so as to blur the pain in his shattered hand.

"Yes."

"Did you find out who's really responsible for your—no, screw that, I sure as hell would like to know: who's responsible for *me being the way I am*? I mean, I killed my old man and my mom, 'cause I blamed them, but that didn't seem to do it, you know? I mean—"

"Shut up. You're tweaking. Yes, I put a bullet into God. Was in consequence reminded that I am you and I am God, and Justice is doing the best

It can, and I myself am the one impossibly responsible, and . . . and the truth is often paradoxical."

"I see. So there's no point in killing me!"

Eric hesitated; and then a burnt feather drifted down from above. His familiar gave a raucous cry and plucked the feather up in its beak and flew to Eric's shoulder. He took the charred feather from his friend's shiny black beak, the gun-burnt feather that had fallen from the final angel, and he twined it into his hair as the Murderer waited for his answer.

Would he let the Murderer go?

The Murderer made another stab at persuasion. "If I am you, and you me, and we're all contained in God, then, eventually, if you shot me—you'd be shooting yourself, right? So you've gotta cop to it: there's really no point in shooting me."

"Wrong. There's a thing called *consolation*." Eric smiled. "It's better than nothing. Shooting you—is the consolation prize."

Then things went as they did in the tale of the Crow, and justice was served, insofar as it could ever be, and the Murderer was shot dead by Eric's will and with metal-jacketed .45 slugs, and Eric's spirit in due course found its way to Shelly and, there, after the human presumptions melted away and Eric and Shelly came out of expectation into the light that is divine attention, Eric found more than consolation, he found completion: in her.

JAMES O'BARR

A self-taught artist, James O'Barr created his character *The Crow* in the early '80s while in the Marines stationed in Germany, where he was on loan to the Army illustrating hand-to-hand combat manuals. He was inspired by such diverse sources as the works of French poets George Bataille and Anton Artaud, the music of punk artists Ian Curtis and Iggy Pop, and the stories of Lewis Carroll and Edgar Allan Poe, and credits his distinctive visual style to his study of classical Renaissance sculpture, '40s noir crime films, and his two years of medical training. James currently lives outside of the Detroit area where he is completing the script for the third *Crow* film, based on his story "Spooky, Codeine, and the Dead Man."

ED KRAMER

An acclaimed editor and writer, Ed Kramer's original anthologies of the fantastic include *Dark Love, Free Space, Sandman: Book of Dreams, Dante's Disciples*, and Michael Moorcrock's *Elric: Tales of the White Wolf*. His fiction appears in numerous collections; *Killing Time,* his first novel, is forthcoming. Ed's credits also include over a decade of work as a music critic and photojournalist; his television series, *Witness,* was recently purchased by Dick Clark Productions. A graduate of the Emory University School of Medicine, Ed is a clinical and educational consultant in Atlanta. He is fond of human skulls, exotic snakes, and underground caverns.

CONTRIBUTORS

ROB ALEXANDER is a Canadian-born watercolor artist who began as an illustrator working on covers for a line of short story paperbacks and doing interior illustrations for magazines such as *Amazing Stories*. His work has appeared on numerous paperback, magazine, and gaming manual covers, as well as popular collectible card games such as *Magic: The Gathering*. Rob's work covers many genres, including traditional and contemporary fantasy, children's illustrations, Tolkien's *Lord of the Rings*, contemporary landscapes, and gothic horror. He lives with his wife, Susan, a fellow artist, and the family cat on a small acreage in rural Oregon.

A. A. ATTANASIO has published eighteen novels, including a science fiction sequence on the importance of Nothing, *The Radix Tetrad*; a prose meditation on death,

Wyvern; a countervailing mediation on love, *Kingdom of the Grail;* a visit to Mars in the year 3000, *Solis;* and two series that approach light and darkness from both extremes of our Judeo-Christian mythography: Isaiah, *The Dominions of Irth,* and King Arthur, *The Dragon and the Unicorn; The Eagle and the Sword; The Wolf and the Crown.* He lives by his imagination on the world's most remote island chain.

RICK BERRY is known for his work in both oils and the digital medium. His work has graced the covers of many novels, including William Gibson's *Neuromancer;* Rick's animation is seen in the cyberspace scenes of Gibson's film, *Johnny Mnemonic.* His work can also be seen on DC Comics's Vertigo line of books, and many trading cards in both the gaming and comics genres. Rick's book *Double Memory,* produced in collaboration with Phil Hale, is a classic retrospective of his work.

TIM BRADSTREET has been illustrating role-playing games, comics, cards, and books for over ten years, and is perhaps best known for giving White Wolf's *Vampire: The Masquerade* its distinctive and haunting look. His cover artwork has graced every *Vampire* Clanbook to date, with the help of colorist Grant Goleash. Tim's work as an illustrator, inker, and cover artist has graced numerous book and magazine covers, including *The Crow: City of Angels.*

DAN BRERETON entered the field of comics and illustration during his last semester at the Academy of Art College in San Francisco in 1989. His first fully painted comics work, *The Black Terror,* earned him the Russ Manning Award for most promising newcomer the following year, and he's been working on one project after another ever since, with such series as *Legends of the World's Finest, Thrillkiller, The Psycho, Lady Justice,* and *Clive Barker's Dread.* His creator-owned *Nocturnals* series has seen several incarnations in print, not the least of which is this anthology. Dan is thirty-two, and lives in the Lake Tahoe area of California with his three kids and all their haunted toys.

EDWARD BRYANT began writing professionally in 1968 and has published more than a dozen books, starting with *Among the Dead* in 1973. Some of his titles have included *Cinnabar, Phoenix Without Ashes* (with Harlan Ellison), *Wyoming Sun, Particle Theory,* and *Fetish. Flirting With Death,* a major collection of his suspense and horror stories. Many hundreds of articles and columns have appeared in such publications as *Omni, National Lampoon, Writer's Digest,* and *Penthouse.* He is also a regular columnist for such magazines as *Locus, Talebones,* and *Cemetery Dance.*

RAMSEY CAMPBELL is one of the premier dark fantasists currently working in the field; his first short story collection, *The Inhabitant of the Lake,* was published by Arkham House at the tender age of seventeen. He has since gone on to author such classics of modern horror as *The Doll That Ate Its Mother, The Face That Must Die, Midnight Sun, Obsession, Incarnate, The Nameless,* and *The Long Lost.* A multiple World Fantasy, British Fantasy, and Dracula Society award-winner, he also reviews films for BBC Radio. Ramsey resides in Merseyside with his wife and two children.

THOMAS CANTY is one of the most accomplished and influential fantasy artists in the field. Recipient of two World Fantasy Awards for Best Artist, he has painted hundreds of book covers, created two children's book series, wrote the children's book *A Monster at Christmas,* and worked as the art director for specialty publisher Donald M. Grant. Tom is also renowned outside the fantasy genre for his modernistic, cutting-edge book designs, which manipulate reproductive and computer techniques to unique effect. These stunning, award-winning designs can be found on mainstream and mystery books from a number of New York publishing houses.

NANCY A. COLLINS is the award-winning author of *Sunglasses After Dark* and the creator of Sonja Blue. Her short fiction has appeared in numerous anthologies, including *The Year's Best Fantasy and Horror* and *Best New Horror.* Writer of DC Comics's *Swamp Thing,* Nancy is also the founder of the International Horror Guild and the coeditor of the erotic horror anthologies *Forbidden Acts* and *Dark Love.* She currently resides in New York City with her husband, anti-artiste Joe Christ, and their dog, Scrapple.

STORM CONSTANTINE is one of the United Kingdom's premier fantasy writers. She has written twelve novels to date, and numerous short stories. Storm is best known for her innovative and exotic vision exemplified by her first trilogy, which introduced the hermaphroditic race of the Wraeththu. The Grigori trilogy, based around the legends of the fallen angels, is published in the United States by Meisha Merlin. Storm lives in the Midlands of England with her husband and eight cats.

CHRISTINE CROWE, Ph.D., is Hon. Reader in French Literature at the University of St. Andrews in Scotland. Her previous works include critical studies of the French poet and thinker Paul Valéry. Her first novel, *Miss X, or the Wolf Woman,* appeared with the Women's Press in 1990 and her main poem is in *Tea and Leg-Irons: New Feminist Readings from Scotland.* She lives on the very edge of the sea in Anstruther, Fife, where she writes poetry, fiction, and paints full-time.

JACK DANN is a multiple award-winning author who has written or edited more than forty-eight books, including *The Man Who Melted* and *The Memory Cathedral*. His short stories have appeared in *Omni* and *Playboy* and other major magazines and anthologies. Other scheduled books include *The Silent*, a novel about the Civil War; *Counting Coup*, a contemporary road novel; the "definitive" Australian anthology *Dreaming Down-Under*, with Janeen Webb; a new edition of his classic anthology *Wandering Stars*; and *Nebula Awards 32*. Dann's latest novel-in-progress is about James Dean; its working title is *Horizon*. Jack "commutes" between New York and Melbourne, Australia.

CHARLES DE LINT is a full-time writer and musician who presently makes his home in Ottawa, Canada, with his wife, MaryAnn Harris, an artist and musician. His most recent novel is *Someplace to Be Flying* (Tor Books, 1998). For more information about Charles de Lint and his work, visit his Web site at www.cyberus.c/~cdl.

JAMES S. DORR's poetry and fiction has appeared in the anthologies *Dante's Disciples*, *Dark Destiny*, *Elric: Tales of the White Wolf*, as well as a number of other publications spanning horror, fantasy, mystery, and SF. He also plays Renaissance music with a semiprofessional recorder consort and has a large, male Himalayan cat that sometimes answers to the name Fang.

BOB EGGLETON is a three-time Hugo Award winner for Best Professional Artist. His work graces many book covers in the SF field, having gained recognition as the artist for Brian Lumley's *Necroscope* series, as well as comics and children's books. Bob was a visual effects concept artist on *Star Trek: The Experience* and is well known for working on *Godzilla* for Dark Horse Comics and Random House Young Adult Books. A new collection of his work, *The Book of Sea Monsters,* is available from Collins and Brow.

ALAN DEAN FOSTER's fiction has appeared in nearly every major SF magazine as well as in original anthologies and several "Best of the Year" compendiums. He has also written numerous nonfiction articles on film, science, and scuba diving, as well as having produced the novel versions of *Star Wars*, the three *Alien* films, and *Alien Nation*. His novel *Cyber Way* won the Southwest Book Award for Fiction in 1990, the first work of science fiction ever to do so. Alan lives in Prescott, Arizona, along with assorted dogs, cats, fish, several hundred house plants, visiting javelina, porcupines, eagles, red-tailed hawks, skunks, coyotes, cougars, and the ensorceled chair of the nefarious Dr. John Dee.

CHRISTOPHER GOLDEN has sold more than twenty novels, including the vampire epics *Of Saints and Shadows, Angel Souls & Devil*, and the imminent *Of Masques and Martyrs*, and a series of *Buffy the Vampire Slayer* novels, coauthored with Nancy Holder. Chris is also a popular comic book writer who has worked on such titles as *The Crow: Waking Nightmares, Spider-Man Unlimited, Shi*, and *Blade*, and has recently been tapped to resurrect the Marvel character *The Punisher*. Before becoming a full-time writer, he was licensing manager for *Billboard Magazine* in New York.

PHIL HALE founded the Newbury Studio in Boston at the age of sixteen, along with artists Rick Berry, Thomas Canty, and Rick Salvucci. His superb brush work garnered him so much attention, by age eighteen he was a pro in demand and commissioned to illustrate Stephen King's *Drawing of the Three*. He has produced artwork for more than a hundred book covers to date. Well beyond the role of an illustrator, Phil also designs racing motorcycles for Harris, and records experimental music in solo. His work is included in the Society of Illustrators annuals and print magazine. He lives in London, England, with his wife and son.

SCOTT HAMPTON never received formal art training, but he gleaned much from his brother Bo, who studied under the great Will Eisner. His graphic novels and comics include *Books of Magic, Batman: Night Cries, The Upturned Stone* and *Destiny: Chronicle of Deaths Foretold, Silverheels, Batman: Legends of the Dark Knight*, and *Sandman Presents: Lucifer Falling*. Scott has contributed to several anthologies including *Books of Blood, Hellraiser*, and *Tales of Terror*, and has done so many trading cards and covers he's lost count. He lives in Chapel Hill, North Carolina, with his wife, Letitia Glozer, and their cat Roxanne.

ROBERT J. HARRIS has a degree in classics from the University of St. Andrews, Scotland, and consequently has worked as a nurse, a bartender, and a TV extra. He is the designer of Games Workshops' bestselling fantasy boardgame *Talisman* and has had stories published in several recent collections. He lives in St. Andrews with his wife, fantasy novelist Deborah Turner Harris, and their three sons.

ALEXANDRA ELIZABETH HONIGSBERG is known for her darkly numinous romantic-gothic poetry and fiction. Anthologies such as the *Dark Destiny* series, *Dante's Disciples, New Altars, On Crusade, Angels of Darkness*, and *Blood Muse* are its literary homes. She is a professional musician, a scholar of comparative religions, and lives with her husband and two cats in Upper Manhattan, land of forests, fjords, and the Unicorn Tapestries.

K. KEN JOHNSTON is a member of Atlanta's subcultural elite, earning a living as a performer, writer, musician, and director. He has appeared in low-budget horror films, improv comedy, Shakespeare productions, TV commercials and movies, children's theater, full-contact jousts, rock 'n' roll clubs, and numerous literary conferences.

CAITLÍN R. KIERNAN was born near Dublin, Ireland, but has lived most of her life in the southeastern United States. Her gothic and goth-noir short fiction has appeared in numerous anthologies, including *The Sandman: Book of Dreams*, *Love in Vein II*, *Lethal Kisses*, *Darkside: Horror for the Next Millennium*, *Noirotica 2*, *Brothers of the Night*, and *Dark Terrors 2* and *3*. Her first novel is *Silk*. Caitlín made her comics debut with "Souvenirs" for DC's *The Dreaming* and is now writing for DC full-time.

LISA LEPOVETSKY has written public service spots for television and a screenplay for a short horror film. She writes murder mystery dinner theater plays for restaurants and teaches writing classes for the University of Pittsburgh at Bradford. Lisa has written several novels; many poems of her creation have been in publications like *Grue*, *Not One of Us*, *Deathrealms*, and *Dreams and Nightmares*.

VALENA LAKEY LINDAHN and her husband Ron are known for their whimscal illustrated books *The Secret Lives of Cats*, *How to Choose Your Dragon,* and *Olde Missus Milliwhistle's Book of Beneficial Beasties*. For the past twenty-five years Val's cover illustrations have graced top science fiction and fantasy books worldwide, and she's produced hundreds of images for *Asimov's* and *Analog* magazines as well as movie posters and video packages. Twice named a finalist for the prestigious Hugo Award and a recipient of the Frank R. Paul Award, as well as numerous other art show awards, her work has been featured in exhibitions and gallery shows throughout the country.

DON MAITZ is acclaimed for his portrayal of fantastic subjects. He has received two Hugo Awards for Best Artist, a Hugo for Best Original Artwork, a World Fantasy Award for Best Artist, ten Chesley Awards, and a Silver Medal of Excellence and a Certificate of Merit from the Society of Illustrators. Creator of the Captain Morgan image for Seagrams & Sons' spiced rum product, his work has been reproduced internationally as book covers, posters, cards, and limited edition prints. He's authored two art book collections, *First Maitz* and *Dreamquests,* and the best-selling screen saver software, *Magical Encounters,* compile his images and his wife's, Janny Wurts.

REX MILLER has received noteworthy success as a radio personality, voiceover announcer, and collectibles entrepreneur. He is regarded as one of America's leading authorities on popular culture memorabilia. Rex's novels include *Slob*, *Iceman*, *Profane Men*, *Slice*, and *Chaingang*. He has also authored over thirty pop-cultural publications, including: *Archives, Comic Heroes Illustrated*, *Radio Premiums Illustrated*, and *Collectibles Quarterly*.

JEFF PITTARELLI's striking images of horror and eroticism have graced the covers of *Cinefantastique*, *Darkchylde*, and *Carpe Noctum* as well as numerous comic books and graphic novels. His illustrations have received awards at both the World Fantasy and the World Horror Conventions, as well as at many additional regional conferences. A selection of Jeff's work is available on-line at www.cobaltvault.com.

IGGY POP was born James Osterberg in Ann Arbor, Michigan, in 1947. Dubbed the "Godfather of Punk," he is one of the most controversial and influential rock musicians today. Iggy earned his title with his group The Stooges in the late '60s, and continuing with his solo career, has created an indelible legacy through over 20 albums of raging, bleeding, brilliant music. His soundtracks include *Repo Man*, *Rock & Rule*, and *Trainspotting*. Iggy starred as the villian Curve in *The Crow: City of Angels*; additional appearances range from *Tales from the Crypt* to *Star Trek: Deep Space 9*.

RICK POPHAM is a graduate of the Georgia Institute of Technology and Atlanta's prestigious Portfolio Center. His photography ranges from large-format high-fashion stills for advertising and print to fine art pieces for magazine and artists. Rick's photographic interpretations of Lisa Snellings's original sculptures, together with the fiction of Neil Gaiman, have been featured in *Fan* magazine.

ROB PRIOR is the award-winning airbrush illustrator of licensed posters for *Star Wars*, *The X-Files*, and many other films. He entered the comics field with Todd McFarlane's *Spawn the Impaler* and his own project, *The Lost Heroes*, which stars likenesses of Mark Hamill, Jason Carter, Patricia Tallman, and others.

RICK R. REED has been, at various times, a grocery bag boy, steelworker, copywriter, encyclopedia salesman, ghost writer, advertising creative director, pornographer, insurance investigator, and novelist. His publishing credits include the novels *Obsessed* and *Penance*. His short fiction has appeared in the anthologies *Dark Destiny*, *Dante's Disciples*, *Dark Destiny III: Children of Dracula*, *The Darkest Thirst*, and *Contra/Dictions*. He writes to support his passions for leather and exotic wildlife.

HENRY ROLLINS was a teenager working as the shift manager for a Häagen-Dazs ice cream shop near Georgetown University in 1980, and was a huge fan of a Southern California punk rock band called Black Flag. One day, he drove to New York City to see them play, and Henry jumped on stage and took the mike for a song. A few days later, he was called back to New York to audition for the band. Henry spent the next six years fronting one of the most primal rock and roll bands in history. Solo since 1986, Henry is a published poet, speaking at universities and theatres all over North America, Europe, and Australia.

JOHN SHIRLEY is the author of the horror novel *Wetbones,* to name his personal favorite. He is also a screenwriter, having adapted James O'Barr's original story of *The Crow* for the screen. His latest collection is *Black Buttterflies,* and his most recent novel is *Silicon Embrace*, both from Mark V. Ziesing books. One of the founding fathers of cyberpunk, John has worked in every genre from men's adventure to erotica to suspense thrillers. For more information, see his Web site at www.darkecho.com/ JohnShirley.html.

LISA SNELLINGS thinks things up and makes them appear in three dimensions. She is a sculptor and, whether she uses clay or paper or glass or metal, everything she makes is a part of herself. Her work is greatly influenced by music, from Hindemith to Tool, Chopin to Swans. Some of her sculptures are disturbing, some are sad, some funny. Each tells a story. Author Neil Gaiman has written seven short stories based on her works and plans to write enough Lisa-inspired pieces to one day jointly release the most disturbing coffee-table book of the early twenty-first century. She has a kind heart and is somewhat dangerous, an unbelievable combination for artistic success.

S. P. SOMTOW (Somtow Papinian Suchariktul) was born in Bangkok and grew up in Europe. His first career was as a composer (his recent ballet, *KAkI,* just received a royal command performance in Thailand), but he is perhaps best known as the author of some 40 books, including the groundbreaking cult classic *Vampire Junction*, named one of the all-time greatest horror books by the Horror Writers' Association. Other novels include *Moon Dance* and *Darker Angels*. Somtow has made some forays into movie directing: his most recent film was *Ill Met by Moonlight*, a gothic-punk Shakespeare film starring Timothy Bottoms.

CHARLES VESS has worked for every major comics publisher, writing and drawing his own material. He participated in the first museum showing of science fiction and fantasy art in America. Charles's illustrations have been published worldwide, and he is regarded as one of the premier illustrators of Faerie and the Fantastic working today. He and his wife live in Virginia on a farm with a whole bunch of animals, and for recreation, he sketches local trees and wildlife, amongst other things.

RON WALOTSKY graduated from the School of Visual Arts in New York City in 1966. His artwork has appeared on the covers of over 400 books, including works by Tom Clancy, Robin Cook, Alan Dean Foster, Thomas Harris, Stephen King, Norman Mailer, and Anne Rice. His illustrations also grace the pages of *Penthouse, Viva,* and *Gallery* magazines. Ron's fine art paintings and science fiction works have been exhibited at galleries on New York's Madison Avenue. He currently resides in a small beachside town, Flagler Beach, Florida, with his wife, Gail, and continues to paint while working on his book, *Inner Visions: The Life and Work of Ron Walotsky.*

KENT WILLIAMS is a painter and illustrator whose graphic novel and comics work includes *Tell Me, Dark,* and *Blood: A Tale.* A selection of his works on paper, *Kent Williams: Drawings and Monotypes,* was published in 1991. His work has seen print in numerous publications, including *Playboy, Omni,* and *The Learning Channel* magazine, and he has received several awards, including the Yellow Kid (Lucca, Italy's prestigious comics award), three medals from the Society of Illustrators in New York, and the Joseph Henninger Award for Best of Show from Illustration West 32. He is currently writing and drawing the graphic novel *Kokoro,* to be published by Dark Horse Comics. He resides in Chapel Hill, North Carolina, with his wife, Sherilyn, and two sons.

CHET WILLIAMSON has also contributed to *Crow* lore as the author of the original novel *The Crow: Clash By Night,* and the novelization of the film *The Crow: City of Angels.* His other recent titles include *The Searchers,* a new paranormal fiction series, and *Second Chance.* More than eighty of his short stories have appeared in *The New Yorker, Playboy, Esquire, Fantasy and Science Fiction,* and in many other magazines and anthologies.

DOUGLAS E. WINTER has written or edited eleven books in the realm of the dark fantastic, including *Stephen King: The Art of Darkness* and the acclaimed anthologies *Prime Evil* and *Revelations.* His writing has appeared in such major newspapers as the *Washington Post, Philadelphia Inquirer,* and *Atlanta Journal-Constitution;* in magazines as diverse as *Harper's Bazaar* and *Gallery.* He won the World Fantasy Award for *Faces of Fear,* and received the International Horror Guild Award twice, for his short stories "Black Sun" and "Loop." The poem/lyric "Joy Divided" melds Doug's musical and writing careers, and acknowledges the creative inspiration, shared with James O'Barr, of the music of the late Ian Curtis.

GENE WOLFE has written mainstream and young adult novels and many magazine articles, but is best known as a science fiction writer, receiving the Nebula Award for his novella "The Death of Doctor Island," the Chicago Foundation for Literature Award for his novel *Peace*, and the Rhysling Award for his poem "The Computer Iterates the Greater Trumps" along the way. His most recent full-length works, and particularly his exemplary *The Book of the New Sun* series, fall into an entirely different category, merging high technology with an almost Dark Ages environment. Meanwhile, his short fiction continues to prove you never know just what to expect from him.

JANNY WURTS is well known in the fantasy field as both author and artist. Her novel credits include *Sorcerer's Legacy*, the *Cycle of Fire Trilogy*, *Master of Whitestorm*, four novels in the *Wars of Light and Shadow* series, and the *Empire* series in collaboration with Raymond E. Feist. An established illustrator, her art appears on her covers both in the United States and in Great Britain. Her painting, "Wizard of the Owls," the cover for a recently released collection of short stories *That Way Lies Camelot,* was also a recipient of a Chesley Award in 1992.

JANE YOLEN is called both the "Hans Christian Andersen of America" (*Newsweek*) and "The Aesop of the Twentieth Century" (*The New York Times*). She has published more than 200 books, and has been awarded a Caldecott, a Skylark, a World Fantasy Award, and two Mythopoeic Society Awards, among others. She lives winters in Massachusetts and summers in St. Andrews, Scotland, around the corner from Robert J. Harris, with whom she wrote this story.